## STATUS: DEADZONE

'WE'VE GOT COMPANY.'

Three robed and cowled figures stood atop the long, flat dune that flanked one side of the path. Behind them stood a line of gangers – House Delaque from the look of their long duster coats and wrap-around goggles. As if on some unheard signal, the cloaked figures pushed back their cowls. Beneath them they wore helmets and eyepieces of familiar design. Not just gangers. Spyrers! – *from* **Descent** *by Simon Jowett*

HIGH ABOVE ME, a shape detached itself from the darkness and dropped. It lunged forwards clumsily but there was no more ground I could give. I planted my back foot, one arm steadying the other, looking straight down the sights. A stance perfect for the first time I would feel the power, the first time I would unleash the cold fury of this most deadly, most beautiful of weapons.

The milliasaur sprang. This was it. Point-blank. Point. Kill.

*Click.*

Misfire. – *from* **Mark of a Warrior** *by Richard Williams*

ON THE SAVAGE factory world of Necromunda, renegade gangs struggle for survival in the shattered tunnels and domes beneath the teeming hive-cities. STATUS: DEADZONE is an awesome anthology of dark science fiction short stories from the devastated urban hell of Necromunda.

NECROMUNDA STORIES

# STATUS: DEADZONE

### Edited by
### Marc Gascoigne
### & Andy Jones

## A BLACK LIBRARY PUBLICATION

First published in Great Britain in 2000 by
Games Workshop Publishing
Willow Road, Lenton,
Nottingham, NG7 2WS, UK

10 9 8 7 6 5 4 3 2 1

Cover illustration by Karl Richardson

A CIP record for this book
is available from the British Library.

ISBN 1 84154 119 2

Set in ITC Giovanni

Printed and bound in Great Britain by
Omnia Books Ltd., Glasgow.

See the Black Library on the Internet at
**www.blacklibrary.co.uk**

Find out more about Games Workshop
and the world of Warhammer 40,000 at
**www.games-workshop.com**

# CONTENTS

# A WORLD ABOVE
## by Alex Hammond

THE FLOOR RACED before him, yellow guide lights casting harsh
shadows across the face of his driver. The thin hum of an electric engine, rubber wheels dashing across the steel, the rush of
the air; the connecting corridors were lonely, humanless places.
Fingering his las pistol, to a passer-by Aldus Harkon would
have seemed to be simply scratching an irritating itch under his
coat. Aldus watched the driver closely; an unimpressive-look-
ing man, but his enemies knew Harkon was cautious of hit
men and his escort ready for anything.

'Shuttle Bay 5b, sir.' The driver spoke with a mid-hive lilt.

'Come up in the world?' Aldus returned his hand to the cane
lying upon his lap.

'Yes, sir. Used to work on the factory floor. Brother went
down-hive; I was recruited up. Saved the foremen from a
Delaque assassination attempt.'

'Made your masters proud, no doubt.'

The man saluted. 'Ran Lo shuttle number five should be
docking shortly.'

The transport's wheels skidded briefly, only to be muffled by
the sound of the rush of depressurising air as the cart entered
the landing bay. Almost immediately a throat-searing rush of

fumes hit Aldus full in the face. He inhaled deeply, painful though it may be – the shuttle bay would be witness to the biggest deal of his life.

The transport cart scuttled away, small wheels competing to keep up with one another. Aldus dusted down his coat and stood, cane in hand, poised near the edge of the eight mile-high precipice. About him men struggled with fuel pipes, prepared magnetic clamps and clung to the sides of the shuttle bay as though at any second the whole thing would lurch forward and toss them out into the night sky, down through the noxious clouds to land a bloodied pulp in the ash wastes so far below.

Aldus loved Hive Primus. If you were strong-willed there were places for you. Places to find greatness, places to make a life for yourself in a giant city almost bursting with the pressure of millions of souls. If you were cast of iron like the city, you could go far. Aldus stepped closer to the edge of the shuttle bay's entrance. Winds battered him, slapping him hard in the face, stinging his old, cunning eyes. Peering out into the night air, he breathed deeply. A freshness unknown to his sickening body filled his lungs. The stars in the sky, every one a new solar system, were each a place for those of iron to reach greatness.

Aldus hacked hard into the front of his mouth. Sliding the phlegm about his mouth he manipulated it with his tongue until it met his approval. Large and heavy. He leaned forward. A bay attendant behind him shrieked. Aldus delicately raised his hand and cast the phlegm from his mouth. The dark yellow globule dropped into the rushing winds and was swept around and backwards into the gusts. Now part of him would travel into the wastes, carried, perhaps, for ten miles or a hundred before it dropped upon the dead earth below. Aldus smiled within.

'Sir!' An attendant, arms replaced by machine loading mitts, screamed into Aldus's ear. 'The hunting party… their shuttle!'

Aldus nodded and began the long walk to the end of the runway.

From beyond, from the dark sky, a bright green light burst into view.

'They're going too fast!' A tech-priest looked up at the flickering, ghost-washed display panels before him, sweat running down his green-lit face, tracing the contours of the electronic sight that replaced his eye.

Aldus remained stationary as the bay was suddenly plunged into bright red light, warning beacons alerting fire safety crews to prepare for action.

The jagged shape of the shuttle grew larger. Aldus could make out the Ran Lo signature on its cockpit, the arcane R and L set in their white circle contrasting sharply with the arched windows above.

'Sir, get behind the fire wall!'

Aldus remained still, with the exception of his calm hands fondling the silver cast at the top of the cane.

As the shuttle continued its wayward plummet towards them, attendants began throwing themselves to the floor, the strobing lights staggering all movement. The tearing of metal screeched about the runway, the shuttle throwing sparks into the smoke-choked air as its wings clipped the sides of the bay. Bulbous wheels screamed like agonised creatures as they struggled to slow the oncoming craft. Small fires leapt up on the floor as the white-hot sparks ignited patches of fuel.

The shuttle sped towards where Aldus stood, noxious fumes pouring from its vents. The shuttle veered off its path for a moment, almost colliding with the wall, only to spin back on line with Aldus.

With an unutterably deafening screech, the wheels finally succumbed to the brakes and the shuttle screamed to a halt, its steel nose cone so close to Aldus' misshapen body he could have reached out and patted its flaking metal prow. The beaming face of a young man smiled down at the stationary figure through the arched cockpit windows. He waved and Aldus shook a hand in recognition.

Attendants rushed about the shuttle bay, pouring foam directly from their augmented limbs onto the spot fires. Meanwhile priests moved in to consecrate the machine's safe landing with oils and unguents. Amidst the flurry of movement, a staircase was lowered from the shuttle's side, its gradual release incongruous with the speed of the men. Four body-suited figures, two boys and two girls, leapt from the access port. Only a robed man, leaving the shuttle last, used the stairs. This, Aldus Harkon knew instantly, was Terrak Ran Lo.

The sage old man walked gracefully towards Aldus, grey hair and groomed goatee painted red in parts. About him the youngsters leapt and shouted, slapping one another on the backs. Their combative prowess was immediately noticeable as they aimed mock kicks and lashed out at one another, pulling short with bladed weapons mere muscle spasms from one another's faces.

'I must apologise–' Terrak Ran Lo began.

'Scared as a cess rat!' The young pilot from the ship grinned at Aldus like a big dog, nodding his shorn head, revealing it to be tattooed with the kill marks of a seasoned hunter.

'Aadon, you oaf, you almost ripped the ship to pieces!' A woman in a tight-fitting body suit, dark, lacquered braid curled tight in the customary manner of all of the women warriors of Ran Lo, spat out the words at her companion.

'Does it matter. What about the thrill?' Aadon snapped back.

'Aadon, you're a genius, did you see them run for the barricade?' laughed the other boy. He was huge, a full head taller than those about him. 'Call me Takarr. Thanks for making this hunt possible, Mr. Harkon.'

'Don't mention it,' Aldus replied. 'You should thank Lord Terrak for having the sense to come to me.'

'You can guarantee that everything will be in place by the time they get down there?' Terrak Ran Lo asked, his voice calm and commanding.

'Yes. As long as they keep to the schedule they'll be having the hunt of their lives.'

'You'd better hope so, Mr Harkon,' the dark-haired woman said snootily as she stepped forward. 'You're being paid a small fortune to make sure this is good.'

'I've had ten years' experience dealing with Underhivers. Four miles below us I have over thirty seasoned contacts; at six I have another forty. I'd like to think that my dealings with these scum has provided me with enough insight to know when something is worth it.'

'Excellent,' the young woman purred and spun on her heels. 'The mice will be in trouble tonight.'

HIGH ABOVE THE Underhive, the air is cold. High above the Underhive you cannot breathe for the lack of atmosphere. Ten miles above the savage wasteland of Hive Bottom is where the city's peak lies. This is where the souls of the dead will travel. This is where they gather. This is where they are blown across

the four winds. Scattered like shards of glass. Scattered souls
bear no memories. Blood...

Blood ran down Knife Edge Liz's face. She could feel it sliding down her chin, charting a course past old scars, through the
valleys of new wounds. Liz reached her hand up to her face. She
might as well have been attempting to lift a steel girder. She let
the limb fall to the ground again. Slow waves of red washed
over her eyes again.

High above the hive the air is cold. Liz no longer felt her legs.
High above the hive you cannot breathe for lack of atmosphere. Liz drew a heavy breath into her lungs. It fell short and
sunk only as deep as her throat. She dragged her hand across
the ground, feeling for something, anything that could help.

Her hand came across something soft and moist. Feeling up
it – a small ring, piercing stone cold skin. Tattered cloth. The
small face of a girl, eyes open. Big round eyes like a cat.

*Kat.*

Kat was dead.

Liz snatched her hand away. Blood rushed to her head. Liz
rose to her feet pushing hard so that she fell away from the
corpse. She staggered forward and fell upon a cushion of flesh.
Arms slick with someone else's blood. Underneath her she
could feel the cold grip of death. Someone was beneath her.
Dead. Liz rubbed at her eyes, grit tearing at her pupils. For each
layer of blood she wiped off, another would arrive – hers or the
corpse's, she could not tell.

'Hive daemons take me!' Liz groaned, rolling off the corpse
in panic.

Liz's limbs struck at the ground, each fist striking in search of
a dry place, a steel place. Somewhere where there was no
blood. A fist ricocheted off a steel case. Pain shot up Liz's arm,
sending spasms about her shoulder and shooting tendrils of
needle-sharp pangs about her. The steel case. Liz ran her fingers
over its mesh texture, searching for a sign. She flipped the case
over and felt again. Small cross-hatches, like the mesh of the
walkways she knew were above her. The criss-cross ended
abruptly; a smooth disk lay in the centre of the case, medical
cross engraved into its surface.

Liz flipped the medi-kit open and rummaged inside it with
trembling fingers. She swallowed pills, wrapped bandages
about her wounds. Took out a hypodermic, shook it and was

rewarded by the slosh of the liquid within. She had to stab four times before she found a vein. Arm rushing with warmth, Liz fell back and continued falling.

In the darkness there was heat. In the darkness the sound of the hive drifted away. Liz rolled around. The painkillers, like the hands of a lover, held her tight and ran their fingers about her body. They sank deep into her skin. Deep into her soul. They traced patterns across her back. Spelt words she could not understand. Rubbed thoughts into her tired brain.

Kat was dead. She'd come from the streets. Wanted to join a gang. Looked for a way to find a meaning. A meaning for the Underhive. Couldn't have been more than sixteen. Dead so young. Half a life is more than none. Half a lie.

Liz rocketed into consciousness. A lie. Somewhere there was a lie.

Liz snapped her eyes open and looked about her. Smoke still rose from potholes in the ground. Electric conduits still buzzed and swung from the platforms above her. Beside her lay the medi-kit, plundered of all its contents. A few bright red stims lay scattered about on the ground. Liz carefully picked these up and secreted them down the side of her boot.

Something bit sharply into her ankle. She struggled with the boot and removed a hard, white card. Guilder credits. The lie was unravelling itself. Liz regarded herself in the sheen of an effluent pool. Her leggings were torn. Deep gashes carved their way through her flesh. Her hair, once dyed blue, was a deep brown, nearer her natural colour.

Liz had fallen close to Bekka, Bekka the Harvester. Liz stared over at her corpse. Deep pock marks had cracked open that seemingly impenetrable body of hers. Hundreds of hours of weight-built work, cast aside like a child's rag doll. For so many Bekka was the paragon of Underhive womanhood: in control, strong, with a mind as strong as steel.

Beside Bekka lay her weapon, its kill markings still as bright as they were the day they were scored. The day they captured that heavy bolt gun from their rivals, the Sump Pirates, had been one of their greatest. An offworld weapon, and ammunition too; an incredible prize! It was a victory that had led them through every bar in Deep Town. They'd got drunk on Second Best and collapsed on the bar-room floor.

From the signs, a story unfolded: the blood-sprayed walls, laceration wounds to her dead comrades. They had come to ambush someone. It should have been simple. A mistake? They took it too easy? Something had gone wrong. Desperate faces, terrified eyes – the dead faces betrayed much. Bekka. Her augmented eyes and powerful weapon would have given her the drop on any assailant. By the ruby scores, sunken into her flesh, perhaps she had been the first to go. A trail of light imprints in the earth belied some rapidly moving assailant. Liz slowly rose and staggered forwards, hand clutching delicately at her leg. With each step the wound tore open a little.

The imprints led to the body of a stranger, wired into a still-pulsing fighting suit. Bloodied mat of hair, disgorged eye sockets. The mechanical enhancements that had once filled these places lay torn on the ground. The stranger was young, Kat's age perhaps. Bladed gauntlets still moist with blood hung by his side. Liz regarded her leg.

'LIZ!' A SCREAM from behind her. She spun around, lasgun at the ready. Kat was holed up behind a rock, heavy shells like blast caps erupting the rock from about her. Kat kept her head down. Liz scanned the smoke-filled tunnels for her assailant. Somewhere above, at the narrowing of the walls. Text-book bottleneck. They were surrounded.

'Liz, hel–' Kat gargled into silence.

Liz spun to catch sight of her comrade. A dark figure stood over where Kat had been hiding. Unashamed, he held part of an Escher girl above his head like a trophy.

'Sonofa–!' Liz threw herself towards the figure that was now dancing about Kat's shredded remains.

Cracking explosions splintered girders, concrete flinging dust into the air. Liz threw herself through this haze and fell upon the figure, unleashing a fiery beam of death from her lasgun. Hot shells crashed about her, some searing her skin as they bounced about the ground. The figure leapt, lightning fast, and threw itself towards Liz, sharp blades like cleavers dripping wet.

Liz spun about, anticipating her assailant's speed, and clipped him. Right arm a mangled pulp, the figure swept hard with its left. Blades sliced across Liz's leg. A sharp pain and sudden dizziness rushed over her. She rolled through the filth, the dirt clogging the wound, blood rush stemmed to a trickle. Liz unsheathed her chainsword and flicked its spinning teeth into action. The figure darted to one side and tumbled across the ground, its suit pumping stimulants into its dying body.

Chainsword buzzing, Liz lightly swept it in front of the oncoming figure's head. Her timing was on line. Like spearing a sump eel Liz timed the blow to anticipate the movements of her attacker. The chainsword caught on the augmentation about the figure's head. Its weapon suit sputtered into a death rattle as armour plates and implants were ripped from its body. Both Escher and attacker crashed to the ground. Liz readied her lasgun and took aim on the hidden sniper's position. Using a bent girder to brace her arm she peered into the darkness.

'Help me.' A voice nearby.

'HELP ME.' A voice nearby. Liz woke. She had fallen by her bladed attacker's body. Her arm lay draped across his carcass. The battlefield was silent, her head and leg bandaged. Liz reached into her boot and pulled out some more stims, swallowed them. The tiny red capsules almost came up again. Internal bleeding somewhere. Forcing the medicine up again. Liz rubbed her throat, making sure they were digested.

'Olaana?' The voice was weaker now.

Liz staggered to her feet and moved towards the noise. Crumpled at the base of a shell-pocked concrete wall was another suited figure. A woman, young... Kat's age. Dark hair tied in braids hung from her head; a las wound to her chest wept tarred blood.

'The mice, Olaana. The mice fought back.' The woman groaned.

Liz watched silently. The woman flapped uselessly at a respirator hanging limp at her side. Liz followed the stretch of conduit cords as they wrapped their way about the woman's suit back to their starting point at the base of her skull. Her face mask was torn and conduit fluid from the cords ran past her brow, across her open eyes. They did not blink but stared white-pupilled into the air.

'Damn suit's got me so high on stimulants that I'm having trouble dying. Olaana?' The woman looked straight at Liz but her eyes made no sign of recognition.

'Yeah?' Liz mumbled, leaning back against a giant girder.

'I– I can't see.' The woman's voice broke into a faint sob.

'I know.'

'Thank the Emperor it's you. Thought you were one of those Underhive freaks.'

Liz paused, mind racing. 'No. They're all dead.'

'We won?' the woman sat forward a little, the effort causing her to gasp.

'Yes.'

'You going to get a head? Take it back?' the woman said, smiling despite her discomfort.

'Why would I want to do that?' Liz crouched before the woman and silently levelled her lasgun at her.

'You've done it after every other hunt.'

Liz blinked. The woman remained still. Liz regarded the nose of her lasgun. Greasy effluent from a walkway above dripped down onto its power cell. The thin hiss of the boiling water was the only noise in the rubble shelter. Tainted rain began to fall. It drowned out the sound of the hissing lasgun. Somewhere in the city above them, the factories were resuming a new shift, emptying spent coolants into the levels below.

'Remember the time we came down and fought those scum at the ash falls? We herded them into that field of razor grass. They were so desperate they ran though it. Remember? Like a pack of mindless sump rats. Only one came out the other end. Lost so much blood he couldn't even pull his trigger. Easiest hunt… we ever had.' The woman's voice was getting weaker.

'This one was bad,' Liz whispered.

'The worst. Wish I'd never come. It was meant to be easier… fun. The plasma's still burning, Olaana. I can feel it through the pain repressors… Olaana? They won't wait at the ash falls for long. You should go… or you'll never get back.'

Liz rocked on her feet. Dizzy.

'Olaana?' The woman reached out towards Liz. 'Hold my hand?'

Liz remained still for a moment. She looked over her shoulder at her dead friends. Her gang. Her responsibility.

'Olaana?'

Liz reached out her hand and took hold of the woman's. It was soft, scarless. Liz stared at it in silence.

'Why was it so hard? They have nothing. No training, faulty weapons. They're animals. Barbarian scum with no right to kill us. We've got noble blood. We own this damn hive. They should be thankful we came down here and put them out of their misery... Harkon promised us an easy hunt.'

Liz released the woman's hand.

'Olaana? I don't want to die.' The woman broke down into tears.

Liz stood up and cast her eyes back over the battlefield. Harkon. Liz remembered that name.

'WHO'S ALDUS HARKON? He's our contact from uphive, Bekka.' Liz's voice echoed through the tunnel as they strode towards the site of their planned ambush.

'And it's a House Orlock shipment?' Bekka asked, strapping tape about her thick, tattooed arms. Liz had always admired her strength in the face of the rat scars she suffered as a child.

'That's right. He's paid us in weapons, up front, to take care of the shipment so that he can offer to finance the deal instead. Least, that's what he told me.'

'Sounds complicated.'

'Uphivers tend to be.' Liz wrinkled her nose like she'd smelt a bad stink. 'Kill their mothers if it paid well. They're worse than mutants.

'We're here.' She turned around to face her gang. 'Take up your positions. We're in a bottleneck, so they won't be able to run.' Liz's colleagues moved swiftly but silently down ladders and ramps into the dried-up canal.

Sometime later, the air still. 'Liz?' Bekka whispered, looked her square in the eyes. 'You trust this Harkon?'

'I–' An explosion silenced Liz. Rubble flew high into the air. Conduits burst and threw gas into the tunnels.

'Ambush!' Kat yelled from down in the bottleneck.

'The Orlocks know?' Bekka screamed.

'No – uphivers! Look!' Liz pointed to a girder high above them. A figure clad in a dark, bladed suit. 'Sniper! Get down!' Liz yelled to Bekka.

Liz's muscled second ignored her. Bekka braced herself against a concrete block and let rip with the heavy bolter. Hot shells spewed from the ejection chamber igniting small chemical puddles about Bekka's legs. The uphiver dashed along a thin girder at full speed. Shells rang after it but failed to make a hit.

'Get down, Bekka!' Liz shrieked over the noise.

Below her Liz could hear the screams of her gangers. 'Harkon, you bastard,' she growled and leapt forward into the bottleneck. She took up cover behind a jutting girder and looked up to the lip of the rise above her.

'Bekka, you coming?' she called over the noise of the heavy bolter. 'Bekka?' The noise stopped. An ammunition belt rolled down the embankment. 'Bekka!'

'Help! Liz!' Kat screamed from across the battlefield.

'Our heavy's down!' Liz howled, trying to be heard above the ricochets. 'Retreat.' Liz looked over to Kat. She was pinned behind a bolder. Liz looked up to the embankment, grabbed hold of the chain of ammunition and used it to pull herself up.

'Bekka?' Liz lay flat in the dust, parallel with a fallen girder. 'Bekka?' she hissed.

A pack of ammunition lay by the discarded heavy bolter. An explosion ripped open the ground about her. Liz peered through the haze smoke. A large figure was lumbering towards the sniper's position.

'Bekka!'

Liz followed as Bekka began her ascent towards the sniper. Liz pressed her back up against a bulkhead and dragged the heavy weapon towards her. Feeding the ammunition over her thigh, she braced a foot against a boulder. Gripping the bolter between her arms, Liz pulled its trigger. Massive shudders shook through her arms and shoulders. Liz dragged the gun around to the sniper's position. She let its bullets ring about the tower.

'I hope this gives you some cover,' Liz puffed as she struggled to stop the weapon spinning loose. Within a few seconds discarded shell cases had piled in a steaming heap about her.

Liz paused and drew breath, watching stunned as the battle continued. Smoke plumes burst from the battlefield, and more of her companions dropped. Thin bursts traced their life fluid through the air. Chips of rubble rose and fell with each new barrage. They were being taken apart.

Liz's ears stopped ringing, thin trickles of blood gathering in them the only reminder of the weapon's ferocity. She looked skyward in an attempt to mark Bekka's position. The girders and walkways rose like an industrial cliff face. Bekka was nowhere. Bursts of light, las fire, flared in a dark recess above her. Liz craned her neck to see further into the darkness. With

unearthly poise never granted in life, Bekka burst out of the
darkness through a curtain of hanging chains and spun for a
brief moment, like a classical dancer, on the precipice. And fell.
Bekka's body curled into a ball, childlike, before crashing into
the battlefield below Liz.

'Bastards!' Liz screamed as she saw for the first time the face
of the sniper: a thin man, wired skull cap linking him to a body
suit of angular metal pieces and bladed edges. Liz grabbed hold
of a new belt of ammunition and began ramming it into the
gun.

The man leapt after Bekka's body. As he fell he unfurled thin
metal meshes, joined from his wrists to his arms. Rather than
drop like a stone as she expected, he glided rapidly towards Liz,
unleashing bolts of burning light in her direction as she struggled to aim the heavy weapon at his slender form.

Links of ammunition fed into the heavy bolter and finally it
kicked into life. The winged sniper dropped faster towards her,
darting between walkways and platforms. Liz reeled and pulled
the trigger, letting the weapon throw her backwards as she
attempted to follow the sniper's movements.

White-hot casings rained about her, leaving scald marks on
her arms as she tried to keep pace with the sniper. The shells
rang about the layers of steel above her, bursting through platforms, cables and piping. The sniper landed gracefully on a
platform above Liz and lowered his las rifle in her direction like
a viper spying a mouse for the first time.

Liz pushed hard against the girder and threw herself onto her
back. The heavy bolter crashed down on top of her. Inside her
chest something snapped. A burst of blue-green light impacted
where Liz had lain. Aching all over and bleeding on the inside,
Liz aimed for the structural supports of a walkway above the
sniper. Her weapon thundered into action again, releasing
burning hot metal at the supports. A second later and the walkway came crashing down. The sniper looked up for a brief
moment. Liz no longer saw him; she didn't have the time.
Flipping the heavy bolter onto its end, Liz huddled about its
base and prayed. The walkway smashed through the platform
on which the sniper was standing and continued downwards
towards Liz. The girders and grated walkways crashed about
her, knocking hard into the heavy bolter and smashing into her
body.

Liz opened her eyes. The bolter remained upright. The sheets of iron, mesh barriers and steel girders had fallen about her, the heavy weapon keeping the heaviest pieces from crushing her. The bloodied ganger pulled on the trigger and let the weapon carve a way out of the rubble.

The battle was going badly in the gorge below. Most of Liz's gang had fallen back into a large crater. Liz scanned the horizon for signs of the gang's assailants as she climbed down the embankment. Crista, one of the gang's veterans, sat spread-legged and slumped upon the ground. Liz reached forward to feel for her pulse. Crista looked up bloody-browed at Liz and shook her head.

'I'll get you outta here,' Liz whispered

Crista shook her head again and her eyes widened. Liz started; reflected in them was a large figure. A trap. Liz snatched Crista's autogun from the ground and threw herself to one side. In that instant, an explosion burst into Crista's body and the concrete about her. Liz was showered with sharp flints and washed in crimson. Liz rolled over, struggling to remove a steel shard from her side. The figure lumbered forward. A man in a massive suit of meshed-plate armour. Oversized arms and shoulders provided protection to all but his head. Fibre cables were attached to the base of his neck. Massive gloved fists clicked and snapped as he walked forward, like a pianist preparing to play. Liz ripped out the shard and pulled the trigger of the autogun. It was light compared to the heavy bolter before it and she over-compensated for recoil. Her shots ran wide and the armoured man rushed her. Liz pulled the spray back and let several bursts impact into his chest.

'Die!' Liz screamed.

The man lumbered on, uninjured.

Liz swung the autogun at his head. Its shoulder stock caught him across the temple, gashing a wound open above his eyes. The man slapped the gun out of Liz's hands and lunged at the ganger before she could fling herself aside. He wrapped his arms about her and lifted her off the ground. He breathed hard into her face. His breath was young, untarnished by years of filtered air. His steel blue eyes were all she could see beneath his combat mask; they blinked at her.

The man's arms flexed and Liz's spine was racked with pain. She slapped at the pouches on her legs, trying to get a hold.

The armoured man bounced her hard to strengthen his position. Liz's hand slapped at her leg again. She had it. Her back spasmed. Her head rushed with blood and the battlefield spun.

Liz looked down into the face of the man, the blood from above his head running into the seamless cracks of his impenetrable armour. His eyes narrowed in strain. She smiled. His eyes widened in surprise. Liz brought her hand into view and opened it to reveal the grenade she held.

With her head spinning Liz punched her hand deep into the fibre cables about the man's head. She felt her hand slip down past his sweating shoulders. Liz pushed hard with her legs, trying to throw herself to the ground. The man struggled to pull her in two. An explosion burst inside the suit. Liz was flung back against a bulkhead. The suit remained untouched, but the man inside it could no longer be seen.

Liz pushed forwards against the bulkhead, a jarring pain running up the length of her arm. The battlefield was silent. She shook her head; perhaps the explosion had unsettled her. Feet throwing up spent shells, she staggered forwards towards the crater where she had last seen her comrades. Liz lifted her head and in that instant her cover burst apart, dust and smoke replacing her protection.

The Escher lurched forward, running blindly through the smoke towards the position she'd last seen her gang. The ground burst open beneath her feet – her assailant was persistent. Her foot collided with a fallen girder. Half-falling, she crested the crater's lip. Liz tumbled over, fortune rather than precision timing throwing her out of the way of an explosion.

A twisted wrist and broken rib later, Liz reached the base of the crater. Her stomach, already giddy with fluid depravation, ran molten hot at the sight of carnage before her eyes. Her gang, some of them with their swords only half drawn, lay dead, lacerations and deep red bruising the signature of their killer. The script was fluid, deep lines intersecting others with deadly precision.

'Liz!' A scream from behind her. Kat lay prone, barely concealed behind a rock. She was now the focus of the barrage of weapons fire. Similar blast pattern, same angle of fire. There was one more assailant. No, there were two: rising up from behind Kat, unfurling like a giant insect, was yet another attacker. Spines stitched in to a lacquered body suit, with two piston pumped blades attached to gauntlets on each arm. The uphiver rose like a mantis about to strike.

The young ganger, pinned down by enemy fire, could do nothing but remain in her position, fumbling with her long fighting knife. An arc of blood rose slowly into the air. Liz ran forwards, drawing her chainsword at the last minute to engage with Kat's slayer. The battle was brief. Wounds were exchanged. The reach afforded Liz by the buzzing, bladed weapon had given her the advantage. The spiny uphiver lay broken on the ground.

Liz scrambled up a crumbling set of stairs, desperately trying to get herself out of the firing line. She scanned the bulkheads, recesses and cables of the walkways and the burnt-out shelters of the bottleneck about her. An air filter ground into action in one of the bulkheads, throbbing dust from the ground up into the air. A slow wind began to pull past her head. Liz paused in silence.

Closing her eyes, she trained her ears first to the noise of the hissing power cell in the weapon in her hand. Small electric sparks, thin and tuneless, rose and fell like ebbing waves. A sophisticated exchange of charged particles, undiscernible to her ears, was taking place in the sword in her hand. The approaching footsteps sounded like a jackhammer in comparison.

Liz remained still. Her head swam and her body ached. She had little time left and would have to make her stand quickly. Hundreds of these seconds would pass every day unnoticed. Now in the stillness of the final conflict they seemed to be glorious hours, dense and full of promise.

Liz waited. There was the crackle of a weapon charging behind her.

Releasing all the tension from her body she dropped like a marionette with its strings cut. At the exact same moment an energy blast rocketed over her head. Liz swivelled on the mesh flooring and kicked a foot into the abdomen of the advancing uphiver.

It was a woman, curving black stealth suit and long braid giving Liz clues to the identity of the masked attacker. The woman's speed was unnatural. Augmented legs kept on pushing, knocking Liz from her precarious balance and sending the woman flying high over her head. They both collided, hard, with the metal floor.

The attacker released several charges from the plasma weapon in her left hand. Liz rolled across the concrete as it was carved up behind her. Pulling a grenade from her leg, she pulled its pin and let it follow the course carved by the plasma blast that had so recently followed her.

The woman leapt high over the grenade's path. The timing was off. The grenade exploded and Liz was thrown back, the uphiver flung after her. In an awkward moment, afforded only by chance, Liz hit the ground seconds before the woman, then the woman from uphive landed on top of her. Their combined weight caused the broken mesh on which they lay to creak alarmingly. A sudden movement and they'd both plummet to the ground.

Liz stared into the eyes of the woman from above. In another life they may have been sisters. For a brief, alien moment they were cast together, their blood intermingling, the danger of the situation something they shared.

The woman did not speak, a quick intake of air the only noise she made. Liz looked to her side. Through the mesh she could make out the smouldering battlefield below. A rivet popped out from the joint where the mesh was anchored to the walkway and spun away for the ground below. The woman gingerly raised herself off Liz. Her eyes darted from Liz to the popping rivets.

The Escher looked back at the ground, calculating. Deciding. She flicked her chainsword into action and severed the mesh in one sweeping thrust. They both dropped through, accelerating as they plummeted. Liz lost her grip on the woman. Neither screamed as they hit the ground.

'I THOUGHT THE fall would kill me.' Startled, Liz turned to face the woman from uphive with a grunt. 'I thought the fall would kill me, Olaana. I fell with one of the prey. No regard for her life. Like an animal. Let us both fall to our deaths.'

'You're… you're going to die…'

'Yes.' The woman's voice was unnaturally calm. 'The suit will try and repair what it can but it's fighting a losing battle. Soon the stimulants will no longer stop the pain. If it's damaged, it will try and knit my skin to its circuitry. It's happened to others down here.'

'I've heard the stories,' Liz lied.

'The pain is meant to–'

'What is it?' the Escher blurted out.

'It's starting.' The woman punched her own arm in agony.

'The suit's damaged?'

'The pneumatic pistons on the right arm. Damn! Nnghh!' The woman punched harder, frantic.

'Let me see.' Liz pushed the uphiver's fist from her wound. A deep wound had cut deep into the arm of the uphiver. The arcane offworld circuitry was attempting to repair both flesh and steel. Stitching bone to gears.

'Nnaaaaagh!!' The woman's scream was something unnatural, alien.

'Get out of the suit!' Liz shouted, hands fluttering over her.

'Olaana!'

'Out!' Liz pulled the woman forwards and begun tugging at the magnetic locks that fastened the suit together.

'My access code! It won't open without it!'

'Call it out! Free yourself!'

'That's against the laws.'

'You're going to die.'

'Olaana, promise you nngh–' Pain forced the woman's words to stop. 'Alpha-two-five… ugh… twelve.'

The magnetic claps hissed open. Liz unwrapped the cords, pulled the skin-tight fittings and unplugged implant interfaces. The woman slid out of the bloody suit like a new-born from its placental sack. Her right arm was a mess of machinery and muscle.

'Olaana…' the woman moaned.

'Here. Take these.' Liz pushed some of the stims into the woman's mouth. 'They'll help with the pain.'

The woman went still. For a moment the Escher thought she was dead. Then the uphiver spat the stims out again. The red colouring from the pills was indistinguishable from the blood in her spittle.

'What?' Liz looked down to the blinded uphiver.

The woman said nothing.

'You know,' Liz said grimly. Her words hung in the silence.

'You're the woman that fell with me. Their leader,' the woman sneered in a wracked voice.

'That's right.'

Suddenly the uphiver flapped her hand about the ground for a moment and came up with a stretch of pipe. She swung wildly at Liz. Stunned for a moment Liz didn't move. The pipe caught her on the knee. Liz fell backwards.

'Stinking Underhive rat!' The woman strained, blood coursing from her wounds. The veins on her temples ran hot, her face contorting in pain. 'You're nothing better than an animal. You're filth to be trodden on by your betters. Thought you could buy your salvation with kindness?'

'No,' the Escher snapped back. 'I'd rather you died like the rest of your kind. Slowly. Let you bleed to death, alone and in the dark. You killed my friends!'

'As did you.'

'We were set up.'

'You thought the ambush would be yours. How are you different to me? I hate your kind and you hate mine!' The woman flopped back in the dirt, spent.

Liz stood slowly. She regarded the woman's damaged body. She looked at the machine-melded arm. At the suit. At her dead friends.

ALDUS HARKON STOOD on the edge of the shuttle bay, staring out into the night sky for the second evening running. The city below him was lit up by thousands of lights from twenty-four hour furnaces. Higher up, the lights of each landing bay, jutting out from the hive like gargoyles. City lights. Star lights. There were almost as many tiny points of light emanating from Hive Primus as there were stars in the sky. Aldus could almost imagine he was staring into a lake.

Aldus spent a lot of time staring. He let his mind wander on these occasions to stop boredom from seeping in and addling his brain. He spent a lot of time waiting. But that was part of the job description. He needed the time to mull over and orchestrate his deals. It was during all the time that he spent thinking that he first realised that the highest price was not always the fastest way to the Upper Spire. Protection, security, special handshakes and powerful patrons were far more useful in the long term.

In the sky above him, Aldus saw one of the stars move. He brushed his lank, greying hair out of his eyes. Minutes passed. The star grew larger until Aldus could make out the Ran Lo symbol on the shuttle's nose. The lights marking the runway lit up. Aldus began his long walk back to the safety barrier at the runway's end, casting tall shadows along the walls as he passed over each guide light.

Harkon sat and watched, reassured to see the shuttle land at a reasonable speed. He began his approach as it settled on its landing gear and jets of steam poured from conduits. The stairs lowered and a lone figure stepped out of the hatch. Aldus recognised the hunter from earlier. Mono-molecular sword sheathed at her side, swagger in her step, braided black hair. Moving slowly; she had been wounded. And her companions? Dead? Aldus stalked forward, rubbing his fingers.

'Welcome home.' He bowed severely before the woman, came up grinning, 'I hope the hunt was as successful as I promised.'

'The hunt, Aldus Harkon,' Knife Edge Liz replied, 'has only begun.'

# THE DAY OF THIRST
## by Tully R. Summers

SURE YOU'VE GOT a heavy stubber. You just better hope Krug hired you to use it, and not for something else.

Oh, I'd rather not say. If Krug hasn't told you – and he obviously hasn't, because you're here – it's not for me to go spilling the beans. Drink your WildSnake, it'll take your mind off that hand of yours.

Of course it stings. The initiate brand ain't meant to tickle. Supposed to impress upon you the seriousness of joining the Black Hand. Don't pick at it, you'll catch spore rot and the arm'll drop off, then they'll have to burn it someplace else.

What? Well of course it's watered down. The way you Black Hand swill the stuff, I wouldn't have enough WildSnake to souse a sump rat.

Uh huh, that's right. Took you on to replace Dramuck. It's in what capacity, you should be worried about.

All right, I'll tell you if you promise to stop calling me 'Weasel' – a most undeserved moniker for such an upstanding gaming den proprietor such as myself, and I don't care what Krug says.

It was a quiet day at the Bonesapper's Lounge–

Yes, that's what they call this old heap of a troop transport.

Why? It's a gambling den, you figure it out.

Nope, hasn't moved for years, ever since whatever it was that blew its left tread off hit it – though some swear it's going somewhere when they get enough WildSnake in them. Look, do you want to hear this or not?

Anyway, it was relatively quiet, with half the Black Hand out working their territory. Krug Face-Mauler sat in a corner with a Guilder from Dead End, hacking out a slag mining contract–

Yes, I'm sure he has a brand somewhere, even if you can't see it behind all that admanterite plate he wears, he started the gang, for sump's sake! Shall I continue or do you want to go and search Krug for distinguishing marks?

Very well. Not far from the hagglers, watching with steely eyes was Horgen, Krug's personal guard.

Yeah, you've seen him before, probably using those two chainswords on some poor gob in the fighting pit at Slimecrawl. Yes, that Horgen. Beside Horgen, Flange was primping and combing his long pink mohawk. He's something of a dandy, quite a feat in a crew of Goliaths. The only reason Krug and the others don't kill him is that he's good with those pistols. Soft moans came from the back room where Agar, who usually takes care of Black Hand's 'business' here at the Sapper, lay sweating on my sheets with the shakes. He'd paid some ratskin to give him a glow mould tattoo the day before, that thing on his face that pulses green with his heartbeat. It's the glow spores under the skin, you see, but it made him sick as a scavvy when he first got it.

On the other side of the room – the others trying to sit out of blast range – was Dramuck, a huge mountain of muscle. That suicidal heavy bolter of his dismantled for cleaning and scattered across my best rat-wheel table. Me holding my breath every time his tinkering set those unstable bolt shells rolling around.

No, I didn't ask him to move. Sure his bolter was dismantled, but his fists weren't, and I didn't feel like eating my teeth just then.

That's when Mother Dark came in, clanging through the two hinged tread pieces of the door like she owned the place. Everyone froze, like a frag had just landed in their lap, and they were waiting to see if it'd go off. Behind Mother Dark strolled in three of her gang, like some kind of erotic carrion bats in black and red leathers.

Who's Mother Dark? You'll find out soon enough. Mother Dark is the High Priestess of the Blood Coven. A secretive Escher gang to the south, practising an obscure religion of their own. Up until recently the Coven had pretty much kept to themselves. Then, for no apparent reason, they began making bloody raids on surrounding territories. The raids themselves seemed rather pointless, with no obvious goal except carnage. Well, carnage and captives. Gangers and settlers taken by the Coven were never seen again. That's when the rumours started of dark magic and unspeakable rituals.

This, then, was Mother Dark, their leader, standing in my entrance, and staring at Krug Face-Mauler like he was the only one in the room.

'Guilder leave!' she commanded, her voice like a razor through velvet.

The Guilder, sputtering indignation at being given orders, gathered his robes about him and scurried out past the warrior women.

Krug rose slowly, the muscles of his jaw working as he bit back his rage. 'You dare break our pact, witch?'

One of the Eschers behind Mother Dark raised a heavy stubber, levelling at all in the room. Horgen's hands flew to the chainswords sheathed on his back, and Flange's pistols were already out, aiming from his lap beneath the table.

'We have held our part of the bargain, and not entered your territory,' Mother Dark purred icily, ignoring the weapon-filled tension. 'But you have yet to deliver one for sacrifice.'

Until now Black Hand had not tangled with the Coven, but by the incredulous looks they directed towards their leader, they obviously had not attributed this to some dubious pact. The shock on their faces quickly turned to fury, and for a moment I thought Krug would be gunned down by his own men.

'You'll get your blasted sacrifice when we capture one of those Orlock scum!' Krug growled back, admirably keeping panic out of his voice.

'No, Krug. The time to sacrifice one of a rival gang is passed. The Day of Thirst approaches! So say the Books of Letting. Preparations must be made. The Sacrifice must be one of your own, one of the Black Hand. You will bring the chosen one to the Drinking Stones in exactly four hours, or prepare for our wrath. The Day of Thirst approaches.'

And they vanished out of the door again before anyone could respond.

Krug turned to his men, who still held their weapons in their hands. All that babble about the Day of Thirst and the prospect of being chosen for sacrifice had done nothing to calm the men's nerves.

'Well, Krug, what's it going to be?' Horgen asked, his finger twitching on the trigger of his chainsword.

'War!' Krug barked. 'No sump-sucking Escher wench is going to give the Black Hand orders! We hit them. Hit 'em hard, and hit 'em now. We'll catch them on the way back to their hide-out.'

Krug's plan, though a relieving alternative to sacrifice, had its problems. First of all, only five Black Hand gangers were present, and with Agar sweating out his glow mould, that left only four gangers to 'hit 'em hard'. That's when I was deputised.

No, I can't shoot or fight worth a damn, but Krug wanted numbers. I refused at first, of course, but when Krug offered to wave his 'protection' fee on the Bonesapper's Lounge for a couple of weeks, well, my credit book got the better of my judgement. By all the gods, if I'd only known... I would've paid Krug twice as much not to go.

The second problem with Krug's plan was time of departure. It took Dramuck an hour to reassemble his heavy bolter, and another hour trudging through chem dust plains, across gantries and down air vents as we made our way into Blood Coven territory. We never caught the Coven on their way home.

We emerged from the air ducts at the Drinking Stones, and a right mess we were too. The chem dust on our clothes had turned to mud in a particularly steamy duct, and our hair was thickly matted with ventmite web, but as we weren't there on a date, it didn't much matter.

The Drinking Stones served as the Blood Coven's headquarters. They lay in an ancient and crumbling dome, filled with debris and rusting catwalks. The Coven had erected the circle of standing stones and a strange altar made out of broken chunks of concrete. Mother Dark and two of the Coven that had been at the Sapper were moving about the stones in bizarre circles. Miraculously, the heavy stubber was not there. We were two hours early, and had apparently caught them in the middle of some ritual.

Dramuck opened fire from the gantry on which he emerged, three storeys up, raining death into the circle of stone with his heavy bolter. I ran to a junction and down the air vent to the next opening about five paces away and began shooting wildly, the borrowed autopistol bucking awkwardly in my hands. Krug, Horgen and Flange leapt down ladders to the rubble-strewn floor.

Things went well at first. The Coven had scattered and taken cover behind the standing stones, and Dramuck's hail of bolts were keeping them pinned there. I can't say my own shooting did much but add to the noise, but I think that was Krug's idea anyway.

He, Flange and Horgen took the opportunity to rush the Stones on the ground. They were almost there when the back of Flange's thigh burst open in a bloody spray. He went down, clutching the spewing wound.

Krug and Horgen spun to face their new attackers. A hatch had opened in the dome wall behind them. Sister Quench, the witch with the heavy stubber, stood in the opening, sending burning chunks of lead into the three Goliaths. Behind her, also drawn by the sound of gunfire, were two more Eschers, charging to their sisters' rescue.

Krug bent, grabbing Flange by the collar, the ground around him flying into sharp concrete slivers. Meanwhile Horgen, chainswords screaming, charged the three Eschers at the door, who wisely sought to avoid the onslaught of the maniacal pit fighter behind its steel jamb. Krug used the brief respite to drag the wounded Flange to the nearest cover, the steel lattice of a catwalk support pillar. Horgen changed the direction of his charge and followed suit.

High above, sweat poured from Dramuck's body, veins bulging like cords in his neck and arms. The heavy bolter ate belt after belt from its huge ammo pack, spitting those bolts from its glowing red muzzle with a sound like chugging thunder. The Coven's reinforcements had come through the hatch directly beneath the gantry that Dramuck had positioned himself on, so he continued his fire into the standing stones, unable to draw a bead on the new threat.

Me, on the other hand, being twenty feet off to the side, could just barely see the bottom of their entry hatch. With a target finally within range, I redirected my fire.

Mother Dark and her cronies, the stones exploding around them, would periodically duck out to snap off wild shots. The two witches with Sister Quench made a dash through the hatch toward Krug and Horgen, my bullets sparking harmlessly off the nearby wall.

Krug aimed his shotgun through the crossbars of the support strut and blasted one of the charging Eschers. The solid slug hit the Coven juve in the neck, practically severing her head. Her lifeless body hurled back and crumpled on the floor amidst a rain of blood and bits of vertebrae.

Sister Quench's crouching form suddenly filled the part of the hatch I could see. Heavy stub slugs began pelting the duct-work around me. I pressed myself to the vent wall, only to hear the metallic shriek of the support lattice giving way.

The whole airshaft I was in twisted, buckled, and plummeted to the ground like some huge rusted worm in its death throes.

When the noise and dust settled, I realised I was somehow still alive. I was on my back, buried up to my shoulders in twisted metal. The ventilation tube was still attached to the wall at the other end, slanting down at crumpled angles to the floor where I now lay, trapped and immobile.

As if things weren't bad enough, Dramuck's pumping bolter finally overheated. The huge machine seized, jamming bolt after bolt together like a tube train crash. It exploded in his hands, sending his body soaring over the edge of the gantry. His fall halted with a sickening crunch, impaling him on the jagged end of a support that had held my fallen airshaft. I frantically tried to free myself, and was rewarded with a new avalanche of debris that covered me completely.

That was it. With two men down and his heavy bolter skewered on a girder, Krug was hopelessly outnumbered. His harried voice came ' Out and back! Out and back! Now!'

The Blood Coven jeered and fired off parting shots as Krug, Horgen and Flange fled the dome through a crevice in its shattered wall.

'Come again, Black Hand!' Mother Dark mocked. 'You're welcome any time!'

My stomach turned with sickening realisation that I had been left for dead. The pile of metal covering me had pinned my head to the side... if only it had broken my neck, I would have been spared the horrors I witnessed next. For though trapped and concealed from view, there was a small hole or tunnel through which I could breathe and see out of, directly in front of my face – staring directly at the Drinking Stones.

Some time went by, in which I assume the Coven were tending their wounds, and scouring the dome for survivors. They did not find me. For that I can give some little thanks. I saw them finally enter the circle of stones carrying two bodies: that of their mangled juve, and Dramuck, who they had somehow managed to drag off the impaling support.

And this is the worst part: Dramuck was still alive.

Any normal man would have died in the blast of his exploding weapon, never mind a careening fall onto sharp metal. It was his massive physique, you see. An iron constitution that refused to let go. The wounds through his shoulder told me that the support hadn't passed through any vital organs. Poor fragging bastard. If only it had hit his heart…

Mother Dark appeared, wearing a robe made of, well, I couldn't swear, but it looked like skin. Yeah, human. No, I don't know for sure. Look, I wasn't that calm at the time… Anyway, she stood before the altar and produced a large bound tome that I chose not to inspect too closely. She began to recite words from the book, strange garbled stuff that I couldn't pronounce, even if I could remember them. A witch with a chainsword began slicing up the dead juve on the floor while four others lifted the groaning Dramuck onto the table-like altar.

I winced and grit my teeth as horrible stone spikes were driven through his wrists and ankles into holes bored deep into the stone surface. This nightmare continued as the rest of the sisters began painting the pockmarked stones with strange symbols and arcs, using the bloody appendages of the dead juve. I could barely watch. This done, the Coven gathered in a circle about the pinioned body of Dramuck.

Mother Dark looked up from her recitation. 'The Day of Thirst is approaching! So say the Books of Letting!' she shouted, lifting the book above her head. 'Preparations must be made!'

With that she opened her robe, revealing a girdle made out of leather. It was covered in dozens of loops and pockets, each holding a gruesome bladed hook, like some horrible surgical instrument. The Coven members filed past Mother Dark one by one, each taking an instrument, and descended on Dramuck.

I thrashed, contorted and beat myself against the restraining pile of metal around me, in a desperate attempt to free myself. Desperate to be away, desperate not to see the hideous dismantling of Dramuck. Chunks of metal crashed to the floor with my exertions, but their reverberating clangs were drowned out by the inhuman screaming coming from the Drinking Stones.

I finally succeeded in freeing most of my body, but the evil piece of rubble pinning my head would not budge. I could not look away. I caught one nightmare image before I clenched my eyes shut to the abhorrent act before me.

It wakes me at night. Screaming. Dramuck splayed out like an anatomy book, the witches with their little hooks and blades, teasing tendon, vein, and organ from their rightful places, rivers of blood coursing down the sides of the altar… and all the while, Dramuck's screaming…

It seemed to go on for hours, tears streaming down my cheeks, my face aching from pressing my lids together so hard I thought my eyeballs would burst. And then it stopped. I lay there, eyes closed, breathing, for what seemed the first time in weeks.

Sometime later, when all was completely still, and I had heard the Coven depart, I chanced a look into the Drinking Stones. Dramuck's remains had mercifully been removed, though the red stone still glistened wetly. Mother Dark knelt at the base of the altar, praying.

Then, as the quiet of the dome carried her voice to me, I realised what I had taken for prayer was conversation. She was talking. Looking closer, I saw the altar sat upon a large drain, like a sewer grate.

She was cooing as one speaks to a dear, small child. 'Yes. Yes my sweet. Drink. Drink deeply, for your day approaches. The day you will emerge and all the Hive will tremble before your glory.'

My blood ran cold. There was something beneath the altar. Something huge. I could hear it, a sloshing gelatinous mass, flopping and banging around in some vast liquid filled metal vat. She was talking to it. And at the pinnacle of my terror, it spoke back. A sucking, gurgling mockery of human sound echoing from the pit.

'THI-I-I-I-I-RST'

In an insane surge of panic driven energy, I wrenched my head free of its vice-like imprisonment, leaving a good portion of my scalp hanging on its edge. Bleeding, I ran like a madman up the twisted tunnel of the hanging airshaft and out of that accursed dome, but not before Mother Dark's sickly sweet voice came drifting up the metal tunnel.

'Yes, my sweet. Preparations are being made...'

SO SURE, YOU'VE got a heavy stubber, but you see the question you should be asking yourself, don't you? Have I been hired to replace Dramuck to fight those sump-sucking degenerate witches...?

Or have I been hired to replace Dramuck as sacrifice to that thing, that abominable monstrosity beneath the altar?

You see, I'm not sure wily old Krug and that witch Mother Dark haven't got together and come to an agreement since our last–

No, wait!

Where are you going?

You haven't paid for your WildSnake yet!

# BAD SPIRITS
## by Jonathan Green

PANIC REIGNED IN the ratskin camp. The great claw swept down again, this time decapitating an old ratskin with a sickening crunch of shattering vertebrae. In the flickering light of the campfire, Grey Spider watched the slaughter in horror. Here he saw the corpse of a squaw, still clutching a mewling infant in her arms. There an elder coughed and breathed his last, as his precious life-blood poured from a gaping wound in his frail chest. And there, silhouetted against the fire in the darkness of the Underhive, was the mountainous outline of the beast. Only the tribe's totem pole towered above it. Grey Spider pumped the barrel of the shotgun and raised it to his shoulder. Now he had the monster in his sights.

Hearing the double click, the beast turned its misshapen head and fixed Grey Spider with its fiery gaze. The ratskin felt the sick chill of fear creep down his spine and seize his stomach in its contorting grip. He found his gun sights wavering – he was shaking. Taking one hand from the shotgun he wiped the sweat from his brow. Roaring, the monster charged. Grey Spider fired.

The report rang out across the vast, empty waste of the dome and echoed faintly from the plascrete ceiling far overhead. Grey

Spider felt the wind punched from him in a rush of air as an iron-hard shoulder rammed into his body, carrying him backwards. The beast slid to a halt and Grey Spider fell to the ground, his chest heaving as he tried to recover his breath. He could hear the beast snorting in great gulps itself as its body was seized by a rage-induced adrenaline surge.

The ratskin still had the shotgun gripped firmly in one hand. Struggling against the pain, he primed the weapon for a second time. This was like no other Underhive creature the tribe had ever encountered. It seemed impervious to weapons and had no understanding of compassion. Why was it attacking their camp? In their search for new hunting grounds had the tribe angered the inscrutable spirits of the Hive?

If only the hunting party had returned that night as had been expected. If only more of the menfolk had stayed behind to protect the camp. But if he and his Braves could not hold off this monster, then who was to say that all the ratskin warriors of the Redsnake tribe would make any difference? If he was to die that night he would die fighting and with honour, as a ratskin warrior!

The monster charged for the last time. Grey Spider pulled the trigger but still the monster would not stop. The great gleaming claw descended and Grey Spider's world exploded into darkness.

The settlement burned.

'IT WAS UNDERHIVERS, I tell you!' Quaking Dome bellowed, shaking his skull-headed staff in fury. As he screamed his anger, the shaman's face turned red beneath the sacred spirals painted on his cheeks.

'Try to be calm, my brothers,' the old chief pleaded, his age-lined brow furrowed in distress. The hunting had not been good, the Giant Rats had slunk off to nest deeper in Hive Bottom this season, and now the warriors had returned to find their families slaughtered. Chief Thunderslag felt powerless in the face of his warriors' grief. Nothing he could say would take away their pain. He could only try to keep them from doing something they would all regret. 'We have always lived on fairly good terms with the hivers.'

'What've they ever done for us?' It was one of the more rebellious Braves who spoke, having found his courage at the bottom of a bottle of Second Best.

'How can you say that, Howling Vent? They have traded with us, buying the skins we hunt for, and our blindsnake pouches. In exchange we have received weapons,' Chief Thunderslag eyed the bottle gripped in the Brave's hand with contempt, 'and that poison you guzzle so much!'

'You call it trade?' Quaking Dome exclaimed. There was no stopping the shaman now. 'It's nothing more than exploitation! The invaders have never respected the sanctity of our lands and now they've shown their true intentions!' He was physically shaking, the bones strung onto his ceremonial armour rattling with every convulsion. 'While we were away providing for our families, they murdered them all to drive us from our homes – so they can steal our territory!'

The shaman's tirade was greeted with a chorus of agreement. Many had sought solace in alcohol since making the gruesome discovery on their return. The shock of what they had found in the cold, oxyacetylene haze of morning had been too much for even these hardened warriors to cope with.

'Stop, stop now!' the despairing chief commanded. 'It is not the hivers who have done this. The spirits have been disturbed and become restless. We must find out why and discover who, or what, has done this. We owe it to the souls of our departed loved ones!'

'You don't know what you are talking about! You are getting old! Your words mean nothing to these people,' Quaking Dome hissed, turning on the ageing chief, his voice full of contempt. Dark eyes flashed in righteous anger. 'Words cannot bring back the dead. Actions are all that can appease their own troubled souls! We must put on war paint and prepare to die taking hiver scalps! It is the ratskin way!'

With that, the shaman turned on his heels and strode out of the camp. 'He who would avenge those who have been slaughtered here follow me!' he shouted back over his shoulder. The rest of the grief-stricken hunting party, high on Second Best, trailed after him.

Chief Thunderslag stood alone by the tribe's totem pole, watching the ratskin warriors disappear from view as they were swallowed up by the blackness of the Underhive.

'You will be renegade if you choose the war-path!' he shouted forlornly after them. 'You will no longer be my people! I will not be able to save you this time!'

No reply came from the darkness beyond the camp.

Thunderslag turned towards the totem. As so often, his eyes were drawn to the grotesque image carved from plascrete beneath the stylised form of a snarling rat. The thing was almost human in appearance and yet there was something monstrous about it.

'Yes, the spirits of the hive have been disturbed,' he muttered to himself. 'They must be put to rest.' Thunderslag instinctively felt a chill in his bones. Something evil was abroad, he knew. He put an uncertain hand to the autopistol holstered in his rat's-tail belt, hesitated and then withdrew it again. The chief looked to the totem with pleading eyes as if turning to it for help. 'But what can I do?' As Quaking Dome had said, the truth of it was that he was getting old. From the evidence lying all around him, even his native skills might not be enough to help him overcome this beast – if beast it was. Yet there had to be a way.

Abruptly, the old chief nodded to himself and grinned. There was always a way.

'SO OLD THUNDERSLAG'S making trouble again? Didn't I always say those ratskins couldn't be trusted?' the toothless bar-prop whistled.

'You sure did, Jemar,' Cooms, his middle-aged and over-weight drinking companion, agreed.

'And this was at the Jaygoth's place, you say, Calem?' Jack Finnian, the barman and proprietor of the Last Gasp Saloon asked, taking up his one-armed lean on the bar-top that he reserved for a genuine interest in what his customers were saying.

'That's right,' the grizzled miner confirmed. 'Old man Jaygoth and his wife and all their young 'uns – all dead. Scalped the lot of them!'

'Savages!' Cooms exclaimed, genuinely horrified. 'They can't be allowed to get away with that!'

'There's talk of some folks leaving town already 'cause of the troubles,' Finnian added, nodding knowingly.

'They need to be taught a lesson, that's what they need,' Jemar decided, slapping his hand on the bar. 'Did I ever tell you about the time I came across that band of ratskins up by Mercury Falls?'

'You did,' Cooms interrupted.

'It's about time somebody did something about them,' Calem said suddenly. 'I would myself, only I'm sure I'm this close to striking a really big adamantorite seam.'

'That's what you said the last time,' Cooms muttered under his breath.

'What about the Guilders?' suggested Finnian. 'They should get their watchmen to sort those ratskins out once and for all.'

'They're only interested in what happens inside the town,' Calem muttered sourly.

With the scrape of metal on metal, the doors swung open and the bounty hunter entered the smoky haze of the Last Gasp Saloon. Silence fell over the saloon, all eyes watching the stranger intently as he strode purposefully over to the bar. The tails of his long leather coat flapped around his knee-length boots. For a moment, the cluster of seals pinned to the inside of his coat that attested to successful jobs was revealed. Everyone in the bar could also clearly see the two, long-barrelled stub guns hanging over the man's hips. He walked tall, his back straight and his steps considered and certain. At the bar, the bounty hunter took the smouldering butt of a cheroot from between his teeth and sucked in a long, hissing breath.

'WildSnake,' he drawled in a voice that was no more than a husky whisper.

'You got it,' the barman replied, hurrying to grab a fresh bottle.

'Hey, mister, you want to kill yourself some ratskins?' Jemar piped up.

'Nope.'

'What d'you mean?' Jemar exclaimed, in disbelief. 'You're a bounty hunter, ain't you?'

'I've already got a job.' The man turned a piercing gaze on the old drinker. In the flickering sodium light, his steely eyes glinted under the shadowy brim of his battered hat.

'Then I would encourage you to finish it and move on, friend,' came a new voice, low and cultured, from the other end of the bar. 'At the moment, Toxic Sump isn't a place where self-respecting gentlemen like ourselves would wish to remain for longer than was strictly necessary.'

The owner of the voice emerged from the smoky gloom. He too wore a long, battered leather coat, beneath which could be glimpsed green trousers. His slender hands were enclosed in thick black gloves; in one he held a drink. He was of medium build, his features angular and well-defined. His carefully-trimmed black beard and moustache were in stark contrast to the bounty hunter's four-day stubble.

'Why's that?'

'Well, to be quite frank, Toxic Sump is becoming a ghost town.' The bearded man placed his glass carefully on the bar and turned to face the bounty hunter. 'The local ratskin tribe have been causing a lot of trouble recently. They are driving many of the settlers away. Claims are being abandoned throughout the dome; there's no work for anyone anymore.'

'He's right,' Cooms piped up, his companions muttering their agreement.

'So when do you leave?' the bounty hunter asked bluntly, fixing the bearded man with a calm gaze as he raised his drink to his lips.

'I am a trader and unfortunately I have a personal financial commitment to fulfil, otherwise I would have departed long ago. When the next guilder convoy arrives I'll conclude my business here, and when it leaves I intend to be on it.'

The bounty hunter downed his drink in one quick mouthful. 'I'm not going anywhere, yet. Like I said, I'm on a job.'

'I was merely looking out for a fellow man's best interests,' the man said with a hint of sighing despondency. 'Let me introduce myself. My name's Cyrus Beckerman.'

'I look after my own interests.' The bounty hunter replaced the cheroot between his lips. 'Now if you gentlemen will excuse me…' He turned to go.

With a ringing crash, the saloon doors were flung open and a ragged man burst into the bar. His grimy face was gaunt and drawn, his hair grey and tangled. His filthy and unhealthy appearance made him look far older than he probably was.

'Quinn? Is everything all right?' Finnian asked in surprise.

'Quick, get me a drink!' the wild-eyed man gasped, slumping down on a stool. 'I need a drink!' The barman didn't need to be told twice. Downing the shot in one go, Quinn slammed the glass back down on the bar. 'Another!' The second went the same way as the first. The grimy character stared directly ahead of him. 'It was terrible, I tell you. I ain't seen nothing like it!'

'What's the matter, man?' pressed Finnian. By now everyone else in the bar was crowding around in concern. The bounty hunter paused. He turned back towards the bar but said nothing. His keen eyes took in the bloodstains beneath the dirt and the sodden red patches on the prospector's filthy clothes.

'I was attacked, out on my claim up on Blackash Ridge,' the prospector whimpered. 'I paid my dues. I don't deserve to be treated like this!'

'Blackash Ridge, eh?' Beckerman interjected. 'Let me get you another drink. WildSnake!' He clicked his fingers and at once Finnian started refilling Quinn's glass.

'There were dozens of them!' the bewildered man went on. 'They were all screaming their war-chants and wearing their horrible rat hides. Their arms were covered in snake tattoos!' The man gratefully accepted the glass handed him by Beckerman.

'Sounds like the Redsnakes,' toothless Jemar offered. 'Didn't I always say–'

'That's them!' Quinn exclaimed, fixing the old man with a wild stare. 'They were mad, gone renegade. Said they were going to scalp me and feed me to the ripperjacks! They stole my finds and all my gear. I was on to something special up there, a really big strike! Then the monster came and I fled!'

'What monster?' Cooms asked.

'He's mad!' Beckerman scoffed loudly, looking around him. 'The man's obviously delirious.'

'Hear him out!' the barman said forcefully. 'Go on, Quinn, tell us more,' he encouraged. 'What was this monster like?'

'It was like some horror from the Sump, big as a test rig, with blazing eyes and one massive claw!' The prospector paused, sucking in ragged breath.

'And?' Cooms pressed. 'Don't keep us hanging.'

Quinn made no reply. Instead the prospector clutched at his throat and his face started to turn purple. He tried to speak but all that came from his throat was a horrible croaking sound.

'He's choking!' Finnian exclaimed. 'Quick, someone help him!'

Before any of the startled crowd could do anything, Quinn collapsed face first onto the bar with a strangled groan and lay still. The drinkers looked on, dumbstruck. Eventually Calem reached over to the prospector and felt cautiously for a pulse on the man's neck. 'He's dead!' the miner announced, in bewildered surprise.

'I guess it was all too much for him,' Finnian suggested, stunned. 'Heart must've burst! Shock'll do that to a man.' He paused, face infused with anger. 'Those ratskins must have done him over worse than we thought.'

'Well, that's it!' Cooms declared. 'I say we raise a posse right now, go up to Blackash Ridge and lynch old Thunderslag. Send the last women and children to Mercury Falls until it's dealt with. The old snake's gone too far this time!'

'Never mind all that,' Finnian interrupted, pointing at the body slumped over his bar. 'What do we do with him?'

'And what about the monster?' Jemar reminded everyone.

'If there was one!' Beckerman snorted.

'Yeah, but what about Quinn?' Finnian pressed.

'I guess we just lay him out back and let the guilders deal with it,' Cooms suggested.

The bounty hunter eyed the corpse suspiciously. His instincts told him that something wasn't quite adding up. Despite the convictions of the saloon's regulars, the prospector's wounds hadn't seemed to be that serious. And anyway, the man had choked, not bled to death.

Realisation abruptly struck the bounty hunter. The last thing Quinn had done before he died was to have a drink. The prospector's glass still stood on the bar. While the others talked, the bounty hunter surreptitiously picked it up and, swilling around the dregs left in the bottom, gave it a cautious sniff. A bitter scent assailed his nostrils. He had consumed a fair amount of WildSnake in his time but the glass smelt strange even for a particularly potent brewing. He thought back: only the barman and Beckerman had handled it. He put the glass back down on the bar and said nothing. Frowning, the bounty hunter looked around the room. Beckerman was nowhere to be seen.

'That trader left in an awful hurry,' he drawled.

'He's a busy man,' Cooms grunted over his shoulder by way of explanation.

Finnian was fidgeting nervously behind the bar, unable to keep his hands still. 'Come on, let's take Quinn out back,' he urged. 'Having a corpse in the bar's not good for trade. Makes customers feel uneasy.'

Between them the men picked up the prospector's body. The bounty hunter surprised everyone by taking Quinn's feet and helping carry the body out to the back room.

'Gotta show respect for the dead,' he drawled. No one saw him deftly withdraw a scrap of paper from the dead man's boot, secreting it in the long folds of his coat.

OUTSIDE THE Last Gasp Saloon, Nathan Creed, bounty hunter, took out the scrap of parchment and unfolded it, grimacing at the stale smell of the dead man's boots. The spidery scrawl and worn lines forming the map were faded with age but their meaning was clear. If the map was genuine – and something in Creed's gut told him that it was – then it would appear that Toxic Sump's dome was built directly on top of another, much older settlement.

Who knew what ancient treasures lay buried beneath the ash? Creed took the cheroot from his mouth and spat into the dust. The prospector had known. Now he was dead, thanks to the aid of a little poison.

*I guess someone else is in on the secret too,* the bounty hunter thought to himself. *Well, Beckerman, or whoever you are, Nathan Creed is involved now so you'd better watch your step.*

There was no one else around: Toxic Sump really was turning into a ghost town. Cocking the brim of his hat, Creed let his robo-sight visor scour the rocky outcrop to the west, beyond the barbed wire topped settlement wall. Beyond the rim lay Blackash Ridge where the dead prospector's claim was situated.

Suddenly he caught the flash of a whiplash coat-tail as a bearded figure slipped around a corner on the other side of the street. Creed grinned.

*Guess it wouldn't hurt to do a bit of poking around of my own before I leave town,* he thought to himself. His suspicions aroused, the bounty hunter set off.

Making sure he kept well out of sight, Creed followed the man in the coat until the furtive figure stopped outside a long, low building. The barn-like construction stood close to where the town wall had been built, almost on top of the rocky outcrop beyond. Its windows were smeared with grime and the structure gave the impression that it had long been abandoned.

As he unlocked the door, the furtive character glanced around to make sure he hadn't been followed. Back in the shadows, unseen, Creed grinned. It was Beckerman, just as he had suspected. The trader ducked inside the building and closed the door.

Creed darted down a side alley, stopping next to a grimy window. Rubbing the dirt from the panes with his coat sleeve, he peered inside. There was no one about – Beckerman appeared to have vanished – but there was plenty to see nonetheless. The building was crammed full of crates that, from their condition, had only been packed recently. Their sizes suggested to Creed that whatever was inside was pretty big – and as a result probably quite valuable.

There was something else. At the back of the warehouse the bounty hunter could make out a large door, slightly open.

'So that's where you've gone… What exactly are you up to?' Creed muttered. The door's rusty surface suggested that the door had been sealed for some time and only opened again recently.

Creed considered his options. He still had a job to do at Blackash Ridge. He crushed the stub of his cheroot beneath a worn boot heel and strode away. Beckerman could wait.

THE GLOW-GLOBES hanging from the ceiling of the dome were dimming by the time Creed crested the ash-covered rise. Before him lay the prospector's wrecked camp. Broken pipes jutted from piles of rubble, leaking steaming green fluid onto the crumbling masonry. Creed surveyed the devastation emotionlessly. The place was a mess: a cooking pot lay upturned next to the remains of a campfire; the prospector's shelter had been demolished; the seismic equipment the man would have used was missing. The dirt and dust around the site had been churned up; here and there lay a feather or scraps of fur. Ratskins had been here all right, but so had something else – something far more sinister.

Among the countless moccasin prints that covered the site, Creed spotted something unusual: boot marks. The pattern of the boot treads had the precision and regularity of a machine press. They hadn't the look of handmade ratskin moccasins.

Something else troubled Creed: why would ratskins steal machinery and seismic gear? His keen eyes scanned the camp. It was common knowledge that the indigenous tribes of the Underhive worshipped ancient archaeotech hoards. They had been known to go on the warpath to recover stolen sacred treasures, but to take modern equipment from a lone prospector? Ratskins had no need of such things. Their knowledge of the treacherous Underhive was unrivalled. There was definitely something strange going on.

It was easy to find where the prospector had been working. Close to a jutting outcrop of rock, a hole had been blasted in the side of the hill. Creed flicked down the photo-visor from beneath the brim of his hat. Peering through the gloom beyond the opening, he could see the pitted walls of a cave and the entrance to a man-made tunnel, shored up with metal props.

Entering the cave, Creed felt a breeze blowing up from the tunnels below. The foetid air testified to the fact that whatever was down there had been there a long time, sealed away with the decomposing effluent that filtered down from the hive-city far above.

The dirt floor of the cave was covered with yet more ratskin footprints and the same boot marks from the camp, leading both in and out of the tunnel entrance. And there, stamped into the dust, were the footprints of something else too, something much bigger. Creed crouched down to study the prints closer but couldn't identify them at all. They were large and flat, and ended in clawed tips. Claws that had cut deeply into the ground with every step. Maybe there was some truth to the old man's monster story after all. Creed grinned in the darkness.

*Getting superstitious, Creed?* he thought to himself. Pieces of the puzzle began to lock together in his mind. Dusting himself down, the bounty hunter began to rise.

'You're not going anywhere!' hissed a cultured voice.

*Beckerman!*

Creed froze in his crouched position, feeling the cold muzzle of a gun pressed against the back of his neck. He had been so intent on his investigations that he had not heard the softly booted approach. Another footprint explained.

'So it was you,' Creed said calmly. 'I guess you aren't any kind of trader at all. What's Van Saar's place in all this?'

The man didn't bother to confirm his identity. 'I thought you were on another job,' he snapped, almost in annoyance.

'I'm sure I can make time for you.'

'You have become a... complication.' Beckerman, or whatever the Van Saar's real name was, was about to kill. Creed
recognised the signs from long years on the trail of untold
killers.

In a fluid motion Creed slid the knife from his boot, the
movement concealed by the tails of his coat. Twisting the blade
around in his hand he jabbed it backwards. The knife sank
deep into the ganger's leg, cutting through his boot, until it
scraped against bone.

Beckerman cried out in pain. Dropping his hands to the
wound, he gritted his teeth and yanked the blade out of his shin.

It was all the time Creed needed. He sprang forwards, away
from the muzzle of the gun and into the tunnel. As he did so,
he turned to his enemy. On his feet again, he faced the ganger,
a stub gun in each hand.

Depressing both triggers he fired off a couple of rounds, feeling the familiar explosive recoil in his wrists. At the same
moment the ganger fired. An instant later Beckerman's bodysuit tore apart at the shoulder, leaving a ragged hole – only a
flesh wound, but it was enough to ruin his aim. Creed threw
himself out of the way as the dust at his feet kicked up in bursts
and the shells impacted against the rocky floor.

Lying on his back in the dirt, Creed pushed himself up onto
his palms. Through the clearing dust he saw the ganger stumbling backwards, his own weapon dropped on the floor of the
cave. Too late, the bounty hunter noticed the wires trailing
away from the tunnel entrance. Before he could aim his stubbers, the Van Saar fell onto the detonating device. There was a
shuddering boom, the roar of shattering rock and the passageway began to shake violently.

The ground quaking beneath his feet, Nathan Creed hurled
himself down the tunnel. Behind him the cave mouth collapsed in a jumble of rocks and wreckage. Creed knew only too
well that an uncontrolled explosion in a weakened dome could
easily cause hivequakes. He had no idea how much of the rubble above him might come down at any second, so he kept on
running. One thing was for certain: the way back was now
blocked by the explosion. There was no going back. Regardless
of what lay beyond, in the twisting network of tunnels, that was
the way he would have to go.

* * *

CREED PAUSED IN the semi-darkness. The artificial lighting in this section of the cave system had failed, forcing the bounty hunter to peer more closely through his photo-visor. Ahead, to the right, the tunnel opened into a larger cave, possibly the remains of an ancient habitation dome or industrialised area. The passage to the left looked like a dozen others he had wandered along for the last few hours, always leading him deeper towards Hive Bottom. He chose to go right.

He was about halfway across the cavern when he heard an unexpected sound that froze him in his tracks. His hands hovered over the holstered stub guns. It was like the sound he had heard when he had once encountered a nest of milliasaurs. They had been picking at corpses from just another badzone shoot-out. The sound was unmistakably the tearing of flesh. Ominously, as he listened, the noise ceased.

Moments later, through the gloom Creed was startled as the half-light caught in the jaundiced eyes of some kind of zombie as it raised its scabrous head to look at him. The creature was half-clothed in filth-encrusted rags, beneath which its diseased skin was visible.

'Plague!' Creed gasped. Everyone knew about what happened to the victims of the neurone plague, but the bounty hunter had never been confronted by the results, face-to-decomposing face.

The once-human thing hissed through its pockmarked lips. Instantly, the rest of the pack left off devouring the corpses, more interested in the prospect of fresh, tender flesh. Half-rotted muscles dragged the zombies towards the bounty hunter, spittle dripping in long strings from their gaping, moaning mouths. As the foul creatures shambled forward, Creed quickly glanced behind him. As he had feared, out of the corner of his eye he could see yet more zombies stalking towards him from behind.

Part of him knew he had to save his ammunition for as long as possible. He had no idea where the endless tunnels would lead him or what else he would have to face before he found a way out. If he ever found a way out. But the likely alternative at the moment was the risk of catching the Zombie plague himself. There was nothing else for it. Aiming a stubber at the head of the nearest horror, Creed pulled the trigger.

The zombie's skull exploded in a shower of blood, bone and brain matter. The walking corpse stumbled on a few feet further

before it collapsed, still twitching. This violent display did nothing to stop the advance of the other zombies. The brain-eating
disease had obviously deprived them of both fear and pain.

A second shell tore a hole in the side of another of the
advancing zombies as it slunk forward, a portion of putrefying
intestine flopping from the wound. Marshalling his strength,
Creed did not run but kept walking at a steady pace. He figured
that until the brainless creatures caught the smell of blood it
was unlikely that they would charge him. Hopefully the occa-
sional shot would keep off the closest of them and clear a path
across the cavern. Whatever, he knew full well that there was no
going back now. He could only go on, despite not knowing
what lay ahead.

Creed felt time slow to a crawl as the interminable zombie-
shoot played itself out. He reloaded as he walked, always
careful to keep a healthy distance between himself and the
zombies. Every instinct screamed at him to run, to put as much
distance between the flesh-eating creatures as he could. But
Creed resisted the temptation. The ground underfoot was
uneven, with hidden potholes and twisted pipes jutting from
the ash, ready to trip an unwary fugitive.

A number of the creatures broke off from their laboured pursuit to feed on the carcasses of the zombies that had already
fallen. Creed smiled his fatalistic smile. Maybe you ugly sons of
bitches have no attention span. He knew he had no option but
to keep going. He just hoped that he found a way out of the
cave system before he ran out of slugs. Creed walked on
through the abyssal twilight.

CREED CROUCHED DOWN behind the crate and allowed himself a
deep breath of relief. He had left most of the zombies behind
in the deeper, darker recesses of the cave system as they lost
interest and began fighting amongst themselves. After several
hours trudging through the underworld, he found himself at
one end of a much larger cavern. As he had reached the prop-
erly lit passages leading up and out of the depths, the zombies
had seemed unwilling to follow. Maybe they feared something
that lay beyond, Creed pondered, something to which they
reacted on an instinctive, primal level.

Hearing the sounds of raised voices, Creed peered over the
edge of the crate, careful to remain out of view. This cavern

stretched out before him for over a hundred metres. Numerous halogen lamps illuminated the chamber, revealing the mouths of distant tunnels leading off into darkness. Twenty metres or so away, a band of maybe a dozen ratskin warriors were in heated discussion with six members of a Van Saar gang, easily identifiable by their familiar padded green body suits. The two groups were clearly in league with each other.

*Hmm... thick as thieves,* Creed said to himself. *Looks like the old man really was onto something.* He scanned the cave for further evidence of his suspicions.

The place was a guilder's dream. It was full of the most incredible archaeotech Creed had ever seen. Bizarre clusters of machinery, dust-covered control panels and chrome-plated artefacts were in the process of being packed into crates... crates like those in Beckerman's warehouse. Creed nodded to himself. *This is bigger than I thought!* It all added up. Creed cursed himself for not piecing the clues together earlier. There was an absolute fortune here. *The credits raised from the sale of this stuff could buy the whole of Toxic Sump, with Mercury Falls thrown in as well,* he thought.

A shout brought his attention back to the discussion taking place in the centre of the cavern. Something was going down: the ratskins and the gangers were almost coming to blows. Every now and again, the breeze from unseen vents carried wisps of conversation to the bounty hunter's ears.

'Not enough trader tokens, hair face!'

'Not enough WildSnake!'

'You agreed to the deal.'

'The spirits are disturbed!'

'Crap – nothing but superstitious fear.'

'The totem beast walks!'

'Rubbish.'

'Our ancestors are watching!'

Creed narrowed his eyes: now things were really getting interesting. The gangers had their backs to him. If he could just get a little nearer he might be able to identify the individuals. Keeping low behind the piles of crates, Creed slunk closer. He closed the distance between himself and the gangers without being seen, before ducking down again. Cautiously he peered around the edge of a crate.

Creed felt his coat tail sweep across the screwdriver just a moment too late to stop the object rolling off the top of a tool box and rattling onto the stony floor of the cave. He cursed silently. Gangers and ratskins all turned in his direction. Creed knew he could not hide now.

'Way too slow!' he drawled as he loosed a fusillade of shots from behind the crate, slamming several rounds into the assembled conspirators. One of the gangers flew backwards as a bullet shattered several ribs; another screamed as a dumdum punctured a lung on its passage through his body.

Then ratskins and Van Saars were returning fire. The chamber echoed with the crack of the tribesmen's muskets and the zinging scream of rounds fired from the gangers' superior weapons. Creed knew he was hopelessly outnumbered, but he was confident that he was by far the better marksman. Despite the dazzling array of targeting devices bolted to the Van Saar's autoguns and bolters, his shots were hitting home. Creed grinned. He liked a good shoot-out. For every ten shots that impacted against the crate behind which he sheltered, one coolly executed shot from him found its target in the form of a renegade ratskin or a corrupt ganger.

The hail of bullets from a bolt gun tore through the empty crate.

'Durability exceeded,' Creed muttered, and bolted for new cover. He ran, wooden boxes exploding in an eruption of splintering planks behind him. Diving forwards he just avoided a glowing plasma burst as it streaked over his head. The barrel it eventually struck, on the far side of the cavern, contained some volatile substance. Forty metres away, Creed felt the wash from the resulting ball of superheated crimson flame. The cave was lit up momentarily by the inferno.

'What the...?'

In the shadows, did he catch sight of something big on the move? Then the scorching blast found the bounty hunter, and even protected by his thick coat he felt its fierce warmth on his back. Creed wrinkled his nose at the rank smell of singed leather. Somebody screamed.

As he lay face down on the ground, he discarded the spent cartridges from his guns and reloaded. Once these precious rounds had been used up there were only enough bullets left for one more reload.

'Looking tough, girls,' he whispered to the stubbers. 'Looks like you're all but done.' His encounter with the zombies had cost him dear.

A bestial mechanised roar suddenly rose above the deafening sounds of the firefight. As Creed looked around, the monstrous noise was joined by the agonised howl of what could only be a dying man. Creed risked a look over the ancient piece of machinery he was hiding behind. To his horror he saw a nightmarish shape. It was fully three and a half metres tall, silhouetted in the bone-white glare of the halogen lamps. The thing lifted a screaming Van Saar into the air by a great curved metal hook. The cruel blade had been thrust through the man's back and was now projecting from his stomach. The hideous monster tossed the dying ganger carelessly aside and ploughed forwards through the mass of men, crushing a petrified ratskin under one of its great, clawed steel feet.

Now or never! Creed thought, and with his adversaries brutally distracted he made his move. Skirting the edge of the cavern he saw the terrible creature revealed in the glare of the lamps in all its startling glory. Once human, muscle and bone portions of the creature had been spliced to a droid chassis, so that the creature stomped across the cavern through the carnage on pistoning legs of solid metal. Something about its shape was strangely familiar, but Creed wasn't about to stop for a closer look.

The psychotic cyborg's visage was a grotesque parody of a human face. One bloodshot eye glared out from a head malformed by a serrated, metal jaw. Its bionic, red-glowing counterpart observed everything unblinkingly with electronic intensity. Atrophying tissue around the artificial implants had begun to peel away from the partially metal skull to reveal the corroded circuits of the endo-skeleton beneath.

Creed saw that the beast-machine's naked torso was crossed with livid, purple scars. The huge, steroid-enhanced muscles of its left arm, coursing with telescoping steel cables, supported the weight of a crude three-fingered talon. The claw flexed spasmodically. The right arm was missing entirely. The massive metal contraption in place of the limb began at the shoulder, plasteel-shielded wire bundles connecting with the monster's spinal cord beneath the skin. From its design and the aged condition of its components, Creed was sure that this was no

modern-day servitor-thing escaped from higher up the Hive.
How long had it been trapped down here, he wondered, its
power cells on standby? Maybe a hivequake had reactivated it.
Its program must have been corrupted along with the slow
deterioration of its body in the inhospitable conditions in the
caves. Now it was loose once more.

The cyborg was proving more than a match for the surprised
conspirators. It seemed to be almost totally impervious to
their weapons. Cauterised holes in its gore-splattered flesh
attested to the fact that both the gangers and ratskins had hit
the creature. However, its armour plating had halted the shells,
and seemed to have stopped them from doing any severe damage.

The gangers and ratskins fought on with increased vigour.
This time it was they who felt out-gunned and out-numbered
by the sheer might of the rampaging cyborg. Their agonised
cries rang in Creed's ears as he ran from the cavern, leaving the
carnage behind him.

The bounty hunter fled along a large, well-trodden tunnel.
Halogen lights illuminated the passage and Creed noticed
power cables running along its length towards the world above.
Desperate, he followed the sloping path upward, his lungs
heaving.

At the mouth of the tunnel, Creed ran into the first and last
piece of his puzzle. Wounded shoulder bound up in a temporary bandage, a bearded man was crouched over a small black
box. Beckerman was trying to make the final connections
between a pair of wires and a small detonator, his lacerated fingers scrabbling. The Van Saar looked up on hearing Creed's
approach and a crazed, leering grin parted his lips. A pair of
twisted wires ran along the access tunnel in conjunction with
the power cables.

'Not this time, Beckerman!' Creed roared, charging the last
few paces.

Ignoring the weapons at his belt, the bounty hunter lunged
forwards, his fatigued muscles fuelled by the adrenaline rush of
exasperated desperation. His hands slick with his own blood,
Beckerman's fingers slipped on the detonator screws, unable to
get a grip. Powering up the tunnel, Creed reached the entrance
and flung himself bodily forward at the ganger before he could
make the final twist of the detonation cord.

As Beckerman fell, he grabbed Creed in two strong hands and twisted. Using his own weight and momentum, the Van Saar ganger flung the bounty hunter over his shoulder. Creed hit the ground hard, cracking his head on the rocky floor. He lay still, momentarily stunned by the shocking pain. As his vision began to clear, Creed looked up. Death looked back.

Beckerman stood at his feet, a great chunk of plascrete raised above his head. The ganger smiled coldly as he prepared to destroy the bounty hunter once and for all. Desperately Creed fumbled for his guns, trying to shake the concussion which all but overcame him.

The bounty hunter blinked suddenly as something splashed against his face. Putting a hand to his cheek he felt a warm wetness. His grimy fingertips came away red with blood. He became aware of a horrible gurgling noise and through the fog of pain he looked up at his would-be killer. Beckerman's feet were hardly touching the ground as his body hung in the air, convulsing, a great, metallic claw thrust through his chest. With a growl like iron scraping on iron, the cyborg took hold of the ganger's head with its vice-like claw. With one savage tug, the man-machine tore Beckerman's head from his shoulders.

In seconds Creed was on his feet, all pain forgotten. He had only one chance. In a supreme effort of willpower he ran towards the monster.

'Chew on this, clawfinger!' he rasped, raising his guns. Both stub guns blasted the last of their precious cargo at the insane cyborg at point blank range. The sound in the confined tunnel was deafening. Under the constant bombardment the creature was forced back by the impact of the shells. With clumping steps it staggered into the mouth of the tunnel as it tried to keep its balance.

Then Creed could hear nothing but the sound he had been dreading: the click, click, click of empty barrels. Flinging his guns aside, the bounty hunter dived for the detonator where Beckerman had dropped it. The cyborg roared and stomped up the tunnel. With one final twist of a screw, the connection was made; with the flick of a switch, the detonator primed. Hurling himself to the ground, Creed thumbed the lit red button then scrambled backward up the tunnel as fast as he could propel himself.

With a distant rumbling boom, the last explosives set by Beckerman detonated. At the echoing sound, the advancing monstrosity turned, confused. The rumble became a roar as the charges set along the tunnel triggered one another in quick succession. A great cloud of dust and stone shards erupted from the tunnel mouth. Face down on the dusty ground, hands flung over his crumpled hat, the bounty hunter waited for the stony hurricane to devour him. Scant metres behind his prostrate form, a hundred tonnes of rubble crashed down on top of the cyborg and Beckerman's mangled corpse alike.

Rocks and rubble rattled about the prone bounty hunter, but the fatal crush of the avalanche on his back never came. As the rumbling din and shaking subsided and finally ceased, Creed thought that perhaps he could hear the whirr of grinding servos for a moment. Maybe it was just the buzzing from his tortured eardrums. Then there was silence.

Coughing, he staggered upright and looked around him. The bounty hunter was covered in a fine grey dust which choked his mouth and clogged his nostrils. He was standing at the tunnel mouth, where it led into another, smaller cave. Through the settling dust he could see a hefty iron door that had been left slightly ajar at the other end of the chamber. Daylight crept around the doorframe, piercing the dust. Cautiously entering the cave, Creed hauled at the rusted door, which opened with surprising ease. Stepping through, he found himself surveying the crated contents of Beckerman's warehouse.

Limping towards the door, Creed winced at the pain from what felt like a hundred bruises. Nevertheless he grinned, a white slash of teeth in his black-grimed face.

'Puzzle solved,' he said to himself. 'Guess I'm about done.'

'THERE'S A WHOLE warehouse full of the stuff,' Creed explained, pointing at the chrome sphere in the open crate at the old chief's feet.

'It shall be treasured and given due reverence,' the ratskin said solemnly. He dropped the bag of oblong, ceramite chips into Creed's hand with a sigh. 'I knew there had to be a way.'

Creed said nothing.

'I feel that perhaps I have betrayed my people,' Chief Thunderslag continued, looking around him. 'Many young Braves have died. Such a pointless waste of life.'

He shrugged sadly. 'But the spirits had to be appeased; our families had been killed. At least now the spirits are at rest once more.' The old ratskin turned to face Creed. 'What do you think? Have I betrayed my tribe?'

'I'm not much of a thinking man,' the bounty hunter replied.

'Does it not trouble you to accept what is no better than blood money?' Thunderslag asked him, a suggestion of anger in his voice.

Creed took the stub of a cheroot from between his lips and squinted again at the totem pole and the grotesque image carved upon it. He saw it now: a creature with one great claw and an ugly, fanged square face.

'A job's a job, old man,' he said, turning his gaze on the old ratskin chief. Creed's expressionless features were an inscrutable mask, giving no clue as to his true feelings on the subject. 'See you round, old timer.'

With that, Nathan Creed secreted the money in a deep recess of his long, trailing coat. Pushing his battered hat firmly down over his brow, he turned and strode off into the fading light of the dimming globes.

# BADLANDS SKELTER'S DOWNHIVE MONSTER SHOW
## by Matthew Farrer

THE CENTRAL THOROUGHFARE of Fever's Break started at the fortified gates and snaked under the huge ridge of metal where the
dome floor had buckled during some upheaval hundreds of
years before. Where it reached the moving stairs into the cliff-
face that formed the uptown, it opened out into a plaza against
the dome wall. That was where all the local hawkers, preachers,
beggars and hoods spent their days, and that was where Skelter
stopped and had his people set up the tent.

Starkey had unhitched the two biggest pack-bison from the
main wagon and was using them to pull the poles upright,
while his brother and daughter ran back and forth with magnetic clamps for the guy-ropes. Skelter's own kids were already
at work, running back and forth through the streets nearby trying to look like locals and shouting, 'Skelter's show is here!
Skelter's show is here!' to each other. They were good at it. By
the time tickets went on sale, everyone would know about
them.

Another half-dozen of the troupe were strolling back and
forth around the tent and the rows of wagons and trailers
parked in a jumble beyond it, relaxed but watchful eyes on the
crowd that was already building up. Skelter glanced out at the

59

faces and did some quick mental arithmetic, and liked the result. In a few minutes he would begin his pitch.

Amongst the cages bustled the rest of them, making sure the covers were closed and the more excitable exhibits were staying calm. Kamusz, the retired bounty hunter, winked at Skelter as he let a fold of tarpaulin fall away as if by accident. Instantly a huge scaly arm shot out and grabbed at him, got him by the front of his jerkin and yanked him toward the bars. There were screams from the crowd. Kamusz yelled as if in fear and Skelter got in on the act, running across and whacking at the arm with a pistol barrel. It retreated and as they put back the tarp Skelter saw Issig the scaly snort through his nostrils in salute before he curled back up to snooze again. They sauntered away.

'That should sell us another couple of dozen tickets,' Skelter murmured.

Kamusz nodded. 'Are you putting Issig in tonight?'

'Sure.' There was a flapping behind them as the banner went up: 'Badlands Skelter's Downhive Monster Show!' They kept walking. 'I don't think the line-up we tried at Rathouse Gulch worked too well. I'm going to bring Issig on last. Most people up here by the Wall are so green they barely know what a scaly is. Remember how they screamed the first time we brought him out at Winchcrag? I'll put on the sump toads early, maybe even have someone walk one around on a leash this afternoon to raise interest.'

Kamusz nodded, then tapped Skelter's arm as a wave of shuffles and muttering rippled through the onlookers. 'Trouble.'

Silent figures were making their way through the crowd, silent figures dressed in heavy cloaks and hats that made them look a head taller than the townsfolk around them. The gawpers melted aside as the leader stalked over. The two showmen tensed. The ganger was easily Skelter's height, which was unusual enough, but his heavy frame loomed where Skelter's long limbs just gangled. Kamusz began idly whistling the little tune that the troupe used as a signal for everyone to get armed and ready. There was a rattle behind them as the doors on the cages were loosened.

'Where is the wyrd here?'

Skelter gave Kamusz a quick 'I knew it!' look, then brightened up and tried to look attentive.

'No wyrds here, sir, I assure you. We have guilder stamps of passage; everyone's been cleared by the Adeptus themselves. Just years of experience in the worst of the Badlands at the very Sump of the Hive, and training that brings out these creatures' natural behaviours. Brought up to these peaceful towns for the first time ever!' He raised his voice a little for the benefit of the crowd. 'For your education, edification and amazement, we give you–'

'There is a wyrd here!' The leader cut him off.

Skelter suppressed a sigh and idly wondered if the man was from a gang he'd heard of. With practice, you could pick the Cawdor flunkies: lovely resonant voices. It was all those hymns and sermons. Not that it made up for the trouble they caused.

'Psykers and carousing and harbouring of mutations! This so-called "show" is a stench in the nostrils of the Emperor. The townsfolk would not listen to our warnings, but I know your kind – thieves and swindlers all.'

Another meaningful glance between Skelter and Kamusz. *Damn, usually it doesn't happen this soon.*

The ranter shoved a hand under his cloak for a weapon. Skelter let his needle pistol slide smoothly from his sleeve to his hand and fired a single, silent shot into the man's throat. The townsfolk yelped and dived for cover as two more gangers fell before they could bring weapons to bear.

Then the cages swung open and Tara ran past, blowing a whistle. Six huge Sump Toads recognised the signal and bounded out of their cages, chasing the last few gangers away down the street, as four of the troupe's wranglers grabbed nets and leashes and took off after them. The crowd parted before them, and Skelter was gratified to hear catcalls and clapping as the gangers scuttled away.

The prone leader was beginning to stir and groan, so Kamusz kicked him hard in the temple. He slumped again as Skelter fitted the little pistol back into its slip-sheath.

'How long have we been working the big-towns circuit, Kam? I can never get over the so-called "settled levels". Call themselves gangers? Soft as spider-gut. I mean, the banner and all our posters say I lived at Hive Bottom for years. Why doesn't anybody ever act as though they believe me?' Kamusz was bent over the unconscious gangers. 'C'mon, best not to rob them.

You know there'll be the Watch along in a second. Let them be the bad guys, hey?'

'I'm not robbing them, Skelter. Recognise these? The way the chamber and sight are set on the stubgun here, the barrel configuration? And look, that knife: chisel-point and no quillions. Only one House makes that design. Give you odds he's got a mask collection at home.'

'Great. Just *great*. Back at the Gulch they told us this was a nice, fat, quiet town.'

'Probably is, most of the time. This whole level is only just within the Underhive by most people's reckoning. The upramps to Hive City proper are only a morning's ride away. Things up here get run pretty tightly. I had people ask around. There are two deputised Watch gangs, the Fireclouds and the Gunsmoke Shadows, and they're both Escher-affiliated. Cawdor loyalties in a town like this mean you have meetings in a cellar and keep your mask under your mattress. We must be something special to bring them out of their burrows.' Kamusz looked around. 'Skel, your crowd's getting pensive.'

The showman nodded, then wheeled around and raised his arms.

'That was no excitement, ladies and gentlemen! That was a scuffle any Downhive child could have won! I hope you think you were entertained before, folk of Fever's Break, because tonight I'll prove that wrong, wrong, wrong! Tonight, at 'Badlands Skelter's Downhive Monster Show!'

Behind him there was a rattle as the shutter went up in a wagon's side and the ticket window opened. Most of the crowd jostled for spots in the queue, and Skelter straightened his waistcoat, twirled his moustache and beamed at everyone.

THERE WAS A grey adamant slab set at eye-level in the far wall of the anteroom, with two lines carved in plain, blunt letters: *We determine the guilty. We decide the punishment.*

Skelter read them for the eighth time, scowled and shuffled his feet. Next to him, Tara gave an ostentatious yawn.

'It was those tickets we sold, wasn't it?' murmured Kamusz from Skelter's other side, and that was too much.

Skelter flapped his arms about. 'Refunds! There are no more hateful two syllables under the Emperor's sun. We had to give *refunds*!'

'Really? No syllables more hateful?' Kamusz scratched his thin white beard as he thought. Tara rocked on her heels, slender hands twitching. They had been disarmed when they were brought into the bunker, and she was missing having a weapon to hold.

'I mean, coming and griping about the show, that was fine. Wasn't that fine? That was OK! I welcome that! I welcome everybody to come and have their say, no one can say I'm unreasonable about that.'

'How about "scavvy"?' Kamusz said while Skelter drew breath. 'That's pretty hateful.'

'I would have been happy to discuss the whole thing with them. Open a bottle or two, sit around a table, discuss any problem they had at all. But noooo…'

'"Cawdor", of course,' Tara put in. 'Two syllables and as hateful as you want.'

'Out they come and they get the bloody Arbites on us! Not the Watch, you'll notice, not the duly deputised guilder representatives delegated to keep the peace and protect the interests of the community. Oh, no, that's too simple.'

'"Lashworm"?' Kamusz suggested. Tara shook her head.

'"Lashworm" is a very congenial two syllables.' She ducked a particularly vehement gesture of Skelter's. 'You can train lashworms, you know. Mother's family taught me. You can teach them to pop out for certain types of sounds or smells. Tricky, though.'

'Really? How about – no, that's not two syllables. How about "No sales"?'

'Even Arbites would be acceptable!' Skelter pointedly raised his voice a notch to try to ride over them. 'I mean, Arbites, OK, we've dealt with them before. I mean, they say they serve the Emperor Himself, even Helmawr can't gainsay them. Oaths of loyalty, upright and true, all the rest of it. Fine! But they waited…'

'Ooh. "No sales." Ooh.' Tara rolled the words around a little. 'Yes, that's hateful.'

'I said they waited until we were almost sold out and then brought every damn thing down! I don't think you two have grasped this yet. Me! Skelter! A showing of the Downhive Monster Show cancelled! We have had. To give. *Refunds!*'

Skelter could see from Tara's face that she was framing a tart reply when the far door clanged open and the Arbites marched in. Hustling after them came the Cawdor leader Skelter had shot, in full regalia now: dark tunic, oiled-leather mask, a stick-patch over the cut the needle had left in his neck. He was fidgeting with triumph or agitation – Skelter couldn't tell through the mask and shapeless clothes. The senior of the two Judges, in black and grey tunic in place of armour, walked to a heavy chair that rose silently through a floor-panel and settled into it in a swirl of his black cloak. His deputy watched impassively through a gleaming, mirror-tinted visor.

'Which of you is Skelter? Stand forward, please.' Skelter took a slow half-step.

'You have had something of a… fraught introduction to this precinct, Skelter. This district is a quiet one. Laws are obeyed. You, however, seem to have aroused some passions.' He flicked the showman an appraising look over steepled fingertips and suddenly pointed to the Cawdor.

'Citizen Jago, of the, um–'

'Light of Fury!' boomed the mask.

'Light of Fury brethren has a number of claims against your, what is it, "Downhive Monster Show"? He has declared it will encourage lawlessness and riot. I understand there was a scuffle when you set your exhibits up earlier. One that it was necessary to bring before the Adeptus.' The Judge's tone was ironic, but Jago had apparently missed that: he nodded in evident satisfaction and folded his arms.

'I can't understand that, sir. No alcohol is to be sold, certainly not drugs, not even food. There are some dangerous creatures, true, Milliasaurs and Ripper-jacks and so on, but we keep those in secure cages and simply charge people to look. I realise that these are settled parts, sir, and people aren't at ease about untamed hive life. That's why we also have acrobats, trick-shooting, more. We will be bringing out creatures from the lower Underhive, but I can vouch, sir, that through tireless training and tight technique that has tamed and…'

He realised he was pitching again, and cut himself short. 'We've been in this business for years, sir. We like order at our shows. If we start trouble, we don't get to come back. Our self-interest is your best evidence, sir.'

'Lies and ever perverse lies,' the voice snarled from under the leather mask, 'told to one who labours in utmost dignity in the service of the Emperor himself!' Jago made an elaborate holy sign at the word 'Emperor' which Skelter didn't recognise.

'The Imperial seal is upon your shoulder, and yet this man profanes it! I came to you, Lord Justice, because surely you must see that the vicious poison of tolerance and loose thought that permits this parade of filth will rot away this town! Mutants and savages lurk in their camp, even show themselves here in a house of the blessed Adeptus! Every hour that the simple people around us are drawn away from prayer, fasting and persecution is an hour that they lose from the path of their Redemption. Consorting with mutants, tricksters and wallowers in pleasure, and those who bring the curse of the witch into the midst of the faithful!'

Skelter shifted uncomfortably. *Good grief! I'm standing in a room with a man who can actually use the word 'midst' in cold blood.*

The Judge nodded, and his gaze pivoted back to the showman. 'And there, Skelter, you have another answer to give. I have ample testimony on the creatures you have in your menagerie, and how co-operative they are. Now there are certain types of outcast with unnatural… affinities with Underhive animals. Outcasts whose names I will not speak here, but against whom I have fought in the Emperor's name. An honest showman such as yourself would have no truck with such, I trust? That is not a common-law crime, Skelter; it is most surely a spiritual one. You must know the penalties decreed for it.'

In answer, Skelter slipped a set of scroll tubes out of his carry-harness and held them out. Jago started to give little twitches of his head as he looked from Skelter to the Judge, trying to work out what was going on, and Skelter allowed himself a little smile. He stood a little further upright as the parchment was unrolled.

'Mutants!' declared Jago, who seemed to realise he'd lost the spotlight. 'Mutants and witchcraft. My brethren and I will soon have the truth. Hand them over to me, Lord Justice.' There was a rustle from the desk as the Judge rolled the papers up again.

'Thank you, Skelter, for bringing these. I understand you have had to do this before?' The Judge's manner had palpably relaxed and Skelter allowed himself to smile.

'Yes, sir. We usually keep them handy whenever we come into a new town. I mean, it's an understandable conclusion.'

'Are you serious, man, uh, my Lord Justice?' Jago pressed. 'With respect, lord, we cannot let the people see that these,

these "entertainers" are tolerated just for having some kind of shady paperwork...' Jago's voice tailed off as he saw the Judge's face darken. Skelter took a discreet step back.

'What I have just seen, Mister Jago, is a certificate from a Primaris psyker' – Jago gasped at the word – 'with one of our garrisons in Hive City. Its endorsement is less than a month old. It testifies that all the members of this troupe have been examined by an Adeptus psyker, mark you, and there is no trace of any psychic spoor that signifies association with a wyrd. There is an inspection chit from a guilder technician stating that all the animal cages and pens are sound and well-built. And I have also just seen a permit to perform, on condition that that psychic examination is conducted every six months to make sure no wyrds are recruited. That permit carries an Arbites counterseal.' He held out the tubes, which Skelter hurried forward to take. 'Mister Jago, downhive I suspect knowing when to quit would be a liability. Up here, it's an asset. Think on that.'

For a long moment Jago quivered in frustration, and Skelter wondered whether to feel sorry for him. Then the man began to speak: 'Though here today a court of my fellow mortals, even under the name and oath of the Great Emperor himself, has deemed my words and my cause unworthy, I shall speak one last time. For though my voice may be as a whisper of breeze in some long-dark corner of this land, one day, that breeze may stir a draught, and the draught may stir a current, and the current will become a great clean wind that shall rise and sweep–'

And Skelter cut him off with a delighted cry. 'I knew that speech sounded familiar! I know that show! We toured with some actors once, it's one of their plays! The Triumph of Grimnar! This cretin's pinching his speech from a children's fairytale!'

Jago stood frozen as a statue, one arm still flung out in front of him, while behind him there were strangled sounds as Tara tried to stay solemn. Then Skelter saw the junior Judge put a hand over his face as if to cough, and couldn't control himself. Jago stamped out of the room and Tara and Kamusz exploded into laughter. Skelter's eyes caught the Judge's and he was sure he could see the faintest of glints.

'SO?' KAMUSZ ASKED after they had walked awhile. What do we do tomorrow?'

They had left the Arbites bunker at the top of the uptown, and were picking their way down through the sloping tunnels back to the plaza. The glow-globes were still in their day cycle up here, giving the three the novelty of light bright enough for sharp black shadows: Skelter's tall and thin like a giant black mantis, Kamusz's the square and jutting outline of his heavy jacket and cap, and Tara's as small and slender as she was. The breeze from the township's convector-fans tousled their hair.

'We go on. I think Jago knows he's lost the initiative tragically, now. And we should have packed out at least three shows in advance after the last couple of hours. Let's do all the shows we can in the next few days and rake it in. Hopefully the fool won't work up the nerve to do anything until we're out of town. I might get you to keep–'

'Extra eyes tonight, sure. What's in the show?'

'Most of the animals. I don't think Tara can spare any to use as guards. And I still think we're safe enough for a while, at least. I'd rather put everything in, have a great show, half a dozen full houses and roll out of here on a high note.' Skelter sighed.

'Why can't we have more places like the Gulch? Lovely, well-policed, cushy settlements who'll pay up for a good show. If I wanted hassle like this I'd still be down-hive wrestling plague-zombies.'

The three of them strolled on. At the plaza gates they stopped while Tara bought a cup of the salty gruel that the downtown markets sold.

A level up, a knot of dark-clad men buying clip after clip of bullets turned to watch them through the barred window of the gunsmith's, staring after them until they disappeared into the crowds.

'OH NO!' THERE was laughter as Tara put her hands on her hips and glared. 'Look what you've done! It's everywhere!'

Behind her, Genca was soaked in a watery brown dye that looked repellent from a distance. Bolitho, wearing a too-tight coverall that made his gawky body even more comical, goggled at her. Tara, in spangled leotard and boots, turned to the audience.

'I'm so sorry, my lords and ladies. We'll carry on for you anyway.'

She waited a few moments for Bolitho to start pretending to clean up what he'd spilled, and after a silent count of three blew a staccato note on her whistle and cracked the glittery display whip. The three pipe-lizards immediately jumped onto Bolitho's bent back, instead of their stools – as they'd been trained to do. More laughter. Genca clapped his hands to his head in mock dismay, paunch wobbling. At the tent entrance, Skelter shook his head and muttered aloud.

'These people are taking forever to warm up! What's wrong with them?'

'Dhunno, Bhozz.'

'Issig!' It always surprised Skelter that the alligator-snout could make words at all, let alone ones he could understand. Issig was peering past him into the tent, where Tara was pretending to scold the two men while the lizards turned somersaults behind her.

'Sss'funnhee. Thhey'rr noht lahhffhh'ng. Ss'ngthnnn whhrd.'

'Maybe they're just not into entertainment in this place. Too straight-laced and well-fed.' Even as he said it, Skelter knew how unconvincing that sounded. There was something about this crowd that made him prickle.

Bolitho and Genca walked out past him, mock-arguing, then stopped, grabbed harnesses and waited. Behind them a mohawked silhouette muttered to itself and did shoulder-stretching exercises.

'You ready, Eva?'

'Yeah.' The ex-ganger pushed her way past the two men into the strong yellow light from the tent. She flipped her pistols out of their holsters, span, juggled, tossed and caught them, then snapped them home without taking her eyes off Issig. Eva had only joined the troupe two months before, and still hadn't come to terms with trusting a scaly – she'd complained bitterly about using quarter-strength ammo for her act. Skelter supposed he didn't entirely blame her.

'Cheev is controlling the targets from the box tonight, and Tara'll stay in there and do the thrown ones for you.' Eva nodded, her bright crest of hair catching the lights.

'Grim-faced crew, aren't they?' she muttered, then shuddered and touched an icon at her neck as Issig loped past her and disappeared into the gloom around the tents.

'You read my mind. But they were fighting for tickets all afternoon. Not a single empty seat.' Eva shrugged as their cue sounded, then sauntered out into the ring as the lizards trotted past her to be leashed and harnessed. Out in the ring, Tara took a large sequin from her belt and flipped it into the air, where Eva nonchalantly shot it in two to gasps and cheers.

*Why are they so grim? Those lizard tricks are sure-fire. They're still not smiling, most of them. Just… attentive.* There was an idea, something big and spiky that his subconscious was trying to push at him, and he found himself shifting from foot to foot and chewing his lip. *Half the audience seemed to have their hands in their laps, fiddling with bundled-up clothes. That made his mind spin a little faster, and he didn't know why.*

*Something is so wrong here.*

Just as he felt the thought begin to come, just as he was sure the piece was about to click, there was a muffled shout from back behind him. Skelter's taut nerves jerked. He crept back a few paces and listened. He thought he heard a voice, and running footsteps, and a word that sounded like 'tent!'. Then his guts lurched as he heard the thump of gunfire.

IT HADN'T BEEN A very good ambush. Kamusz had been scanning a pile of tarpaulins when he noticed a shadow that hadn't been there before. He was too old a hand to raise a shout straight away. He let them think he hadn't seen them, wandered back into the space between two trailers and ran like hell. Zian and Travis came at a quick whistled signal and they started back as a flash of light came from the perimeter. Kamusz roared and unslung his shotgun. Ten, twelve more paces and he was in cover behind a giant steel track as masked figures broke from the nearest pits and buttresses.

*Damn damn damn!*

Zian was squinting into a darkvisor. 'Nine, ten… no, just nine. Hey, Kamusz, this is a pretty spineless effort for a mob that knew we'd be on guard. There's gotta be more than this.'

Kamusz's mind worked faster than Skelter's had. His eyes widened.

'The tent! The tent! Back to–'

Then the darkness was alive with running, shouting figures and a shot spanged over Kamusz's head. He snarled and dropped back behind his cover as his gun came alive in his hands.

Behind them in the tent, a roar began to rise.

Realisation screamed in like a dislocated joint sliding back into place. For the first time that night, Skelter's head felt clear. He stared into the tent with his mouth open. For a moment he simply couldn't believe they would – had – tried it. But the fidgeting, the solemn faces, the watchfulness, and those little folded bundles in their laps. They were waiting for the signal. To put on their masks.

Skelter's searching eyes settled on one of the biggest men in the crowd, sitting at the most visible point, high in the central stands. Arrogant set to his wide shoulders, rich black hair, thick arms folded – and a stickpatch on the left side of his throat.

'Jago!' Skelter croaked, and then found his voice and strode into the tent, bellowing, 'Get out of my tent, Jago! Take all your Sump-damned bloody undercover foot-soldiers with you! No Cawdors! Out! GET OUT!'

Skelter whipped his head from left to right. He thought of shutters closing over windows, or a shroud of fog descending on the silt wastes. Suddenly all across the stands there were no eyes to meet, no expressions to watch – just rows of featureless masks. There were no eyes visible, just dark holes, but he could still feel their stares burning into him. His hand squirmed by his side where his holster normally was.

There was a rush of words from the befuddled, unmasked faces left sitting – less than a third of the crowd now.

'Hey what–'

'But why are they all–'

'Is this part of the–'

'Get your guns, this is–'

Skelter ground his teeth, and then Tara punched his arm and yelled 'Run!' As gunmetal glinted all around the ring, they sprinted for the entrance and the curses, battle cries and prayers of the Cawdor mob rose to a roar.

THEY PELTED OUT of the tent and scattered into the dark. Around the rim of the camp they could hear gunshots and shouts. A flash and a shower of sparks from inside had them moving again, racing for weapons. People were at the trailer ahead of them. Starkey was scrabbling at the gun locker, half-sobbing to himself. Skelter grabbed him and spun him around. His hair was sweat-slick and his eyes stared.

'What's happening? What's happening?' Tara pushed past them.

'They went after the kids. They started shooting at the south side when Kamusz found them over to the west. They fired past us at where the kids were. This isn't a terror raid, Skel, they mean business!'

Skelter felt his stomach churn. 'Alright, we're going to fix this. Take an autogun and get back out. You and Genca cover the sideshow enclosures, where you were.' Starkey took a breath and nodded. Tara stood up, pulling a drab grey coverall on over the sparkling suit she had worn in the ring.

'Who's hurt, Starkey, who'd they get?'

'Gia got burnt when one of them fired a hotshot shell and it splashed, uh, they were, oh Emperor's name, they were throwing grenades, Kantor, you know, my son, they shot my son, he was screaming–'

'Who's dead?' Skelter fought the urge to shake him.

Starkey shook his head and wiped sweat from his face. 'Nobody so far, I don't think, people were hurt, the kids were hurt and we had to carry them to the wagons...'

Tara turned around with a shotgun in her hand and revenge written in her face. He heard a scrape and clack as Eva locked a live clip into each of her pistols.

'Genca, you and Starkey get going. Eva, cover the tent entrance as long as you can!' The fat man nodded and led the way off through the camp, and Eva ducked back the way they'd come.

A fresh burst of gunfire made Skelter and Tara spin around. The Cawdors were trying to storm out of the tent, but the mass of regular punters had its own ideas. There were just enough bystanders to clog the narrow aisles and create knots of shouting, brawling people at each tent-flap. Skelter grinned despite the sick anger building up in his gut – the advantage was to the bystanders, and the Cawdors couldn't fire in the swirling mob without hitting one another. The erstwhile show-goers were punching, stabbing and pistol-whipping with impunity, and the stands were rocking and threatening to give way. There was a crunch and a chorus of screams from inside, and Skelter realised that Cheev had used the controls in the master booth to drop the target gantry for Eva's act onto the rioters below. He let out a hiss of triumph and grabbed two autopistols from a rack, just as Cheev himself came scampering out of the tent with three Cawdors on his heels.

Tara dropped to one knee and put a man-stopper shell through the first, and Skelter cut down the second with a quick double-burst. The third dropped his chainsword and sprinted for the gates. Cheev gave them a grin, white teeth flashing, then reached for his pursuers' weapons.

'They were shooting at the kids!' Tara yelled. 'We need to get to the main trailer and make it safe.' Skelter bit back a foul taste in his mouth and ran after her as she flitted through the dark maze between metal wagon-walls.

'Tara, this is my fault! Emperor's eyes, Tara, I played stupid games with that Cawdor bastard, I pushed him too hard, they came back and they–'

'Not your fault and you know it! Shut up and– *down*!'

Tara dropped and Skelter followed her. A smear of plasma hissed overhead, splashing the wagon behind them. A grinning, dwarfish Cawdor took aim again as, behind him, a hulk of a man in nothing but leggings and mask hefted a grenade launcher. Skelter tried to move even as he thought won't make it before it recharges but then something thrummed by his ear. There was a solid *chank* and both Cawdors seemed to loll oddly in the dim light until Skelter realised they had both been speared into the metal wall behind them. He looked around.

Behind him, Issig had already put the butt of his harpoon gun on the ground and had pulled another shaft, solid steel and wrist-thick, out of his quiver. His arms bulged as he forced it down, then the spring clicked into place and he pulled the weapon up under his arm, disappearing into the twilight again. They clambered up and Tara pointed ahead: the main trailer lay just across from them.

'I thought you'd made Issig get rid of that thing.'

'I thought he had! I vote he keeps it after this.'

They scurried across the open ground. Skelter, moving backward with pistols hunting the air, thought he saw gun-muzzles in every shadow and hunched over. Behind him, Tara hauled a door half-open and he heard children's cries.

'Kray!' Tara called. 'Who's in there with you?'

Kray was supporting a baby in one arm and cradling a tri-barrelled laspistol in the other. The bandage around the baby's chest was spotted with stains that looked black in the dim light. 'We got the kids away, they'd all been playing out by the fire. They ran right up there–'

'We've got that area covered. I think they're gone again. Who's in there?'

'All Starkey's kids, not badly hurt, just shaken up. Gia, and Eva's baby niece and Cheev's little brother, and Jayden's little girl. An-wei and her three are down the back there. Jayden's in here with the medical stuff, she's working on the hurt ones.' Skelter could see Tara's eyes narrowing, and he knew his own looked the same.

Kray looked stricken. 'I couldn't see Lee or Canda. They went running off to find you, Skelter, and the masked men were shooting–'

Tara slammed the door and spun around, grabbed shells from the pack at her hip. Her voice was clipped and level. 'We go to the hotspots first, then? Once we know they aren't there, we double back toward the tent and start looking.'

Skelter nodded and they were running again.

KAMUSZ STEPPED OVER a dead Cawdor, his shotgun on his back, stub-gun in one hand, power-maul in the other. Around him, the mutant cages howled and rattled under their armour-cloth tarps – no chance of letting the animals out into the teeth of a firefight, not like this morning.

Two gangers were crouching by the corner of the wagon, intent on priming the bombs they carried as shells ricocheted around them. Kamusz began the maul on its arc even as he glided forward and the first dropped in a shower of sparks. The other spun around and Kamusz drove the stubber into his gut. His body silenced the shots, then he dropped and Kamusz stepped out of the alley.

This was where they had had their campfire. Three Cawdors were here still, their backs to him as they shot at shapes lurking among the wagons. The troupe's fire stopped when Kamusz appeared and the Cawdors stood up to give chase, thinking their enemy routed. Kamusz dropped two of them with quick headshots and clouted the third with the maul: he had thumbed the setting up and the flash of power took the man's face along with his mask. Issig and the others ran forward from their positions and then stopped. The massive figure slowly pointed over Kamusz's shoulder.

Kamusz didn't need to ask why. He could tell what the looks on their faces meant. He was lowering his weapons even as the voice from behind him boomed: 'You move and he dies.'

TARA AND SKELTER had split up at the mech-shop wagon and now she headed for the perimeter. The shooting was tailing off and there were no fires. A shape appeared balanced on a shoulder-high trailer coupling.

'Repent and Redeem!' the Cawdor howled as he raised an autogun, but Tara didn't slow: she swerved in, pulled her knees up and ran two paces up the side of the trailer, kicked out and backflipped. The burst ricocheted off the metal behind her and she hit ground, rolled and fired a hotshot shell that toppled the Cawdor down next to her. He screamed and kicked in the flames, but weakly, and she took the time to spit an old ratskin curse her grandmother had taught her. The man let out another cry, and she crushed his knee with the stock and left him to burn. She rounded the corner and hurdled a dead, masked body, but the scene by the remains of the campfire turned her limbs to lead. The shotgun sagged in her grasp and she stopped.

SKELTER FIRED A long burst from each pistol, and the masked woman with the grenades staggered back and fell. He took two steps forward and looked at the little crowd beyond her: all hooded and armed, but stymied and uncertain.

Amateurs playing at gangers, he thought, who don't know that in real life people shoot back. One began to raise a gun. Skelter saw the little girl with bloodied bandages around her in his mind. My fault.

He raised the gun before they could fire and began long, sweeping bursts that scattered them and felled them and chased the rest of them, yipping and wailing, off into the dark. His pistols juddered and jammed, and he let them drop to his sides. He felt exhausted, and turned toward the camp... and heard Jago's voice roaring out his name.

'SKELTER! SHOW YOURSELF!'

Jago held the boy in one elbow, the muzzle of his plasma pistol grinding back and forth against Lee's temple. One of

Jago's boots pinned Canda's hand to the ground; she whimpered but would not cry.

'*Skelter*! I know these are your children! Let me see you NOW!'

'No need to shout, Jago. Just turn around. Look, no pistols this time, no needler in the sleeve.' Skelter walked slowly into the firelight, hands spread by his sides. Jago lifted his foot, and Canda withdrew her hand. He kicked her hard as she got up to run: she cried out but moved fast. The Cawdor dragged Lee back until the two of them stood by at the very edge of the camp, his back to the side of their one, prized power-wagon.

'There you are, vermin, you see? The little bitch back as a token of faith, although Emperor knows the only faith she'll know is that of the scum who spawned her. What faith do you know, any of you? What? WHAT FAITH?'

*Holy Emperor and all the saints and primarchs,* Skelter thought, *if you can hear me, help me now. This man has a gun to my son's head, and I am watching as he goes mad before my eyes. Please, help me now…*

'Your filth may have broken my dearest brothers and sisters, but you will be the ones to weep and cry when the Emperor gathers us up! He will say to us "How have you proven your rotted souls that I might deliver you from the fire and agony", and we will point to where you wallow in your, your decay and your corruption and the, the spittle and vomit in which you have coated your souls, and we will say to our Emperor: We have lived by your Word, we have spread fire and anger and blood everywhere we looked, and when they came to spoil us with laughter and wine and lust and mutants and… and… We are Cawdor. We are *Cawdor*!' The hand holding the pistol was starting to shake, and Jago's voice was growing jagged.

'There's a latch by your shoulder, Jago.' Tara's voice seemed to jolt the man out of a daze. He looked at her and Skelter thought he saw his arm loosen. He prayed Lee would run when he had the chance.

'Open the flap there. Are we really going to be able to pull anything before you can fire?' She glanced at Kamusz as she spoke, a look that said *Try nothing.*

Kamusz nodded. Moving like a sleepwalker, Jago tapped the cover up and looked at the brass scrollwork.

'It opens the hatch next to you. Lee knows how to work it, and if you let him, he will. We'll all move back while you get in. You can walk down through the wagon to the cab. It'll take you out of town and away from the Watch. And then you can sell it or burn it or whatever you want. And you'll be away.'

Skelter looked from Jago to Tara. Her eyes were wide and dark and watchful. *What the hell is she doing?*

'Lee, it's alright, trust me. You can open it. I know you're normally not allowed to, but it's alright.' Jago's arm loosened, and the boy wriggled free. Lee's little hand went out, twisted the switch. There was a clunk and the hatch jolted as it unlocked. The window in its top reflected firelight. Tara started to say something, and then Jago gave Lee a gentle little push. The boy took an uncertain step, shot a look over his shoulder, and ran.

And behind him Jago raised the pistol.

'And as a reward, child, I am going to send you to the Emperor and save you from these–'

They never found out what he was going to call them. Skelter ran forward but Tara was quicker. His feet seemed to slow and there seemed to be time to look around and see everything happening around him with stately, dreamlike pace. Tara dived and grabbed, spun to protect Lee with her back. Next to Skelter, Eva's arm dipped and her laspistol was in her hand and a single silent trail of light drilled through Jago's elbow and sent his own shot into the girders high over their heads. The man had time for one scream before he staggered backward and heaved the hatch open, scrabbling for the machete at his belt.

By the time Skelter's roared curses could pass his lips, Jago was backing through the hatch, craning around as though he'd heard something move behind him... And Issig scooped up his empty speargun, eyeing the distance as he did so, and threw it underarm in a lazy, end-over-end arc that knocked Jago sprawling into the wagon. Light flooded out as the movement triggered interior lamps, and the hatch thumped shut again. Skelter took his first breath in what seemed like hours, ran to his son and rounded on the rest of them.

'What are you waiting for? Get to the cab and get him!'

Still no one moved. Tara raised an eyebrow.

'You never do remember where anything is parked, do you?'

Skelter stared at her.

'That's the ripperjack wagon.'

As he turned, despite himself, to stare, the shouts of the Watch and the Arbites klaxons sounded from the surrounding tunnels.

And something appeared at the little window in the wagon hatch. Something red and tattered that screamed and beat at the glass… until it collapsed against the window, leaving a scarlet stain as it was dragged out of sight.

IT WAS WARM when they rode out for Ashclam. Skelter and Tara sat together on the steering platform of the lead tractor, the wagons and trailers spread out behind them and the buggies with their rattling little methane engines scooting past to take point. Issig had been allowed out when they were out of sight of the settlement and had dozed off on the roof of his trailer, a half-gnawed bone in his hand. Skelter had wondered if it really had been a Cawdor icon he'd seen dangling on a bracelet around that bone that morning, but he'd let it slide.

Tara yawned. 'What's Ashclam like? I only want quiet places for a while after this. At least with one thing and another no one thought to stir up trouble about Issig the way they normally do. But we were lucky to get out of it as well as we did, you know.'

'I know.' Skelter's face was set.

'I didn't mean it that way. It wasn't your fault, Skel. Jago was a freak, something was wrong with him. He'd have come out shooting, no matter what we did.'

He nodded, and they rode in silence for a while.

'We'll be fine. We're doing well. We're making money, got our permits. One day soon we'll get a Hive City gig, just like you said. And from there, it's just up and up.'

Skelter nodded again. They could just see the distant dot of light that was the giant road-pipe leading uphive to the Ashclam trail, and around them the dome walls curved up into dimness. After a while, Tara put her head on Skelter's shoulder. The lights of the buggies criss-crossed in the middle distance. And above their heads, the bloodstained Cawdor mask hanging from the roll bar swung and twisted on its thong. Skelter always had been a sucker for souvenirs.

# MARK OF A WARRIOR
## by Richard Williams

I COULD SEE them both from where I sat, the two dark figures crouching in the shadows. They had stalked one another for an hour now, round and round the mining settlement, sneaking quietly between buildings, senses alert, each waiting for a stray sound or smell to betray the position of the other. Now, it seemed, the end was at hand. One of them was huddled down on the ground, peering between two battered yellow cargo containers. He was scanning the open space barely visible through the crack, hoping to catch a glimpse of his quarry, but there was nothing. I saw him shift his weight and edge sideways a fraction, so he could scope the rest of the buildings. As he did a stud on his belt grazed the hard metal surface of the crate, and his enemy, a few paces behind him, took the opportunity to ease himself a little farther around the corner.

The huddled one looked down at the stud. A wire-thin strip of yellow paint twirled away from its point. The silver line of fresh metal glinted back in the darkness. Then he realised, I don't know how, the danger he was in. I saw his body clench as he strained his ears for the softest brush of skin on cloth, of someone else's breathing suppressed to almost nothing. His eyes slid sideways in their sockets and he gripped his gun tighter.

There it was, the swipe of skin on skin, of an arm bringing a
gun up to firing position. All pretence aside, he dropped forwards, boots kicking up dust, and rolled to his back. He
whipped his arm around until he was staring down the barrel
straight into his enemy's eyes. Their gazes flashed across one
another for an instant before they both inhaled savagely, gasping for every last bit of air, 'BANG! BANG! BANG! BANG!
BANG! BANG! BANG!'

The pieces of piping jerked in their hands as the vocal bullets
spat forth. Once again, their chests heaved as they cried in perfect unison, 'GOT YOU FIRST!'

Another game of 'Outlaws and Watchmen' ends, the same
way they always do. The kid standing had dived at the one on
his back and they were wrestling on the ground. Their 'guns',
pieces of scrap, had been forgotten, as the two settled their
argument in a far more physical manner. When I looked back
at them, one nearly had the other pinned, who, in turn,
grabbed the tuft of hair on the other kid's head and slammed
it down. Young skull met hard dirt with a thud and the struggle continued,

'You're DEAD!'

'You MISSED!'

'Did NOT!'

'GET OFF!'

I didn't know their names, but I knew who they were. I'd
been the same a few years ago; creeping through settlements,
hunting my friends. We thought we were just like the gangers
who came through town everyday, either trading at the post or
lounging in the bar, and every single one with a gun strapped
to their hip or slung over their back. The mark of a warrior, that
set them above all the rest of us.

They all knew that no one makes it in the Underhive without
one thing.

Respect.

To get respect, you have to fight.

To fight, you need a gun.

Even we Goliaths know that. The biggest, the strongest of us
would never go into a fight without packing something. It was
kind of comforting to me when I was a kid, my little rebellious
thought whenever some seven-foot, man-mountain of a ganger
ordered me to fetch this or carry that. You may be larger than

me, you may be louder, but without that piece of metal stuck in your belt, that piece of metal that looks so ridiculous when your oversized fingers are crammed around it, you would be nothing.

I remember the feel of having a gun in my hand, even a make-believe one. To only have to point, to kill as if I were the Emperor himself. Now it was going to happen. Today was the beginning. I ran a hand over my shaven head. Already I could feel stubble, the tops of stiff hairs poking through the skin. I wanted to look my best, nose stud polished up, my thin strip of hair freshly dyed. Trying to look like the warrior that I would become, if the gang judged me worthy. There was only one thing missing: on my belt hung a knife and a holster, an empty holster.

I tried to relax, tried to calm down, waiting for them to get started with whatever. After all, I couldn't look too wired, they might think I was scared. I dropped my head back on the pile of iron slag I lay against, staring up at the far away ceiling. Then again, it would be worse if I looked like I was snoozing or day-dreaming. I shifted onto my side and propped myself up on my elbow. I squirmed to try and find a comfortable position among those sharp little rocks. A flash of pain stabbed through my side. I looked down. My braces had got twisted, the studs that lined them were digging into my flesh. Clambering to my knees I began adjusting the few clothes I was wearing, making sure everything sharp pointed outwards and looked keen, rather than pointing inwards and being... inconvenient. Distracted, I didn't notice the shadow fall across me. I sure noticed the meaty hand dropped on my shoulder, though.

I didn't leap up; that would have been the worse thing to do. I knew who it was. The harsh metallic grating of respirated breathing and the edge of Second Best mingled with stale sweat in the air left me in no doubt. It was the ganger sent to test me. First impressions matter. He'd caught me off guard and if he saw me jump out of my skin he'd know I wasn't up to it, might even refuse to let me try. I didn't know whether he could do that or not, but I wasn't taking any chances. So, instead, I let him wait a second, like I knew he was there all along, and then I turned my head, slowly.

His hand gave him away; he was old. It's always the hands that show it most. He must have been nearly forty. Long past his best, still just a ganger with no hope of ever becoming anything more. He had become everything a young man dreaded. No wonder he reeked of cheap Second Best. I got up off my knees and his hoary limb fell away. I swung around to him. His head was shaven and the respirator covered most of his face. No, his head wasn't bare by choice, he didn't have any hair at all. I tried to stop staring at his gleaming dome. He didn't flinch. His scarred and hairy body still looked powerful, the two pistols hung at his belt and the studs and spikes and the ammo chains on his clothes would have made him an impressive figure indeed. As it was, though, I couldn't help but feel embarrassed to see such a man.

His hands rose to his face and his thick fingers undid the straps on his respirator with practised ease. He pulled it to the side of his face, revealing a gold ring through his nose and an old, faded tattoo on his cheek. His lips twisted and words emerged in his low, damaged voice: 'You ready?'

WE HADN'T WALKED far from the mining town before he stopped in front of me.

'This is it.'

What was it? The place was deserted, nothing apart from a pile of planks dumped nearby. What was the test supposed to be, single combat? Fine by me, I guess, I would just have to be careful not to kill the old man. He glanced back at me and must have mistaken my confusion for fear.

'You better not be wasting my time, juve. You still wanna do this?'

'Yes, sir,' I snapped back instinctively and hated myself for giving him the respect he didn't deserve.

'Cos it's easy by me if you wanna quit. Save me waiting around for you.'

I held my mouth in check. I didn't trust what would come out. He finally turned away and padded over to the planks. He crouched down and fumbled for his respirator. After a drag he took a hold on the top piece and heaved. Nothing moved. I couldn't believe it, even a piece of recyc-plastic was too much for this guy. No one could be that puny, yet there he was, he wasn't grunting or anything but I could see the strain through his body, his muscles rippling along his back and the trembling of his head. Suddenly an almighty crack resounded around the plain and the old man shot up. He stood back and I peered at what he had left behind. The plastic plank had snapped in two, and this wasn't cheap package plastic either, but the reinforced kind. It had been bolted to the stone in the floor. I was stunned. Looking back on it, he could have weakened it before he collected me, or maybe it had already been damaged. But that didn't stop me reconsidering my opinion of him. He took another breath through his respirator, then let it hang to the side as he wiped away a bead of sweat that had formed on his brow. If he noticed the change in my expression, he didn't show it.

'This,' he announced, pointing at the planks, 'is what you're gonna do.'

Suddenly, for the first time, I wasn't sure whether I would make it, whether I could match such a feat.

'This leads straight into one of the mine shafts.'

Now the broken plank had shifted I could see that it had covered a small hole beneath. It looked like it dropped straight down but in this light, I couldn't see more than a few feet.

'This shaft used to be worked, along with the others. But it got infested and the rock-worms inside started to come out for dinner. The main entrance was buried by the locals, and when they found that some of the nasties had burrowed out through this hole, they boarded it up and hoped nature would take its course, that everything inside would eat each other. If you want in, you go down there, you scrag one of the worms and you drag yourself back here with proof, something it couldn't live without. Get it?'

'Yes, sir.'

My mind raced, digesting the information. A mine infested with milliasaurs, kill one and bring back a trophy. Simple and straightforward, just like us Goliaths, but was I only going to have my knife? In answer to my unspoken question the ganger pulled one of the pistols, a stub gun, from his belt and offered it to me. My breath caught with anticipation.

'Here. Take this.'

I did so, with a careful reverence.

'But remember, we do not need such things. We are Goliath. Where others are weak, we are strong. Where others rely, we merely use.'

His grotesque voice carried on with its dogma. I'd heard it often enough. I concentrated instead on the magnificent object

I held in my hand. A G40K revolver-style stub gun, a standard
product of the Goliath heavy industries. Cheap, hard to break,
easy to repair, there were thousand of weapons identical to this
one in Hive Primus alone and countless millions of variants on
the design across the planet. But as my fingers curled around
the moulded plastic grip and brushed against the trigger I knew
this one was unique, because it was the only one of that multitude that was in my hand. I hefted it and felt its comforting
weight. I slid it into my holster and it fitted perfectly. I let my
hand rest on my hip, tensed in anticipation of the quick draw.
My hand leapt forward, the pistol in its grasp nothing more
than a streak of silver. I aimed it, clenched one eye and looked
straight down the barrel. I felt the power, the power of life and
death for whoever crossed those sights.

A red shape blocked my vision. Suddenly I was hauled from
the ground. I dangled from my bracers which were sandwiched
between the gnarled fists of the ganger. His eyes displayed his
lack of amusement.

'Get it?' he demanded

'Yes. Yes, sir,' I stammered in response, my feet struggling in
the air.

He snorted and released his grip. I felt the drop jar all the way
up my body and collapsed to my knees in front of him, coughing in the dirt.

'You will.'

I FELL THE last few feet or, at least, I would have done if my belt
hadn't caught on a small metal spur poking out of the tunnel
wall. The moment I spent hanging in mid-air, suspended by my
trousers, screwed up my timing and so, when the inevitable
happened, I clattered to the ground, landing one limb at a
time.

I'd shot to my feet, whipped the pistol from its holster and
was scanning my surroundings for danger before my brain
kicked in. I have to admit, after the wave of adrenaline had broken over me and my pulse settled down, that I felt pretty smug
about that recovery. Yeah, I'd looked a fool but that happens
sometimes and all the smooth moves after, pure instinct. After
years of playing, it felt so natural to be doing the real thing.

A spark flashed across my eyes, jolting me from my self-con-
gratulation and illuminating the dimly lit area. The sharp

odour of ozone briefly overwhelmed the underlying smell of dank stone and rusting metal. It was a storage room, if the crates and barrels were anything to go by. The main support column in the centre of the room had collapsed, more than that, it had been virtually felled by the explosion that had destroyed the tunnel entrance. As a result most of the other end had caved in. The sparks flared again. Something had been ripped off the wall, leaving circuitry exposed.

There was only one way out, apart from the hole above my head of course, and as I put my gloved hand on the frame to look through, I discovered what this exit had been, a window. It crunched and I felt, not pain exactly, just the threat of imminent pain if I gripped any tighter. Ever so gently I peeled my hand away and brushed off the pieces of glass embedded in my glove. Keeping well clear of the jagged edges, I leaned forward and peered down. It was quite a drop but, luckily for me, there were stacks of containers that would make the descent easier. I eased myself through the gap and moved onto the topmost box. It moved with me. With ponderous inevitability the stack gently began to topple away from the wall. Quickly I jammed my other foot back to steady the pile and rocked it back. Regaining my balance, I grudgingly tucked the pistol back into its holster and used both hands to lower myself cautiously down.

Damn, I assumed the crates would be full, it never occurred that the miners would have emptied everything before they left, just as they had stripped whatever had been of use from the last room. Feet now firmly on the floor, pistol and knife in hand, my eyes searched. Nothing. Nothing but the piles of boxes and a big hole in the ground in front of me. A ladder was attached to the lip, leading down into the darkness. I slowly edged round the circumference of the opening, stub gun trained on the shadows. Nothing again, except this time there was the faint whiff of an effluent stream.

Once I'd got down there I had to follow the smell to find the source. Buried in the shadows in the corner there was a tiny crawlspace. As I leaned down into it I was hit by the reek of the sewage. It was dark, damp and a perfect place for milliasaurs. Now, you couldn't survive in the Underhive if you were claustrophobic. Everyone has his limits; and having to squeeze through a passage only big enough for a child, full of the

stench of liquid garbage, to hunt monstrous worms who'd
paralyse you and then drag you home for a slow digestion, is
getting close to mine. Still I had no choice, and I had my gun.
That was enough.

I dropped to my hands and knees, then to my belly. I coughed
with the extra weight on my lungs. There would be barely be
enough room for me to lift my head to see where I was going. I
pushed my knife-sheath and holster around my belt until they
were beside my hips, I couldn't have them dig into my waist as
I pushed myself along. Steeling myself, I entered, nudging my
pistol and knife in front of me. With my shoulders pressed
against the sides, I put arm in front of arm, then swung a hip
forwards and dragged my legs along behind me.

I struggled onwards. My chest scraped along the bottom, my
hair was flattened against the top and it brushed dust down
into my eyes, making me blink. When I finally had the full
length of my body inside, I realised exactly how narrow the
shaft was. My only way out would be to push myself backwards, completely blind. If something got behind me there was
no room to turn around. Nothing I could do. What use would
even a meltagun be if something bit me in the leg? And if it was
a milliasaur, one bite would be all it needed for its poison to
cripple me.

My breathing quickened, I couldn't fill my lungs and I was
gasping for air. My body heat reflected off the surfaces that covered me; it was hot, and the smell, I might as well have been
drowning in it. I knew I was panicking, and that made it worse.
My head was beginning to feel light. Deep breath, the thought
sprung suddenly into my mind, that's what I need, a good deep
breath. I stopped gasping for a second, closed my eyes and
gripped the butt of my gun. Whoosh; the dust-laden, stink-rid-
den air was blown into my lungs until my chest had expanded
so much that my back was driven into the roof of the tunnel.
Then I let it flow out, until I felt quite deflated. I felt at peace
for only a moment, then my nose began to itch, my head
sprung back and a sneeze exploded from my face. My forehead
bounced off the floor and the back of my head ricocheted into
the top of the shaft. My hair softened the impact but my temple throbbed. After taking a moment to recover I wiped my
nose on my hand and dragged myself on.

* * *

THE POOL OF filth gurgled and lapped against its metal banks in a hideous mockery of water. Pressed to the ground as I was, my nose was unpleasantly close to it. There was no way across so I spun round on my belly and made my way back. The tunnel had opened out into the crawlspace proper. In fact the ceiling in the corner had fallen in so I clambered out, up into the room above. Another storage room. A column had collapsed across it, or it could have been a beam which had fallen from the roof; whatever, it had smashed the stairs, forcing me to climb along its length until I could drop off onto the floor above. I was confronted with a lift, twisted at an angle that gave no doubt as to its state of repair. I carried on, this time through a hole in the wall which led onto the rock face.

Pleased as I was that I hadn't encountered anything down in that crawlspace, I couldn't kick the feeling of... having been cheated. There should have been something there, even if not a milliasaur, there should have been at least rats or spiders – or even a face-eater. I shuddered at the thought of bumbling across such a monster unexpectedly. Still, it was odd I hadn't seen signs of any activity at all. Perhaps, after the mine was collapsed, the milliasaurs had retreated deeper. Maybe the locals had been right and the creatures had turned on each other once their ready supply of food had been cut off. Maybe there'd never been anything and the gang had put me down here because they'd already rejected me, to go and scrag something that didn't exist. No, they wouldn't have spared the effort to tell me to get lost. I'd show them. I'd show them I was worthy of their gang, hell, I could lead their gang, given a chance.

Even as I ventured on in my hunt, my mind was miles above as I sketched out my glorious career.

It wouldn't take much. After I'd passed this stupid initiation and shoved a half dozen rock-worm trophies down the old man's throat, we'd be hired to guard a guilder trade caravan. The gang leader would have set the route, I'd have warned him that it took us too close to a fortified tower in scavvy territory but none of them would've listened to me because I was so new. I would be ready when the first shots of the ambush rang out and would have sprung forwards, rushing the scavvy raiders.

I jumped up on top of a crate to simulate climbing the tower.

They'd be surprised by how quickly I reacted and I would slaughter their leader's mutant bodyguards and put a gun to his head, demanding the rest of his ramshackle band give themselves up. As soon as they had, I would kick him off the top level – I booted the air for emphasis – and the rest of my gang would slaughter the rest of the degenerates. Our only casualty would be our foolish leader, cut down in the first few seconds. The guilders would shower me with goods and cash and I would become the new gang boss.

Getting down from the crate, I continued on.

Would I be content then? With a female in one hand and a bottle of WildSnake in the other? Hardly. I would purchase from the Van Saar techs two of their finest bolt pistols, for an exorbitant fee. They'd try to double-cross me, of course. Insist I come alone and then try to leave with both their weapons and my corpse. I would be too quick for them.

Two imaginary pistols leapt into my outstretched hands.

The Van Saars in the room would fall in seconds, before any of them had time to draw. The rest of the gang would burst in and meet the same fate.

I crouched behind a barrel, picking off phantom enemies with my stub gun.

Another victory, and then on and up, until I rested on a throne in the Hive City itself.

Spectral smoke coiled up from the barrel. I drew it up to my lips and gently blew it away.

High above me, a shape detached itself from the darkness and dropped. It clubbed me over the back of the head. My jaw smashed into the muzzle. My teeth howled in pain and blood spurted into my mouth. I was knocked down, hard. The stub gun tumbled away.

I was stunned for a critical second, not knowing what had happened. I thought the roof was caving in. Then I looked over my shoulder into the gaping mouth of the milliasaur, and I moved. Its first poisonous bite went wild as I spun onto my back. It shot back as fast as a snake, rearing to strike again. Its tiny legs stood out like horns running down the side of its rocky carapace. I saw the next strike coming and flattened myself against the ground as its incredibly powerful muscles rocketed it through the air.

It didn't even bother to draw back before it struck again. It lunged forwards clumsily but there was no more ground I could give. The fangs bore down and I threw my other arm up for what little protection it could provide. The monster, seeing something shoot into its mouth, crunched down early. The knife I'd held was shattered between its teeth and it flinched away. I struggled up and scrambled into the corner, scooped up the pistol and whirled around. I planted my back foot, one arm steadying the other, looking straight down the sights. A stance perfect for the first time I would feel the power, the first time I would unleash the cold fury of this most deadly, most beautiful of weapons.

The milliasaur sprang. This was it. Point-blank. Point. Kill.

*Click.*

Misfire.

That was the last thought to scurry through my brain before the monster punched into my shoulder and slammed me back against a wall. I went down. Its writhing body fell on top. I had no escape. Its spasms pummelled me, its rock-hard hide crushed my body and pierced my skin and its steaming hiss assaulted my ears. I protected myself as best I could. Screwed into a ball, battered by its throes, I cowered. Then, an unseen lightning-fast blow. My face exploded. My head bounced off a stone and I was plunged into oblivion.

I LAY THERE. The weight of the milliasaur's corpse pressed down on me. I don't know how long it was, I'd lost track of time. To begin with I didn't even know it was dead, that my broken knife blade had torn open its throat as it had tried to swallow the pieces. I was just grateful that it had stopped, I didn't care why. I was lucky it hadn't collapsed on my chest or I wouldn't have been able to breathe. Instead it had finished up lying over my entire right side, literally pinning me to the ground with the sharp edges of its hide. I was bleeding underneath it, but the weight of the creature cut off my blood supply, like a tourniquet. First I felt the warm fluid cooling, then, as the minutes crawled by, it began to scrape away in clots on my fingers. The gritty residue got under my nails.

I had to move. Even if I wasn't too badly hurt, I needed a drink. My raging thirst had been made worse by the acid taste of the blood I'd swallowed. An image resurfaced in my mind, of me, with a beautiful woman in one arm and a bottle of Wild snake in the other. Well, there was no booze and the only thing in my arms was... well. My half-hearted laugh turned into a

splutter, which devolved into a coughing fit, a painful coughing fit as every movement pulled at my limbs and dug the
milliasaur's hide in a little more. I had to move. I figured what
with a worm being basically one big cylinder it would be easiest to roll it off. Slowly I brought my free left leg up and around
to get my foot against the corpse's side and squirmed my body
to brace my shoulder against the wall, then I tried to move it.
It was easier than I thought it would be. It had been its speed
and power that had done the damage, not its weight. There
wasn't much pain to begin with; everything was too numb. But
when it rolled off my shoulder and thigh and flattened my
hand I screamed myself hoarse as the rocks on its hide dug into
healthy flesh. A swift kick fuelled by agony drove it off me completely as I yanked my injured hand clear. The limp tube
flopped away.

You can't cut off the circulation to a limb without expecting
some payback. I knew what was coming. With the arteries clear,
the blood flooded back through my system. I rolled in torment
on the rocky floor. I felt angry, angry that I had won. I had won,
and all I got was pain and more pain. I knew this would pass,
though. My real fear was that the scabs over my wounds would
burst under the pressure and I'd start bleeding again. When it
finally passed I struggled up against the wall, the wall that had
kept me trapped against the dying milliasaur, so I was sitting
upright. My arm was a mess; the dried blood had been scraped
off in some places, leaving streaks of brown, alternating with skin
either rubbed raw or bruised blue. My shoulder and elbow were
sore, but I flexed my fingers fine. I couldn't see my leg through my
trousers, but I guessed it looked pretty much the same.

Gingerly, I tried to get to my feet. I took it slow. I drew my left
leg under me, then the right. I gasped; there was something
wrong with that knee. Pushing myself up onto my hands, I
tried to keep as much weight as possible off it. Then, leaning
into the wall to balance myself, I got my left foot on the ground
and stretched out that leg. My head swam and I fumbled for a
firmer grip on the rock. Only then did I gently lower my battered right leg. It was stiff, and the knee hurt, but I figured that
if I kept it straight I could make it.

I limped over to the body of the milliasaur. I needed proof
that I had killed it and as sure as hell I wasn't going to drag the
entire thing out of here. Something it couldn't live without, the

old man had said. Now I'm no great student of worms, and I've heard stories of how you can cut them in half and make two of the monsters, but I know that in the vast majority of cases taking off the head is a pretty safe bet. It sounded simple when I thought of it. later I realised how difficult it was to carve through a neck made of rock with a few shards of a broken knife. But that thought would wait, because I'd just seen my gun.

It was hiding underneath the body, it must have been dragged down there by the worm when I kicked it off me. I felt sick, betrayed. A misfire. I didn't want to pick it up, but I had to, if for no other reason than that it had been entrusted to me and it had to be returned. I eased myself down and grasped it with my bloody fingers. Maybe I could fix it, for the journey back. I flipped the barrel open and six empty chambers stared back at me.

WHEN I FINALLY heaved myself out of the pit, the breeze cooled the sweat on my body. He was standing there looking for all the world as if he hadn't moved an inch. I thought I noticed something in his eyes when he saw me, a... softening, only for a second and then it vanished.

Bruised, battered, blooded, with the face of a milliasaur strapped on to my belt. I must have been quite a sight. I limped towards him, my broken knife in one hand, the pistol in the other. Every single step back out I'd been thinking of what I would do. Should I get mad? Should I thank him? Or maybe act like I'd never noticed? I'd done what he asked, I'd got my trophy, I should just say what I was supposed to say, what he wanted me to say, and then I'd be in. I'd be one of the gang. But part of me wanted more, wanted to demand an answer, wanted to rip his head off. It drove me mad. The choices whirled round and round in my mind until I said to myself; no more, when I got there, when I could look in his eyes I would know what to do.

Now that time had come. I let the gun slip from my grasp, it thudded in the dirt. I wrenched the dripping trophy from my belt and dropped it on top. There. My victory, my knowledge, my questions were plain for him to see. I waited for a flicker of response. There was none. His aged, bloodshot eyes returned my gaze impassively.

'Get it now?'

The hard, metallic words whispered from his respirator. No praise. No apology.

What little blood remained in me boiled. The fist came out of nowhere, I didn't even see it until his head slammed to the side.

I couldn't believe what I'd done. I stared at my hand as if it were another's. I was shocked, but I felt good. He turned back to me, his respirator hung uselessly off the side of his face but his expression was the same. My pleasure turned to ashes. Had he even felt it? But then, there it was, a tiny drop of crimson emerged from the shadow of his nostril. It edged its way past his nose-ring and began the long journey down to his cracked lips. I smiled. I soared.

He didn't even bother to wipe it off before he picked me up and drove me into the ground. Then he hauled me on to his shoulder and started back. His laughing made it a bumpy ride, and he didn't stop for long damn time.

# THE DAEMON BOTTLE
## by Alex Hammond

'AND THERE WILL be fire from the heavens and righteous bolt guns will quicken and purge even the deepest crevices of the Underhive. All that is foul and pestilent will be washed away! For this is the teaching of House Cawdor of the Redemption.'

First there was a sound. Like a burst of fire that stirred the dim mutterings of my mind to action. Somewhere in the back of my head, a woman from my dream, beautiful body scarless and soft, still danced in the upper hive.

'Look upon this scum. The deepest slag pits could not out-match his sins in their filth and perversion.'

Thoughts swelled. My dancing girl disappeared.

'See – though he wakes from his slumber, he does not release the bottle from his hand.'

The voice was closer than I remembered in my sleep. Louder too. Enraged. I opened my eyes.

Legs. Lots of legs, some bound in cloth, others wearing heavy boots, stretched out before me. I followed them upwards and discovered the hard, ash-worn faces of a crowd of settlers. Their attention flitted between my recumbent form and someone behind me. A preacher? I began to stand, bow-legged, still recovering from a bottle of WildSnake.

'On your feet and face the prophet of universal destruction!' A solid boot in my back sent me floundering forward into the reeking mud.

The crowd cheered. I rolled over onto my back, elbows deep in the sludge. Through mud-splattered eyes I made out the robed preacher – thick burgundy cloth ran in torn strips from ground to neck. A leather mask covered all but a pair of rabid eyes and a mouth spitting blood. A House of Redemption preacher had come to town.

'Vermin man! Stand and answer to the House Cawdor, the true prophets of the flames of salvation.' Through the black leather face mask one eye caught my attention. Bloodshot streams ran their course to a pupil as dark as pitch. Another boot struck me full in the face.

'Look,' my voice cracked, from behind the haze of last night's drinking, 'I'd be able to stand if you'd stop practising ratball with my face, old man.'

Stunned silence behind me. The preacher staggered and began to shake violently on the spot. Theatrical performance or the jiggling of a religious psychopath, I wasn't going to hang around to find out.

Slowly I stood. The Cawdor preacher stopped moving. The crowd clustered well back.

'Emperor damn me,' I muttered, as a leathered fist pulled out a hand flamer.

'Talk back will you, rat man? Mock those who herald cleansing flame?' A white tongue slid in and out of the priest's mouth. 'Seek ye retribution?'

'Look, I'm happy to go sleep in some other part of town.'

The preacher pointed his flamer in my direction. The crowd scrambled wide. 'This town is in no need of ratskin scum. Go converse with your blasphemous hive spirits!'

'That's *half*-ratskin, slimehole!' I rushed for the crowd hoping the distance and their bodies would afford me protection from the flames.

*\*Click\**

'Aaaaagh!' I threw myself into a pile of scrap.

*\*Plop\**

No wash of flame. I turned to look over my shoulder.

The zealot stood there. The antiquated weapon still levelled in my direction had failed to discharge its round. An empty fuel canister came to rest in the mud beside me.

The old man began to reach for a reload amongst his tattered robes.

A lead pipe, thick bolt rusted to one end, felt good in my hand. I wrenched it from the mess of ancient metal about me and whirled it about my head.

The priest, rustling about his drapery, produced another canister.

'Aaaaargh!' I screamed in terrified panic.

'Aaaaargh!' The Redemptionist thrust his hands together, loading the weapon.

A warm trickle of liquid down my leg. My only source of comfort. I swung towards to the preacher and reconsidered my options…

…this man had friends…

…*too late*.

The pipe sunk deep into the leather mask. Somewhere in his head something cracked. A muddy thud later, the preacher lay on the ground. I grabbed his flamer and spun to face the rabble. Only a silver snowfall of effluent ash from somewhere overhead – not a settler in sight.

The silver ash fall began to thicken. Somewhere in the hive city, miles above me, ancient machines were grinding over, pulling on pistons, driving cogs and starting the thousand year-old machines of Hive Primus.

THE ASH FALL had worsened. I watched from inside Karag's Saloon as desperate underhivers ran for cover, trying to keep their particle intake to a minimum. Push your annual quota too high and you'd reduce your life span by as many rads as you'd inhaled. Inside the bar, smoke hung momentarily before air filters dragged it into the bowels of Downtown's evaporation tanks. I had used the old zealot's money to purchase a fresh bottle of WildSnake and a few pills from a fixer I knew. I began to think things over. Life was getting bad for settlement-dwelling ratskins – so bad, it appeared, that even half-castes like myself were now the targets for retribution. I should move uphive, work in an Orlock factory till I had enough creds to pay for some nu-flesh and a day on a serum drip. (I had no need of a lung pump: the respirators I'd scavenged when I was young had kept me free from noxious air.) Once I'd had a wet overhaul, I'd have a better chance of getting employed by one of the spire noble families.

Karag's extraction fan above the bar spluttered, gave a grinding death rattle and stopped. Almost immediately all eyes turned to me. Karag – big man, lots of teeth – stretched out his hand towards me. His two real fingers held out a stack of guilder credits.

'Sarak, we'd all appreciate it if you'd go in there and fish out whatever's got caught in the fan.'

'I've quit cleaning ducts.'

'Even for your friends?' Karag flipped out a couple of extra coins.

'You try wrestling a Catchacan face-eater one day and then see if you're keen on going back into an air duct.'

'There's another bottle of WildSnake on me if you'll do it.'

SOMEWHERE IN THE duct, something was half-alive. Its squeals echoed down through the steel lung that fed air into the bar below me. The humid conditions of the air ducts of the underhive were home to creatures that just could not bear to live anywhere else: albino milliasaurs, phosphorescent lashworms and all manner of tropical spores and bugs.

A few tiny carapaces cracked beneath my hands as I inched further towards the bar's extraction fan. The squealing stopped. It had heard me. I struggled with a flashlight and shone it forward onto the mechanism.

*EEEEEEEEE!*

Like a leathery bolt, something rushed forward, needle teeth snapping at my face.

'Wha–' I slipped forwards.

The flashlight spun out of my hand sending spiralling patterns about the air vent. It came to rest dead on the creature. Four eyes perched in a row across its brow stared into mine, unblinking. A multitude of legs, wing flaps strung between them dipped – the thing sprung again.

'Aaagh!'

*Snap! Snap!*

Its teeth were just inches from my face. But no further.

Looking over the thing's back, I followed its tail, like a large welt of flesh, to the extraction fan. It was caught.

'Karag!' I called down to the mumbling bar through the vent.

'Quiet!' Karag poked at the air duct from below with a broom. ''Zat you, Sarak?'

'Karag, notch your fan up a few dots.'

'You sure about that?'

'Karag, this thing is going to eat my nose if you take any longer!' Hurried footsteps somewhere below.

The fan ground a full revolution, pulling the creature eight inches towards the rough blades.

'Again!' I called.

The creature squealed and lost its footing, scrabbling on the metal. The fan, now free, whirred up to full speed, sucking the thing backwards into its blades. It ground the thing up like a paste, spitting its entrails, many legs and bright yellow ichor into the vents, all over me and down into the bar.

'It's dead!' Karag's voice observed astutely from below.

A FRESH BOTTLE of WildSnake in hand, a few off-cuts of giant rat skin tucked around my feet, I settled down in an alleyway behind a tanner's shop. I opened the stopper on the bottle and let its pungent odour hit me full in the face. I had done well: the distiller had let part of the brewed snake slip into this bottle. Looked like a rib. I took a swig and swallowed one of the pills I'd acquired earlier.

Somewhere in the distance, gunfire rattled out a staccato beat – the gangers were waking. Leaning back I looked skyward. The thousand walkways of the underhive disappeared up into the darkness like a thousand steel-black arteries feeding the life blood to the Hive City's dark heart. I could make out under-hivers moving along the lower levels.

Little people moving. Little people with more scar tissue than sense. This place swarmed with the very worst humanity had to offer. Here I was, knee high in effluent with only a bottle of WildSnake, a dust-respirator, a dead man's weapon and a rad-counter to my name. I had to move uphive. I'd almost lost my life twice today and wasn't going to settle for a third. In the hive spire they don't have bugs. No bugs, no wounds either.

The tiny lights of the hive city above me looked like a galaxy of stars, a glimpse of greater things. A gentle breeze washed over my face and… and I knew I was in. The soft sound of music, light as though touched by the fingers of air – a small coloured bird in a cage – a clear night sky free from poisonous cloud cover – star freighters, bright blue thrusters propelling them deepspace – the woman, injury free and white skin dancing, turning around and around, calling out my name, soft melodious voice – no rattle of gunfire – just the soft wind, the dancer and the smell of real plants.

I WOKE FOR the second time that day. With the visions of the hive spire still playing through in my mind, I walked out of the alley way into the city streets, holding the fur off-cuts tight around my shoulders. For the first time in years, I smiled at a woman and child as they passed me by, fresh rats hung off their belts. I knew where to go and how to do it. I was going uphive.

WHEN YOU'VE GOT little that you own and are still getting over the euphoric effects of a drug cocktail everything seems a lot easier. Perhaps if I had been straight I would have gone about my exodus a little differently. Perhaps I wouldn't have gone to the front gate.

'You Ratman Sarak?' Masked man. Three others with him

'Huh?' I stared through the two ancient pillars that denoted DownTown's front gate – it was five metres away. The drugs in my system tripled that distance.

'Ratman Sarak your name, half-breed?' The man was dressed in robes; a pair of ape like lips jutted out of a leather mask.

'Ah, yeah?'

'Someone paid a lot of money so that they could have a problem with you instead of us.' One of the other men, cradling an auto pistol in his hands, spoke tight-lipped through a similar mask to his friend.

'Oh?'

'Enough of this.' The big man was giving the orders. 'Pack him up and let's make that delivery.' I couldn't remember where I'd tucked the flamer. One of the men stuck me with a syringe filled with black liquid. My body sagged – and then I realised what I'd done.

'HELLO, MY SWEET.'

The dancing woman? I'd be able to open my eyes if I could stop my head from rotating. There were others in the room.

I caught hold of my head and snapped my eyes open.

'Oh?' A bloated neck lead in rolls of flesh up to the back of a shaven head. 'He's awake.' The figure turned around to face me. A pair of bespectacled eyes stared down on me from within a wealth of flesh. A large guilder badge predominated a costume of rich cloth and precious metals.

'Greetings, Mr Gunta,' I slurred.

'Oh Sarak, there's no need for formalities. No, debts as steep as yours make us business partners. Call me Otto, do.'

Otto Gunta, the Black Tongued Guilder Prince of the Underhive. First time we'd met, although I knew his agents well. A guilder with as many kills to his name as he had guild bonds.

'OK, Otto.' I attempted to reach out a hand but found it tightly constrained by an iron brace.

'Silly boy. You're in no state to move. There's enough spore venom in your blood to have you flapping about like a fish on the floor if we don't keep you restrained.' His pitch-black tongue licked his lips.

'Which spore?'

'Lugtekk, what colour was it?' Otto turned back over his shoulder.

'Yellow.' A metallic voice in the shadows, the only other thing in the big, empty warehouse.

'Now, Sarak. I have the antidote to this poison if you'd just pay up your debts.'

'Nothing.'

'That used respirator, rad counter and that hand flamer you so cleverly hid on your belt make up at least, say, thirty credits? Now if you could make up the other one sixty?'

'I don't have any money.'

'Oh yes? Well this is no good. Discovered any archaeotech recently?' The guilder's pudgy fingers danced at the mention of ancient technology.

'No.'

'Some green hivers I could extort?'

'No.'

'Well I guess I'm going to have to sell your carcass to a body bank–'

'Wait... I could offer you my services.' Perhaps I didn't sound desperate enough.

'I'm afraid you're a little under-skilled. You're the town drunk and a chemhead to boot. You're worth about ten credits to a generous body harvester.'

'Seriously, I take care of infestations.'

'Infestations?'

'Pests.'

'Pests? … Alright Sarak. You've got yourself a job. You take care of an infestation and we'll wipe the slate clean. I might even see about that dancing girl.'

'What?' Otto's nasty little mouth broke into a smile. 'You dare touch my mind with an unsanctioned psyker and I'll–'

'I don't deal with psykers, Sarak. You spilled your guts to us when you were under – once metaphorically and the second time, well…'

'I'm not laughing, fat man,' I slurred.

'You're in no position to laugh, you mincing turd!' Otto's spittle sprayed my face. 'Lugtekk, give him the antidote and get his sorry behind rigged up to infiltrate those scavvies.'

'What?'

'Your chosen vocation is pest exterminator? Well I'm up to my armpits in mutant scum from the bottom of the hive and they're costing me profit.' Otto spat out the words, slapping the guilder badge on his chest. 'What did you think I'd do, send you into my warehouses with a stick and a rat quota?'

'Yes.'

'Baha!' Otto wobbled as he broke out into a high shriek. 'Let's get this show on the road.' The warehouse suddenly came to life, lights cast the shadows aside and the ground shook and began a steady rumble.

'Where are we going?' I stumbled over the words, my fear obvious.

'We're taking this rig deeper into the hive.' Otto smiled.

'WHAT MR GUNTA wants is simple. And when Mr Gunta wants something simple done, for a lot of money, we do it. Right?' A strap was pulled tighter across my chest.

'Look – Lugtekk?' The man comprising more machine parts than real flesh stared across at me. 'You don't want to be leading an assault against these depraved cannibals – just like I don't want to be sneaking into their hide out and poisoning them.'

'Not all of 'em. Just the leader. Without him they're toasted rat.'

'That's a moot point. I'll be dead before I get close to any of them.'

'Not with this you won't.' Lugtekk fastened another strap across my chest and placed an electrode on my head.

'What is it?'

'A holo-suit. Mr Gunta was planning on selling 'em to the Talloran rebels,' Lugtekk's metal fingers pressed another electrode roughly to my head, 'but an Imperium patrol clamped down on his spaceport and the stock ain't moved since.'

'What's it do?'

'Re-routed to make you look more like a skavvy. Here.' Lugtekk flashed a piece of mirrored glass in my face.

Woah. Welts and a third eye adorned my head.

'Come on, Lugtekk. You know I would look more realistic with sludge meal smeared on my face.'

'It's still configuring to your dimensions.'

'You really want to go into battle? Come on, we could ditch this caravan and head uphive together.'

'Sorry, little man. When exactly did you become a friend of mine?'

'Bu–'

'See these?' Lugtekk flashed out a series of pictures.

'Aw, no, frag–' Skinned like sludge rats.

'These are the faces of gangers Mr Gunta had me ride out of town. These holos are all that's left. Right now they're eel food. I'm not in the business of being pleasant. I'm a hired gun, little man. Now get ready to go.'

I didn't speak to Lugtekk again. Otto, seated behind a control panel in his head caravan, issued orders to a band of mercenaries and hired scum, a posse he'd pulled together from the toughest bars in the Underhive.

I pondered my predicament. In my sweat-drenched palms I held five melting capsules. Poison, Lugtekk had said, but I had my own suspicions. Through the shimmering light of the holo suit I pulled on the fuel canister Otto had reimbursed me as part of the hand flamer. It was fresh. Brand new.

Otto finished his commands. 'Now Sarak.'

'Ah-huh?'

'We're going to equip you with that flamer to give you a little confidence. Pep you up some. Nothing is going to go wrong.'

'Ah-hah?'

'We've been planing this for weeks. So all you have to do is mosey on up to them with that carcass and its juicy piece of bait in your hands, pop those pills in their leader's food and, hello hello, come home to mummy.'

THE GRINDING OF the machines above had always been of comfort to me. But down here at Hive Bottom I could not hear them, only the soft squelch of the mould carpet underneath me. Huge pillars bored into the ground, like the trunks of a steel forest. Fluorescent bugs scuttled up and down them like blood in the veins of an ancient giant.

In the darkness I regarded the dead ganger I had dragged all this way. His eyes were bloodied, a pock mark of jagged flesh torn through his jaw. His death had been slow. Into his belt was tucked a map and a guilder schedule, pretty good ones – even I couldn't tell they were fakes. I hoped the smell of blood hadn't attracted the nasty things from their recesses.

'Skav you're?' A voice in the darkness. A stunted figure.

'Un,' I replied trying to give as little indication of my uphive origin.

'Big eat on. Hoegas's kin?'

I didn't understand a word. 'Un.' I stuck to what worked.

'Sludge meal, manflesh to eat.'

'Oh, splendid,' I muttered under my breath.

The dark figure led on, stumbling towards a dim glow in the distance. We approached the skavvies' stronghold, twenty figures gathered about a large fire in the middle of a shanty town. I nearly retched when I saw the faces of these depraved souls, the garish light the fire threw up highlighted their pustulent limbs, encrusted skulls and infested wounds.

Upon the fire was a giant, spent ammunition shell, used as a cooking pot. A stray limb fell out as a bloated skavvy stirred. Not even the visions of my worst drug-induced stupor with its skinless apes and pit-eyed marionettes compared to this spectacle.

'More for pot?' A plastic-wrapped man, jagged smile and pointed teeth, stepped out of the mass of cannibals. 'You bring good eatin'?'

'Un,' I muttered, sticking with the routine.

'Me Hoegas, I lead.' The half-man reached out a wrapped hand.

I passed him the body.

'You kill 'im?' His eyes shifted.

'Uh-ha. Look like guilder.'

Hoegas looked down. His smile dropped. For a second the holo suit shimmered. 'What?' The skavvy leader reached towards the body and removed its torn flack jacket. 'He got words!' The skavvies left the pot. They huddled close, small luminous worms digging about their flesh. I closed my eyes. 'Words tell of more guilder kin, travel slow through old walls. Got good stuff!' Hoegas translated.

'Good stuff!' the skavvies cheered, moaned and shrieked in near unison like a daemonic chorus.

'Bring new skav down front. Let 'im eat sum.' Hoegas flapped a claw at me.

I would have been happier if I had been buried alive in a mass grave. These freaks gorged themselves for an hour on the half-decayed carcasses of former companions and the fresh kill I had delivered to them. The leader sipped periodically from a private keg of WildSnake by his side. His plastic squeaked and rustled as he stood to fetch another bowl of flesh gruel from the pot. I stumbled towards it through the crowd of skavvies, half-rotten hands slapping me on the back as I moved. I reached for the keg. Its neck in my grasp, all sound and movement stopped. All eyes were on me.

Hoegas spun about. His eyes met mine. Thin wisps of psyker–electricity played across his fingers. I had to think quick. I unplugged the lid of the keg and, dropping to one knee, offered it to him.

'Hail Hoegas, witchman king!' I was fast running short of ideas.

'Hail!' chorused the skavvies. Hoegas grinned a jagged-toothed smile at his monstrous comrades. In the moment his head turned I crushed Otto's pills through the gaps in my clenched hand. 'Hail Hoegas!' Hoegas chuckled and reached towards the keg of WildSnake.

A shot rang out. The skavvies fell to the ground, drawing out ancient blades and muskets. Hoegas fell to the ground – clutching at his chest.

A large scaled skavvy stood up, smoking pistol still in his hands. 'No hail Hoegas. Hail Blotta, hail all skavs!'

Oh great. I was in the middle of a skavvy revolution. A cannibal collective.

Hoegas gurgled, shimmering blue light dancing about his chest wound.

'Blotta!' Hoegas cried, then erupted in a rush of blue flame and sparks. The cannibal pot spilled its gore into the sludge. I slipped on a rotten intestine.

'Blotta good skav, let other skavs drink!'

Blotta – three arms, one eye – snatched the WildSnake from my hands and took a deep swig. I scuttled back from him, eyes roaming the skavvy crowd for an escape route. Blotta grinned across both his mouths.

'Good drink!' His eye caught mine, 'New skav drink up. All skavs drink!'

I shook my head. Blotta wasn't showing any signs of being poisoned yet; perhaps it took a little time to wear in.

'Drink!' Blotta waved his gun at me.

The other skavvies fell silent. I fingered the trigger of the hand flamer tucked inside my shirt. An arching spray would hit most of them – what was I saying? I'd never shot a gun, let alone a highly volatile antique.

*Click-chink* 'Drink!' Blotta cocked and thrust his pistol at my head.

They must have been getting suspicious. I reached forward, taking as long as I could to reach the bottle. Still no sign from Blotta. Slowly I grasped its neck, and held it to my lips. A small clock was ticking down the time in my head, I tried to move its hands. I let only the smallest amount of the WildSnake touch my lips and trickle down my dry throat.

'More!' Blotta grabbed my hand and upended more of the drink into my mouth.

I spluttered backwards onto the ground to a burst of laughter. I lay there while the skavvies drank themselves silly on the WildSnake. I was poisoned. I tried forcing my fingers back into my throat but nothing happened.

'New skav. Come kill guilder kin!' It was Blotta. Looked like Hoegas's old plan still stood.

I staggered to my feet. Perhaps Otto had an antidote. All I had to do was circumvent the holo-suit and get up to his caravan. Half a chance was better than none. The skavvies armed themselves with stolen weapons and rust-encrusted blades. As they busied themselves I struggled with Hoegas's body, trying to find some evidence of his death. In the end I cut a ring from his finger.

'New skav?' Blotta and his mutant comrades were ready.

'Un.'

GLAD TO BE running. Good to be running. Perhaps we'll make up time. But what if there is no antidote? No means of stopping the poison that runs through me. I'm not feeling ill but it could be one of Otto's nastier concoctions, something seeping into my system and eating away at me from inside. Otto must have planned for the poison to kick in when the skavvies arrived in his trap. Why didn't he tell me about it? How could he know they'd come straight away? What if–

We arrived. An old dome town, the metal braces that held its roof still remained like an old iron skeleton. The perfect place for a trap. A guilder caravan sits in the centre of the dome. The skavvies cheer as they see it below. Guns blazing, they rush at it. I follow, keeping my distance, trying to catch sight of Otto.

Nothing... and then it starts. Before the skavvies even reach the caravan one falls to the ground. It clutches its head and thrashes about on the ash floor. Dust kicks up at its feet and thin wisps of light crackle about its head. One last kick and it lies still, electricity tracing along its lifeless body. Blotta begins to scream, firing shots wildly into the air. One gets lucky and hits one of Otto's mercenaries hidden in the iron braces.

A volley of gunfire, heavy weapons and red hot lasers rains down on the skavvies. A few shots are good but the mutants seem to have an uncanny speed. Blotta still screams and then begins to slowly rise from the ground. A wyrd? Spiralling upwards, his shotgun buckles as forces beyond his control wrack his body. Other skavvies, hidden amidst the old machines and broken concrete slabs, begin to cast fire from their fingers, burn white hot and float.

'Gunta!' I yell over the sound of the screaming skavvies and the gunfire. A red dot traces its way across the ground towards me. I struggle with the electrodes stuck to my head. I start running. Bullets pepper the ground behind me, throwing up ash and ricochets from scrap metal. I duck into an old doorway and slump to the ground.

A skavvy's hiding here too. It draws out an old musket.

I wave my flamer at it.

'Skav?' It moans. 'Others think in my head.'

'What?'

'Big man laughing, metal man shoot metal from above. Skavs think of dead.' It slaps its brow. 'All in my head. All in my head.'

Suddenly I work it out. *Spook*. The street name for what wannabe psyckers hit up on in order to get some psychic action. It was banned throughout the Underhive, but some still couldn't refuse the chance of wielding a bit of nether-forces. Otto must have wanted to fry the skavvy boss's mind, make him overload on psychic juices or something. But now it was messing with everyone's head.

'You think man-thoughts. You not skav. You friend of laughing man!' The skavvy levels its musket at me.

I let my finger run the flamer's trigger as far as it will go.

*\*Flaaaash\**

The flamer begins spewing blazing napalm across the Skavvy and throughout the burnt-out room we were in. I leap from the flames. A bullet grazes my head from above. The sniper must have been waiting. I start running again, panting and desperate. One of my legs catches alight from a lick of flame that comes rushing down from above.

The scene outside is rife with destruction and carnage. Skavvy turns on skavvy hallucinating wildly as the mercenaries gradually tighten their stranglehold. Bullets fall in waves about the dome. I drop to the ground and beat at the flames on my legs. I rip the electrodes from my head and hit the holo-suit's release button. Blood trickles down across my eyes.

'Gunta! You slimehole!' I scream.

*Don't worry. He'll get his.* A voice in my head.

'What?' I groan, flat on my back, the ancient dome above me. My head spins. Some thing is inside my head. Hive spirit?

*Not exactly.*

'What're you doing in my head?'

*You eat those pills?*

What? Uphive. Dreams of uphive. Think... Focus!

I pull myself across the ground. Skavvies lie twisted and contorted in the shapes of painful death. Many are alight.

*You're the last one alive.*

'How do you know?' Voices in the distance. Outside my head.

*Trust me. I was there when each of them died.*

Otto Gunta the Black Tongued Guilder Prince strolls about the corpses, surrounded by men, marking each dead skavvy off on a clipboard.

'We've done well, Lugtekk.' Otto addresses the mechanoid man beside him. 'Quite well.'

'Gunta!' I call out.

*He can't hear you.*

It's true – he doesn't react.

'Gunta!' I scream so loud I think my lungs will burst.

*I won't let him hear you. Not until we've had our chat.*

'Who are you?' Sharp pain shoots throughout my body. 'Get out of my head.' I roll over, face-first in the ash.

*She dances pretty well.*

'What?' Ash tastes like burnt bones.

*The girl in your head.*

'Leave her alone.'

*Oh-ho, silly boy! The Spire looks nothing like this. No no. Scrap the coloured birds and the warm breezes. They're all hooked up on life support systems up there. Air's too thin to breathe.* The voice is jagged with cynicism.

'Liar!'

*How'd you know?* A pain in the back of my head. *Don't cry now.*

'Damn you!'

*That's better, use those emotions all up.* I feel my body being lifted. *Now let's get us moving, eh?*

I stand to my feet, legs propelled by forces other than my own. The men move with suspicion. Otto is undeterred.

'Well done, Sarak.' Otto approaches.

'Why'd you use Spook?' My voice rings loud like a roll of thunder.

'Oh no. I don't deal in illegal substances.'

*\*Crack\**

A pain through my chest. 'That's your payment done.' The obese guilder slides his pistol back into its holster.

*Did that hurt? It had to hurt.*

'You're dead!' I stagger forwards, thrusting the flamer at Otto.

'Wa–?' Otto turns, my sudden actions making the fat man dance on his feet. 'Kill him!'

A hail of gunfire jousts with the wave of flame that I launch from the weapon in my hand. I'm struck all over, hot metal boring into my flesh. The bullets feel warm inside my cold body. Not too much pain.

*That's the spirit!*

I burst alight, the flamer dropping at my feet. Otto's men roll and writhe on the ground slapping at the flames.

*Let's dance.*

The few remaining mercenaries rush at me, controlled bursts breaking into wild fire as I fail to fall to the ground in a bloody heap.

'What are you doing to me?' I scream as I am flung about like a puppet on a string.

*You're possessed from the warp, man. It's a lesson in messing with psychic drugs.*

Claws I never knew I had begin to cut the fighting men to ribbons. Only Lugtekk fights on. Blood and oil streams from his body, his machine limbs clogged with his own life fluid. All too soon he falls to a burning heap on the ground.

This is it, I think, I'm going to die. But I have one last trick to play.

*What trick?*

'Never you mind,' I say aloud.

I take a few deep breaths and rush Otto. He screeches and tries to run, but I do not let him.

'Take my credit badge! Sarak, I can fix it! I have friends in the spire. I can get you work there!' Otto weeps like a child.

'No,' I reply calmly. I feel pain. 'No, Otto. We're both going to die.' The hurt runs in waves across my body.

*What are you doing to me?* The voice is fading.

'I have a present for you, Otto.' I release hold of all that I care for; let my emotions slip into nothing. Slumping forward, I fall on top of Otto, crushing his body to the ground.

Otto shrieks. Already a death spasm grips my body.

*You're dying.*

'I know.' I thrust a bloodied arm down the screaming guilder's throat. And let go of the dancing girl.

My eyes are glazing over. Consciousness slips away with the last drops of blood. A final image burns into my retina – the screaming guilder, possessed to die and burn for eternity.

# RITES OF PASSAGE
## by Gordon Rennie

HEREK ROSE PAINFULLY to his feet, trying to rub some sensation into the stump of his left arm. The wound had healed long ago but down here, in the dank air of the deepest tunnels of the Underhive, it continued to trouble him, reminding him painfully of the place where, years ago, a rusted scavvy blade brought his career as leader of the Orlock-affiliated Steel Skull gang to an end. It was time once more to deliver The Speech.

He cast a shrewd eye over the fearful young faces looking at him in the dim light of the tunnel. Generations of Underhive dwellers had left their marks here, and the walls were covered in ganger graffiti: arcane symbols, faded boasts of warriors now long dead and dire warnings of what lay beyond the ancient blast-doors at the end of the tunnel. 'From here on in, you go alone,' Herek told them sternly. 'Anyone who wants to back out better speak up now. There's no shame in it. You won't be the first, and I don't expect you'll be the last...'

As he had expected, Dorn, the largest and strongest of the pack, was the first to step forward, eagerly seeking his mentor's approval. Dorn was a born warrior, his face already marked with his first battle scars, proudly won in teenage rumbles against fellow gang members in the gang's fortified settlement, a kilometre or so above this desolate place.

'We will not disappoint you, Herek,' Dorn declared loudly, not waiting for the others. 'In two cycles' time, we will return to you not as children, but as warriors! This I swear to you, on the honour of House Orlock!'

To his right, Mikhal, already as tall as his father and potentially as good a fighter, with just a little more experience under his belt, nodded his assent. Alongside him, Lan, as wiry and intense as a sump rat, did likewise. Both were keen and brave enough, Herek knew, but in all matters they followed Dorn, tying their fortunes to his. As he rose through the ranks of the gangs – as he surely would, if he survived the coming ordeal – he would take them with him as able lieutenants. Herek smiled to himself, fondly remembering other, similarly commanding warriors from previous years who had gone on to earn greater glories for the gang.

Herek turned towards the two remaining youths. 'And you, young Jaal, are you and your brother ready for what waits for you on the other side of those blast-doors?'

Jaal Rinn shifted uneasily, barely raising his eyes from his new, ill-fitting boots. As ever, it was his brother, Mallin, who answered for him. 'Aye, Master Herek. Show us our enemies, and we will prove our worthiness to our clan.'

Herek nodded, looking at the pair appraisingly. Such a different pair, not even truly brothers! Mallin was strong and capable, and wise beyond his young years. The other, Jaal, was small and pale-skinned, and bore none of the inherited traits of strength and hardiness normally associated with the House of Iron. The boy's parents had died when he was but an infant, killed in a raid upon the Skull's settlement by Cawdor gangers, and he had been taken in by Mallin's family and raised as their own. Quick and agile as he was, Jaal had never been the equal of his more confident brother and Herek suspected that it was only with Mallin's help that Jaal had made it this far through the training.

'Let the runt speak for himself!' Dorn sneered, his hands clenching into fists. 'Must he always hide in the shadow of his brother?'

Jaal blushed in anger – the runt of the litter, they called him! – and spoke out, his voice shaking with emotion. 'My clan has raised me and protected me. All I ask is a chance to serve it in return and reclaim the blood debt owed to me by the murderers of my parents.'

Herek smiled in satisfaction, quietly impressed by the young ganger's resolve. He would need it where he was going. 'Brave words, young Jaal. Now let us see if you can make good on them. The enemies you go to face do indeed carry the colours of House Cawdor. Let your hatred give you strength, but never forget that we have more need of live warriors than dead heroes.'

At Herek's signal, the two gangers who had accompanied them down to the entrance to Hive Bottom – seasoned veterans who had once fought under Herek's leadership – moved to haul open the immense blast-doors at the bottom of the shaft. Beyond these doors, their outer surfaces scarred and pitted by the centuries of ferocious assaults from the things that dwelled on the other side of them, lay a world of darkness and danger.

The young initiates crowded around the open doorway, eager to see what lay beyond. Hive Bottom. A place that, until now, they had only heard tell of in childhood stories tailored to frighten them into obedience. A fearful place populated by mutants and witches, and where deadly traps – toxic waste pools, poisonous mists and grotesque mutant creatures – were always waiting to ensnare the unwary.

Back when he was leader of the Steel Skull, leading raids on Goliath merchant convoys and Cawdor settlements under the flag of House Orlock, Herek had braved the dangers of Hive Bottom many times. Even now, though, he still remembered his very first sight and smell of it during his own rite of manhood, and understood exactly the fear and apprehension his young charges must be feeling now.

The two gangers silently scanned the darkness around the doorway, their weapons primed and at the ready for any sign of danger. Satisfied, one of them waved the young bloods forward with a sharp gesture. Dorn looked around at his fellows with a wide, brave grin and strode into the darkness; the others followed with more nervous steps.

'Go easy on 'em, Dorn,' one of the veterans said, slapping the lad on the shoulders as he passed.

'Nah, give those Cawdor scum hell, Dorn,' the other grinned. 'Get yourself back in one piece and I'll give you some of my winnings!'

Herek watched the slight figures disappear from view, knowing that there was no more advice he could give them. For two day-cycles he would remain here, waiting to see which, if any, of the young juves returned.

'Good hunting – all of you!' called Herek into the gloom, stepping back and signalling for the two gangers to close the doors. He offered up a silent prayer, calling on the Emperor to watch over the young warriors. He had tried to teach them everything he knew. From now on they were on their own.

THE HUNTER MOVED easily through the crumbling ruins, more at home here than it had ever been in the palaces and landscaped parks of the Upper Hive. If it had ever had a name, it had long ago forgotten it. It paused, checking the information relayed to it through its armoured body and savouring the thrill of the replay images being fed directly into its mind from the suit's memory systems. Steel claws punching through flesh. The feel of laser bolts and bullets ricocheting harmlessly off armoured skin. The screams of its victims and the images of their faces as they died in agony.

It had been too long – scarce two hours – since its last kill. It felt its body's auto-systems activate into life at the joyous replay of those few bloody seconds. Fibre-bundle muscles twitched with life, armoured plates clicked and flexed together and its claws slowly unsheathed themselves as memory circuits sent an electronic thrill of pleasure through its body. Sensor systems flared into life, invisibly scanning the area and locking on to a distant group of targets moving through the darkness.

The prey was still far off, but coming closer. The Hunter turned and moved silently towards it.

'LAN, GO AHEAD and check the way in front of us. Make sure your laspistol is armed and charged,' Dorn insisted. The juve gang crouched near a barely lit glow-globe, taking cover amongst the twisted girders of a long-ago collapsed structure. Dorn barked orders as if it were his given right; he had already assumed natural command of the group. 'Mikhal, stay beside me. Mallin, cover our rear – and see that the runt doesn't get lost in the dark.'

Their destination was the ritual duelling area out in the wastes of Hive Bottom – the ruins of a one-time settlement long abandoned to bands of mutants and outlaw gangs. It was here they would meet their chosen opponents, but this coming battle was but a small part of the test. Any journey through Hive Bottom was hazardous, and the young warriors were only too well aware that anything could be waiting for them in the velvet darkness.

At the rear of the band, Mallin sensed his brother's uneasiness, and laid a reassuring hand on Jaal's shoulder. 'Ignore him,' he said levelly. 'Stay by me, and we'll both survive this together. Remember what Herek taught us. Fear is the greatest killer of all, more deadly than any weapon. Conquer fear, and you will be ready to call yourself a true warrior.'

Jaal nodded, realising the worth of his brother's words. He was afraid, but not of the coming battle. He was afraid of this place and the things that roamed its shadows. He pulled nervously at his bandanna. A strange uneasiness filled him – a gut instinct that he had come to recognise as a warning of imminent danger. Such instincts had saved him from a knife in the back more than once, back when he was running with the younger juves of the Steel Skull's settlement, learning how to stalk and fight in the relative safety of the tunnels around the compound.

Now he felt that same familiar sensation of lurking danger again, coming from out there in the surrounding darkness. Somehow he just knew that something dark and deadly was out there – and it was coming closer.

THE HUNTER CROUCHED in the shadows atop a ruined metal shack, watching its prey. The chameleon scales on the surface of its body suit shifted to blend in perfectly with its surroundings. Thermally sealed inside its body suit, it was invisible even to infrared detection. Its armoured suit had been crafted in the finest artificer workshops of a far distant world, and the suit's enhanced adaptation systems meant that it now possessed extra-evolved abilities that not even its creators could have predicted.

The Hunter activated its own infrared systems, watching the heat patterns of its prey dance through the darkness. Five of them. Five lost children, all alone down here in the dark. It paused to consider its options, strategy simulations composed from the stored memories of previous hunts flickering through its hard-wired consciousness. The Hunter ignored them. Memories of old kills no longer satisfied it. The prey was so close. It hungered for the thrill of fresh combat.

It leapt from its perch like a jaguar, sensor systems allowing it to track its prey's position effortlessly through the landscape of ruins. So confidently they moved, so unaware of the potential terrors that surrounded them down here!

Inside the skin of its suit, the Hunter smiled. They were sent down here to learn, and so it would teach them a lesson in terror. But first, in order for the lesson to begin, they must discover the surprise that lay in wait for them at their destination. After all, thought the Hunter, it had gone to such lengths to prepare the scene, and it did not intend for such effort go to waste…

'DEAD! THEY'RE ALL DEAD!'

At Lan's shout, the rest of the gang came running with their weapons drawn. They found their terrified comrade standing in the centre of the abandoned settlement. Its crumbling walls and burned-out dwelling holes were a testament to the destruction that had long ago been visited upon it by the marauding mutie gangs that roamed the wastes of Hive Bottom.

'Dead! They're all dead!' Lan repeated over and over, gesturing at the scene of bloody carnage around him. 'Look at them, Dorn! What kind of thing could have done this to them!'

Dorn looked, stunned by what he saw. He had been prepared for some kind of ambush – the rules of the ritual allowed for almost anything, and victory often went to the first gang to reach the duelling arena and set a trap for their opponents. But this… This was something he could never have foreseen.

So far he had counted five dead Cawdor gangers, although so many body parts were spread across the ground that it was difficult to tell exactly how many of them there may have originally been. One of them hung high above their heads, impaled on a steel beam jutting out of a shredded walkway. They had all been killed at close range – that much, he was certain of – ripped apart and their remains left for the scavengers. But killed by what, he asked himself fearfully?

Dorn glanced around him, checking the positions of the rest of the gang. Mallin and his runt brother were searching amongst the bodies, but he became uncomfortably aware that

Lan and Mikhal were looking to him for some sign of reassurance. As the appointed leader of the hunt, he knew it fell to him to assert his authority over the situation. 'An ambush,' he said, not feeling as confident as he tried to sound. 'Something was waiting for them before they arrived here. Scavvies, most likely. No ganger would kill like this, not even Cawdor scum. Whoever they were, they are long gone from here...'

'No. This was no ambush. Look at the evidence, Dorn. It is lying all around your feet.' Dorn turned at the sound of Mallin's voice, seeing his rival bending down over the butchered bodies of the dead gangers. 'There was a full-scale battle here. These Cawdor gangers died bravely as a warrior should, fighting to the last with a weapon in their hands.'

Mallin stood up, holding up the fused remains of a laspistol marked with House Cawdor battle emblems. He held it out for them all to see, a grim look on his young face. 'The power pack on this laspistol has been burned out. Whoever was carrying it kept on firing until he'd exhausted its power-charge.

'And those two juves–' He gestured with his arm at a pair of sprawling bodies. 'The ground around them is littered with spent cartridges from their stub pistols. Jaal and I count at least ten cartridges apiece for each weapon. That means they had time to reload and fire again before they died.'

Mallin paused, looking directly into Dorn's eyes. 'No, Dorn, this was no ambush. These warriors all died fighting an enemy they knew was coming at them.'

Behind Dorn, Mikhal and Lan exchanged nervous glances and raised their weapons. From his position behind Mallin, Jaal surreptitiously released the safety catch on his own laspistol, hearing the reassuring hum that told him it was fully charged.

Dorn stepped forward, locking eyes with his challenger, but none of them could have failed to notice the new note of uncertainty in his voice. 'Not an ambush, then. But I still say this was nothing more than the work of mutie scavengers.' He continued to glare at Mallin. 'Either way, we have nothing to worry about. Everyone knows scavvy packs never stick around after a raid. Even now, they'll be far away in their lair licking their wounds and counting their plunder.'

All eyes were on Mallin as he crushed Dorn's words with the cold logic of his argument. 'Then where are the bodies?' he retorted. 'All these shots fired, and not one dead attacker? Everyone knows scavvies leave their dead and even their injured behind them.'

Mallin paused, pointing towards the dead bodies around them. 'And, if it really was scavvies that did this, why haven't the bodies been stripped of their weapons and equipment? Jaal and I have checked the area for tracks. All we can find are those of the Cawdor gangers.' Mallin stood defiant, awaiting Dorn's answer.

'Then what are you saying?' sneered Dorn, running his hand over his close-cropped hair. 'That a ghost, a ghost that can walk through bullets and las-blasts, came here and killed them all?'

It was Jaal who answered, stepping forward to name the unspoken terror word on all their minds. 'No, not a ghost.' he stuttered hesitantly. Everyone turned to stare at him. Mallin nodding reassuringly at him to continue. 'It's a spyrer. A single spyrer did this. We are being hunted, Dorn. All of us. It killed every single one of these Cawdor juves, and now it's coming after us.'

THE HUNTER WAS close, closer than any of them dared imagine. From its position high above, perched on the underside of an overhanging walkway, it could look down directly upon them to study its prey. Watching them, selecting which one would be the first of its victims.

Its sensors tuned into the sound of their voices, storing them in memory. The words were unimportant – it had been years since the Hunter spoke or listened to the voice of another human being, save the sound of its victims' screams.

It listened only to the tone of their voices, realising after a moment that two of them, the two biggest, were arguing. Let them argue, it thought. As if the question of which of them led the others would make any difference to the final outcome!

The Hunter chose its target, sensors zeroing in on it to study and record. This one was stronger than the others, and the rest would look to it for leadership. The other one talked bravely, but the Hunter's sensors detected the nervous beat of its heart and the frightened tone in its voice which betrayed its words.

Let these striplings follow their new leader, it thought. It would soon show them just how vulnerable they were, when he would be the first to die.

The Hunter uncoiled itself from its hiding place, scuttling along the underside of the walkway as it moved silently towards its first chosen victim.

SPYRER!

Everyone glanced fearfully at each other as Jaal dared to mention that dreaded name. Spyrers: cruel hunters from the Upper Hive, descending down into the depths of the Underhive in packs to hunt their prey, seeking enough kills to return back up the Spyre to be recognised by their kind as rightful members of the Hive's aristocratic elite.

All of the young Steel Skull gangers had heard fearful tales of the exploits of these most hated of killers, knowing that even the most battle-hardened veterans of their settlement were afraid of such enemies. But, it was whispered, there was one sort of spyrer even other spyre hunters feared: the lone renegades. Those who had developed too much of a taste for death and never returned back to the Upper Hive. Instead, these lone killers remained in the Underhive, adapting to the environment of their new home and mercilessly hunting down all that crossed their path. When such a renegade was discovered, even the bitterest enemies amongst the gangs would join forces to destroy it.

'He's right, Dorn,' said Lan, panic breaking his voice. 'This is the work of a spyrer!'

Mallin nodded in agreement. 'We have no other choice. We must abandon the ritual and return to Herek. He will know what to do. We have to warn our people that there is a spyrer on the loose!'

'No!' Dorn snarled, gesturing wildly with his laspistol. 'The test is not yet over! To return now, without any kills, would bring shame upon us all.' He paused, staring hard at the other juves and daring any of them to contradict him. 'Our enemies are dead, but we have been offered a far worthier opponent to face. The test goes on, and when we return it will be in triumph to present Herek with the head of a spyrer!'

'This is madness, Dorn!' Mikhal interjected, trying to reason with his leader. 'Even the bravest gangers would not choose to fight such an enemy. I say Mallin is right. We should—'

Mikhal's voice tailed off as Dorn silenced him with a single threatening glance. 'I am the leader here – and I say the test goes on. I thought you were loyal to me, Mikhal. Are you siding with this coward and his runt brother?' Mikhal stepped back a pace as if he had been physically struck, staring shamefacedly at the ground and unable to meet Dorn's eyes.

Unnoticed, at the back of the group, Jaal's head buzzed with sudden pain. That feeling again, a sense of utter dread, only stronger now than he had ever felt before. And, with it, something else: strange alien thoughts – violent and predatory – crowding into his mind from elsewhere. Jaal's vision blurred and the ground span beneath him. Suddenly he was no longer standing with the others. He was hanging in the darkness high above, looking down on them all. His body was not his own. Instead, he felt himself sheathed in a cold metallic shell, powerful fibre-bundle muscles responding to his every move. He could hear Dorn's challenge to Mikhal. See Mallin backing off, his hand moving towards his pistol holster, unaware of this new danger above him. There was a rush of air. Jaal felt himself falling, no, leaping.

He snapped back into his own body. Numbed, he tried to shout out a warning as the thing descended down from the darkness towards its target. 'Mallin! Above you! Look–'

Too late, Mallin looked up to see the spyrer dropping down towards him. Jaal caught a glimpse of a dark spider-like shape, its outline blurred as though it was a living part of the darkness from where it came, and then it was upon his brother.

Mallin raised his weapon to fire. Something impossibly fast and terrifyingly sharp flashed through the air. Mallin screamed, the las-blast from his weapon discharging harmlessly into the air. Jaal fumbled for his own weapon. In the split-second it took to draw it, Mallin was gone.

More laser blasts lanced through the darkness – Dorn, Lan and Mikhal firing upwards, their shots ricocheting off stonework and girders and illuminating the hellish scene in bright flashes. Jaal caught strobing glimpses of the spyrer carrying the screaming figure of Mallin with it back up into the darkness. At first Jaal thought the spyrer was actually floating through the air but, looking closer, he saw the gleam of something thin and silvery reflected in the light of the las-blasts: a metallic web-line anchored to some point in the darkness above and spun out from the spyrer's wrists, strong enough for it to carry both it and its prey out of range of its enemies' weapons.

Mallin. It had taken Mallin!

Jaal sank to the ground, knowing that the others were wasting their shots and that his brother was already lost to them. With a sickening lurch, Jaal saw the object lying on the ground where, only seconds ago, his brother had stood. Mallin's severed hand, still clutching the useless laspistol in its lifeless grasp.

Jaal doubled over and retched violently, this final horror too much for his shocked senses. He had known that the spyrer was out there. He had seen it in his mind, known it was coming after them. He should have said something earlier, tried to warn them what was about to happen. If he had, Mallin would still be alive…

Dorn's boot crashed into his ribs, sending Jaal sprawling across the ground. With a shock, Jaal realised that he had been babbling to himself, speaking his thoughts out aloud.

'Traitor!' screamed Dorn. 'What do you mean, you knew what was going to happen?'

Dorn turned towards Lan and Mikhal, pointing in fury at the figure of Jaal lying at his feet. 'You heard him! You heard him say he knew it was out there. He knew, and he led it straight to us! He's one of them. A witchling! He's been in league with this thing all along!'

*Witchling.* Jaal knew the word. *Psykers*, some called them. To be so named was a death sentence, the Redemptionists ruthlessly hunting down anyone suspected of possessing such feared powers.

'Then we should take him back, Dorn,' stammered Mikhal, staring at Jaal as if the youth could strike him dead at any moment. 'The elders should judge him. It is not for us to decide…'

'No!' Dorn raged, aiming his laspistol directly into Jaal's face. 'He has betrayed us all and led his own brother to his death! He is a traitor, and I shall judge him where he stands!'

Terrified, Jaal closed his eyes, fearing he was only seconds away from execution at the hands of the wild-eyed Dorn. But the expected shot never came. Instead, he heard the sound of an echoing voice calling out from the darkness around them.

'Help me, Dorn. Help me, Jaal. Help me…' It was Mallin. Mallin was still alive! Weak and in pain, judging by the agonised pleading of his voice, but still alive.

How could that be, thought Jaal? Spyrers never spare their victims. Perhaps Mallin had escaped. Perhaps–

'On your feet, traitor,' said Dorn, dragging him to his feet by his clothes. 'It seems your spyer master still values the life of its servant.' Dorn jammed the barrel of his laspistol painfully against the back of Jaal's head and hissed into his ear in a voice full of anger and loathing. 'It has spared the life of your brother. Maybe it wants to trade his life for yours.'

'HELP ME, DORN. Help me, Jaal. Help me…'

The Hunter looped the recording through its suit's vocal systems, mimicking the voice of its victim. An old trick, but one that had often served it well in the past. The trap was set. Now it would wait and see if the prey took the bait.

THE YOUNG STEEL Skull gangers moved warily through the ruins, following the distant sound of their comrade's pleading voice.

Mikhal and Lan took the lead, cautiously scanning the overhead ledges and structures for signs of their enemy. It had taken them by surprise once already. They were determined it would not do so again. Dorn brought up the rear, roughly pushing Jaal in front of him, his laspistol trained on his captive's back.

Jaal stumbled, risking another blow from his ill-tempered captor. 'Dorn,' he dared to stammer, 'you're making a mistake. You're leading us into a trap. I don't know how, but that can't be the voice of Mallin out there…'

Dorn silenced Jaal with a painful prod from the barrel of the laspistol. 'Shut up, runt. Try and warn your ally that we're coming, and I'll blow you in half.'

'Help me, Dorn. Help me, Jaal. Help me…'

Dorn signalled for silence, trying to get a fix on the location of the voice. There, up ahead. Through the ruins of a tumbled archway they saw a walkway across a bubbling pool of toxic sludge, its acrid vapours giving off a noxious stench. Through the poisonous mists they could see something waiting for them on the other side of the walkway.

They shuffled closer, covering their mouths to avoid breathing in too much of the foetid air. A couple of paces ahead of his fellows Lan was the first to see it. He stopped dead, barely able to believe the sight that awaited them. It was the body of Mallin, hanging puppet-like from a metal web of razor-edged wire that cut through his body in a dozen places. Mallin's head lay on the ground in front of him, that same mocking voice sounding as if it was coming directly from his lifeless lips. 'Help me, Dorn. Help me, Jaal. Help me…'

The spyrer exploded out of waste pool. It landed nimbly on the walkway in front of Lan and Mikhal, its armoured body streaming with burning pollutants and corrosive acids. Jaal howled in terror as it reared up before its prey. Its sinuous body was composed of black armoured plating which flexed and locked together as it moved. Jaal was reminded horribly of the stories he had heard of the monstrous spider-things that inhabited the deepest reaches of the Underhive. Cruel diamond-edged claws extended from each of its wrists, their blades glistening with lubricants and deadly venom. Its horn-crested head swivelled round towards them and, with a sudden lurch of fear, Jaal realised that it had no face. Its human features were hidden behind the blank shell of its armour, guided by electronic senses the extent of which Jaal could only guess at.

It came at them at an impossible speed before any of them had time to react. With one sweep of its claws, it cut through Lan's throat. The ganger was dead before he even had time to scream, his body hitting the walkway and his blood jetting out of him in one long spray.

Mikhal spun to bring his laspistol to bear, but the spyrer was faster, thrusting the wrist-blade of its other hand deep into the juve's stomach. Servo-mechanisms tensed as the spyrer lifted its still-living victim off his feet, raising him high above its head in a superhuman show of strength. Mikhal did scream, a long agonised howl from the very depths of his soul, as the spyrer released the blade's venom cells into his body.

With a dismissive gesture, the spyrer hurled its victim over its head, ripping the blades out from the juve's body. Mikhal landed on the walkway behind, his body already starting to convulse and contort into agonising shapes as the deadly venom coursed through his veins. Then the spyrer turned to face its two remaining victims.

'You bastard!' Dorn hurled Jaal aside and charged the spyrer, blasts from his laspistol ricocheting harmlessly off its armour. At the last moment, Dorn dropped the pistol and drew his knife, throwing himself at the spyrer with a roar of defiance. The ganger crashed into the spyrer, catching it off-balance and sending both him and his enemy backward into the waste pool.

Jaal turned and ran, knowing that Dorn's attack had been a brave but hopeless gesture. Behind him, he could hear Dorn screaming in rage and agony as he tried to pull the spyrer down with him into the corrosive depths of the waste pool. Jaal knew the spyrer would survive – nothing could kill it – and it would be coming after him next. He snatched up Lan's laspistol, realising the futility of the gesture but wanting to at least die fighting with a weapon in his hand.

THE HUNTER PULLED itself out of the waste pool, leaving the burning and dissolved remains of Dorn behind it. Neural links ran a damage check on its suit systems.

Its armour was corroded in several places and the burning acids had destroyed its chameleon camouflage system. In time, the suit would repair itself, but the Hunter, driven by the need to kill, was oblivious of all thoughts of rest or repair.

Even now, its last victim was escaping, and the Hunter was determined to finish its game.

JAAL RAN THROUGH the maze of ruins, knowing that the spyrer was close behind him. He could feel its thoughts buzzing in his head; whispering horrors that he barely recognised as coming from anything human. Occasionally, he would feel his mind spiral out from under him. Then he would be inside the mind of his enemy, seeing and experiencing everything around it as it moved across the top levels of the ruins, leaping from structure to structure and scuttling, insect-like, up the sheer sides of walls and shafts.

He found himself running towards a rusting metal walkway, maybe a metre wide, spanning a chasm from some long-past hivequake, its sheer sides dropping away into nothingness. The spyrer was hunting him, he knew, probably herding him into another of its traps. If only he could control this new ability; focus these visions that flashed through his mind…

His boots made the precarious walkway echo beneath his pounding feet. A voice in Jaal's head suddenly screamed a warning, telling him to stop. Jaal threw himself onto the reverberating walkway, seeing in an instant the deadly trap he had almost run into: strands of the spyrer's metallic web-line, strung out across the walkway. If Jaal had kept on running he would surely have been sliced apart.

A wave of terror washed through the young ganger. The spyrer was just playing with him, toying with him like a cat until it closed in for the final kill. What chance did he, Jaal the runt, the weakling of the litter, stand against such an enemy?

A dark shape swooped low over his head and Jaal felt a vibration as it landed on the walkway behind him. He hauled himself up and span around to face the spyrer, steadying his stance on the walkway and gripping the laspistol in both hands. The nightmare stalked slowly towards him, venom-dripping weapon claws slowly extending from their armoured casings.

Jaal knew he had nowhere to run. Before him was the spyrer. Behind him, the barrier of razor wire web. Below the walkway, on either side, a long fall into oblivion. The final trap had been sprung and the game had reached its end. A terrible sliver of ice ran the full length of his spine.

'Fear is the greatest killer of all,' the spyrer said mockingly, perfectly imitating the voice of his dead brother. 'Conquer fear and you will be ready to call yourself a true warrior.'

At the sound of Mallin's voice, something convulsed inside Jaal's head. Fear gave way to fiery rage and hatred as he heard this creature, this foul thing, speak with the voice and words of his dead brother. His fury opened up something within him, blossoming like a match igniting kerosene. Something that had been there all along, waiting to be set free. Power – pure, unfocussed power now channelled and released by his rage.

Jaal was thrown backwards onto the hard, cold metal, as he felt some uncontrollable energy erupt from his body, a wave of enormous concussive force spreading out from him in all directions. The walkway beneath his feet buckled as the aged metal was rent by the supernatural force Jaal had somehow released. With a scream he realised he was sliding down towards the spyrer's web of razor wire.

Jaal scrabbled up the slope of the collapsing walkway, grabbing hold of a bent support beam. Turning he saw the spyrer leap from the shifting platform as it gave way under its feet.

A thin web-line shot out from its outstretched wrist, seeking a secure anchor to the structure at the other end of the vanished bridge. 'No. Not this time,' swore Jaal, determined that the spyrer would not escape him. 'This time the hunt ends here.'

Unthinking, Jaal raised the laspistol in his free hand, aiming not at the spyrer but at the web-line supporting it. He reached out with his mind, focusing his expanded senses on the thin strand of metal glittering in the darkness, and pulled the trigger. A searing bolt of laser energy leapt from his gun, his mind flying out with it, leading it, taking it to its target. The shot hit true, vaporising one segment of the web-line in a flash of white-hot energy.

Caught in mid-swing, the spyrer tumbled down into the darkness, diamond-edged claws throwing off sparks as it tore at the sheer wall of the chasm, vainly striking out to find a desperate handhold.

'Nooooo!' Mallin's dead voice cried as the creature fell. 'Jaaaaaaal!'

And then it was gone, its death-scream amplified by its suit systems, an electronic screech that seemed to echo forever across the Hive Bottom long after the spyrer itself had been swallowed by the chasm.

'HEREK? FACE IT. If Dorn ain't coming back, none of them are.' The Steel Skull gangers waiting by the open blast-doors looked more worried about losing their wagers than any real sorrow.

The old man sighed to himself, and turned back toward the light. 'Very well. Seal the doors,' he ordered. 'They've had an extra day-cycle. We've put ourselves at too much risk already by waiting here so long.'

Herek watched as his two lieutenants carried out his orders, and silently swore under his breath. He had lost whole parties of juves to the ritual before, but he'd had high hopes for at least some of this group. But, at the last, there would be other tests and other initiates, all of them eager to prove their manhood amidst the dangers that lay in wait on the other side of those doors.

FROM HIS HIDING place, Jaal watched the gangers haul the blast doors closed. He wanted so much to shout, to run towards them, to tell Herek and the others that he was still alive, that it was over – that he was safe and just wanted to go home. But he knew that would be madness.

Everything had changed. Now that he knew what he was – a psyker, a witchling – he knew he could never return home. Not that his stepfamily would mourn him, not when they had lost a real son. He was orphaned again. He was an outcast, a renegade, doomed to dwell in the darkest places with the others of his kind – the freaks, monsters and mutants of Hive Bottom.

After a long moment, Jaal turned and walked away. He did not look back at the final clank of the bolts when Herek's men sealed the doors shut behind him. Silently, he slipped off into the shadows, already welcoming the protection and anonymity they offered.

# SISTERS
## by Neil Rutledge

BLADES STARED DULLY at the beaker in front of her. Why was she drinking this filth? She knew only too well but pushed the thought away from her along with the empty cup.

'Another one, princess?' Licksy, attentive to a fault, called softly from behind the bar. His scarred, crumpled face, pressed against the grille, looked like some penned animal, his huge, dark eyes filled with the sadness of resignation.

Staring at him, her own eyes tormented, dark-ringed with more than paint, she felt her heart constrict. Her throat felt like choking but, knuckles white against the pitted plastic of the table edge, she fought it down. Not trusting her own voice she simply nodded. He turned, hunched over the battered flasks and she dragged herself up from her stool and over to the bar. There were no worms in, word must have got round fast, and Licksy didn't have the cage door shut, but affection for the old man and a wish to save his twisted feet got her up. As he passed her another full beaker through the slot, his thick fingers gently touched hers. His face looked even more yellow and riven than normal and his mute anxiety jerked back her memory. Ages back he had looked at her just like that as she was about to leave on some juve foray, but back then she wouldn't have been alone at the bar. She quickly sat down and took a long slug.

Out of the corner of her eye, she caught the movement as Sasha glanced over at her, but by the time Blades looked up the big woman's head was back down. Without war paint, Sasha's jowly face looked oddly babyish as, apparently rapt with concentration, she studied the stripped-down stubber laid out in front of her. But Blades hadn't missed the glance. What was it? Concern, warning, disapproval? Was she sizing her up, thinking she could take her, thinking it was time Blades's Gang needed a new leader?

She knew she shouldn't have any more Wild Snake. The ratskin could be back at any time with news of the zombie but, sump it! She felt wretched and needed fire from somewhere. The cloying smell of the slug oil Sasha was using carried over the bar, even over the acrid stink of Wild Snake. Again Blades felt her stomach contract. Why did the stupid bitch have to slip? This time she could not fight the memory away. The numbness was wearing off. The armour of habit that had seen her through the aftermath of the fight and brought her back to Licksy's place had flaked away. The jagged blade of memory slashed across her eyes, even as she screwed them tight shut against it. The vision of Katz dancing nimbly across the gantry, bullets skipping around, was seared into her eyelids. Oh, Katz had got the Orlock all right, burnt him clean in the forehead, the last one of the schlokk-baggers. Then her sister was traipsing back gleefully when she slipped.

Spire! She could still see the expression on Katz's face. Just a startled smile, not even a yell before she hit the chem sink and was gone. Why, damn it? Blades's stomach heaved again and she staggered upright. It took all of her willpower to make herself walk to the midden and she only just made it before throwing up. Her body shook as, white-knuckled, she steadied herself against the cold, corrugated iron wall.

Weakly she punched the tap, vainly trying to get enough water to clean her face and rinse away the smell and the memories. She straightened up and started as she caught sight of herself in the grimy mirror. Spire! She looked dreadful! Her eyes stared wild from dark pits and her paint had run in purple smears where she had tried to wipe away the vomit. Get a grip! This was life, not a dream tab. Blades realised she hadn't cleaned up since she had got back. Her hair, once extravagantly plumed, now stuck in a dank, clotted mass to the side of her head, green dye mixed with blood from the last juve she'd scragged. With a sudden stab of bleak humour, she thought she would have no problem surprising the zombie – the chugger would take her for one of its own! She felt a little better at that and, smiling grimly, she set about battering the tap into supplying enough for a more thorough clean up.

Blades managed her face well enough and got painted up again, although her hand refused to stop quivering when she was applying the stick. Not an ace job, but better than before. Her hair would have to wait for the full treatment but she cleaned it as best she could and pulled it back in a tight snake, binding it with a spare plasticuff. Moving to the door, Blades took a few deep breaths and walked back into the bar.

Again she sensed quickly averted gazes but she walked calmly back over to the cage. If there was to be action it was better not to face it on an empty stomach. 'Some of your best stew and a couple of slormcrusts, Licksy,' she asked softly and smiled at the old ex-ganger.

'Coming right up, princess,' he grinned back, obviously reassured.

Of course, she could always send some of the girls to hunt down the zombie. The worms, as the citizens of Ashcliff were known, looked to Blades and her gang for protection but that didn't mean that Blades herself had to deal with every rogue slime gator or crazed mutant personally. The odd wandering zombie wasn't extraordinary. Sometimes they just stumbled vaguely about and were easily torched. Sometimes a meaner one would show and scrag a careless worm or two, but they were still no big deal. Normally, in fact, she would have sent someone else, maybe even a couple of juves eager to notch their sluggers. Today, though, despite the sick feeling still lurking in the pit of her stomach, or perhaps even because of it, she knew she would go after the chugger herself. She flexed her fingers. They felt barely able to lift a spoon, never mind a shotgun, but maybe the action would help her get a grip on herself. Maybe? It had to.

Blades turned and looked down the bar hall. The bright, comforting light glared back off the pitted metal tables and the lurid murals. Angie and Torsh, their faces bleached spirit-pale

by the light of their booth, were close as always. Their hands
flickered over one of their interminable games of thornback,
played, as usual, in silence save for the gentle rustle of cards
and the soft scrape of counters being exchanged. Faye looked as
if she was dozing at the vid desk but Blades knew better.
Yooshie, she assumed, would be running the surprise box, out
of sight, ready for gatecrashers, just in case. The rest of the girls
were keeping out of her way. They were all behaving normally
enough but, Blades wondered, was she imagining the tension
in the air? The covert glances? Lips pursed with worry, or disapproval? Yes, this time she'd better go after the zombie; show
she was still in control. Or some girl might just reckon she
could take Blades's gang off her.

'Here y'are.' Licksy passed the stew and crusts through the
hole in the security grille. Blades took them, smiled her thanks
and sat back down by herself again. The stew at Licksy's was
near legendary in quality and for a while Blades lost herself in
enjoyment of the spicy stodge. She was assiduously mopping
up the last juice with a hunk of slormcrust when Faye called,
'Ratty's back.'

Blades stuffed down the crust and quickly took the bowl
back to the cage before seating herself again.

The flickering green light showed Yooshie was ready in the
box. One of Faye's hands hovered over the pit flick while she
pushed the door button with the other and then grabbed up
her stub gun. The double pairs of security doors clanked and
wheezed through their cycle and eventually the ratskin padded
in. Angie left her game and followed him as Blades beckoned
him over.

The ratskin stood across the table from her, silent as the darkness. Like most of his kind he was short and slightly built, but
Blades knew the appearance was deceptive. The ratskin might
look scrawny but he was tougher than boiled milliasaur, with
sinews like cured slime stringers and the reactions of a rubble
snake. But now he just stood and stared, the blank eyes looking through her.

'Well?' the gang leader snapped. The ratskins always quaked
her a bit. There was no getting used to their silent, staring ways.
She even preferred a rowdy ratty, tanked up on Second Best, to
this sort of sober spook. The scout fingered some sort of amulet
at his neck and for a moment his eyes seemed to focus on her.

'Found empty one,' he stated plainly, using the ratskin word for a zombie.

'Where?' Blades was still sharp.

'In the pipes-that-echo by Joe's Crack.'

'Take me there.'

The ratskin shrugged. 'It got foolish lone worm,' he added, unconcerned.

There was a metallic rattle as Sasha finished re-assembling her stubber. 'Want me, Chief?' she asked with a smile that Blades could not read.

'No.' The gang leader rose. 'It's only a chugging zombie. Ratty and I'll manage.'

The ratskin shrugged again.

'I'll take your night-sight, though,' Blades said to Sasha again. 'Save me a walk to the glory hole.' The big girl thought for a moment, then nodded and passed over the visor.

'Scrag it, Chief!' Sasha encouraged and watched approvingly as with ease, almost graceful, her leader checked over her gear and lifted the faithful shotgun she'd carried ever since her first juve outings.

Then with only a soft, 'See you ladies,' Blades followed the ratskin through the asthmatic security doors and out into the Necromundan gloom.

THE GLOW-GLOBES had never been great around Ashcliff and recently they seemed to have become even dimmer. Blades shivered as she followed the silent ratskin away from the last of the sheds and along the rough pack trail that wound through the slag dumps towards Raggy Gap. It was completely quiet. Sleep time and fear of the zombie had kept all indoors. Well, fear of the zombie and perhaps fear of her, Blades reflected. She smiled darkly – and just then heard the moaning.

It was an eerie whining, rising and falling, just audible; felt more on the neck than heard with the ears. Blades tightened her grip on the shotgun and paused. A few paces ahead the scout had stopped too. He turned, and with the skin over his head silhouetted against the sickly radiance that came from the ailing skylights it seemed as if some giant rodent had thrust its shoulders up through the clinker.

'The worm,' the ratskin hissed.

'Why isn't he dead?' Blades demanded angrily. 'If the zombie wounded him then he should be scragged. Can't take chances with the plague! Blasted worms! You'd think living here they'd be tougher.' She thought the ratskin shrugged but couldn't be sure in the gloom. He had turned again and was making off down the sidetrack that led to Joe's Crack.

JOE WAS LONG dead but the ash-brick and rubble hovels that he had built were still there, inhabited now by the extended family of his grandson. As they crested a low ash ridge Blades could see a few lights glowing ahead. The crack that Joe had given his name to and had made his livelihood from was still there too. It was a jagged scar between fifteen and thirty feet deep, narrow, sheer-sided and twisting through the ash for almost half a mile. Joe had discovered that various hapless creatures – snakes, rats, lashworms, and so on – would often fall in it and be unable to get out. With care and the aid of a rope hoist, he made a good living out of the unfortunates. Well, until he was scragged by a huge slime gator that had fallen in while wandering from pool to pool. Jake, his son, climbed down and got the gator; he made so much money from it that it went to his head and he'd run off further down-hive with one of the duster girls from Peeky's Palace. Hanko, Jake's abandoned wife, was a tough old tunnel chicken and she and the kids had kept the place going. Jakey, the eldest, pretty much handled things now. He was all right, Blades recalled. None too sharp, but he kept out of trouble and paid his dues.

Almost bumping into the ratskin's back jerked her out of her reverie. Careless, she bitterly admonished herself. Blades girl, what is wrong with you? She continued her mental self-castigation. But she knew what was wrong and again had to fight back unpleasant thoughts. The ratskin was saying something.

'Tracked from here. Not big. Staggering.' He was whispering. Just ahead, Blades could see the overturned hopper of the bagger, its noxious cargo split across the path. Something was skittering among the rubble behind the hopper. The scout muttered a salutation in his own tongue and, fastidiously stepping around the spilled garbage, headed on up the path.

They soon reached the steading and were waved into a small rubble shed where a disturbing sight met their eyes. Lying on a trestle table was the injured bagger. He was still moaning but only quietly now, and he seemed only semi-conscious. The unfortunate victim had been stripped to the waist and Blades could see a long wound running down from his head, across his shoulder and over his ribs. His right ear and part of his cheek had been sliced away and the white of bone showed through the gash in several places. The table was slick with his blood and it had pooled beneath it too, but the worst of the bleeding had been stopped. Presumably this was thanks to the woman bending over the prostrate man and attending to the wound.

'Spire!' Blades swore, recognising the distinctive, bitter smell of stinger mould paste even over the sooty stench of the slug oil lamps. 'What are you doing?' the gang leader snapped at the woman. 'He should have been scragged and torched. You know the law!'

The woman did not look up but replied in a quiet voice. 'It's just a cut. The zombie only slashed him. The wound's clean and there are no bite marks.'

Jakey, the big prospector who had waved them in, whispered from behind Blades, 'It's Uncle Zot, Ma's brother.'

Blades swallowed, 'You know the rules, Hanko. He's been got by a dead one, a zombie. The plague's too much of a risk. He's got to go.'

The woman turned. She had a slight, pinched face. It had been beautiful once but time and the Hive had taken its toll. The once-delicate features were now harsh and lined. Grey hair flopped listlessly from under a grubby red scarf. 'We can watch him.' Her voice was clipped into a challenge.

'Ma...' Jakey's voice tailed off.

'The rules are to protect all of us, Hanko,' Blades said firmly, gripping her shotgun. 'I can't allow this. What in Spire's name possessed him to be out with the zombie about anyway?'

'Four hungry girls.' Hanko's voice was bitter.

There was silence for a moment. One of the lamps spluttered and the distorted shadows flickered on the rubble wall. 'You'd better leave, Hanko,' Blades spoke softly now but still firmly.

'I'm not going,' the older woman turned and started dabbing at the wound again.

'Ma...' Jakey mumbled once more, then shuffled outside.

'You too, out!' Blades waved her gun at the ratskin. He shrugged, his perennial gesture, and left.

'Hanko–' the younger woman began.

'I'm not leaving.'

Blades moved around the table opposite Hanko, who was now deftly stitching the widest gash.

The bagger lay quiet, now quite unconscious. Blades bent over him. The lamp smoke and the stinger mould brought back an echo of her former nausea. Even so, her stiletto had pierced the man's heart and had been withdrawn before Hanko even noticed. The bagger gave one twitch and his sister looked over at the gang leader in silence.

Her face was blank and her voice flat as she asked, 'What about the youngsters?'

'We'll take any fit girl juves.' Blades voice was strained. 'If you can't take the others, Peeky probably will. It sucks as an arrangement, but better than starving.' The ganger turned and went out, wiped the stiletto on a patch of basket fungus and sheathed it. 'C'mon, Ratty,' she instructed, 'let's get the chugger.'

Jakey stared after them. They could hear his shaking voice. 'Ma…'

'PIPES THIS WAY,' hissed the ratskin. Blades knew without having to be told. The pipes had been considered a good play area. Close enough to the hab zone so that it was unlikely that you would find anything really nasty holed up there but often housing snakes, rats and spiders. A good place for a sub-juve to cut her teeth. Then she and her sister, Katz, had often explored the pipes, after letting Joe know they were there. Blades's memory flashed to the feeling of pride when they had sold their first four-footer to Hairy Mary. How the old hag had given each of them four shots of Second Best, 'One for each foot, my dears,' in a bottle of algae juice and they'd been ill all night. They were there… They had sold… They'd been ill…

The sob caught her unawares and escaped before she could choke it back. The ratskin turned.

'Just ash in the throat,' Blades mumbled and quickly pulled the visor over her eyes. Detail sharpened immediately. No wonder she preferred not to wear the chugging things.

BLADES WAS GLAD to have to concentrate on her footing as she climbed the treacherous slag slope up to where the pipe holes stared out, two black pits. She had a fleeting image of Hanko's eyes but quickly turned her thoughts to trying to remember the pipe layout. No one knew what the pipes originally were. Nearly a mile of man-sized tubes running in and out of each other. The pipes echoed alarmingly and to the uninitiated seemed a maze. The appearance was deceptive, though, and they actually followed a fairly regular grid pattern. Even now, years after, Blades could remember it. There had been five entrances. Three had been down the other side of the hill, near the pack trail. They had been buried in the avalanche which renegades had triggered during a daring ambush of a guilder caravan a couple of strokes back. Now there were only two holes and they connected pretty soon.

The climb had been a steep one and the ganger was panting slightly as she gave her orders to the scout. 'You take this pipe, Ratty. After a bit there's a junction. The left fork only runs about ten paces and then stops but check it. Then go right. After a while it runs into the other tube. I'll meet you at the entrance and we can clear the rest together.' The ratskin shrugged, half-cocked his musket, and disappeared into the pipe. Blades had no doubt he could handle the zombie if he met it. She laughed mirthlessly as she reflected that, in fact, he could probably sense better and move far more quietly than she could.

She toiled on up and to the right where the other pipe opened. She felt better now. The adrenaline was beginning to flow. Blades felt her lips tighten and the familiar prickle of thrill in the pit of her stomach. She checked the magazine of the shotgun again, man-stopper and incendiary mix. The chugger was going to pay for having picked her patch. She adjusted the fit of the borrowed night-sight visor and stepped cautiously into the pipe.

Using all her skill, the ganger moved stealthily into the hill. There was a fresh looking patch of gunk on the pipe, just inside the entrance. Could be the zombie, she mused. Could be just about anything.

Not far into the hill, she thought she heard a noise. Blades pulled up, raising the shotgun. Creeping slowly forward towards a twist in the passage she became positive. Something was around the corner. Could it be the zombie already? Shotgun cocked and moving with extreme caution lest she start the pipes reverberating, Blades crept around the corner.

A short way up the pipe, a large rat was nosing at something. Alone, it would probably be no problem. Blades stepped out.

The rat froze, then turned and sniffed towards her. She took a step forward. The rat skittered off into the gloom at the edge of her visor's range. Still very cautious, Blades moved on. There was another splash of gunk on the pipe. It must have been what the rat was investigating. Blades stooped over it. In the eerie green universe of her passive visor it was hard to tell anything about such goo; it was just that, a splash of gunk. She daren't poke at it and so, straightening, she moved on.

Blades was amazed at how the old habits came back: The strange shuffle that kept one to the bottom of the pipe and avoided the echoes. The careful sweeping ahead of the shotgun to check for webs that were almost impossible to see even with the visor. There were other memories of those juve days too, but she pushed them firmly out of her mind. She must be near the intersection now.

'These pipes clear.' The sudden hiss caught her completely off-guard. It was the ratskin warning her in advance before she stumbled into him. Stepping closer she could just make out his watery green form in the blank hole that was the mouth of the connecting pipe. Right at the limit of the visor's range. How in spire's name had he detected her? Blades again reflected how the ratskins quaked her. How did he see anything in here? They were spooks all right, but you had to be impressed.

The ganger controlled her voice carefully. 'Clear down here too. Follow me.' She was tempted to send the ratskin in front but it smacked of weakness. And she was not weak, she wasn't. She was the leader, it was her gang, damn them! She couldn't help feeling a prickle of unease with him behind, though. Blades couldn't even hear a rustle from him, yet every slight noise she made roared in her ears. She had to fight the impulse to look round and check he was actually there.

Perhaps it was this preoccupation that made her miss the web and only the discipline of years stopped her crying out as it slapped into her face. She stopped and checked carefully. No spiders. It must just have been a remnant. She shuddered slightly as she pulled the thick, sticky threads from her skin and hair. She had just cleared the last one when she thought she heard a noise. A light tap on her shoulder made her start but showed the ratskin had heard it too.

It came again, a lisping, sucking, breathy noise half way between a whisper and a gurgle. Her heart pumped harder.

Odd, zombies were normally quiet. Very slowly, shotgun at the ready, Blades shuffled forward. The noise was coming from a pipe intersection further up on the right. Tightening her grip on the shotgun, Blades slid round the corner.

There was a clatter as the shotgun fell and the echoes rebounded along the pipe. Blades stood frozen, jaw slack and speechless, her hands held feebly out in front of her. Only when the figure in the pipe began limping towards her, stiletto raised in its one good hand, did the scream burst from Blade's throat, rising from her belly, rising from the past, drowning her as she slumped against the pipe wall. She was only dimly conscious of the flash and thunderous crash of a musket firing.

WHEN BLADES CAME to, she tried to scream again but all that came out was a groan. Not a zombie at all! The full horror swamped her. She knocked the visor aside and pressed her fists into her eyes trying to blot out the image of the ruined face that was burnt into her brain. The relentless, undying image of that chem-burned wreck dragging itself towards her. No recognition in its blank eyes, only mindless death.

Spire knew what agonies the chem sink must have inflicted to turn her into that wandering killer. Was she dimly still fighting that last gang fight? Was she in some insane hell dimly trying to battle her way home? Had some twisted memories from childhood drawn her back to those pipes?

Flushed, chest heaving, the ganger fought to stop the shaking that convulsed her. Gradually she controlled herself and lowered her hands, opened her eyes.

The ratskin was sitting opposite her, re-priming his musket, face a blank, unreadable mask.

'You killed her?' Blades asked weakly.

'It dead,' the scout replied.

'Let's get out,' Blades panted, struggling to her feet and straining to lift the shotgun. The ratskin started off and she followed shakily, the visor making the world dreamlike once more

The effort of walking concentrated her thoughts. Blades's mind raced and her body physically reeled as she thought about what the scout had witnessed, and not just here in the pipes. He'd been there when she'd scragged the garbage-bagger! Because of the risk of plague. Spire! Spire! Chugging Spire!

Her brain was racing; before she was aware of it she stumbled. The scout turned. Through the visor his eyes were just black pits. Like Hanko's! Seeming to her to accuse and condemn in a look... Spire! This would not do!

"Right, girl?' the ratskin asked softly.

'Oh yes, Ratty! I'm all right,' the ganger replied, and there was steel in her voice.

The scout turned without another word and continued up the pipe. Smoothly Blades raised her shotgun and put a man-stopper into the back of his head. He went down like a scragged zombie.

She leaned against the pipe wall until the echoes had subsided. 'Not much chugging use, your lucky amulet!' she muttered viciously at the lifeless body. Then the ganger forced herself to turn back and head down the pipe again.

She only threw up once before she'd pumped three incendiaries into the already half-charred body, barely daring to look where she was aiming, not daring to miss and let it lie around for anyone to find. In the ghastly glow and stench of the flames, she made her way back to the dead ratskin.

'Thanks, Ratty,' the ganger spat as she fired more incendiaries into the scout's body.

EVENTUALLY BLADES dragged herself to the pipe entrance. Bright through the visor she could see a figure at the bottom of the hill: Jakey. The gang leader forced herself stiffly upright and made herself walk calmly down to where he was waiting.

'Get it?' the prospector asked nervously, fingering his own shotgun.

Blades did not raise the visor. 'Yeah,' she replied, her voice hollow. 'It scragged the ratskin, but I got it.'

Jakey shuffled. 'Ma said to say thanks,' he mumbled, unused, perhaps, to talking so much. 'Says she's sorry she was weak. Knows you can't take any chances with that zombie plague.'

Blades stumbled slightly and sat down hard on a flat rock.

'You all right?' Jakey said with obvious concern.

'Yeah... fine, fine. Go back to Licksy's and tell Sasha to bring some meltas and kraks. I'm sealing those pipes for good.'

Jakey headed off into the glow globe twilight without a word, and the tears started.

'Oh, Katz,' she sobbed. 'Oh my sister!'

# THE LAKE
## by Tully R. Summers

LORD ORL LOOKED down at the viscous purple slime lapping at the side of the skiff in the light from the sputtering flares. He spat in disgust, thinking of the sorry chain of events which had brought him to such a humiliating endeavour.

He had started his gang, the Brassers, with the grand intent of becoming the first Orlock Slag Lord of the Underhive. Centuries of mineral-laden chemwaste and solidified sludge lay hidden in the bowels of the Hive, just waiting for a man of will and vision to take it and turn it into the foundations of an empire. The House of Iron would echo with the name of Lord Orl. The fat, preening Metal Barons of the upper hive would bow and scrape before him, once he had completed his conquest. A fine vision, though easier said than done.

True, his band of highly disciplined men had taken their first slag pile with ease. Red's Tower, a huge stalagmite of compacted ore, had been wrested from a barbarian Goliath gang, the Black Hand. The yellow metal mined from the tower had proved perfect for making clothing, gear and equipment, thus giving name to his crew: the Brassers.

But Black Hand's retaliation had been brutal. Months of bitter fighting had reduced the Brassers to a handful, and left Orl

with a pitiful stash of credits. Then the blasted Hive decided to
settle, one of the ancient subterranean domes crumbling under
the weight of nine miles of vertical Spire. The resulting quake
dislodged house-sized chunks of concrete onto the Brassers'
water still, crushing the gang's only means of survival. Without
water for his gang, and without enough credits to buy a new
still, Orl's dreams had been flattened like the sails of the
vapour collector.

Then came the guilder.

Rorget Ahn was a devious but powerful merchant lord, known
widely for hiring the many gangs of the Underhive levels to carry
out his dubious business transactions. Lord Orl had long before
vowed that the Brassers would never deal with such a sump-
snake, but desperation now demanded he break his word.

Rorget Ahn had found a new dome. The very same Hive
quake that had brought ruin to the Brassers had opened a tunnel to a deeper part of the ancient city that had been closed for
untold centuries. A dome, completely filled with liquid, a vir-
tual lake. A lake filled with mulk spiders.

Rorget's plan was simple: the Brassers would go spider hunting. They would harvest the gem-like eyes from the mutant
arachnids and bring them back to the guilder. The fortune
gained by fencing the jewels through Rorget's uphive contacts
would be split with the Brassers. Orl could buy his new water
still and have plenty of creds left to revive his atrophied gang.
It wasn't much, but it was a plan.

SO HERE HE WAS – Lord Orl, future Slag Lord of the Underhive,
bobbing across the surface of a stinking slime lake like some
sump-sucking algae farmer. He turned to regard Kar, in the rear of
the fungus-wood boat. Kar, one of Rorget's hired guns, had been
sent along to make sure all harvested spider eyes were accounted
for. The grizzled, white-haired warrior at the rudder coughed and
sputtered, choking on noxious green smoke as the little outboard
motor burnt its fermented algae fuel. Orl almost laughed aloud
as Kar activated the mechanical counter on his wrist.

'I'm not the only one who Rorget's demeaned, bean-counter,'
Orl sneered, pulling his patched mesh-link overcoat around
himself.

Kar glared back in silent resentment, eyes dark and murderous, and Orl turned his gaze back to the lake-filled dome

around him. Behind him, lurching through the purple ooze were the other two boats. R'daff, his trusted second-in-command, Husker, Ferren and Hack were all straining sweatily at their oars. Orl hadn't had enough money to buy more than one motor. He spat again into the lake. That was the worst part. Rorget had made them pay, actually pay for these rickety fungus-wood rowing boats, barely big enough for two men. The conniving guilder had taken him for every one of his last measly credits.

Still, better these bathtubs than trying to swim in this filth, Orl thought sourly, regarding the stinking substance filling the dome.

It was unlike any effluent he had ever seen, even down here in the depths of Underhive. Its purple surface rippled constantly in strange oily patterns, as if the liquid had a life of its own. The dome itself was relatively small, less than half a mile across. The intricate metalwork traceries that covered its looming walls were incredibly ancient. He had seen their like before, these vast, metallic webs built from what looked like the skeletons of millions of extinct metal insects, shattered remnants of the myth-shrouded founders of the Hive. The technology to make such walls and machinery had all but vanished along with the memory of their makers.

Orl found himself wondering what lay beneath the purple surface of the lake. Up ahead, the end of some vast machine jutted from the ooze. Solidified chemical deposits encrusted what seemed to be the top of an enormous tube-covered tank, creating a small island in the centre of the lake, possibly the source of the flood that had filled the dome.

'Spider sign!' R'daff's shouted warning came from behind. Twenty feet away from Orl's flimsy boat, the surface of the lake was boiling in the flickering flare-light. Kar veered the skiff toward the disturbance as Lord Orl knelt up in the prow, pumping a shell into the chamber of his shotgun with shaking fingers.

The bubbling surface parted, almost like an eye opening. Glistening purple chitin emerged amidst flailing, many-jointed legs, and the air filled with an eerie wailing like a dying infant. Flat, paddle-like limbs slapped the water as they propelled the nightmare creature swiftly towards the skiff, razor sharp mouthparts clicking hungrily. A virulent purple spray fountained beside the creature as Orl's first shot went wide. The shotgun's recoil rocked the skiff dangerously. Kar fought with the rudder, struggling to control the craft as Lord Orl chambered another shell. Before he could slam it home, the immense, reeking monster was upon them, crawling up the side of the boat, blade-tipped legs clawing into the wood.

Orl jammed the barrel of his shotgun into the slavering jaws and pulled the trigger. Chitin flew apart in a rain of blue-black blood as the creature blew inside out and fell back into the slime.

Orl stared at the floating carcass. A spider maybe, but not any kind of mulk spider he'd ever seen, and he had seen many. Its body was strangely asymmetrical. External gills fanned out along the sides of its ragged abdomen, along with a number of other unidentifiable fleshy appendages. But the eyes were there, five glistening black jewels staring from its dead thorax.

As Orl cut the diamond-hard gems from the spider with the curved knife he had brought along for just such a purpose, Kar's mechanical counter ticked five times. Behind them more strange wailing echoed it across the darkness. Three more of the creatures came to the surface, buoyed by the air trapped in their external gills. Orl saw that the same weird asymmetry had warped these in other ways. Though presumably of the same strain, each animal was drastically different from its fellow. Autogun fire mixed with searing laser blasts as R'daff and Ferren entered the hunt, their partners rowing wildly.

Another spider flew apart in a black splash as Ferren's laspistol hit home. Ooze kicked up around R'daff's spider as it scuttled towards them in a hail of lead. An orifice under its belly suddenly jetted a stream of liquid in a convulsive spasm that sent the creature hurtling inside their boat. R'daff tumbled to the deck, a tangle of slashing legs on top of him. Dropping his oars, Husker fumbled the stub pistol from his holster. R'daff's screams mixed with that of the spider's as bone scythes sliced into his flesh. Husker's stub shells smashed into the creature, hurling it overboard.

R'daff, blood flowing from many cuts, rose shakily to his feet. A severed chitinous leg hung from his shoulder, its bone hook still embedded in flesh. R'daff gritted his teeth and wrenched the still twitching member out, tossing it overboard in disgust. It sank into the mire.

All three spiders lay dead, the Brassers bringing the boats along side to carve their booty from their hides. Kar's counter dutifully clicked away.

'Head on back and get those taken care of. We'll finish up here,' Orl commanded, waving at R'daff's seeping wounds.

'What? These scratches?' R'daff panted back, smiling through bloody lips.

Orl shouted back fondly, admiring the warrior's bravado: 'Row his rump home, Husker, before he catches spore–' Orl screamed wildly as his shoulder exploded, spattering Kar with blood and gristle.

'Hey, lads! Looks like them sissy Orlocks are tryin' to jump our claim!'

Lord Orl spun to the hated voice, clutching his ruined arm, face white. 'Krug!' he roared, his voice breaking with pain and rage, 'You Helmawr-damned sump-slug, this is our claim! Guilder sanctioned! Show him, Ka–'

He stopped his bellow in mid sentence, gawking in disbelief at the sight of the leader of the Black Hand gang standing on the prow of a large, algae-powered garbage scow – the very same garbage scow Rorget had tried to sell him two days earlier. Lord Orl had opted for the three fungus-wood skiffs instead, fearing the seaworthiness of the pressed bonemeal hull of the scow.

'That double-crossing bastard…' Orl muttered darkly, as the firefight blew apart the semi-darkness of the flooded dome.

Lasers, bolts and bullets churned the lake into purple froth as both gangs fought for ownership of the hunting grounds. The Brassers' three skiffs made difficult targets, positioned behind the centre islet for cover. The whole Black Hand gang seemed to have come on the garbage scow through the sludge-filled canal at the far end of the dome. Though they made a relatively easy target, massed on the deck, their numbers were prevailing, a new gun replacing every one that the Brassers downed.

Autopistol slugs tore into Ferren's thigh, almost pitching him overboard. Chips of fungus-wood flew as the Goliath's fire slowly ate the Brassers' skiffs from under them. Then the withering rain stopped, replaced by alarmed shouts.

Lord Orl raised his head from the deck. The garbage scow was melting. The bonemeal hull was slowly dissolving in the viscous purple slime, affirming Orl's choice of boat purchase.

The Black Hand frantically scurried about the softening craft, jamming its motors into reverse and desperately trying to keep it afloat. Lord Orl breathed a sigh of relief as the scow turned back and disappeared into the canal from which it had come, the Black Hand making a last-ditch effort to reach dry land before they sank.

A scream from the back of the skiff cut Orl's reverie short. Another mutant spider had leapt out of the lake onto Kar, attaching itself to his flesh with its bone hooks. Orl watched in horror as saw-like mouthparts chewed through Kar's face. Kar's gun went off in his convulsing fingers, the plasma beam hitting the fuel tank of the outboard. The vast, flaming green explosion obliterated the skiff.

ORL SWAM DESPERATELY for the surface with awkward strokes, crimson clouds trailing from his limp left arm. Somewhere below him, his shotgun sank down into the viscous darkness. The mysterious liquid was like hot needles on his skin, fire in his mouth, and razors in the wound of his shoulder.

His head broke the surface. Kar's body bobbed beside him amidst pieces of the skiff. Ten feet away, through stinging, slime-clogged eyes, Orl could make out the misshapen hump of the island.

Something jerked Kar's body beneath the purple murk. One moment it was there, the next it was gone. Orl began swimming toward the island, pumping his three good limbs with all his might. A fountain of bloody bubbles erupted where Kar's body had been and Orl redoubled his efforts.

Orl heaved his body onto the island's sedimentary shore, thanking all the gods he could think of that his skin was still there. The purple liquid, though stinging painfully, was not terribly corrosive; there were parts of the sump that would have eaten the flesh off his bones.

'Orl! Behind you!' R'daff screamed in panic from across the semi-darkness. Lord Orl quickly rolled onto his back to find himself facing the huge lake spider that was looming over him. Its sickening mouthparts descending toward his face, clicking like knives being sharpened. Orl's numb fingers scrabbling at his belt, desperately seeking the hilt of his knife.

Lead slugs from R'daff's autogun slammed into the creature as Orl's blade repeatedly crunched into its chitinous belly. The spider collapsed bodily on top of Orl, drenching him with its hot, black blood.

Husker rowed the skiff to the shore, R'daff leaping over the side to aid his leader. Heaving the spider's corpse off Orl, the ganger helped him gingerly to his feet. Ferren and Hack, in the other skiff, anxiously scanned the lake. The malevolent surface was calm, for now.

LORD ORL FINISHED prying the dead spider's eyes into the cupped hands of R'daff, grimly noting the absence of Kar's beeping motion detector device.

'Let's get the sump out of here,' Orl snarled, his men eagerly nodding in agreement. Both men boarded Husker's skiff, bringing the gunwale dangerously low. The Brassers worked the two gun-battered boats toward the half-submerged gantry from which they had entered.

Five feet from the makeshift dock, the shimmering purple surface of the lake erupted one final time, the dark blur of a spider leaping from the slime behind R'daff. In a lightning fast strike the creature's bladed leg hooked through R'daff's cheek, emerging again under his chin. Before the gang could even raise their weapons, R'daff was dragged into the ooze, vanishing with his attacker beneath the oily waves.

The rest of the gang flew to the gunwales, helplessly aiming their weapons at the slime, shouting R'daff's name until it echoed around the ancient cavern. Three minutes later they stopped. Nothing. No spider, no R'daff. Not even bubbles.

Pulling the skiffs from the hated lake, the remnants of the gang began the long trek home in mournful silence.

DOKKER FINISHED CLEANING the end of the brachial vessel and placed the severed arm in the cryo pod at his feet. It had been eleven months since he had 'jumped the wall', fleeing the glittering halls of the Spire after that fatal surgery. Yes, eleven months and no sign of the dead Noble's vengeful family, their lust for his head obviously overcome by their aversion to the teeming filth of the Underhive levels. All told, his new practice, cleverly located in an abandoned gantry crane, was doing quite nicely down here, with the ceaseless gang warfare providing him with a never-ending supply of patients and body parts for transplants. He had even come to grudgingly accept the moniker the gangers had slapped him with: Dokker Hack'n'Slash.

A loud metal clanging roused Dokker from his thoughts. He went over to the balcony of the crane, and peered over the railing. Four storeys down, he could make out the copper form of a Brasser, the yellow metal mesh of his garments glinting dully in the chemlight of the dome.

'Hack, my friend!' Dokker cheerily greeted the familiar ganger. 'More spare parts for me?' he asked eyeing the body Hack carried.

'No Dokker, it's Lord Orl. Something's wrong with him!' Hack shouted back in a worried voice. 'Let me up!'

Dokker hit the large red button beside him, lowering the ancient, winch-driven access platform to the ground below.

LORD ORL FORCED his eyelids open. The familiar plates of the ceiling came into focus.

'Awake at last, I see,' Dokker Hack'n'Slash's reedy voice piped from nearby.

'How long have I been out this time?' Orl croaked through split lips. His throat felt like he had drunk acid.

'Three days now, if the glowglobes are to be trusted.'

Orl turned weakly in the sick bed. His body felt like an aching lump of lead, and there was a searing pain in his left shoulder. He slowly moved his undamaged arm to clutch the throbbing wound. His fingers sank into the sickly white flesh like wet clay. He let go with a start, and was horrified to see the skin refuse to spring back, leaving deep trenches where his fingers were.

'What the hell's happening to me!'

'I don't know.' Dokker leaned over him, shining a light in his eyes. If his expression was anything to go by, he seemed almost amused. 'It seems to be some sort of extreme cellular deterioration. At first I thought you had advanced stages of spore rot, but you failed to respond to the anti-fungal treatments, worse luck, and I can find no traces of fungal spores in your bloodstream.'

'Damn it all!' Orl groaned. Dokker prattled on, but the room began to swim before Orl's eyes, and purple-drowned darkness engulfed him once more.

* * *

'LORD ORL. CAN you hear me? Lord Orl?' Orl's eyes fluttered open to the concerned visage of Ferren. 'That rat-faced guilder, Rorget Ahn, has been asking for you, lord. What should we do?'

It took Orl some time to untangle his muddled thoughts. The lake... spiders... eyes... Rorget Ahn!

The backstabbing sump-slug had sold them out, purposely pitting the Brassers and Black Hand against each other. Profit, nothing but profit for the guilder, selling his gear to the gangs so they could destroy each other. The weaker the gangs, the easier for the guilder to control them. All this, plus the promise of impossibly rare spider eyes brought back by the survivors...

'Don't give him the eyes, Ferren, what ever you do, don't give him the fragging eyes!' Orl wheezed through cracked lips.

Ferren's face became more troubled. 'They're... they're gone, lord.'

'What?' Orl rasped forcing himself up into a sitting position. The way Ferren started back in revulsion did nothing to ease his consternation.

'They're gone, sir. They melted. The day after we got back from the lake. Melted away like ice.'

Orl shook his head in disbelief, pressing his good hand to his forehead. 'What the hell kind of spiders were those? What the hell was in that lake?' he asked himself, staring at the pus on his palm that had oozed out of the corners of his eyes. 'The lake...' Orl looked up at Ferren, 'I'm dying. Whatever's in that Helmawr-damned lake poisoned me, Ferren, and now I'm dying.'

Ferren fidgeted uncomfortably. 'Word has spread about... what happened. The ratskins are in an uproar. Seems they've known about the dome for generations. It's taboo. They say it's evil...'

'You don't fragging say?' Orl snarled contemptuously, then paused. A tooth had dislodged from his gums. He spat it onto the bed sheets in a gob of bloody pus.

'They say the ancients practised evil sorcery there. Sorcery brought from, from off-world.' Ferren breathed the word like it was sacred. 'They say they made things there. Wrong things. Things contrary to the sacred spirit of the Hive.'

'Enough, Ferren! Enough fairy tales! I'm dying. Let me rot in peace.'

Ferren slowly walked to the door. There he paused as if to say something.

'What?' Lord Orl demanded.

Ferren sadly shook his head and stepped out of the door.

ORL AWOKE ONCE again, but he was not in bed. He was crouching in the corner above an open cryo pod. He suddenly realised what he was doing and dropped the cold, dead hand that he had raised to his mouth. Waves of nausea shook him as he staggered back from his gruesome meal. He began to sob.

Dokker's cheery voice came from the back room 'Lord Orl? Is that you? Are you all right?'

Orl could hear the surgeon's footsteps coming closer, and his mouth began to salivate. 'No! No stay back!' he screamed and lunged out through the door.

He shivered as he lowered himself down on the access platform. On his way out he had seen his reflection in a polished metal wall plate. Huge misshapen lumps covered his body, pestilent fluid running from where the skin had stretched and split.

Dokker called after him from the balcony as he ran into the maze of tangled masonry, fleeing on cracking painful joints. He ran through the Hive's artificial night, the dimmed chemlights concealing his decaying form.

HIS HEADLONG FLIGHT ended hours later on the metal dock. The dreadful purple lake lay quietly before him, as if it was waiting for him. The skin of Orl's knees had sloughed off in the many stumbling falls he had taken on his journey. It hung in bloody tatters around his shins. The exposed bone of his kneecaps seemed to have turned a sickly mauve.

His gaze fell on the dark island jutting in the centre of the lake. What's done is done, Orl thought, and leapt into the oily slime. Strangely, the liquid did not burn, but felt oddly comforting, filling the gaping wounds of his body with soft warmth.

Driven by some inexplicable intuition, Orl swam to the protruding machinery of the island. He crawled onto the shore, violet liquid streaming from the mesh of his overcoat. Making his way to the jumble of pipes and steel before him, he began clawing away the solidified deposits on the face of the tank.

Flesh flaying off his fingers he finally managed to break a large sheet of encrusted filth from the tank's surface. He stared numbly at what lay beneath.

Black arcs and crescents crossed on a yellow field. As Orl's ruined fingers brushed over the insignia it burst into life, flaring with ancient energy. His mind was hit with a jolt of terrible knowledge. Words and images he could barely comprehend flooded his brain as the ancient device pumped the memories of lost gods through his tortured nerves.

They had called themselves Gene Lords, and had plundered the known galaxy from frontier to frontier, collecting not ore, not gems, but the life-blood of every living horror they found haunting the abyss. There was something in this blood they needed, something for which Orl had no words. An infinitely small spiral, a twisted double chain they needed for some vast secret experiment that was far beyond his understanding.

That was it then, this lake around him, this stuff coursing through his poisoned veins. It was a vast alien soup, stolen from creatures beyond imagination, brewing for centuries inside this infernal vat, finally bursting forth to flood this age-old dome.

Turning from his mind shattering discovery, Lord Orl realised he was not alone. Dozens of the spider-things clustered on the shore in a rough semi-circle around him. They did not attack, but stood motionless, staring with their black jewelled eyes.

Orl took in their warped and varied forms, each so different from the other. This one with countless extra limbs, that one covered with dripping blue mouths that sucked hungrily at the foetid air, this one sprouting tufts of black hair and trailing a giant, rat-like tail.

Understanding did not come to Orl until the spider wearing R'daff's face stepped out in front of the others – or was it R'daff with a spider's body? They were all something else, all these spider-things, all originally some other creature that had happened across the lake. This alien soup had taken them, and absorbed them, just as Orl himself was being absorbed.

He was not dying, he was changing. He could feel it. The substance in his veins churning, shifting organs, changing bone to chitin, inexorably marching toward its alien purpose. No, the spider-things would not attack him, he was one of them. Orl could feel their silent, beckoning call: *Come down with us, down into the sweet depths, down with us, where you belong.*

*Yes, my new brothers, but not yet,* Orl thought back. Fighting the desperate, all but overwhelming urge to follow the spider-things, Orl withdrew something from the inner pocket of his overcoat.

'Not yet,' he repeated aloud. 'I have something I must yet do.'

RORGET AHN'S SUAVE, aristocratic features were knitted in concentration as he pored over the curling guilder contracts laid out before him on his antique writing desk. The silken flap of his caravan tent blew silently open as if blown by a subterranean breeze.

Rorget was on his feet in an instant, shouting in alarm: 'Guards! Guards! Intruder!'

'Scream all you want, Rorget. Your guards won't hear you.' The voice of the dark figure standing in the door flap was strange, as if something was obstructing its vocal chords. The dim light glinted off the torn links of the figure's overcoat.

Fear flooded into Rorget's handsome face along with recognition. 'You can't kill me, Orl,' Rorget reasoned, pleading, sliding an ancient, off-world bolt pistol from his silken robes. 'You know the consequences of killing a sanctioned guilder.'

'I'm not going to kill you, Rorget.' Orl charged across the tent on three insectoid legs, crashing through Rorget's portable desk and pinning the terrified guilder to the floor. A scythe-like bone hook lanced through Rorget's wrist, sending the bolt pistol skittering across the floor.

'I'm not going to kill you, Rorget,' Lord Orl hissed again, forcing the guilder's head back and withdrawing a small object from the depths of his overcoat. 'I have something to give you.'

Orl poured the contents of the glass vial into the guilder's choking mouth.

'Welcome... brother!' he spat, as the viscous purple liquid slid down Rorget's throat.

# RAT IN THE WALLS
## by Alex Hammond

'I'M GONNA DIE,' Knife Edge Liz moaned, staring at her distorted reflection in the blood pooled at her side. 'I'm gonna die in this stinking hole.'

Her face was pale, the scar tissue of countless wounds now unnoticeable in its fading pallor. Her hair was matted with blood and her dark eyes glazed, irises unable to maintain their focus on even the closest objects. The ancient, rusted air duct around her was moaning and sighed like the lungs of some great beast, like she was trapped within the pumping vessels of a giant. A rush of chill air welled up through another tunnel behind her, thrusting siphoned air all about her, cooling her fever, then rushing away on its journey through other parts of Hive Primus.

Liz gazed down at herself, at the wrecked combat suit which she had pulled down to hang lifelessly around her waist. She wore her gang colours underneath. They clung to her with a combination of sweat and blood -- life's vital ingredients, like the filtered air that swirled around the Hive, slipping away with pulsing regularity.

Liz rolled over and pulled herself forwards again to the edge of the mesh grille set in the floor. The sirens had stopped howling some hours ago. The Uphive security systems had plainly got over their initial surprise at her arrival. A tangle of wires trailing from the combat suit caught on a jagged metal edge, somewhere in the dim-blue darkness behind her.

'Damn it...' Liz sighed. She pulled roughly at the cables. They tore suddenly and starting spurting a thin chemical mist around the tunnel. Pneumatic coolant turned part of the wall to ice, the frozen nitrogen-spewing pipe spinning perilously close to her left leg. Before she had a chance to try and grapple with the cable, the arcane suit's dying mechanisms stepped in. The cable self-repaired and the gas stopped hissing. As the static-white haze settled, Liz returned her gaze to the grille.

Below her, a vaulting fresco-covered corridor revealed the hourly happenings of the uphive denizens. These were nothing like the people Liz had grown up with in the Underhive. She lay mere yards above a breed of people intent on her destruction, who thought her to be no more than a base animal. These nobles and their ladies wore soft cloth, not the scavenged pieces of armour and mesh that could be scrounged to afford some protection. A gentleman in a brightly coloured silken robe strode past. His hand rested gingerly on a small, leathery ape-like creature, naked except for a steel face mask which guarded passers by from its vicious jaws. A woman in a translucent dress with a trail twice her length passed next. A huge, studded mail collar led up to her neck, where it was incorporated into an enormous lacquered hair escutcheon.

Liz marvelled at all she saw. The people moved and gestured with wide flamboyant strokes, they let their eyes wander to observe strangers, they congregated in open places, they spoke loudly rather than whispered in hushed tones. They did things that could bring about their death in the Underhive. Men and women paraded their affections in public. Much of their clothing revealed vital body parts that would, were this Deep Town or the Sump Hole, beckon assailants and encourage their blades and gunfire.

Liz rolled onto her back. 'These people are insane... and I'm dying among them,' she whispered and fell unconscious.

LIZ DRAGGED HERSELF awake. She could feel her arms and legs but could not make them move. She attempted to focus on something in the duct, latch onto something to steady her spinning head. Like a whirling vortex, like the gaping maw of Chaos, the roof above her twisted and spiralled, snickered and creaked. The weight of the hive was too much. It would collapse, crush her and all those below, everyone the entire ten miles down.

'No,' Liz moaned to herself. She knew these were just delusions, fears unchecked, but they would not stop.

Something sighed in the clammy darkness around her. The soft glow of the stolen combat suit's power cells ebbed; flickered; waned some more. Liz reached wearily for the small medi-pack lying at her side. She'd torn it open when she first staggered into the duct, blood flooding from an open wound. The hypos helped to coagulate, the pills reduced the pain and the staples did their best to keep her innards where they belonged. Fever or no fever, these things were running thin. The bag was empty; the life support in the suit almost flat. To sleep was to die. But it would be painful, slow.

Let death take as long as it must, Liz thought, but damn the pain.

'I need some drugs,' she said aloud, her voice a croak.

Liz wound the suit's coils around her waist. Their small warmth was some help against death's cold. The rubber hissed as it pressed against her bleeding side. The shreds wrapped around her, Liz crawled slowly, like a cat bloated on sump rats. Her legs and arms shook with every move. Sweat ran from her body.

Dehydration. She wiped her hand across her face as she crawled, and tasted the salt and iron. Vital fluids. The dawning pain was intensifying, like a thousand steel spines protruded from her bones every time she placed a limb on the ground. Was she sweating blood now? Had the fever penetrated so deep that her heart was seeping life now? The noise in her fog-bound head intensified. The rush of static, buzzing as though every synapse was burning out, flaring like match heads, popping like overloaded transformers.

The dim light flickered, reflected from a slowly rotating fan set in the roof of the tunnel. Ancient dust hung in dirty stalactites. The floor was suddenly cold and jagged under her hands: another grate. Liz peered down. Quarters. Rich tapestries, colours so bright they burnt her retinas. A vast, solid table, dark as midnight. The vaulted ceiling; a thirty foot drop. Too far.

The pain kicked up another notch and Liz screamed. She wept. The drugs would run out, and she would die. Perhaps the fall was worth it? Perhaps it would end the pain quickly?

She struggled with her combat knife. The shakes intensified. She gripped the blade handle tighter, hoping her remaining strength would be enough to wrest control of the quivering knife tip as she tried to place it close to the grate's screws. Her hand slipped and the blade scored a jagged scar out of the ancient metal with a screech like a sump-rat thrown onto a campfire.

Liz jerked her body, rammed the blade under the mesh and kicked at it with her foot. The blade snapped backwards, part embedding itself in her boot. The grate flipped open. Liz pulled at the knife. She was uncertain if it had sunk into her flesh. The combat suit's boots were light, designed for speed, so they afforded little protection. Liz had no time to investigate. She leaned forwards, her plan knitting together, despite the fever.

The slowly rotating extraction fan above her head paced its circles. Liz jammed it still with the knife. Uncoiling the combat suit's life wires, Liz lashed them to the stilled blades of the fan above her. Slowly, she leant forwards over the drop to the room below, the ebony table below her. No one was visible in the room; no obvious security system was in place.

With a sudden motion, Liz dropped forwards, then jerked to a halt like a marionette, her strings – the cables from the combat suit – pulling taught behind her to break her fall. She swayed six feet from the table, the last of her blood rushing to her head.

Liz wriggled from those parts of the suit that held her, slick, dripping, until she lay on the table. Her cocoon swayed slowly from the hole above her. She lay there for a moment, red and green with the liquids from her body and the suit. She left hand and foot prints on the table as she crawled to the edge and fell further. The room's floor was like ice beneath her feet; its cross-hatched steel bit into her bare feet. In the Underhive, you never removed your boots; it was a cardinal sin. Underhivers who wanted to live slept with their boots on.

The wall to her left was free of tapestries, and covered instead with antique weapons. Liz removed a three-pointed blade, and staggered forwards to the nearest door.

Sleeping quarters. A lush bed with dark red cloth hanging about it covered most of the floor space. A giant insect, the size of a man's hand, hummed softly in a large gilded cage in the far corner of the room. Its multi-faceted eyes reflected her bloodied, near naked form back at her a hundred times as she staggered across the floor. An adjoining room, white with back-lit tiles, stretched out in front of her. It was small, near empty except for a steel hose and a wall mirror that opened to a reveal a series of pneumatic drawers. Liz flicked at each of these, letting the cool air of their opening hisses wash over her face. It did little to help. The pain was intensifying. Her legs turned to rubber and gave way. Liz grabbed hold of the nearest open drawer as she went down.

Pills and hypo sprays covered her prone form in a rain of brightly coloured pebbles. She turned her head to one side, fighting all the way. It was as though her spine was soldered to the floor. She tried to reach for one of the pills, it didn't matter which, but she fell short, her arms weak. Powerless, she saw the bright lights above her head intensify. And fell into blackness.

A LIGHT BUZZED above her, hygiene white. This was not the after-life. The light was the length of her body, long and sharp-cornered. Liz could only part-open her eyes; whatever was in her system was making even the slightest movement an effort. She became aware of a gas mask pulled across her face, its copper base hard against her flesh. The air being filtered in was sweet, perfumed. When she breathed, her side no longer ached. Someone had been in there, fixed the ribs. She lay on a bed, her bloodied gang colours replaced by a blinding white robe. A series of hypo sprays and operating equipment were set out by the bed.

Liz could not move her head. Braced or drugged, she was not capable of scanning the room. But she knew without looking there was someone in the room with her. They were good, but the near-silent movements of their clothing betrayed their presence. Someone was observing her, watching her, concealed by her incapacity and the regular grinding from the medical equipment about her. She felt naked without a piece in her hand. The figure stirred and moved about the recesses of her vision in the corner of the room. Something warm pinched into her arm and spread about her body, dragging her eyes shut.

The medi-crib droned its incessant rhythm, its pulsing bladders and hissing pistons like the staccato of an autogun peppering the walls of an Underhive bar. The Underhive wound around Liz, twisting and arching, pulling her back.

Liz stood knee-deep in sump waters, the warm oily liquid spreading throughout her body, the brief pinch of the hypo spray at her side.

'You'll need to overhaul those lungs if she's going to survive beyond the week.' A voice echoing at the side of her head, like steel ringing against a structural support.

Liz was not standing but floating in the sump, bobbing lethargically.

'Some butcher has been at her. Most of this scarring is from poor sutures. I don't know how they could still use those medi-staples. We have fibre tape ten years old that'd do a better job,' another voice bubbled up from the sump.

'Who's there?' Liz asked.

'She's stirring, Althar. Give her another hypo of anaesthetic,' the steel voice replied.

The machine drummed out a heartbeat. The water beneath her stirred and Liz sunk beneath it.

'HOW YOU GOING, boss?' Liz was sitting around a camp-fire lit in a burnt out artillery shell, deep in the Underhive. 'Boss?'

The smell of fire-seared concrete filled the air. Dark shadows were cast from broken buttresses and twisted supports. Liz looked up from the warm flames to the face of a woman she hardly recognised. Thick purple dreads, rich brown muscles like iron, arms as thick as a structural girder. It was Bekka.

'You're dead–' Liz said.

'Don't think so,' Bekka smiled.

'–or I'm dreaming.'

'What do you mean? Dead?' Bekka scratched at the ground in front of her with a foot long, stainless-steel combat knife. She traced a skull and crossbones.

'We were ambushed. Everyone killed,' Liz said, feeling awkward in the light medical shift she wore. She pulled its edges to cover her bare feet.

'You?'

'No.' Liz could smell harsh disinfectants and sweet anaesthetics. 'I'm dying now, though. Uphive.'

'You gone Uphive? You're up there with the rat nobles?' Bekka flicked the knife into the ground, between the skull's cross-hatched eyes.

'I went there to kill the men who set us up.'

'You get 'em?'

'Yes. Aldus Harkon.'

'Harkon? Never liked him. Glad you got him Liz.' Bekka stood and stretched her back. She began to walk away from the fire. 'Even if you don't get the others, you've done a good job, girl. Sounds like you've revenged us pretty good.'

'Yeah, I guess so,' Liz said, watching her friend disappear into the darkness.

'YOU GUESS WHAT, my dear?' Liz opened her eyes. A tall, lean man, with brutal but charming features, leaned over her. He was scar-free, with eyes older than his skin suggested. She now lay in the four poster bed, its soft mattress cradling her. Liz dragged an arm down the white gown and pulled a sheet up over her.

'I wouldn't concern yourself with all that fuss,' the man said turning away from her to examine a holo-projector, 'I've seen your insides.'

Liz could only make out small details in the room around her. To gaze too long was a strain. A dull pain behind her eyes forced her to take it slowly. The rise and fall of the machine beside her occasionally jostled the fluids and sedatives suspended from a wire frame. Their shiny brass exteriors rattled, sending small tremors down the metal cords bolted to the body plugs in her arm.

The man examined the readings and flicked through a pad of reports, written on real paper. 'Says here that you're doing well. That's hardly surprising: my doctor is a genius when it comes to rejuvenation.'

'Rejuvenation?' Liz murmured.

'Yes. A complete overhaul.'

Liz touched her face, gingerly at first. 'My scars–'

'Scars, lungs, blood, liver – the whole system. You've brushed up quite nicely for such a ragged piece-of-work.'

Liz brought her hand round to her neck. The mark from the near-fatal blow Alquath the Viper had dealt her in a duel remained.

'Couldn't leave you without one reminder of where you came from. It has a certain rugged appeal to it, I think,' the man said without turning around.

'You know who I am?' Liz said, examining the hard copper-coloured wires that ran from the heavy medical systems to a socket set in her arm.

'Oh yes,' the man replied his back still turned to her. 'I know you. The terrorist from the deeps, who's been picking off the Emperor's good children from air ducts. Yes, I know who you are.'

'You didn't kill me.' Liz returned her attention to the man. He was dressed in an elegant suit, made from a material that changed from a deep purple to a rose colour as he shifted. A robe set over it trailed to the ground around him billowing on the floor.

'No.' The man turned to face her. 'No. I didn't kill you. I must say, it is not every day that one finds a half-naked woman lying bloodied in their en suite. At first I thought you were a threat by some enemy. I thought you were Ursula, truth be told. You're about her height and build.'

'That counts for an explanation in these parts?' Liz said quietly.

'Explanations later,' the man stood and walked towards her. He adjusted the brace behind Liz's head. 'Rest now.'

'You gonna give me your name?' Liz sneered.

'Kassat. My name's Kassat Ran Lo.'

'My name is–'

'Liz. I know who you are,' Kassat said, leaving the room.

LIZ WOKE LATER to find the pipes hanging loosely next to her, gone from her arms, the socket removed and only a faint red circle remaining. Beside her rested a mesh platter with welded plates that bore strange, unfamiliar foodstuffs. In the centre of the tray a translucent, plastene card was inscribed with some words: *Eat well. Get your strength up. XXX. Kassat.*

Liz picked up a moist plant. It was brightly coloured with soft leaves and a sweet smell. Its touch was like the soft skin of those Uphiver brats she killed. Liz grabbed it and stuffed it into her mouth. It tasted good. The other food was less delicate. Some of it she recognised from stories she had heard. There was a bug-like creature, its hind shell cracked open to allow access to pulpy flesh that trickled down her throat. Small ovoid bones which, when bitten through, revealed a twin coloured marrow, white and yellow. Liz devoured these morsels and sat with the tray for some time.

Later, Kassat arrived.

'Awake?' he said by way of greeting. 'Eaten everything. Flower included.'

'What?' Liz looked up at him, still chewing her food.

'A flower, from Catachan.' Kassat produced another of the fragile, sweet tasting plants. 'A deathworld with the most exquisite flowers. They're not traditionally eaten, but savoured for their beauty.' Kassat placed it behind Liz's ear, stroking her face as he did so.

Liz considered smashing the mesh tray across his face but stopped herself. 'What does "ex-ex-ex" mean?' she said, waving the card at Kassat.

'It's an expression of affection,' Kassat purred, brushing dust from a lapel.

'Where I come from they're kill markings.'

'How very ominous.'

'Why would you express an affection for me?' Liz pushed the grate onto the floor. It crashed loudly to the steel ground.

'It is my way. Keep your friends close and your enemies closer. It's a philosophy I have long followed.'

'Don't make sense to me.' Liz crossed her arms.

'Oh dear. Call it a clash of cultures.'

Liz spat on the too-clean floor. 'What do you want from me, Kassat Ran Lo?'

'You'll need to learn the art of conversation,' Kassat said, wiping the spittle from the tiles with a handkerchief.

'I don't need to learn anything.'

'Oh, you will. You owe me your life. You owe me a favour, and in order to perform it with any grace you will need to be prepared.'

'I'm no mistress. I'm a killer,' Liz said removing the flower from behind her ear. She crushed it.

'I know what you are and what you do.'

'I won't do anything for you.'

'Then you will die,' Kassat said coldly. He spun on his heels and left the room.

Liz stared at the modular, steel plates that made up the ceiling. She had counted the rivets in a brief moment of lucidity some days earlier, at one of the cold points in her fever. She reached out and took the tray, sliding it under the covers with her, keeping it close. After a moment, she also tugged free one of the tubes that had been in her arm, and secreted it in the same place.

Kassat strode back into the room. In his hands he held a locked, iron-bound casket. 'This is what I need from you, sump rat.' His manner was rougher now.

Kassat leant forward and slipped his fingers into the case lock, a pair of hollow eyes on an embossed skull. Liz flicked the tray from beneath the bed and swung it at Kassat. It caught him in the face and the noble staggered backwards, crashing through a rack of medical equipment and falling to the floor. Liz struggled forwards, tripping onto the floor beside him. Kassat slammed the casket down towards her and caught her in the chest. Liz screamed as something snapped. Her arms couldn't co-ordinate. She rolled across the floor towards him. Liz grabbed both ends of the tube and slipped it around Kassat's throat. The noble struggled and managed to stand. Liz gripped him around the waist with her legs, driving her heels into his kidneys.

Kassat started to laugh.

Liz pulled harder on the makeshift garrotte.

Kassat just laughed louder.

'Harder! You're going to have to pull harder than that!' he shouted, spinning violently around, driving Liz into the bed.

Pain coursed though her back and she released the tube. Kassat grabbed her arms and held her to the bed.

'Drugs, my girl. The harder you struggle, the more you fight them, the worse they get. Right now you couldn't even raise a lasgun if I put one in your hand. You're mine,' Kassat Ran Lo sneered. 'You'll do as I say or die.'

Liz lay still. 'You wouldn't have brought me here, saved my life, if you were gonna kill me straight off. It's a bad investment.'

'Perhaps I wanted to see how well you'd take the news? Perhaps I had other plans for you. Trade you as a pleasure slave to House Helmawr?'

'Nah,' Liz said, 'You ain't that smart.'

'Perhaps,' Kassat said, letting go of her shoulders and sitting up. 'Perhaps I'm not. So let's say we make a deal? You are a mercenary, after all.'

'You're wrong, Kassat. I was ready for death the day I smuggled myself Uphive.'

'How about revenge?' The nobleman resumed opening the elaborate steel case and produced a small holo-monitor. He tapped some switches and a spectral image flickered into light. Men and women, Uphivers, moved about one another in a large chamber, drank from elaborate fluted glasses and watched as slaves, tethered together at the ankles, fought for their pleasure.

'This is a ball I gave some week-cycles ago. I had a holo-recorder inserted into a servitor, keeping him alive long enough for me to get this recording.' The image bucked and swayed as it moved throughout the crowd. 'There is a man who will be present at the next such occasion. His name is Terrak Ran Lo. I want him dead. I want his place at the Ran Lo council.'

'And you want me to do this for you?'

'For yourself as well. He is the man who employed Aldus Harkon, the man whose money sponsored the ambush that saw the death of your friends.'

'What?'

'You may not consider me to be smart, Liz, but you, my sweet thug, are as dense as concrete. You talked and talked during your malaise. I know all about your gang, the hunters, your friends' deaths, coming Uphive and killing Harkon. I had to increase your dosage just to keep you quiet when night came.'

Liz stared at Kassat, tracing his calculating features with her eyes. His face was alight with satisfaction. He could barely suppress his grin.

'This man–' Kassat hit an inlaid rune and froze the device's image. 'Terrak Ran Lo is the man who organised for the deaths of your friends, organised their deaths as a blood sport, as entertainment for his young proteges. It was a hunt, Liz, and you and your gang were the animals.'

Liz stared at the image. Terrak was old, his face soft and unthreatening. His eyes looked calm, like tranquil waters.

'Doesn't look like a man with murder on his mind, does he?' Kassat growled.

Liz fixed her gaze on those eyes; still, unfathomable, unmoving. 'What do you need me to do?' she whispered.

* * *

'IT'S SIMPLE. REALLY,' Kassat pressed, restrained, patient.

'Really?' Liz sneered, her face close to his, eyes reflecting the bank of grid lights above them. Kassat stood in the centre of his living quarters, his elaborate furniture pushed to its edges, the ornately tiled floor cleared of clutter. She stumbled in the awkward shoes Kassat had given her to wear and landed on her rump. She had never seen anything like them, so impractical: spindly, elongated heels forcing her forwards, up onto her toes. The hum of the lighting grid droned behind the thin music Kassat had set piping from a cone-shaped machine that ran off a rotating copper disc. It echoed though the high ceiling and around the ironwork gargoyles which clung to the corners of the room. Liz noticed that the table, onto which she had crashed the other day, had been replaced.

'Yes,' Kassat said, stepping backwards for a moment, brushing down his silk coat, 'the man leads. You simply follow.' The noble held his arms out again.

Liz spat on the floor. 'What is this thing anyway?' she growled.

'This dance is called a vaults. It is an elegant practice many millennia old.'

'I don't get it.'

'I don't understand,' Kassat said.

'Oh yeah?' Liz replied, crouching down.

'No, you should say "I don't understand",' he chided.

'Look! All I need to do is kill this guy and we're square!' Liz said, bending to pull off a dress shoe and shaking it at him. 'I don't get... understand why I need to do all this,' she sighed, rubbing at her blistered feet.

'You will not infiltrate Terrak's guards at his quarters. At the ball he'll have only one guardian. He will not be expecting an attack.'

'Because it's suicide?' Liz pulled at the muscles in her neck and rolled her shoulders.

Kassat paused, considered the woman at his feet, and adjusted his cuffs. 'For some, perhaps.'

'And for me?'

'You were born with an animal's instinct for survival. Uphive assassins are less–'

'Cunning?' Liz said, standing and replacing her shoe.

'No, they're cunning all right. Rather, they are less crude.'

| 12 | 11 | 10 | 9 | 8 | 7 | 6 | 5 | 4 |

| NAME: | | | | | | | | |
|---|---|---|---|---|---|---|---|---|
| **ADDRESS:** | | | | | | | | |

**DATE:** 12 / 11 / 00

1598

| | CASH | C.O.D. | CHARGE | ON ACCT. | MDSE RTD. | PAID OUT |
|---|---|---|---|---|---|---|

| DESCRIPTION | PRICE | AMOUNT |
|---|---|---|
| STABS: 12 | | |
| | tax | 6 85 |
| | | 59 |

'Crude,' Liz said coldly, 'Yes, I think I understand.'

Kassat returned to his position. 'You need to appear as though you have been an Uphiver all your life. Not some savage from the lowest level. You will have to tame some of your feral impulses.'

Liz sighed, then slowly sashayed forwards with small, fluid steps. Kassat's eyes widened in delight. She took him by the arms and held him gently at the small of her back.

'Excellent,' Kassat purred. 'And again...'

LIZ STARED AT her reflection in the window of Kassat's private chambers. She could hardly recognise her reflection. She was clad in a bodysuit, cross hatched with nano-filaments that cast a cascade of changing colours, primarily intended to accentuate her figure. Kassat had provided her with a pair of those elaborate, impractical shoes, that revealed much of her feet. Her broken toes, she had noticed, had been reset, the missing two replaced. Kassat had employed some woman to spend many hours reconstructing and painting her toe and finger nails. She couldn't see the point.

A dark blue, feathered head-dress was strapped to Liz's shoulders. It fanned out around her face, which was the part that Liz least recognised. Her hair was slicked back and bound into a tail and painted completely white. Her face was similarly covered, bar her lips, which had been painted a bright blood red where they met.

Liz turned to one side and then the other. She looked through her reflection, through the window to the night sky outside. She had never been in these private quarters before. They were filled with strange devices, antiques and furniture made from an organic substance Kassat called 'wood'. They had the only exterior window in Kassat's quarters, but even the one spoke of quite unimaginable wealth. They would provide a good view of the sunrise, they were that high above the toxic ash clouds. At the moment, outside Liz could see the sad little stars. They were like nothing she had imagined, more like pin-pricks in the darkness. The way the merchants had spoken of them she believed that they were massive planets of fire. But she was glad it was dark now. She could not really imagine what the view would look like during the day, but she knew she could not help but be unnerved by the vast openness of the view, all these miles above her natural home.

Kassat entered the chamber, clapping his hands together happily. 'They've done fantastic work, don't you think?' he grinned.

'It's impractical.'

'Nonsense, my dear. Kick the shoes off and you're in a fully functioning combat suit. Much like the one you stole from those hunters. That padding isn't simply there to flatter you. That's mesh armour. Finest quality. Lighter than those feathers.'

Kassat was attired in a material that adjusted its colours to match the background as he moved throughout the room. 'Latest thing, adapted from Imperium camouflage,' Kassat said, noticing Liz's scornful gaze.

'I'm going to need a weapon,' she sniffed.

'Ah yes. But I don't quite trust you to give you one now. No offence,' Kassat said.

'None taken,' Liz said, gazing at the immense desk set before the window. Kassat had it piled high with papers, holocards and locked files. It was the only place in his quarters that was in disorder.

'Besides they are still somewhat security-minded at these things. No one gets in without being scanned. I've arranged for your weapon to be hidden in the centrepiece of the main banquet table,' Kassat said, walking face to face with Liz.

'The point exactly?' Liz starred back at him.

'They wouldn't dare break a fragile object of such beauty. They wouldn't expect that a weapon would be hidden in an ice sculpture that took hundreds of hours to create. It's simply not within their nature,' Kassat said, adjusting the head-dress on Liz's shoulders.

'But I'm crude?' she replied.

'You can be,' Kassat returned, unfazed. He placed his hand on Liz's cheek. 'Looking at you now I'd never guess that you weren't born Uphive. You're a remarkable woman, Liz.' Kassat stroked her face gently.

'The gun is in the ice statue,' Liz said as if to herself, stepping away.

'That's right.' Kassat turned to the door.

'How long now?'

'Twenty minutes or so before I am expected.' Kassat moved towards the door his back still turned to Liz.

'And me?' She took one last look at herself in the window. Part of her wished that she had a record of this woman, this new incarnation of Liz from the Underhive.

'I've arranged for you to go with another party of nobles. Eddas Ulanti owes me a favour. My people will take you to them,' Kassat said, partway through the door.

'I'll see you there then,' Liz said quietly, returning his gaze.

'Yes. Emperor bless you, my dear. I hope to see you safe at the end of all this,' Kassat said, turning to face her for a moment, before he strode out of his quarters in a rush of shimmering cloth.

'Liar,' Liz said, and spat on the tiled floor.

GIANT DOORS, THREE storeys high, driven by huge pneumatic arms decorated with ornate crests, slid open, the air from the hydraulics purring out across the floor. Liz walked amongst the Ulanti, at the back of a procession arranged according to a hierarchy she didn't start to understand. She took a place amongst the body slaves, the dancers, courtesans and pit-fighters. She had remained close to Eddas Ulanti, a rat-faced man, the whole while keeping her mind fixed on her objective and her way out.

The noble's ball was in full sway by the time she arrived in the vast ballroom, as wide as an entire Underhive dome. All present, with only one exception, were dressed in a kaleidoscopic collection of fabrics and colours. Liz could not believe the complexity of some of the garments, nor the shapes worked from the hair and bodies. All around her, men and women moved about in the same states of undress she'd expect of an Underhive pleasure bar, not a nobles' ball. The exception was a man, plainly an off-worlder, dressed in dark grey robes and bearing a heavy iron talisman around his neck. Where he strode, the crowds parted; even the most arrogant looking of Uphivers bowed their heads and averted their eyes. Aside from the guards, this man was the only one to openly carry a weapon. A heavy pistol hung alongside the talisman. He was dangerous. Liz tried not to stare at him.

At the centre of the great room was a gaping hole that plunged deep into the heart of this part of Hive Primus. It was covered with glass a metre thick, so as to give the illusion that those present were walking upon the Hive itself, thousands of feet above the foundries below. Gingerly Liz took a single step

out on to the glass. On either side, pillars of rough-hewn stone
and iron soared high up into the air above, creating an equally
dizzying effect. This openness was unfamiliar to her, the
expanse of space oppressive and dizzying. The only cover
afforded were the frail, carved wooden tables at which many of
the nobles sat, gorging themselves. They wouldn't stop a shell
from a juve's first pistol, let alone automatic gun fire.

Kassat, from within the crowd, caught her eye. She followed
where he was looking and caught sight of her prey, Terrak Ran
Lo, just as Kassat had described him. She looked back, wanting
him to nod, confirm it, make it real, really happening – but
Kassat was already striding away. Liz followed, to another open
area over which hung a giant structure made of crystals of many
colours, hanging from spider web-thin chains, that reflected
shimmering spotlights about the room. In the centre of this
space was a pit. A barbed, steel cage was part-sunk into the
ground. In it, two bloodied men chained at the necks fought
with dulled, stabbing blades. Nobles stood at the edges and
threw paint, nails and fruit at the fighters, jeering and snigger-
ing at the trapped men. They were desperate men, their lives
sold to slavery, death a certainty for one of them tonight.

Kassat approached Liz and took her by the hand. She followed him beyond the pit, onto a polished dancing floor. As
they whirled, Kassat clasped her close and pulled her face close
to his. Liz tensed.

'An ancient bolt pistol, custom design – explosive, caseless,
laser sighted and recoil compensated…' Kassat whispered. Liz
could feel his heartbeat, the micro-conduits of the combat suit
amplifying its pulse. His heart was racing – as was hers.

'Who's the man in grey?' she hissed.

'A witch hunter. An Imperium inquisitor, from off-world.
Come to inspect the nobility, root out mutations and deviance.
Needless to say, he is not pleased with this event.'

'He has a weapon,' Liz growled.

'Yes. You may have to kill him too.'

'What? Did you know he would be here?'

'No!' he spat. 'I knew nothing about it until just now. There
are others too: Arbites, Ecclesiarchs, military men and those
with something invested in the Imperium. Unlike these nobles,
they are men who are prepared to fight.' Kassat pulled away
from Liz.

She dragged him back, in close, staring deep into his eyes. 'Kassat, if this is a set-up I will kill you,' she said softly.

'You know,' Kassat smiled, 'I will have to fight back.' The noble patted the small of her back and released her. 'Good luck,' he whispered, then bowed his thanks for the dance.

Kassat slipped quickly back into the bustling crowd. Liz stood alone in the middle of the dance floor, close to the fighting pit. The combatants' arms were locked in a strained grapple. The release system on the cage was a simple catch. Liz started to think. The ice sculpture was thirty or so paces away. One, two... five guards, all armed with autoguns, stood by the doors. The exit route Kassat had mentioned, through a vent set in the wall, was another hundred strides beyond the table where Terrak Ran Lo was flirting with a young woman, hand on her shoulder, laughing.

'Time,' Liz sneered and headed towards the cage. A dancer tripped over her as she strode purposefully across the floor. He fell backwards in alarm, hundreds of tiny beads cascading from his suit. Liz flicked the lever on the cage.

'Hey, rat-bait!' she called down to the men.

They stared for a moment only, their tired eyes enlivened at this opportunity. The men burst out of the cage, flailing at the nobles standing closest to them. One gripped a young boy by the neck and drove his duelling-blade into his throat. Nobles screamed.

Liz ran for the statue.

The guards reacted slowly, The fighters started slashing a red swathe through the crowd. Their necks still linked by chains they crashed through the nobles like loosed bulls, their awkward, bleeding bodies slipping about on the polished steel floor.

Liz turned to the ice-statue. The carving was of her, Liz, dressed in her gang colours, a naked man at her feet. It was placed in the centre of a table, two score of dishes spiralling out from its centre. She could see Kassat's mocking grin in her mind. The ganger collided with a fleeing noble and rolled over his back as he fell, kicking off the stupid shoes. She landed solidly on her feet and sprinted hard for the table.

The guards began firing at the freed slaves, their shots taking one down. The other, tied to the dying man, tried to drag his body across the floor.

Liz leapt up onto the table, knocking a sallow-faced trader face-first into a platter of eel spawn. He looked up, the tiny eggs spitting from his mouth. Liz grabbed the ice-statue and hurled it at the trader, knocking him onto the ground. The ice shattered, slivers spinning wide and far across the floor. A noble woman screamed as Liz leapt from the table like a feral cat.

Trapped in a deadly embrace with his now-dead opponent, the live slave thrashed like a trapped animal, growling and swiping wildly at the nobles as they clustered around him. The inquisitor stepped through them and calmly shot out his leg, sending him slipping to the ground in a cascade of blood.

'To raise a weapon against an agent of the Emperor is heresy,' the inquisitor said. The guards massed at his back opened fire, tiny red explosions erupting all over the slave.

Liz landed on her hands and feet. An Arbiter came at her with a club. She rolled onto her back and kicked him hard in the gut. Over his doubled-up back she saw the inquisitor turn to face her. Liz used the momentum from the roll to smash her elbow into his face, letting her body weight carry him to the ground. They both fell into the shattered ice. Liz crawled onto her hands and knees, and swept about on the floor scrabbling for the gun.

The inquisitor rose, his hands thrusting his pistol at her. Liz dived between the legs of a panicked, fleeing noblewoman. The shot clipped her and her hip burst red. Liz caught sight of the bolt gun as, in the pandemonium, it was kicked into the clearing before the inquisitor. He raised his gun at Liz again. She dived forward and rolled across the ice. A shot spat over her shoulder. Sliding through melting slush, she snatched up the assassination weapon and swung it wide towards the witch hunter. He pulled his trigger.

A flash almost blinded Liz. Something knocked her hard in the chest. Like someone had pulled the floor from beneath her, she fell to the ground. Her heart ached like she'd been knifed. The inquisitor stared. His mouth opened but he said nothing. A few feathers from Liz's headdress floated to the ground.

Liz looked down at her chest. The mesh armour had stopped the blow. Slowly and deliberately, Liz levelled the laser sight between the inquisitor's eyes and pulled the trigger. Nobles behind him were showered in gore and brain matter. She ran for the crowd and it parted about her. She dived beneath a table. A wave of gunfire tore through the table, disrupting Liz's dark world with violent keyholes of light.

Liz stood, throwing the table back off her shoulders. Liz closed on Terrak Ran Lo. The old man was moving for cover, crouching behind a side-table.

'Terrak!' Liz screamed.

Her prey did not notice her. She leapt from above the table and fell upon him, dragging him to the ground. His breath was wine-rancid, his eyes glazed with age.

'Who?' He looked at Liz, her white face sprayed with the blood of the inquisitor, and his eyes span.

'A message from the Underhive,' Liz spat and pulled the trigger. The blast tore the old man from her hands, throwing him up into the air. The guards, moving in formation through the thinning crowd, began shooting. Liz was clipped twice; the wind was knocked out of her but neither shot pierced the body armour. She grabbed her injured arm and returned their fire, running parallel to the guards, shooting around stricken nobles and courtesans. Her shots flew wide, but the explosions forced the guards to seek better cover. Liz ran full sprint for her escape vent. An Ecclesiarch stepped in front of her, blocking the entrance. The guards returned fire as Liz span the man in front of her. The blasts impacted through the light robes the priest wore. His body shook as Liz held him close to her. She returned fire and clipped one guard in the shoulder; he fell to the polished dance floor. The guards hit the ground again. Liz rolled from underneath the dead Ecclesiarch and dived for the grate.

She slid across the polished floor, crashing face first into the wall. The grate was fixed at its corners. A snaking line of bullets traced across the ground towards Liz. She flicked her pistol to full auto and blew away the grate. Metal shards spat past her face as she dived for freedom. One final, hopeful shot hit her full in the back and blew her forward.

KASSAT SAT IN his study, staring blankly at desk-top before him. Audits, mercantile reports, credit transferrals both above and below board. A dizzying array of numbers, estimations and processed units, many hundreds of hours of work to process, but he could not concentrate enough to dive in.

Now he waited, staring at the antique timepiece on his wall, which sat on the wall between his weapons cabinet and an ancient brass-and-leather vox-caster. It was very old and could not keep true Imperial hours. He turned in his chair to look out into the dawn sky. The sun would rise above the cloud cover soon, sending its yellow rays to touch the Spire, lighting up the dark, nebulous mass drifting in swirls below. The ash clouds could be quite beautiful if the light was right. However, like the brightly coloured arrow frogs of Catachan, they were also poisonous. Nevertheless, he had the clouds to thank. They had been the reason for Hive Primus and her sisters. If it weren't for the clouds he would not have been a powerful man.

He fingered the pistol on his lap. Should have been back by now. Wild thoughts of her capture ran though his head. In his head, he ran a possible scenario: the inquisitor uses his years of experience of information retrieval on the Underhive girl. She is strong, but not without the frailties of the flesh. Pain can be very real. What's more, she has no reason to conceal him. She reveals all, the plan, his involvement – the truth is released. He is sentenced to death. His only chance, to escape now? His bags are packed, his shuttle readied. Three more minutes and then he can take flight. He has some guards on his books. he can find out what is happening.

Kassat turned from the window and glanced again at the grate through which he expected her some time ago. Perhaps she had not found the section schematic he had left for her.

He pressed the button on his communication relay.

'Sir?' the voice crackled.

A filth-covered form crashed in through the vent in front of him.

'Never mind,' Kassat said, flicking the switch back.

'Kassat,' she said standing.

She was dripping blood on his Talleran rug. She had been cut on the hands and feet, but the suit had held. Her face was no longer pristine white, but stippled red and black with blood and oil.

'You look quite daemonic, my dear. Are you successful?' he asked.

Liz brought her gun up to face him. It was bent and dented, the sight destroyed. Perhaps it had only a few rounds left.

'What's the matter, my dear?' Kassat said smoothly.

'Just checking,' Liz said with a thin smile, and lowered the pistol.

'You kill him?'

'Oh yes.'

'Excellent.' Kassat cocked the gun silently beneath his desk. 'You've done good work.' He pulled the trigger and she span to the ground.

'Whaaa–?' Liz screamed.

Kassat peered over his desk. She lay there, clutching her leg.

'Weak spot at the right knee. Sorry. Failed to mention it,' Kassat grinned.

'You bastard!' Liz screamed, bringing her gun up towards him and staggering to her feet.

'Liz, Liz, what do you take me for? That won't work in here. I have a suppression emitter dialled in to that weapon. It won't fire.'

Liz pulled the trigger again and again. It clicked over lifelessly. She screamed and threw the gun at him. He nimbly stepped aside, then levelled his own gun at her head.

'Just think of the honours I'll be awarded for capturing the killer of Aldus Harkon, four Ran Lo hunters – and of course the mighty Darlon Ulanti.'

'Who?' Liz groaned.

Kassat stood, pressing the gun barrel to her head, twisting it so that it cleared a patch of pink flesh beneath the white and blood. 'That wasn't Terrak Ran Lo, silly girl. You killed Darlon Ulanti, a man intent on stopping the hunts. On stopping my business.'

'What?'

'Oh, I thought you would have got that one. *I'm* Terrak Ran Lo,' Kassat smiled, bowing his head slightly.

'But–'

'I knew who you were the minute you arrived,' Terrak said, delicately wiping the grime from Liz's face with the gun. 'You can't believe the harm you've done to my business. So many of these whinging nobles are now reluctant to send their useless whelps off on the hunt on account of one rat-loving ganger.'

Now, in the dawning light, Liz could see Kassat change before her. His movements were no longer refined and practised, but harsh and savage. His eyes narrowed and intensified like laser sights. There was no ambiguity any more, just her and Terrak Ran Lo.

'Why didn't you kill me?' she yelled.

'So much to be gained, my dear. Besides, like a cat, I prefer to play with rats before I kill them.'

Faster than he could react, Liz slapped the gun away from her forehead and stepped to one side. Terrak brought his weapon back to face her but now she was standing before him, her leg trembling... and with the inquisitor's bolt pistol in her own hands. Terrak growled.

'Something I picked up along the way... dear,' she hissed.

'You can't win. The Arbites will be here in a few seconds. If you shoot you'll kill us both. Those are explosive shells. The window will break and the air pressure will suck us out.'

'Good,' Liz replied, aiming over his shoulder and pulling the trigger anyway. The glass behind Terrak burst outwards, throwing the room into mayhem. Caskets, papers and hangings were ripped out through the window.

As the air sucked at him, Terrak fired back, catching Liz in the arm. She spun like a swamp lizard and fell to the floor, the debris sweeping her towards the window. She crashed into Terrak's table and a wide gash opened up on her forehead. The Arbites rushed into the room, shouting something that was lost in the howling torrent.

Liz slid towards the howling window frame but managed to grasp the edge. The shattered glass cut deep into her hands. Something was tugging at her legs. Liz looked over her shoulder. Terrak clung to the body suit, legs flailing in the rush, his hands a vice around her ankle. His icy face was shot through with fear.

'Save me!' he screamed.

An Arbiter swept out through the window, knocking Liz's right arm from the sill. Her other hand was being shredded by the remaining shards of glass.

'Liz!' Terrak screamed. 'Pull us in... and I'll give you anything! Anything!'

Liz looked back towards the noble. 'No, Terrak! You will die today!'

She let go of the window and spun around as the gale swept her away from the building. She grabbed Terrak tight around the body and together they sailed out into the air.

'Why? Terrak screamed, his face white with fear.

'A promise to a friend!' Liz screamed back, the air screaming around them, slapping Terrak's coat into her face. 'Doubt your doctors can piece you together... after you land... if they find you!' she yelled.

Liz pushed free of Terrak. She sailed out into the howling rush of air, her arms spread towards the rising sun, its orange rays lighting up soft fissures and rising peaks in the boiling ash clouds below. She smiled as the winds swept her out over this landscape, through its gullies and down into the darkness.

# DESCENT
## by Simon Jowett

### One

'SO THE OLD pus-bag was telling the truth after all.'

Cullis Chan, master of the *Queequeg*, stood at the conning tower rail, sweeping the lantern beam through the tunnel's gloom. Another, larger lantern had been slotted into its mounting at the prow of the boat shortly after they surfaced; now its more powerful beam stabbed through the deeper darkness ahead. Slick rainbows painted the surface of the water as the twin beams played across it, moving steadily from one side of the tunnel to the other, then back.

'Like sliding down a reef-eel's gullet,' muttered Barak, the *Queequeg*'s first mate and self-appointed Voice of Doom, who was standing to the rear of the stubby conning tower, next to the brass columns of the periscope assembly. A man of few words, all of them pessimistic, he was probably the longest-serving member of the crew. Probably, because there wasn't a member of the submersible's crew who could remember a time when he hadn't been first mate. Given his pit-fighter's physique and the almost inhuman level of violence of which he was capable, Chan couldn't imagine that anyone would ever be stupid enough to challenge him for the post.

Tilting the lantern in its U-shaped mount, Chan ran the beam up one side of the tunnel's gentle curve, across the low dome of its roof.

'It's too regular to be natural,' he said quietly. 'Must've been drilled centuries ago. Virad said the plans he saw dated back to the Great Crusade.'

'"Great Crusade" my puckered end!' Barak spat sourly. 'That treacherous old–'

A whistle from the communication pipe cut across his words. Barak flipped open the hinged cover and bent to listen.

'About time!' he barked into the pipe. 'And make sure the batteries are charging. We don't know when we'll have to duck and run.'

As he snapped the cover back into place, a violent shudder ran the length of the vessel, followed by a volley of congested explosions from the stern as the *Queequeg's* surface engines coughed into life and expelled whatever Sump matter had collected in their exhaust tubes while submerged. Most of this voyage had been spent running as deep as possible to avoid the possibility of being followed, relying on the echo sounder to avoid collisions and only surfacing when the air inside the vessel had become too clogged and rancid to tolerate. As a result, the batteries that powered the ship while submerged were dangerously low on charge.

Unconsciously, Chan adjusted his balance as the ship wallowed, then settled and moved forward at greater speed, the sudden lurch an indication of how depleted the batteries had become.

'Time we unlashed the skiffs,' Chan said.

Now they had surfaced, the crew would be expecting something to happen. They had been confined within the long, narrow teardrop of the *Queequeg's* hull for far longer than was usual – not hunting, just hiding from those who would rob them of the information that had brought them this far. They knew this voyage promised the richest pickings of their lives and, as time had passed beneath the water of the Sump, anticipation had begun to turn into impatience. Chan wasn't the first master of this vessel, and he knew that at least one of his predecessors had been tossed overboard because of the crew's dissatisfaction with their takings under his command. As ever, Barak had the final say over his replacement, just as he had had over Chan's assumption of the captaincy when Waylan Gaff was reduced to a smear of organic slurry by the venom of a raft spider large enough to rival the mythical White Mares of Varan.

'The skiffs? Why? We don't even know what's at the end of this tunnel.' Barak had stepped over the open hatch in the conning tower deck and now stood beside Chan at the rail. He was peering ahead, as if trying to see beyond the range of the prow lantern. 'Could be we just find another shaft, this time heading straight down. I wouldn't be surprised if Virad gave us directions to hell – anything to get us off his back.'

'If he did, he'll be the first person to greet us when we arrive.' Chan smiled up at the puzzled look on Barak's face. 'After he handed over the maps and bearings, I had Bryll slip a little extra something into his drink.'

Like all ratskins, One-Eye Bryll, the *Queequeg*'s most experienced harpooner, revered the venom of the raft spiders as sacred, a source of ecstatic visions to their hybrid kind and of death to all others. He had been sitting slumped in a corner of the ramshackle drinking hole, a half-empty jug of gutrot clutched loosely in one hand, before either Chan or Naz Virad, the broken-down information broker, arrived for their meeting. After Chan had left, taking Virad's oilskin chart-case with him, Bryll had hauled himself to his feet and stumbled unsteadily in the direction of the bar. One more drunken ratskin wouldn't attract anyone's attention in this place. Bryll had lurched against a group of Sump dredgers, who were arguing over whether to accept the price they had been offered for their latest haul. He was rewarded by several curses and a kick, which propelled him towards Virad's booth. Catching himself before he sprawled full-length across the pitch-blackened ironwood of the table, he had slurred an apology, righted himself and stumbled away, this time heading for the door. Virad showed no sign of having seen or heard him. As he left the bar, Bryll glanced back to see Virad lift his tankard and drain its contents – ale and the vial of spider venom Bryll had emptied into it.

'I was halfway to the wharf when he started screaming. It sounded like the Arch-Zealot had come for his soul. That or he'd just caught a look at Bryll's wife.'

Barak grunted – the closest he ever came to expressing amusement – and moved back to the communication tube.

Flipping open its lid again, he barked out another order to those below. Seconds later, the fore and aft hatches clanged open. The crews of the hunting skiffs moved with practised speed along the slick, sloping hull of the submersible, towards the narrow five-man skiffs that were secured, keel-up, by bolts and spider-gut lines, like sharp-edged metal blisters on the *Queequeg's* outer skin.

Working more by touch and memory than by sight, the almost total blackness of the tunnel lightened only by the backwash from the prow and tower lanterns, the skiff crews removed the bolts and loosened the hawsers. Five soft splashes sounded in quick succession as the skiffs were tipped over the side, landing in the thick Sump water right side up, now tethered to their mother ship by a single line. Their crews swarmed aboard them, checking their benzene-powered outboard motors and fitting harpoon guns into their binnacle mounts. Each boat's ratskin harpooner intoned a ritual invocation to the mysterious gods of the Sump and the hunt, their monotonous chanting punctuated by the cries of 'Ready!' from each skiff's leading hand.

'What are you going to buy with your share, Barak?' Chan asked vaguely. The prospect of an imminent hunt always prompted him to think ahead, past the danger, to the profit on the other side. 'A ship of your own? If Virad's information is only half-right, we should all come out of this with enough to buy a fleet each.'

'The *Queequeg's* all the ship I need,' the first mate growled in reply, then leant over the tower rail to bellow orders to the skiff crews. A less confident man than Chan might detect a threat in Barak's words. A reminder that, on this ship, captains were expendable, that Barak always had the last say in their appointment and, without his support, they wouldn't last long past the first unsuccessful hunt under their command. And he would be right. Chan was under no illusion about who was the true master of the *Queequeg*. He knew that his role was to gather information, to point the ship towards its next quarry – be it spider, human or some incomprehensible technological relic from an earlier age – and let Barak and his crew do the rest. All that mattered was the reliability of the information and the size of the profit to be earned.

And the information he had taken with him from his last meeting with Virad promised riches that would make the Emperor blush.

'Light! Dead ahead!' Roark called back from his post at the prow lantern. Chan peered ahead. A faint, nacreous glow was visible, almost at the limits of vision.

'Some other skag get there before us?' Barak had joined Chan at the front of the conning tower. 'Maybe Virad made more than one copy of the charts.'

'No. He knew what I'd do to him if he did that.' Chan blinked, then tried to focus more tightly on the light. It was still too far away to make out whether it came from a single source.

'You did that to him anyway!' Barak snorted, as if pleased to have found something else to be pessimistic about. 'Maybe he decided to get his revenge in early.'

'That's glow-moss, I'm sure of it.' Chan hoped that he sounded as confident as a captain should. He turned to face the first mate. 'Full ahead, Master Barak. Tell those rats in the engine room to push it to the red line.'

Barak reached once more for the communication tube.

'And Barak…'

'Cap'n?'

'Break out the auto-cannon and shotguns. Just in case.'

The pounding rhythm of the engines echoed back from the tunnel walls and shook the deck beneath Chan's feet. The ship surged forward, the still-tethered skiffs dancing in its wake, as if the *Queequeg* was a vast and ancient spider, and they, all five of their harpoons having struck home, were riding it down, waiting for it to tire before moving in to deliver the killing stroke.

With every beat of the engine, both the light ahead and Chan's confidence grew. The luminescence was too diffuse to come from another ship's lantern. It filled the tunnel ahead, swallowing the beam that reached out from the *Queequeg*'s prow. Chan called for Virad's charts to be passed up to him. He checked and re-checked every bearing, sounding and hastily-copied extract from the log of the last ship to pass this way, decades, possibly centuries before. Virad had claimed access to a forgotten Imperial archive, but that old liar would say anything if he thought it might save his life. And, since he'd sold details of the *Queequeg*'s last voyage to not one but two sets of would-be pirates, only to see the ship return, still in the hands of its original crew, he knew his life was in desperate need of saving.

'SPIDERS.'

The word was barely recognisable. Virad's voice sounded strangled, high-pitched and fearful.

The captain sat across the table from him, in the booth he had used as an office for as long as anybody could remember, buying and selling information, settling his percentage of any salvage rights. Virad had never liked Chan. He smiled too much, like many of the merchants he had known in his younger, wealthier days. They would smile, pat you on the back and buy you a drink – then stab you in the back, relieve you of your merchandise and hand you over to the Judges on some trumped-up charge. Virad still bore the A-shaped brand of the Adeptus Arbites on his left shoulder, albeit faded and blue now with age. It was a sign to all who saw it that he had spent time on one of their correction gangs, shackled together with other offenders and set to work clearing debris from the latest hivequake, wading unprotected through the effluent from ruptured conduits and fighting off giant rats and milliasaurs with pick and shovel. Ever since then, he had been wary of men who smiled too much.

But Chan wasn't smiling now. His right eye was swollen shut and half of his right ear was missing. Virad imagined he could see bite marks on the bruised flesh of his cheek and neck. Human bite marks. There were fresh scorch marks on his heavy spider-pelt jacket as well, as if a volley of las-fire had recently come much too close for comfort.

*Not close enough,* Virad decided.

'I don't see any spiders in here,' Chan hissed, keeping his voice low. 'Just a treacherous old has-been who tried to sell me, my ship and my crew to the highest bidder. Now, are you going to come quietly or am I going to have use this?' He opened his jacket far enough to reveal the knurled grip of the laspistol holstered across one side of his chest.

'F-fire that in here, you'd never make it out alive,' Virad stammered.

'You really think anybody in here'd want to take a shot for you?' A thin smile lifted the corners of Chan's mouth. 'Even if they did, you'd be past caring.'

'Just business, that's all it was,' Virad decided to change the subject. 'Look… I owed some people. I– I want to thank you for getting them off my back.'

Chan's smile grew, as if he was actually enjoying Virad's stumbling attempt to talk his way out of the slow, painful death the *Queequeg*'s crew had planned for him.

'Oh, it was our pleasure,' he replied, his voice dripping with irony. 'Now you owe us – in blood.'

'I… I can do better than that.' Virad's voice cracked, jumped to an even higher pitch. 'I can give you spiders. More than you ever dreamed of…'

'We can find spiders without your help,' Chan cut across Virad's words. His smile had faded, his patience exhausted. 'Get on your feet. You're coming with me.'

'No!' Virad's sudden cry caused several of the dive's other occupants to turn, hands unconsciously twitching towards their weapons. Upon seeing the tableau in the booth, however, they turned back. A business deal gone sour – nothing new in this part of the Underhive.

Virad realised that Chan was right. If he drilled Virad where he sat, all anyone would do was complain to the bar owner about the smell of over-cooked meat.

'Wait!' Virad raised his hands in abject surrender. 'Listen. The information I have could set you up for life. Your crew as well. I'm not just talking about one or two spiders, or even a nest. I'm talking about a nursery – a hundred spiders, maybe more, all laying their eggs in one place!'

'I'm too old for bedtime stories.' Chan sounded impatient, dismissive, but Virad, who had spent his life listening not just to what people said, but how they said it, knew that he had just extended his life expectancy by a few more minutes at least. Chan was the master of the *Queequeg*, the most extraordinary vessel ever to sail the waters of the Sump, but he was just another freebooter and all freebooters were interested in only one thing: profit.

'It's true! I've got the charts and bearings. Been under Imperial Seal for centuries. But I knew someone who knew someone who wanted something I could provide and…'

Something in Chan's expression made him falter. Time was running out.

'L-like I said, hundreds of spiders, thousands of eggs. All in one place. I don't know why – maybe this is a more sociable kind of spider. Anyway, inside each egg is a baby spider, too young to defend itself. Thousands of baby spiders. Tens of thousands of eyes. Sure, they won't be a big as a grown spiders' eyes, but with that many of them, who cares? Captain's share of that haul would make you the richest man in the Underhive. Hell, you could buy the Underhive!'

Virad paused.

For what seemed like forever, Chan said nothing.

'Of course, you don't happen to have these charts with you,' he said at last, his tone flat, expressionless.

'Well, no. They're way too valuable. I always wanted to put together a crew of my own, but…'

'But you can get them easily enough. Bring them here.'

'Yes! I could be back here in an hour, maybe less.' The sense of relief that rushed through him was so great that when it came time to stand, to leave the bar, Virad feared his legs would be unable to carry him. 'I swear, you won't regret this.'

'You'll be watched. Get clever, try to run and, charts or no charts, it'll be your head that's delivered to me.'

'I WAS RIGHT,' Barak growled, the light from the glow-moss painting his face with a sickly greenish tint. 'Virad sent us to hell.'

Chan looked out across the glass-flat pool into which they had emerged. The size of a small quay, it might almost have been carved out of the rock for exactly that purpose. An uneven ledge ran around the half of its circumference that faced the tunnel entrance, leading back into inky shadows. Rust-red glow-moss coated the ragged dome of the stalactite-heavy ceiling, grown so dense in places that it hung down in iridescent strips like threadbare chandeliers.

'If you're a spider, maybe,' Chan said, indicating one of the inert carcasses that floated a short way off the starboard bow. There were nine of them, floating like massive, grey-pelted islands in the pool. Judging by what was visible above the surface, each one would have taken all five of the *Queequeg*'s skiffs to bring it down, aided by a volley from the submersible's auto-cannon. Nowhere in the log fragments that Virad had handed over along with the charts had there been any mention of fully-grown spiders acting as guardians of the nursery – although, had he been thinking beyond the vast wealth on offer, Chan should have expected it. Maybe Barak was right. Perhaps Virad, assuming that Chan would kill him anyway, had left any such warning notes in their hiding place, hoping to send him and his crew to their doom.

But something had intervened to frustrate Virad's plan. Each of the floating corpses exhibited massive wounds, tears in their pelts and the tough tissue beneath, exposing ruptured organs or else forming hollows into which a glutinous ichor of blood and venom had collected and begun to coagulate. Roark, the harpooner aboard the skiff Chan had ordered to take a closer look at the nearest of the corpses, had taken one sniff of the mixture and recoiled, babbling wildly about sacrilege and corruption. He had even refused to harvest the beast's eyes, leaving the job to the rest of the skiff's crew. Every other harpooner, even the normally strong-minded Bryll, had done likewise as the other skiffs moved among the submerged carcasses, their non-ratskin crew members carving the fist-sized gems from the spiders' eye sockets.

'Whatever did this could still be here,' Barak replied, looking resolutely on the dark side.

'We don't know that,' reasoned Chan. 'How do we know that they didn't do this to themselves? Perhaps there was some kind of dispute over whose egg sacs got pride of place.'

Barak stared at him as if unsure whether or not he was joking, then waved a hand in the direction of the ledge. Looking past him, Chan noted that Jostin's skiff had almost reached the ledge, towards which he had directed them. He also noted that Bryll, Jostin's harpooner, whom he had seen stand up and roar his defiance into the jaws of living spiders at least as large as those that floated inertly around them now, had retreated to the rear of the boat.

'And that's why there isn't an egg sac left whole?' Barak asked. The wall that curved up over the water's edge was draped with the tattered remains of more egg sacs than it was possible to count from this distance. The milky white skins of the sacs hung flaccidly, like punctured bladders and ragged festival banners, their contents reduced to streaks and smears on the rock all around them.

Chan turned his gaze back to the first mate. There had been an edge in his voice that Chan hadn't heard there before: unsettled, almost fearful. If this place was having such an effect on the normally stolid Barak, Chan could be sure that the rest of the crew were feeling it too.

*Time to calm things down,* he decided. *Take control, gather what booty we can and get out of here.*

'Look,' he said out loud. 'I'm no expert on the child-rearing habits of raft spiders. We came here to kill them, didn't we? Well, it looks like they saved us the trouble. The eyes from these beasts alone are double a normal year's takings. Let Jostin and his men take a quick look on the ledge – there might yet be some young ones over there with eyes worth having. Call back the other skiffs, get them lashed down. We can be under way as soon as Jostin's had his look around. You know as well as I do: nothing calms the nerves like a share from a good haul.'

The first volley of gunfire from the ledge was followed by a chorus of alarmed shouts and the splash of a body hitting the water. There were more shouts, but these were swallowed by the combined reports of the landing party's shotguns.

With a muttered oath, Barak cupped his hands to his mouth and began bellowing orders to the other skiffs to move in on the ledge and support Jostin's crew. Chan directed his attention to the source of the sudden confusion, but couldn't make out what was going on. Three of Jostin's crew stood on the ledge, firing wildly into the shadows; Bryll was still aboard the skiff, not showing any sign of wanting to climb ashore. The fifth member of the skiff's crew was nowhere to be seen – Chan could only assume that he was in the water and therefore beyond help. The noxious chemicals beneath the pool's faintly iridescent surface would already be eating through the crewman, rendering his body back to its component parts. Whether he had been pushed or had merely missed his footing was irrelevant – this expedition had claimed its first casualty.

Chan lifted the macro-glasses that hung on a leather thong around his neck. Pressing the twin cylinders to his eyes he spun the knurled brass wheel set between them and the scene on the ledge jumped into sharp focus. He saw the three crewmen, two of whom were still firing while the third – Jostin – was digging in the pocket of his jerkin for fresh shells. Shifting his gaze slightly, he tried to detect some sign of who or what it was they were firing at. At first all he saw were shadows, then a hulking figure stepped into view. It appeared to be human, wearing armour that gave its arms and shoulders an over-developed, ape-like outline. A shotgun blast hit it in the shoulder, the impact causing it to take a step back and flex both arms, as if to check for damage, before continuing its progress towards the crewmen.

It wasn't alone. Other figures stepped into the light: two more that shared the heavy-set aspect of the first and another pair that were more lightly armoured, but no less menacing. One was armed with a sword and a shield that flashed with reflected light; the other appeared to possess long, tapering claws instead of hands. This last figure took a single step, then leapt to avoid a volley of gunfire, which passed harmlessly beneath it. Too high, too fast to be merely human, the sight made Chan think of the sudden leaps he had seen spiders make when surprised in their lair. The moment its feet touched down, it flung one arm forwards as if hurling a projectile at the crewmen, who had begun to retreat towards the lip of the ledge. Chan saw nothing leave the figure's hand but, switching his attention back to the retreating crewmen, he saw one of them drop his shotgun, arms pinioned as if by some invisible force, before being jerked from his feet and dragged, kicking and screaming, towards the figure.

By now, the sword-wielding attacker had advanced ahead of its hulking comrades. Fending off a volley from Jostin's rifle with its shimmering shield, it sliced through the gun's twin barrels with a single downward sweep of its sword. Jostin raised the truncated shotgun in an attempt to club his attacker with its butt, but was grasped around the throat by one of the heavy-set creatures and lifted off his feet.

At that moment, Chan knew there was only one thing to do.

'Barak, call the skiffs back. Now!' he shouted at the first mate, then leant over the rail to address the crew of the autocannon that had been brought topside and fixed in its mounting mid-way between the prow and the conning tower. 'Aim for the ledge!' he ordered. 'Push those bastards back and give us time to secure the skiffs!'

The skiffs were already executing tight turns in response to Barak's shouted orders when the autocannon opened up, its deep throaty coughs followed by the explosive impacts of its shells on the rock above the ledge. Adjusting their aim, the gun crew fired again, this time throwing up a curtain of rock shards from the ledge in front of the advancing creatures. Eyes once again pressed to the macro-glasses, Chan was surprised to see the creature, one of whose over-sized hands was clenched around Jostin's throat, turn as if to shield the struggling crewman from the rain of shrapnel kicked up by the autocannon's second volley. The razor-sharp shards of stone ricocheted off the plate armour covering its back.

The third crewman left on the ledge, faced by the other two hulking creatures, which were advancing on him from either side, obviously decided to follow the skiffs' example. Dropping his shotgun, he took a running leap off the ledge in the direction of the landing party's skiff – only to discover that Bryll had already gunned the boat away from its temporary mooring. He hit the water, disappeared beneath its surface with a splash. A second or two later he reappeared, flailing uselessly, mouth open but his shouts drowned out by the autocannon's roar, before sinking once again.

The *Queequeg's* hull rang as each skiff returned at speed to their mother ship. Unconsciously, Chan counted the impacts, calculating how long the crews would take to secure the boats and how quickly the submersible could be underway. Only the landing party's skiff remained, powering across the water towards them, Bryll crouching low in the stern as the autocannon shells pounded over his head.

The figures on the ledge had retreated under the barrage from the autocannons. They stood on the threshold of the shadows as if frustrated by the flight of their last potential victim. Bryll was halfway between the ledge and the *Queequeg*. Chan could tell by the shouts that came from the aft deck that the last of the skiffs had been secured, their crews tumbling through the aft hatch. Barak was barking orders to the engine room; the idle hum of the engines changed, becoming heavier, more insistent, as if impatient to be away from this place.

'Keep them pinned until we're underway!' Chan shouted down to the autocannon crew. 'I don't want to find out whether any of those monsters can swim!' Chan would take the *Queequeg* out of the grotto at flank speed, then dive soon after entering the tunnel. If any of the attackers were able to follow, by the time they reached the tunnel's mouth it would seem that the submersible had vanished.

Then he saw it, arching upwards from the ledge like a jet-black bird of prey. Jet-black except for its wings: stiff, sharp-angled pinions that shone with a shifting iridescent blur of colours, mirroring the sheen on the water below. Its fast, rising trajectory took it over the angle of the autocannon barrage, almost to the glowing, moss-hung roof – and then down, arrow-straight, towards a point roughly midway between the ledge and the *Queequeg*. Straight at Bryll's skiff.

'Bryll! Evasive!' Barak had seen it too and was bellowing a warning to the harpooner. Bryll, either deafened by the noise of the autocannon, or simply too intent upon reaching the *Queequeg* to register the first mate's warning, showed no sign of having heard. He kept the skiff on its original course, making no attempt to throw the airborne menace off his tail. Chan doubted that the ratskin was even aware of the armoured raptor that was bearing down upon him.

Watching through the macro-glasses, tracking the metal-winged apparition as if it were merely some interesting new avian species, Chan saw its wings shift, the spear-pointed sections of each wing parting to slow its descent. Mere heartbeats before impact, its body swung down towards the vertical, arms and legs reaching out like the finger-like pseudo-limbs of a ripperjack, moments before fastening around the head of its prey.

Bryll was plucked from the speeding skiff like a true rat, caught by an airborne predator before it could reach the safety of its lair. Too surprised to even cry out, he was carried upwards, as the skiff slewed drunkenly off-course, heading for a collision with the grotto wall while his captor executed a combined roll and turn that dazzled Chan with its elegance and careless ease. He noticed idly that the backs of the creature's wings were coloured solid black, as if in readiness to melt into the shadows from which it had come.

The sudden roar of a bolt pistol next to him on the conning tower jolted Chan from his fugue state. Barak was pumping bolt after bolt into the air, apparently heedless of the fact that, should he bring the creature down, he would also doom Bryll to a corrosive death in the pool's shimmering, deadly water. Perhaps he didn't care. Perhaps all he cared for was to exact some kind of revenge upon the monstrosity that had taken a crewman who had served aboard the *Queequeg* almost as long as him.

Chan, however, cared for something else: escape. Stepping to the communications tube, he screamed the order to submerge, to be answered, almost immediately, by the high-pitched whistle of air venting from the dive tanks.

Taking their cue from the sound, the autocannon crew ceased firing, unpinned the weapon from its mount and hurried below decks. They were followed by the prow lookout, who slammed the forward hatch shut behind him.

Barak was still firing uselessly after Bryll's winged captor, which avoided the bolt pistol's shells with almost contemptuous ease, sliding through the air in a zigzagging evasive pattern with flick after delicate flick of its wings.

'Barak, get below!' Chan shouted but the glassy-eyed first mate showed no sign of having heard him. The sound of the venting tanks had changed from a whistle to a thick bubbling as the ship began to submerge; in a matter of seconds, the Sump water would wash over the conning tower rail.

'I said get below! Bryll's gone! We're leaving!' Chan repeated the order and backed it up by thumping Barak on the shoulder. The first mate turned, his face a grimacing mixture of murderous rage and stark terror. He stared at Chan for a moment, during which time the master of the *Queequeg* wondered if he might receive Barak's next bolt in his gut, then blinked, nodded quickly, holstered his weapon and dropped through the conning tower hatch. Chan allowed himself a moment of relief at having been spared the sight of his own intestines smeared across the periscope assembly, then followed Barak inside, slamming the hatch shut above him.

Chan had never felt so glad to feel the familiar melange of old sweat and engine oil coat the back of his throat. It meant he was wrapped within the cramped metal cocoon of the *Queequeg*, out of sight of their attackers, soon to be beyond their reach, protected by the waters of the corrosive sea that would lead them home.

Chan issued orders to the helmsman and the operator of the ping-board, the brass-coiled echo-sounding device whose signals, transmitted from the antennae arrayed around the ship's mid-line to the jug-shaped apparatus clamped to the operator's ears, would guide them back into the tunnel mouth and from there, through the tunnel's twists and turns, past the reefs and sudden changes in its width and depth, to the open Sump. Then, after shouting a mixture of threats and encouragement to the engine room via another communication tube, he stepped up to the periscope.

As a crewman cranked the handle set into the rear of the periscope assembly and the viewing glass rose to eye-level, Chan glanced across at Barak. The first mate leaned heavily against the curved hull, still glassy-eyed, as if unable or unwilling to acknowledge what he had seen. Chan knew that every crewman who had been aboard the other skiffs would share at least a portion of Barak's horror. Jostin, Bryll and the others would be missed but, once the sparkling, multi-faceted eyes they had torn from the floating corpses had been sold and the profits divided among the crew, Chan knew that the money would work its magic upon their memories. The day's events, the loss of their comrades would be told and re-told, gradually becoming one more legend to add to the multitude of legends that formed the *Queequeg*'s reputation among the other Sump-farers. There would be glasses raised in toast to the dead, many glasses. And there'd be women, Chan promised himself. Lots of women.

The view through the cracked eyepiece moved sideways as Chan scanned the surface for any sign of the armour-clad enemy. Nothing. The ledge was empty, the spider-corpses floated as before, receding as the submersible sped towards the tunnel mouth. Satisfied, he flipped the handles up against the periscope tube and motioned for it to be lowered. He was about to say something reassuring to the control room crew when Stavek, the ping-board operator, called out:

'Contacts aft, moving in fast!' He turned, the nest of cables that connected his earphones to the board swinging around his shoulders like a particularly luxuriant head of hair. 'And there's something else. It sounds like… like insects.'

The tone of Stavek's voice and his puzzled expression showed that he was aware of how ludicrous the last part of his report would sound. He held one earphone away from his head and invited Chan to listen.

Chan bent down, placed an ear against the grill that ran across the top of the metal cup… and heard it too. A high-pitched jumble of insectile clicks, punctuated by a sudden squeak or wave of what sounded like white noise from an untuned radio receiver. Stavek was right to compare it to the noise made by a large number of insects. Chan had heard a similar sound when a swarm of steel locusts had descended upon the settlement of Carter's Crag, his childhood home, and stripped every piece of metal from roof and wall, causing over half the settlement's buildings to collapse. But there was something else about it, something unnatural. Something mechanical. Chan suddenly felt as if he was overhearing a high-speed conversation going on between several piece of delicate machinery.

'Evasive manoeuvres!' Chan ordered.

Then they heard it: a rhythmic banging, transmitted through the dense metal of the hull. Then another, emanating from a different part of the ship's outer skin. Then another. Something was out there.

Something that wanted in.

## Two

'Times of strife are the proving ground of the Redemption.'

The words of Pastor Zydo's last sermon rang in Poldar's memory as his autogun chattered and bucked in his hands. Three of the four rag-wearing scavvies who had jumped down from the wagon to avoid the cleansing fire of the flamer that had washed over their transport danced an absurd jig, blood erupting from the stinking folds of their clothes, before falling in separate ragged heaps. The fourth, somehow unscathed, continued to run along the downward slope of the cinder track, until he was punched sideways by the impact of a shell from Hastor's stub gun. Hastor appeared around the front of the ancient tractor that had been pulling the wagon down the track until a direct hit from Malec's grenade launcher had turned its wheezing, arthritic engine into just so much slag and signalled the beginning of the attack.

Poldar raised a hand in acknowledgement of Hastor's marksmanship. The latter, breaking open his weapon and inserting another shell, smiled in reply, his lopsided grin visible beneath the ornate fringe of his mask, then disappeared back around the other side of the tractor.

'Times of war and civil unrest,' Zydo had addressed the assembled gangers in a warehouse on one of the lower levels of House Cawdor's industrial holdings. 'At times such as these, each man must look into his heart and make a choice: does he stand with the Redemption, with the manifest destiny of mankind as decreed by our One High Lord, the Emperor of Man. Or does he side with the darkness that is all around us, and which threatens to engulf us all?'

Gangers in various parts of the warehouse shouted their answers, every one the same: 'Redemption!'

'I am here to tell you that the Last Days are all but upon us. The Underhive is rife with rumours of yet another manifestation of the sin and corruption in which all but the faithful wallow. Creatures that walk like men, but speak with the tongues of the insect and the machine. Once human, they have taken all that is inhuman into their hearts, their very souls, in preparation for the apocalypse, the final fire, which shall surely soon be upon us!

'These creatures skulk among the refuse of the hive bottom, biding their time, gathering their forces. Now they are but few, but they stalk the dark between the settlements, the waste hollows and slag plains, seeking converts. They must be denied!

'All who are unholy, whose lost souls might provide a welcome to the new darkness that would use them to its own ends must be saved. Must be cleansed by bolter, sword and fire!'

'Redemption! Redemption!' The warehouse rang to the gangers' chant. Poldar punched the air with his fist, over and over. From his makeshift pulpit atop a container that bore the marks of House Cawdor and the Merchants' Guild, Zydo surveyed the sea of raised fists. He nodded in satisfaction, then raised his own hand for quiet.

'Go forth and seek your destiny, the destiny of Man. You are touched by the fire of Redemption. You are instruments of its cleansing touch. You are blessed!'

'You are blessed!'

Poldar remembered the pastor's final benediction as he moved along the length of the wagon, heading towards its rear, alert for any other scavvies who might have escaped the fire. Ahead of him, a short way up the cinder slope, stood the second tractor, forced to a stop by the destruction of the vehicle which had preceded it down the track. The tractor driver had been armed, as were several of the wagon's pox-faced passengers. The driver had already been reduced to a bleeding, broken-stringed marionette, his pistol clutched in a dead man's grasp. Weapons' fire from the wagon's passengers, however, had forced Poldar's brothers to pause in their attack, find cover and return fire.

By the time he reached the end of the first wagon, Poldar was sweating heavily under his cowl, due to the intense heat from the burning bodies of the wagon's passengers – the only fitting end for all scavvies, whether or not they had embraced the new darkness of which the pastor had spoken.

The sickly odour of roasting flesh descended on Poldar in a wave, causing him to gag. Why didn't Malec pump a grenade or two into the midst of the remaining scavvies, he wondered as he spat in a useless attempt to rid himself of the heavy, oily taste? Peering around the end of the first wagon, he saw why: Malec lay in open ground, his face and mask torn away by a scavvy's bullet. His grenade launcher lay a few feet from him.

Poldar swore an oath to the Arch-Zealot and opened fire on the second wagon. His first round caught a woman high in the back, exiting in a spray of blood and bone from her chest. Some final nervous impulse caused her to arch up and over the side of the wagon. As she fell, a rag-wrapped bundle tumbled from her grasp. It hit the ground with a high-pitched squeal, which thickened into an unmistakable ululating wail: a child, another of its mother's twisted, mutant kind.

Poldar ignored the child. Too small and harmless to be worth a bullet, he would come looking for it after the battle was won. He continued to pump rounds into the wagon, hoping to draw the fire of some of its armed occupants and give his comrades a chance to move in, to bring the flamer into range.

The dull concussive thump of the flamer's fuel tanks exploding took everyone by surprise. In the momentary lull in the weapons' fire, Nerran's screams were clearly audible, almost as high-pitched as those of the baby that still lay beside one of the tractor's wheels. Without realising it, Poldar had advanced into the gap between the first and second wagons. By simply turning his head, he was afforded a clear view of Nerran as he staggered forward, still screaming, completely engulfed in the tanks' volatile, flaming liquid. The wretch managed three or four steps before his legs buckled and he fell forward, still burning, but silent.

Poldar's first thought was that the flamer had malfunctioned. The gunfire that kicked up ash all around the sheltering gangers changed his mind. Tearing his gaze from the still-twitching form of Nerran, he saw them racing down the slope of the slag heap that rose at the gangers' backs, one of the succession of such heaps that loomed over both sides of the track. Some of Poldar's brothers shifted their positions behind the smaller heaps of ash and clinker that they had been using as cover from the scavvies' bullets and returned fire. Their attackers, however, had the advantage. They had already found their range and were moving too fast for the gangers to draw an accurate bead on them. They were, in fact, doing to the gangers exactly what the gangers had done to the two-vehicle convoy – and were showing just as much mercy.

What felt like a punch in the side of the neck caught Poldar by surprise. He stumbled sideways, legs suddenly unsteady, only to collide with the rear of the first wagon and bounce drunkenly back. One knee gave way and he sprawled in the cinders.

Struggling into a semi-recumbent position on the granular surface of the track, he shucked one of his gauntlets and pressed his bare hand to his neck. It could only have been a glancing hit, perhaps from a ricochet, but it had opened something vital. Hot blood pumped between his fingers, painting the ground with broad strokes.

More confused than fearful, Poldar noted absently that his legs had gone cold and numb, while his chest seemed to have caught fire. Blinking away the mist that now edged his vision, he looked again at the firefight that was taking place at the edge of the track. Caught in a crossfire between the ambushers and the scavvies in the wagon which, though only a couple of paces from where Poldar lay, might as well have been parked on one of the highest levels of the Spire, the gangers were being cut to pieces. Horror, despair, righteous anger – Poldar knew he should feel something as he watched Hastor, the last of his comrades, cut down. He just didn't seem to have the energy.

As his brothers' killers reached the now silent ganger positions, Poldar watched as they searched the bodies, collecting guns and ammo packs. There looked to be ten of them: Underhivers carrying autoguns, bandoleers slung across their chests. They wore a motley of various kinds of protective gear, probably scavenged from the industrial levels – hard hats, anti-splash jackets and leg-guards, metal-tipped work boots – but no gang colours. Just a bunch of freelancers, then, out for what they could get.

No. Not ten. Eleven. Poldar hadn't seen this figure during the attack. Taller than the others, broader in the shoulder, evidently the product of a more comfortable upbringing than was the norm in the Underhive. He carried a bolter, an unusual and expensive piece of equipment for an unaffiliated freebooter to possess, and was dressed differently, too.

Poldar's vision swam. The fire in his chest had burned out. Blinking rapidly, he regained focus for a brief moment, during which he saw, with almost unnatural clarity that, beneath the bandoleers slung across his shoulders and the cartridge belt cinched about his waist, this last figure wore the tattered but still unmistakable remnants of a Redemptionist's robes.

A Redemptionist? Impossible! The House of Cawdor was the House of the Redemption. No acolyte of the Arch-Zealot would lead an attack on a Cawdor gang!

Then he heard it. The victorious freebooters were singing – no chanting – something. A single word, a name perhaps: Vex.

The word meant nothing to Poldar and he was much too tired to give it any more thought. He slumped onto his back and discovered that someone was standing over him. A scavvy, its face pockmarked and dotted with sores. A scavvy with a gun.

Staring into the barrel of the scavvy's weapon, the darkness seemed to rush towards him. From somewhere far away, he heard again the words of Pastor Zygo: 'You are blessed.'

*Oh*, Poldar thought. *Really?*

VEX SPUN ROUND at the sound of the single gunshot, senses alert to another possible threat, bolter braced in both hands. In the gap between the burnt-out wagon and the tractor that had escaped the attentions of the gangers' flamer stood a young scavvy woman, holding what looked like an antique single-shot rifle. The rifle was angled down at the headless body of another ganger. The woman threw the gun aside, then moved behind the tractor. Seconds later she reappeared, cradling a ragged bundle in her arms. A faint exhausted mewling came from among the rags.

'Someone exacting a little righteous vengeance, pastor.' Slant-Eyed Micc stood beside him, stuffing scavenged autogun cartridges into the pouches of his bandoleer.

'Vengeance is a sin,' Vex replied as he lowered his bolter. Several other scavvies gathered around the young woman, cooing over the child in her arms as if it was a talisman, a good luck charm or just some vague promise for the future.

'But a holy sin, surely,' Micc smiled, his unevenly-set eyes and crooked mouth giving the impression that his features were all crowding to one side of his face, 'when one is avenging an evil deed?'

'Has the Crusade issued some new edict of which I am unaware?' Vex asked.

'You mean, since the one that called for the delivery of your still-beating heart to the dinner table of the Arch-Zealot? I don't think so.'

'At least it stopped that chanting. The last thing we need is to advertise our location.' Vex paused, then added: ' Don't the men know that it makes me uncomfortable?'

'Hey, I've told them,' Micc replied, mock-defensively. 'Even offered an alternative. They pointed out that shouting "Micc" is nowhere near as inspiring as shouting "Vex". And besides, I'm nobody's saviour.'

'Don't you start with that nonsense.' Vex slung his bolter over one shoulder, then scanned the slag dune on either side of the track. 'Post lookouts and get the rest to help shift that wreck.' He indicated the burnt-out wagon and tractor. 'We should already be on our way. Emperor knows how many other gangs are lurking round here, looking for blood.'

'Let 'em come,' Micc commented before leaving Vex's side. 'We'll give 'em blood. It'll be their blood, sure, but who can tell the difference when it's running all over the floor?'

IT WAS A story Vex had heard countless times before, but with greater frequency over the last few months: Redemptionists sweeping through a sector, armed to the teeth and psychotic with self-righteous anger, backed-up by an army of Cawdor foot soldiers. Rich or poor, human, ratskin or scavvy – no one was spared.

Ironically, it was the scavvies' place at the bottom of Underhive society that saved them. Living in a small tent ghetto in the shadow of a forest of pipes leading from the sector's waste treatment complex, they heard the sounds of the massacre before it reached them. Striking their tents and gathering their belongs, they climbed aboard the wagons and headed off, descending through a maze of tunnels and access ramps until they reached the slag dunes.

'The gangers came at us out of nowhere,' the scavvy named Neesa told Vex as she walked with him ahead of the wheezing tractor. Her voice was coarse, phlegmy, as if the sores that covered her skin also afflicted her inner surfaces. She was still carrying the child – her sister's, she had explained when he suggested that she let someone else carry it for a while. Her fellow refugees were riding in the wagon, apart from those who were already armed or had scavenged weapons from the dead gangers; these had joined forces with Vex's men, either scouting ahead or covering the rear.

'They probably weren't part of the force that attacked your sector,' commented Micc, who was striding along beside them both, autogun carried casually in the crook of one arm. 'More than likely, they were just roaming around, looking for trouble. That's happening a lot, these days.'

'They believe the Last Days have come, when the Underhive shall be purged of the sinful and unworthy.'

'By sinful and unworthy, they mean anyone who isn't a Redemptionist,' Micc added sardonically.

'Your grasp of the complexities of the Crusade's theology continues to amaze me,' Vex returned. Micc snorted his amusement and shifted his weapon to the crook of his other arm.

'But you're a Redemptionist,' Neesa finally asked the question Vex imagined she had been wanting to ask for some time. 'Your robes…'

'Indeed,' Vex replied. 'Or, at least, I was. My brothers and I had what you might call a falling out.'

'A theological disagreement,' Micc chipped in. Vex shot him a look.

'Quite. It's enough to say that we're no longer on speaking terms.'

'With them that can still speak, that is,' Micc added brightly. His grin faded at the sight of Vex's expression. 'I'll go check on the scouts,' he muttered and moved on ahead.

'So why do you still wear the robes?' Neesa asked. It felt like a very long time before Vex answered.

'As a reminder.'

* * *

THE SETTLEMENT SAT in a natural amphitheatre formed by a towering, curved rock wall and a depression in the earth that might have been scooped out, aeons ago, by some vast godlike hand. Several tracks ran through the shantytown of tents and ramshackle huts that huddled around the circular wall that enclosed the settlement's more permanent-looking buildings. The wall itself appeared to have been thrown together using wrecked vehicles, and wagons, rocks, girders from long-derelict buildings, each and every kind of industrial detritus. All the tracks led to a set of double gates which long ago might have been the doors to a spacecraft's loading bay.

Neesa stood at the point in the track where it began a steep descent towards the settlement, listening to the noise that rose up from it, focussed and amplified by the rock wall.

'Hope's End,' Micc stood beside her. Vex had gone on ahead. The wagon was moving away from them down the track. He was waiting for the rear-guard to reach them. 'Last working privy before the Sump and home to the homeless, courtesy of Pastor Vex.'

Neesa looked at him. 'He built this?' she asked.

'Well, there was a settlement here before he arrived, but he got things organised. Got the wall built, stuff like that. Made it safe to grow. Ordinarily, one of the gangs would've moved in, or the Redemption might have come a-cleansing, but Vex is smart and tough – and I do mean tough. He must've been a holy terror when he was a believer. Had quite a reputation, I'm told.' Neesa could tell from Micc's voice that he thought highly of Vex – more highly than the wiry, crook-faced little man would ever let on.

'He organised the militia, comes out with us on patrols like this, but I'd swear it's his reputation that keeps most of the trouble away – or has done till now.'

'Why do you say that?'

'Something's changed. Surely you can feel it? A whole new bunch of rumours are flying around – creatures that look human but aren't – and I don't mean zombies. And then there's the Redemption. Even Vex says what they're doing now is more serious than anything they've tried before. One of their plans for the Last Days is what they call the Final Crusade. Vex reckons that's what they're doing now. Those tents and huts outside the wall, they weren't there a month ago. A lot of people are on the move – like you. Something's going on and I'll bet it's coming our way.'

A shout from back along the track caused Micc to start. The rearguard had come into view. Micc waved to them, then turned to Neesa, the unhappy, distant expression that had come over his face as he spoke was gone, replaced by another lopsided grin.

'Come on,' he said, leading her down the track, towards the settlement. 'Let's get you settled in.'

## Three

THE CLOCKWORK bird spiralled down through the shaft of sunlight, its jewelled wings alive with multicoloured fire. Spinning down from the high vaulted ceiling, it chimed a harmonious yet melancholy series of notes. A dying fall.

Ty Helios Kayne watched the bird's descent and wished that he could be somewhere, anywhere else but here.

The bird's downward path looked to be taking it towards one of the series of ornamental fountains that ran the length of the gallery, whose waters caught the light that streamed in through the high arched windows, transforming it into a thousand small rainbows. A metre or so from the fountain, the bird suddenly changed direction. Its inner mechanism, rewound by the motion of its fall, drove it once again upwards, towards the vaulted ceiling and the flock of similar toys that inhabited the gallery's upper reaches. As it rose, on a gentler trajectory than it had taken during its descent, it chimed again: a rising, more cheerful cadence.

Kayne left the bird to its flight and looked out from his position on the dais that had been erected in front of the altar. The hunters stood in a line before him, helmets held in the crook of one arm, trying not to shuffle and twitch with suppressed excitement. He knew that their minds would not be on the ceremony taking place in their honour. They would be trying to imagine the hunt to come, trying to conjure up the sights and smells of the Underhive, the world below the Wall, below the Spire in which they had lived their whole lives. No more practice bouts with each other and members of the House Ty militia, learning the rudiments of combat in their offworld-crafted battlesuits. The next fight they found themselves in would be for real and upon their success or otherwise would depend much of their future fortune. A successful hunter would not be short of supporters in the kaleidoscopic land-scape of shifting alliances and petty politicking between the noble families of House Ty and, by extension, between the Ruling Houses of Hive Primus.

Kayne caught himself on the verge of a yawn – easily dis-guised when one was just one of the hundreds of attendees that filled the body of the gallery, unforgivable when one stood before the altar, representing one's family. He clamped his jaws shut and fought to suppress the impulse. How did his father manage to endure these things? If the old man wasn't confined to his bed amid the usual rumours of poison and attempted assassination, Kayne wouldn't be standing here alongside the other Nobles of House Ty, feeling more keenly than ever the unwelcome attention that had been directed at him since his return alone from the last hunt that was sanctified in this place.

*Old Man Cal might very well be poorly*, Kayne could almost hear the whispers that were passing among the assembled con-gregation, their bellies full from the banquet that preceded the blessing, tongues loosened by wine, *but Bael should be standing there in his place, not Kayne. Bael was pureblood, not the fruit of some concubine's loins.*

It didn't matter that fully four-fifths of those present were also the products of semi-official liaisons in their families' seraglios. All the surreptitious talk of bloodlines, 'fitness' and 'honour' was coded language, disguising the one word whose utterance could lead only to a formal challenge and to blood: cowardice.

'May the Emperor who watches over us all grant you courage, luck and cunning,' intoned the priest, standing at the altar, overlooking the dais and the gallery beyond. The massive carved monolith bore a representation of the Emperor in Glory, triumphant after his defeat of the Heretic, Horus. Looking out from the dais, Kayne spotted the black-robed ret-inue of the Emperor's living representatives, standing out like a patch of unnatural shadow among the brightly-dressed throng.

Inquisitor Cinar had come to the end of his tour of the Spire and was awaiting passage on an Imperial transport due to arrive in this Segmentum in a few days. He and his acolytes had moved from House to House, accepting the ritual entertain-ments that were his due and, apparently, doing little else. The rumour mill had, of course, ground out stories of clandestine meetings, even journeys beyond the Wall, but there had been no arrests, no show trials; none of the noble families had been exposed as a nest of heretics.

Kayne wondered whether his own story had reached Cinar's ears. *Seven of them descended into the Underhive, as is the custom among young House Ty noblemen, yet only he returned. His older brother – their father's true heir – was among them. He claims he saw his comrades slain, that he barely escaped with his life. The Underhive is a dangerous place, to be sure, but…*

Kayne could imagine Cinar, moving among the crowd at yet another interminable banquet, nodding absently as a fawning noble, anxious to be seen as a confidant to the Inquisition, poured out the tale in a conspiratorial whisper. A footnote to be added to the inquisitor's report on his visit, perhaps, or just one more piece of gossip to be discarded, forgotten moments after Cinar moved on through the crowd. Kayne knew which of the alternatives he would prefer.

'Good hunting,' intoned the priest.

'Good hunting,' repeated the congregation. Kayne realised with relief that the ceremony was nearing its end. Soon the hunters would leave the gallery, conduct the final checks on their suits and begin their descent.

'Go forth and return in–'

The priest's last word, 'glory', was destroyed by the sudden bark of gunfire from the far end of the gallery, followed by a strangled scream and a crash as one of the ornate, tempered-glass doors was torn from its hinges.

The noise caused an immediate reaction in the packed gallery: panic. Those nearest the source of the commotion surged towards the far end of the gallery. Those already standing closer to the altar did likewise in an attempt to avoid being trampled. From his vantage point on the dais, Kayne watched as a tidal wave of richly dressed bodies rolled towards him. There were more gunshots, more screams as people fell beneath others' feet. A uniformed figure flew through the air, over the heads for the fleeing crowd, legs and arms pinwheeling brokenly. Kayne, straining to make out what was going on at the far end of the gallery, caught sight of a hulking figure with broad, armoured shoulders, lashing out with an oversized fist in a blur of piston-driven motion and slamming another militiaman into the backs of the terrified mob. A rain of auto-gun shells broke against the intruder's breastplate, fired by a militiaman who was back-pedalling frantically. The armoured hulk closed in on him, its other arm outstretched, and was lost to sight behind the furthest of the fountains.

Time froze, then ran backward, taking Kayne with it. The gallery's glass-and-gilt dissolved, to be replaced by the shattered landscape of the Underhive. For an impossible, endless moment, Kayne found himself in the time and place that he had last seen such a figure, moving with the same deadly purpose...

The impact drove Kayne to the very edge of the dais, almost tipping him into the clear floor space at the feet of the hunters who, after a second spent exchanging confused glances, were locking their helmets in place and powering up their suits. Kayne turned and saw that his erstwhile companions on the dais were engaged in an undignified scramble for the higher ground of the altar. The priest had already retreated behind the monolith; Kayne caught sight of his pale, wide-eyed face, staring out from one side of its bulk.

At the foot of the dais, the line of militiamen, seconded to form the hunters' honour guard, struggled to turn and face the attack, only to be confronted by the onrushing tide of terrified nobility. In an ill-advised attempt to bring the wave to a halt, one of the honour guard fired his autogun over the heads of the crowd. The wave broke, people scrambling in all directions, pushing, kicking and clawing at those around them. There was an almighty crack as one of the ornamental fountains was dislodged by the sudden force of bodies slamming against it. Water plumed from the broken pipe, knocking people from their feet, washing them back under the well-shod heels of the mob.

Homing in on the tell-tale hiss of las-fire hitting flesh, Kayne spotted the inquisitor and his retinue, backed up against one wall in the space between two plinths, each topped with the bust of a past ruler of House Ty. Each of the black-robed retinue had produced a laspistol from within the folds of their robes and was cutting down any member of the mob unwise enough to seek sanctuary in their direction. At occasions such as this, all but ceremonial weaponry was forbidden – Kayne himself was wearing his father's jewel-encrusted, blunt-edged and utterly useless sabre. Presumably no one had dared attempt to apply this restriction to the Emperor's representatives. The cowl had fallen from the head of one of the retinue; Kayne glimpsed the ruby glow of a tech-adept's ocular prosthetic before the deep-throated cough of a bolter launcher, followed by a chorus of renewed shouts, screams and curses wrenched his attention back to the area immediately in front of the dais.

The monster stood in the middle of a suddenly clear space, as if it had emerged from a trap door in the marble floor slabs at the behest of a stage conjurer. In one oversized metal paw it held the limp body of a member of the family militia. Once again, Kayne was assailed by memory: the intruder wore an Orrus-class battlesuit, as he had done when he travelled below the Wall, as did three of those hunters this ceremony was intended to honour. But this suit bore the scars of innumerable battles. The once-smooth surfaces of its plating were heavily pitted and gouged; the plates covering one shoulder appeared to have been peeled back by far heavier ordnance than was available to the militiamen in the gallery, exposing some of the suit's wiring and the actuator mechanisms. Having emerged from the throng to one side of the dais, it seemed to pause. Its head swung from side to side, as if searching for something. Tilting its head upwards, its gaze fastened on Kayne, by now the only person standing on the dais. He half-expected it to emit the growl of some feral animal about to pounce.

Two of the Orrus-clad hunters fired their glove-mounted bolters, hitting the intruder mid-chest. The interloper was punched backwards, but managed to retain its footing. Several unarmoured bystanders and a militiaman fell, caught by shrapnel from the twin impact. It was a good strike. By rights, the threat should have been eliminated – its chest had been reduced to little more than a smoking ruin. But, impossibly, it stood there, stubbornly refusing to die.

Worse yet, it struck back. Firing bolts from both fists, it blasted both its attackers back into their fellow hunters and the chaotically milling crowd beyond. Under other circumstances, it might have been comical – some of the brightest lights of House Ty, clad in combat rigs assembled at vast expanse by off-world expertise, thrown into an ungainly heap of servo-driven arms and legs. However, as the monstrosity, the fresh wounds in its carapace still smoking and leaking drive-fluid onto the floor, turned its gaze back to the lone figure on the dais, Kayne could find little to laugh about.

There was no point in trying to run. To turn his back on this thing was to invite a bolt between the shoulder blades. Feeling like a prize fool, he drew his sword. Even the intruder seemed to appreciate the absurdity of Kayne standing above him, brandishing the antique weapon in the face of an opponent who, wounded or not, bore enough firepower to smear him across the altar stone and all those who were currently sheltering behind it.

Kayne hurled the sword at the intruder and leapt from the dais, landing beside the prone body of one of the hunters' honour guard. As Kayne bent to pluck the autogun from his nerveless grasp, the fallen man twitched and moaned. Kayne ignored him and levelled the autogun on the intruder. A headshot might work, but down a foot or so, at the point where the flexible mail protecting the neck and the more solid plates that covered the chest...

The interloper rocked back on its heels as the bullet slammed home, then righted itself. For a moment, it seemed as if this shot would also be shrugged off. Then both knees buckled. Twisting as it fell, it slammed onto the floor face-up.

Kayne was first to the body, autogun still held ready. His target might have been a statue, fallen from its plinth. Kayne bent, reached out with one hand and unfastened the clasps on either side of the helmet, then wrenched it away.

The pale grey eyes were still open.

'Brother.'

A fine mist of blood accompanied Bael's words, bubbling up from his throat, ruptured by Kayne's single shot. 'We're still there... where you left us.' He coughed, struggled to continue, the light fading from his eyes.

'Waiting for you.'

## Four

'WE'RE STILL THERE... *where you left us.*'

What else could he do? Ever since his return, there had been rumours, unvoiced suspicions that followed him everywhere, ranging from cowardice to fratricide. His father's declining health had done nothing to calm them; his solitary return from the Underhive had put Kayne in the position of heir apparent.

All he could do was go about his business, pretend not to hear the whispers or see the sneers that marked his path, until the court gossips tired of the story and found a new, undamaged reputation to tear to pieces.

That was before Bael returned to the Spire – and Kayne killed him.

Bolum, Kayne's personal manservant, checked his master's suit's systems and seals before he entered the gallery. Normally, another of the hunters would do this, but Kayne felt safer knowing that the person testing his suit's integrity had no interest in its sudden, mysterious failure shortly after entering the Underhive. Leaving his personal chambers, Kayne strode fully armoured through the corridors, annexes and galleries of the Ty House apartments, the suit's servomotors humming as he marched. He wanted them all to see, to believe: Ty Helios Kayne was returning to the Underhive to rescue his lost comrades, or die in the attempt.

The gallery was silent, empty. All sign of the previous day's mayhem had been erased: blood washed from walls and floor, the damaged fountain repaired. The clockwork birds still rose and fell, chiming mindlessly. Kayne resisted the temptation to blow one of them out of the air with a shot from his suit's glove-mounted bolters as he strode the length of the gallery, his heavy-booted footfalls echoing on the marble.

There were six of them, not counting the priest: Mot, Gyse, Schular, Telmac, Maas and Nikol. They sported Malcadon, Yeld, Jakara and three Orrus; he would be the fourth in such a rig. The complement of each hunting party was determined by ancient tradition. The fact that Fidor, the party's fourth Orrus, had been injured during the brief exchange of fire with Bael had been taken by some to be an omen. Fate, it seemed, had decreed that Kayne should accompany them below the Wall.

The priest raised an eyebrow when he saw that Kayne had already donned and secured his helmet, his eyes invisible behind the iridescent sheen of the photo-visor, nasal filter plugs in place. For a moment, Kayne thought the priest might order him to remove his helmet, standing as he was before the altar of the Emperor, but, after a moment, the priest composed himself and began the blessing. He jogged through the ritual with almost irreverent haste, Kayne thought, barely giving the hunters time to utter the prescribed responses. There was none of the stately pomp of the previous day, no visiting inquisitor to impress.

'In the Emperor's name I ask you: what is your vow?'

'To seek those who went before us and are lost,' the hunters replied in unison. This vow replaced the traditional: 'To seek honour and glory in the name of Ty House'. It had been composed late the previous day, by the priest and a conference of family heads. Kayne's father had, significantly, been excluded from the discussion.

'To return with them,' the hunters continued, 'or with news of their fate.'

Kayne did not join in with this last section of the oath. Raising his voice, he spoke over their words:

'Or to die!'

Heads turned. Mot, another of Ty Helios Cal's harem-brood, opened his mouth as if about to rebuke his half-brother. A rangy, undernourished-looking man, his Malcadon suit accentuated the angular aspects of his physique. Kayne remembered him as being a quiet child who had grown into a sly man, always looking for ways to ingratiate himself with their father.

Kayne returned the others' gaze for a moment, then turned to the priest.

'Are we blessed?' he enquired.

'You are blessed,' the priest replied, taken aback and anxious to conclude the ritual.

'Good.'

Kayne stepped around the line of hunters and marched towards a door set to one side of the altar. It led from the gilded outer surface of the Ty House apartments, to the more functional service areas, to corridors and elevators used by the vast numbers of servants and menials whose families could trace their lineage as far back as those of noble blood, should anyone be sufficiently interested to ask. And beyond those areas, there were other shafts, deserted, half-forgotten, whose purpose was simple: descent.

Just like the last time...

'You're quiet, brother,' Bael had said. 'Worried?'

'No,' Kayne had replied, his voice faltering. The rusty cage of the elevator car rattled and jolted as it descended. Already the Ty apartments were far above them, the pitted and discoloured links in the elevator chain their last remaining link with that world. And, when the cage reached the foot of the shaft, even this would be gone.

'Probably just feeling queasy from all this jerking around,' Aidor said, moaning as usual. 'You'd think they'd send someone down here with a pot of lubricant.'

'Who'd waste it on a rickety old elevator?' asked Volk, her wicked leer distorted by her Malcadon mouthpiece.

'Not you, from what I've heard!' laughed Pitar. Even in the confined space of the elevator cage, Kayne found it almost impossible to make out the outline of Pitar's body, cloaked as it was by his Yeld wings, whose chameleonic skin mimicked the rising bands of light and dark through which the elevator was descending. Only his head was clearly visible and seemed to float, unsupported, in mid-air.

The banter had been almost continuous from the moment they left the high gallery, as if in reaction to the solemnity of the pre-hunt ritual. Their path through the service corridors had been cleared by the House militia. As they bustled along, their armoured figures looking bizarrely out of proportion with the passageways they passed along, they laughed and joked as if they were just a group of friends on their way to the theatre or a party. The laughter continued when they reached the elevator shaft and ran through the final checks on each other's suits before cramming themselves into the too-small metal cage.

Under other circumstances, Kayne would have joined in. But, this time, he found himself with little or nothing to say.

'He's looking forward to the hunt,' Meela said. 'The sport to come. I know how he feels.'

'I know how I feel,' Bael said. 'My nose itches. But how do I scratch it with these?' Everyone laughed as he held up his hands, clad in the massive gloves of his Orrus armour. Even Kayne laughed at last, easing some of the tension that had gripped him as the priest pronounced the final blessing.

'The sport to come.' Georgi's monomolecular sword was slung over one shoulder. The jewels on his Jakara suit's buckler gleamed dully in the flickering light, which was weaker than before, an indication that they were almost at the bottom of the shaft.

Bael suddenly slapped Kayne on the back, making him jump. He hoped no one noticed.

'Honour and glory, eh, brother?'

Kayne looked at him and nodded, glad that his visor prevented Bael from seeing the uncertainty in his eyes.

'Honour and glory,' he replied quietly.

THE CAGE SLAMMED to a halt at the foot of the shaft, jolting Kayne back to the present. He looked at his fellow travellers on this new mission. Though their armour looked familiar, their faces, where visible, were the faces of strangers. He stared long and hard at the Malcadon mask to his left, reminding himself that behind its rubberised mouthpiece and the circular lenses of its goggles, he would find Mot's features, not Volk's.

'Is there a problem, brother?' Mot asked.

'No, Mot. No problem.' Kayne turned to Nikol, standing pressed against the concertina-mesh of the elevator's gate. 'Open the gate. Proceed with caution.'

Turning with some difficulty in the confined space, Nikol clamped an armoured hand around the gate's handle and slammed it aside – too hard, as she over-estimated her suit-enhanced strength. Several of the hunters, Mot included, started at the noise of the gate crashing open. The sound echoed down the three enclosed serviceways that led away from the elevator.

'Why not tell the whole hive we're coming?' Gyse joked weakly. He wore his wings folded back as he followed Nikol out of the cage.

'All the better sport, if our quarry knows we're coming.' Maas slapped Gyse on the shoulder as she followed him. On the way down, she had done most of the talking. The others had been quiet, stealing – Kayne was sure – surreptitious glances in his direction.

Kayne was the last to leave the elevator. The low light level had already triggered his photo-visor, which cast the area in a pale greenish glow. He saw that Maas and Telmac were running through a short series of exercises designed to prepare both their bodies and their suits for the coming hunt. The others were staring into the mouths of the serviceways, debating in low voices which one to take.

Kayne stepped between them and strode into the square mouth of the left passageway. Light panels were set flush with the top of the metal tunnel; all were dead except for one, a hundred paces or so ahead. Kayne didn't need the light, or the enhanced vision provided by his visor to know that, another hundred paces beyond the solitary light source, he would find a junction, another serviceway running across the end of this tunnel at right angles.

'Stay alert.' Kayne's voice drifted back to the others. 'We don't know who might have been sniffing around down here since last time.'

At the mouth of the passage, Gyse turned to Mot.

'Maybe having him along will have its uses after all,' Gyse muttered, then stepped into the tunnel which Kayne and his companions had taken last time.

'CLEAR AHEAD.'

Bael and Pitar had been gone for close to an hour, scouting the levels below. Since stepping from the elevator, their progress had been uneven. One of the three serviceways that had greeted them at the bottom of the elevator shaft had quickly proved useless, its metal walls twisted and warped into an impassable dead end by some unguessable force. The second led them to an open-sided ramp, angled upwards across a pitch-black abyss. Bael edged several steps along the incline before his foot met only emptiness. Another dead-end.

The third tunnel proved more promising, leading them through an enclosed maze of passages, then out onto a web of open walkways, latticed metalwork being all that kept them from what promised to be an endless fall.

'At least it'd be quicker than walking,' Volk joked as she peered over the rust-pitted railing of one of the walkways. Warm air rushed up from below, causing the metalwork to hum gently. From above – a long way above, Kayne thought – came a dull repetitive beat.

'Some kind of ventilation shaft,' Aidor speculated. As if in response to his words, the shaft resounded to a sudden broken grinding. The hunters froze, heads jerked upwards as if waiting to see doom, in the shape of some vast piece of mechanical debris, finally freed from its moorings by age and neglect, come crashing down.

The noise faded, to be replaced once again by the regular beat.

'Time we were somewhere else,' Georgi muttered, as Bael and Pitar appeared at the far end of the walkway, beckoning the others across. As well as scouting a route, they had been checking for possible threats, either natural or man-made. It was not unknown for two or more groups of hunters to meet unexpectedly in the no-man's land these ancient shafts and passageways had become. Sudden close-quarters combat between hunters from rival Houses had claimed the life of more than one young noble before they ever reached the Underhive.

Kayne followed the others across the remaining walkway towards the far wall of the shaft, where Bael was waiting for him.

'Soon, brother, I'm sure of it,' he said. 'We'll be done with this scurrying about like vermin. Then the real sport can begin.'

Kayne nodded. Bael smiled, then turned and followed the others into the service tunnel. Kayne made to follow, then stopped, cast a look behind him. The way home.

'Honour and glory,' he muttered, then hurried to catch up with the others.

LIKE THE MEMORY of a nightmare made flesh, the blade plummeted out of the darkness, accompanied by a rain of smaller pieces of debris. Gyse saw it first. Yelling a warning over the cacophony of tearing and falling metal that filled the shaft, he launched himself over the railing, unfurling his wings and shooting upwards on the rush of heated air.

Lost in his dark memories, Kayne was already standing at the threshold of the service tunnel towards which he had been leading the hunters. At Gyse's shout he turned and saw Telmac leading the race along the companionway towards him. Fragments of dislodged metal and concrete were bouncing off the walkway, ricocheting from the hunters' armour. First Telmac, then Maas raced past him into the tunnel. Mot and Schular were close behind. Kayne looked up, trying to locate Gyse.

And then he saw it: a narrow teardrop of tempered steel that had spent countless decades as part of a ventilation unit, set high in the shaft, now arrowing downwards.

*Time we were somewhere else*, said a familiar voice from Kayne's memory, seconds before the free-falling blade hit the companionway.

The shock of the impact hurled Schular past Kayne, into the arms of Telmac and Maas. Mot stumbled, regained his feet as the walkway tilted sharply, threatening to spill him back along its length into the pit, and launched himself towards his half-brother. Kayne reached out, caught Mot's arms just above the bulge of his suit's mono-fibre dispensers and hauled him into the tunnel.

'Nikol!' Telmac was shouting over the sound of falling metal. 'Where's Nikol?'

Kayne looked back along the companionway, now inclined downwards at a suicidal angle, its ragged end swaying drunkenly. The falling blade had struck the walkway like an executioner's axe, severing it close to the halfway mark, tearing away a section and carrying it down the shaft. The last time Kayne had seen Nikol, she had been working her way along the companionway towards him. Now all he saw was empty space.

'Kayne, get back!'

Kayne jerked his head up at Gyse's shouted command. The winged hunter was several metres above the tunnel mouth, describing a ragged figure-of-eight in the air as he fought to descend against the flow of heated air that was rising up the shaft. Without waiting for a reply, he glided towards the far side of the shaft, executed a sharp turn, then folded back his wings and arrowed towards the tunnel mouth.

Back-pedalling quickly, Kayne shouted a warning to the others. As he retreated, Kayne kept his eyes on the square of the tunnel mouth and the winged figure that grew to fill it. The slightest miscalculation would slam Gyse into the shaft wall on either side. To lose one hunter so early in the hunt was bad enough. To lose two...

With a sharp crack of unfurling metal, Gyse's wings scooped at the air, bringing his flight to a neck-breaking halt. Swinging his body to the vertical, he shot feet-first into the service tunnel, re-furling wings ringing and scraping against the tunnel's sides. He tried to hit the ground running, to absorb his remaining momentum, but there was just too much. He slammed into first one, then the other wall, before ploughing into Kayne, who had braced himself in the middle of the tunnel.

It took a moment for Gyse to realise he had come to a stop. Then, with a curse of surprise and relief, he eased himself out of Kayne's oversized embrace.

'Good catch,' he said, then coughed. 'I think you only broke half my ribs.'

'At least you're still breathing,' Maas muttered. Gyse shot her a puzzled look and she gestured towards Telmac, who stood a short way further down the tunnel, staring blankly at the wall. Without warning, he slammed a piston-driven fist into the tunnel's thin metal skin.

'Where's Nikol?' Gyse asked. Kayne shook his head. With another curse, Gyse stepped past him and moved to comfort Telmac.

'Nikol and Telmac… were they close?' Kayne asked.

'Good guess,' Maas replied sardonically.

'We should move on. This isn't a child's game. These things happen.' Kayne strode away from her, passed Gyse and Schular, who were still comforting the grieving Telmac, towards Mot, who stood waiting for them at the next junction.

'I guess you'd know about that,' Maas muttered after Kayne's retreating back. Kayne turned; his suit's comm-link must have picked up her words.

'What?' he asked.

'Nothing,' she replied, stone-faced. 'Let's get moving. I really want to kill something.'

## Five

BACK THEN, the first time, they had emerged from the maze of apparently forgotten shafts in a sector that looked like it was dedicated to hydroponic agriculture. Below them had been a series of low domes, their canopies opaque, the colour of eggshells, lit by vast arrays of luminescent elements designed to mimic the even, diffuse radiance given off by a sun not obscured by mile upon mile of dense industrial emissions. Some of the domes were well-maintained, the long ranks of nutrient vats full of densely-packed staple crops. Many more were all but derelict: dead lighting elements hung over ranks of cracked, empty nutrient vats. The plants that should have been growing, suspended, in these vats now hung limply over their sides, brown-leafed and decaying. In places, the floor was slick with a brown-green layer of reeking vegetable mulch.

The hunters moved cautiously from dome to dome, hugging the shadows that were more numerous in the neglected areas. Bael was the first to take point, then Kayne, edging between the vats and nutrient storage tanks, ducking under ropes of tubing thicker than a man's chest, his suit-enhanced senses alert, heart pounding, mouth dry.

The vats, storage tanks and connecting tubes all bore Van Saar markings – no surprise, given that House's reputation for technological achievement – but many had been scratched away or overlaid by the crest of House Escher. Evidently such a valuable installation as this had been the subject of a good deal of territorial haggling.

And – judging by the sound of gunfire that drew the hunters like night-flyers to a flame – the argument was far from over.

From the look of things, the Orlocks had bitten off more than they could chew, or else they simply lacked the infiltration skills of Bael, Kayne and their fellow hunters. Either way, they now found themselves pinned down by a vicious crossfire from the Escher women atop the service gantries that flanked an area given over to production control machinery. Half the Orlocks' original number lay dead in the aisles between the ranks of levers, gauges and valve assemblies that might normally be manned by members of Escher House's servile, intellectually-deficient male population – were it not for the fact that their bullet- and bolt-riddled corpses also lay sprawled across the tiled floor. It was only a matter of time before the Eschers picked off the intruders, or until reinforcements arrived and they moved in on them en masse. The Eschers knew it. The Orlocks knew it.

The hunters knew it too.

Bael, of course, had a plan. The hunters split up, three heading for the foot of one gantry, three for the other. Only Kayne remained, crouching among the tangle of pipes that marked the end of the last rank of vats before the production area.

Though he knew his heart was racing, the time between each beat seemed to grow ever longer. His mouth, already dry, now felt impossibly arid; he imagined his tongue as a cracked and swollen thing. Stinging sweat ran into one eye as he triggered his suit's targeting mechanism. He blinked it away as he raised his right hand and brought the twin crosshairs that now floated before his visor-enhanced gaze together on the curve of a valve assembly, midway between both gantries, behind which a beleaguered Orlock sheltered.

The blood being spilt in the open area before him might as well have been a play, a mock-battle staged in recreation of an episode from the Imperium's history for the amusement of a noble audience, high in the Spire. Kayne was waiting for the whispered signals from his comm-link, telling him that the others were in position.

'We're ready.' Bael's voice crackled in his ear.

'On your mark, Kayne.' Meela's voice followed in quick succession.

Kayne tried to speak, swallowed, tried again.

'Kayne?' There was concern in his brother's voice.

'Honour and glory,' Kayne croaked through a dry, constricted throat then triggered his bolter. Despite the recoil-suppressing mechanism built into the forearm-mounted weapon, he felt the shock of its discharge run back up his arm and down the length of his spine.

Trailing vapour from its reservoir of propellant, the bolt shot through the crossfire like a shuttle through a loom and slammed into the valve assembly. The pipework was peeled back by the impact, releasing a pressurised stream of superheated vapour. The Orlock who had been sheltering behind the valve leapt to his feet and staggered away from the scalding geyser. By some fluke, he had escaped injury from both the blast and the flying shards of red-hot shrapnel that followed. The Escher gunners on both gantries saw to it that he had little time to enjoy his good fortune. He danced first one way, then another as hundreds of autogun rounds slammed into him from both directions, before finally hitting the floor like a slab of half-chewed meat.

Taking Kayne's shot as their signal, the other hunters attacked. Sparks erupted from the supports of the gantry to Kayne's left as Georgi sprinted between them, slicing through them with the irresistible blade of his monomolecular sword. The walkway above him sagged then, accompanied by the sound of shearing rivets and twisting metal, came crashing down. Those Eschers who survived the fall found Aidor and Bael waiting for them on the ground, oversized, piston-driven arms open wide.

From atop the second gantry came shouts of surprise, quickly followed by cries of terror and pain. The shock of seeing Pitar, climbing spider-like over the gantry rail, clad in the body-hugging Malcadon suit, would have bought his companion enough time to select a target. To buy herself more time, Kayne imagined she would pinion more than one victim with the iron-hard pseudo-silk from her suit's spinnerets before moving in, claws extended.

Over the sound of screaming, the audio-enhancers in Kayne's helmet picked up the soft fizz of las-discharge as Volk, wings open, dived upon the Eschers from above. Any lucky enough to make it to the gantry steps would find themselves confronted by Meela, pounding her Orrus-shod way up to the walkway by the more usual route.

Realising with a shock that he hadn't moved since firing his first bolt, Kayne broke cover. Head singing with a sudden exhilaration, he raced towards the collection of consoles behind which the Orlocks had been cowering and from behind which several of them had already emerged, wearing almost comical expressions of puzzlement at the unexpected turn of events.

Spotting Kayne's running figure, one of the Orlocks turned, levelling his autogun. Kayne loosed off a wild shot. The bolt flashed past the Orlock and blew a gaping hole in a bank of gauges. The Orlock didn't flinch, even when a figure raced past behind him, shield held up to deflect a ragged peppering of gunfire, blade descending. Nor did his expression change as his body fell in two, neatly bisected from shoulder to opposite hip.

It took a heartbeat for Kayne to realise what had happened but, by then, he was already pumping bolts in the direction of the Orlocks who had been foolish enough to open fire on Georgi as he raced to Kayne's aid. One of Kayne's bolts hit a ganger square in the chest, turning him into just so many litres of blood and liquefied bone. The sight of their comrade's explosive dissolution was enough for the rest of them. They raced away, disappearing among the vats, preferring to face their gang boss's wrath than certain death here.

'Emperor's blood!' Aidor's face was alight as he and Bael strode towards Kayne and Georgi. 'The trainers never told us to expect this! I've never felt so alive!'

'It's feedback from your suit, boosting your neuroware,' Meela told him as she and Volk walked towards them from the opposite direction. From the look on her face, Kayne could tell she was feeling it too.

'Like I care what's causing it!' Aidor laughed. 'I just don't want it to stop!'

'When our suits' memories are purged, the record of this hunt will be preserved,' said Pitar after she had dropped lightly out of the air, folding her wings as she did so. She walked over to join them. 'Every trainer will use it to show every hunter what it means to hunt for House Ty.'

'No one hunts like House Ty!' Aidor bellowed, broke into another peal of hysterical laughter, then slammed a fist into a control panel, ruining it amidst a shower of sparks.

'We're going to have to watch him,' Georgi muttered.

'He'll get used to it,' counselled Bael. 'But now we really ought to be on our way. We're here to hunt, not fight pitched battles with Escher reinforcements out for revenge.'

The hunters moved off, heading out of the hydroponic domes in a different direction to that taken by the fleeing Orlocks. Aidor didn't stop laughing until they had left the sector.

NO ONE HUNTS *like House Ty!*

Aidor's laughing face, never to be forgotten, flashed before Kayne's mind's eye as he closed his steel-gloved fist around the lower jaw of the Underhiver with the flamer and squeezed. Blood, teeth and fragments of bone squirted between his fingers. Ignoring his twitching victim, Kayne flicked the ichor from his glove. The Underhiver had been edging between the stanchions of the overhead conveyor system that seemed to run the length of the derelict smelting plant into which he and the others had followed the hunters. Accompanied by two other scavengers, each armed with an autogun, he had been trying to outflank Schular and Gyse, who had become pinned behind the coils of a vast chain, long since fallen from the complex of pulleys and tracks that still ran across the plant's high ceiling, now half-buried in the grey metallic dust that covered the floor. They had darted from stanchion to stanchion, unaware that they, too, were being outflanked.

Kayne took the time to target the first of them, then charged forward as the remaining two stood frozen by the shock of their comrade's sudden, apparently spontaneous, explosion. Batting aside the second autogun-wielder with a chest-crushing swipe of one hand, he then closed in on the last before he had time to bring the flamer nozzle to bear.

*No one hunts like House Ty?* he thought grimly. *We'll be lucky this time not to end up as trophies traded in some vermin-ridden pit-market.*

Telmac must have been asleep on his feet or else too busy brooding over the loss of Nikol to notice that someone was on their trail. Given the number of scavengers who had descended upon them shortly after they had entered the smelting plant in search of a down-shaft, they must have made as much noise as a particularly ill-disciplined army on the march. When they had emerged from the service shafts in this derelict industrial zone, rather than the hydroponics sector Kayne had been expecting – though he was sure he had followed the same route through the forgotten labyrinth that he had taken with Bael – Kayne had given Telmac the rearguard in order to give him something else to focus on, to distract him from his loss.

*Bael wouldn't have made that mistake.*

He brushed the thought aside, but the suspicion remained: that it should have been Bael who returned to the Spire after the last hunt, not him. But that would never have happened. Because Bael would never run.

'Maas here. Can anybody hear me?' Her voice crackled in Kayne's ear, followed by calls of acknowledgement from the other hunters. Only Telmac didn't reply.

'I'm with Telmac. We think we've found a way off this level,' Maas continued. A loading ramp, heading down. Follow the conveyor, magnetic west.'

'Easier said than done,' replied Gyse. Off to Kayne's right came the sound of another fusillade from the scavengers who had pinned Gyse and Schular. Focussed on the hunters hiding among the fallen chains, they were apparently unaware of the fate that had befallen their flanking team. Kayne moved to a nearby stanchion, peered around it.

The scavengers had sought cover among the scattered wrecks of various trolleys and bins that littered the smelting plant's floor. There were too many for him to try to pick them off with his bolters. They'd range in on him as soon as he started firing, force him back. All it would take would be one lucky shot and his hunt could end here.

A rush of memories assaulted him: Bael, laughing Aidor and the others, overwhelmed by a tidal wave of chittering Underhive scum, heedless of the hunters' firepower, as irresistible as an ocean.

And he, Ty Kayne, standing momentarily in the clear, the comm-link ringing with his brother's screams.

The force of the memories caused Kayne to take an involuntary step back. Feeling his foot strike something, he turned, looked down. The faceless scavenger lay at his feet, ruined head surrounded by a halo of rust-brown blood, seeping into the grey dust that carpeted the floor. The body lay face-up, back arched over the flamer's tanks and feeder assembly.

Kayne knelt by the corpse, tore away the weapon's straps and rolled the corpse away. As he stood, flamer held in one hand, he realised that he was being watched.

The scavenger stood several paces away, autogun held limply in one hand, his other arm pressed tightly across his chest, where Kayne had swatted him. His breathing came in ragged gasps and his face was pale beneath the layer of dust that covered most of it. He stared at Kayne, as if unsure what to do next.

'Well?' Kayne asked, intending to distract the scavenger while he swung his free hand into a firing position. The crosshairs of his targeting system edged slowly towards a point in the middle of the stooping figure's chest.

'Spyrer!' the scavenger croaked brokenly. It had been a long time since he had been called that. The word was both an insult and the name that had been given to those like himself, unbidden visitors to the hell beneath the Wall.

Either way, the scavenger had made up his mind. Letting the autogun fall into the dust, he turned and ran, weaving between the metal boles of the conveyor supports with a painful, limping stride.

Kayne watched him go for a moment, then turned back to the firefight. Barely pausing to consider factors of distance and trajectory, he hurled the flamer in a high arc that would take it over the heads of most of the scavengers who continued to rain fire on Schular and Gyse. As it approached its apogee, he targeted and fired.

The flamer's tanks exploded with a dull concussion, spilling fiery rain onto the scavengers' ranks. Several of them jumped up, heads and shoulders alight, flames licking hungrily at their clothing. Kayne watched as they ran about like frantic marionettes, screaming, batting uselessly at the flames, colliding with those of their number who had not been touched by the fire and passing it on.

Las-fire cut down one such blazing puppet – Gyse had obviously decided to exact a little vengeance of his own.

'Don't waste your time,' Kayne barked into his comm-link. 'Head for Maas's position. This isn't what we're here for.'

He saw Gyse and Schular emerge from the chain's coils, head off, following the line of the conveyor. He cast a glance behind him, along the path the fleeing scavenger took, felt a sudden pang of envy, then turned again and pounded after the others.

They were still too high, even here, in the midst of the seemingly endless darkness of the Underhive. They had to move on. Move down.

## Six

THE BROKEN PILLAR against which he had slumped was surprisingly comfortable. Not as comfortable as his usual seat in the Grog Bucket, but… But that was where this fool's errand had begun! The dark, smoky drinking hole had been alive with gossip, as usual, but one subject kept cropping up.

Archaeotech. A new motherlode.

He coughed and spat, wincing at the feeling that shot through his chest: something in there was loose. It ground against something else every time he breathed too heavily. It was a wonder he'd made it out of the old factory without passing out from the pain. Judging by the screaming that erupted shortly after he ran from the Spyrer, he ought to count himself lucky that he could feel anything at all. Until he reached the wide doors leading to the factory's deserted yard, he had expected each step to be his last – the first thing he saw when he came round, nose and mouth clogged with dust, chest on fire, had been Frenc's corpse. He had recognised it by the jacket – the bloody ruin of its face could have belonged to anyone. Luckily for him, the Spyrer must have had other things on its mind.

'Damned if I ain't the luckiest guy in the Hive,' he muttered, then wished he hadn't as the broken pieces inside him ground together.

If he'd known what they were tracking, he would never have followed the others into the factory. He'd heard the stories, how they were souls damned by the Emperor himself, hiding from his wrath in the depths of the Underhive – that, or else they were just rich kids from way up in the Spire, looking for thrills. Either way, they were bad news.

A wave of nausea rushed through him, causing his guts to clench and his vision to swim and fog.

'Oh, yeah,' he muttered through clenched teeth. 'Real lucky.'

'I'VE HEARD THE damn stories,' Klyde had said, sitting across the table from Frenc and Clemm. 'An' you know what I think? I think someone's been list'nin' to too many Redemptionist sermons.'

'You don't have ta be a Redemptionist ta believe in blasphemy,' Clemm replied defensively.

'If your mother had believed in it, she'd have taken one look at your face and strangled you at birth!' Frenc laughed, then took a swig from his tankard. He stopped mid-swallow and peered suspiciously at its contents.

'I mightn't be the prettiest of fellas,' Clemm agreed – and anyone catching sight of the ludicrously misaligned set of features that hung beneath his patchy, uneven hairline would be hard pressed to disagree, 'but I ain't a complete fool, neither. There's things movin' about down here like as no one's seen before.'

'There's something moving about in here, all right.' Frenc upended his tankard. A bug the size of his thumb hit the tabletop, along with the dregs of his ale, and scuttled away before he had the chance to bring his tankard down on top of it.

'I know I've asked this before,' Frenc continued, 'but why the blazes do I drink in this place?'

Frenc didn't belong here, this far down in the Underhive. Word was, his family had connections with the Guilders. His manners were those of someone who'd had the time and money to acquire such things. He'd been doing well for himself, people said, until he got into some kind of tangle with a merchant's wife. Or daughter. He was a good-looking lad, so it might have been both. One day, he had just turned up at the bar – Klyde must have been one of the first people he spoke to. Since then, he'd been doing the same as everyone else down here: getting by.

'These things ain't your reg'lar muties or zombies.' Clemm stubbornly persisted with his tale. 'I heard, they don't kill ya. They do stuff to ya. Make ya like one'a them.' His already deep voice dropped a level. 'They take away ya soul.'

'I've heard other stories about these so-called monsters,' Frenc said, ignoring Clemm's baleful gaze. 'I've heard they're just like you and me – only they've found something: archaeotech, still functioning, and they're using it to secure their territory so they can dig out some more. I know a man who's putting together a little hunting party. Says he's got a Guilder willing to pay very well for a sample.'

At the mention of archaeotech, Clemm got up and left. While not very intelligent, his loyalty and bravery were beyond question – he wouldn't think twice about walking into a pit-fight with Bull Gorg himself – but he drew the line at having anything to do with archaeotech. To his uncomplicated mind it smacked of the unholy. Klyde watched him go, then turned back to Frenc.

'You haven't been over at the Two Tunnels, talking to Jerico, have you?' Klyde asked. ''Cause he ain't ta be trusted. Always got a plan, that one, but when the waste hits the walls, he's always got a way out. I know plenty a' people who've been left in the lurch by him.'

'It's not Jerico,' Frenc replied, 'though I hear he might be getting together a hunting party of his own – and he's not the only one. Clemm, the Redemptionists and every other superstitious half-wit in the Underhive can shout "blasphemy" all they want. I want to make some money.

'Bevan's group is meeting at the old filtration works in an hour. He says he's getting some heavy gear from a dealer he knows, but to bring along any hardware you've got.' Frenc got to his feet. 'Interested?'

Klyde looked up at him for a moment then, without really knowing why, shrugged and said: 'Why not?'

WHY NOT? 'CAUSE *if you do, you'll end up unarmed and alone, with a chest full of broken ceramite.*

The world swam back into focus in time for Klyde to see, in vivid colour, the red-veined gobbet of mucus he had just hawked onto the dirt… between the pair of scuffed boots that he was sure hadn't been there a minute ago.

It took an enormous effort for him to raise his head from where it had fallen forward on his chest. His chest felt as tight as a drum. He wondered if he might be bleeding inside, as well as just feeling all broken up. He'd seen that happen to Torus, another old drinking buddy from the Grog Bucket. There'd been a fight – over a game of dice? – but Torus had come out of it without a scratch on him. Then, a while later, he just keeled over. Apothecary opened him up and found his lungs were full of blood. A little piece of rib had done the damage, must have been cracked in the fight...

Dragging his mind back to the present took almost as much effort as raising his head. Everything was slipping away. The ground in front of him, the ground on which the owner of the scuffed boots was standing, might look pretty solid, but it was slipping away, too, he could feel it.

The boots' owner was a woman, a scavvy by the look of her. The skin across her pale flat face was pockmarked; it looked as if someone had held a candle too close to one of her cheeks – the skin there fell in uneven folds. She held her head at an odd, tilted angle as she looked down at him.

Klyde tried to speak, coughed, spat more red-tinged phlegm into the dirt, tried again.

'I... I got nothin' worth stealin' but... but, if you help me back to the Grog Bucket... I can show ya how to get there... I've got money... landlord keeps it behind the bar for me.'

The woman continued to gaze down at him. Klyde noticed how her lower lip hung limply from one side of her mouth. Was she some species of imbecile? If so, he was surely going to die here.

'Name's... name's Klyde,' he tried, feeling both desperate and foolish. 'What's yours?'

The woman opened her mouth with a sudden, almost mechanical snap. The stream of high-pitched clicks and squeals that issued forth from somewhere inside her was like nothing Klyde had heard before. Mechanical? Almost. Insectile? Almost. But not human. Definitely not human.

As the woman bent towards him, Klyde wanted to get to his feet and run, as he had run from the Spyrer, but his legs refused to move. The woman reached out a hand, palm first. Moments before it covered his face, he was sure that he saw something move beneath the dirt-caked skin.

Her hand pressed over his mouth and then he felt it, pressing against his lips, forcing its way between them, prising apart his clenched teeth, moving over his tongue.

Something sharp stabbed against the roof of his mouth and Klyde found that he could, for the last few seconds of his life, move his feet again. He kicked frantically at the dirt, clawed at it with his hands, but it was too late.

His last, absurd thought was that this wasn't how he imagined it would feel to die, to be killed. It felt more like… more like being drained.

THE WOMAN TOOK her hand from the corpse's mouth, the slit in her palm closing of its own accord, and stood up. Information, newly acquired, sang through her veins: images from a solitary life, lived among hundreds of thousands of other lives, but still, like them, alone. She heard voices, snatches of music, fleeting memories of fleshy pleasures. Conflict, too: arguments, brawls, gang fights. One such memory captured her attention, one voice: *Well?*

Details of the face and body were obscured by the heavy combat suit, though the type of suit was familiar to her. But the voice. She *recognised* the voice.

Tilting back her head she emitted a stream of sound. Shifting to a pitch beyond human hearing, it drove vermin of every description to seek shelter and feral dogs to howl in anguished, frightened protest, caused airborne insects to spiral crazily through the air, suddenly unable to navigate.

The acknowledgement came in similar fashion, informing her that her message had been received and was already being passed on. Her mouth snapped shut and she experienced a moment of what she would once have called anticipation.

He had returned. Ty Helios Kayne.

The prodigal.

## Seven

'THIS IS WHAT we're here for, isn't it – to hunt?' Mot held up the length of Malcadon silk so that they could admire the three human ears that had been threaded along it. He could tell by the set of Kayne's mouth that he was not impressed.

'Not this time,' Kayne insisted through gritted teeth. 'Do you know how much time we've wasted waiting for you? You'd do well to remember your vow.'

'I remember it!' Mot spat back. From the tone of his voice and his body language, Kayne could tell that the bio-boost from his suit was having an unsettling effect on his nervous system. 'Perhaps, if you had remembered yours, we wouldn't be having his conversation. "Honour and glory" – is that really what you've brought to House Ty, brother?'

'Think you could do better?' Kayne growled, closing the gap
between them. Mot took a step back, already half way into a
fighting stance, but Maas stepped hastily between them.

'We all remember our vow,' she said. 'We have the chance to
do more than earn honour and glory. If we stay focussed, work
together, we might bring home our lost hunters – think of
that!'

Staring levelly into Kayne's visored eyes, she continued: 'Bael
said they are still alive. You can lead us to them – or at least to
where we might begin our search.'

She turned, now fixing Mot with her steady gaze.

'And there'll be other hunts, Mot, when you'll be able to
wrap yourself in even greater glory.' Kayne remembered that
Maas's father was a respected diplomat, always involved in
negotiations between House Ty and the other Ruling Houses,
the Merchant Guilds or other off-world bodies. Evidently she
had inherited some of her father's skills.

'What I want is last on everybody's list,' Mot muttered petu-
lantly. Maas raised an eyebrow. 'Other hunts,' he conceded,
then fell silent.

'That's right,' she said, gently, then continued more briskly:
'we should be on our way. We don't want to be caught flat-
footed by any more of the locals.'

The smelting plant was several levels above them by now.
The loading ramp found by Maas and Telmac led down to a
multi-layered complex of warehousing. Some of the units had
been echoing and empty, others had been crammed with containers, discarded parts for vast machines. One level had been
chosen as a nest by an extended family of rats the size of children and had been the scene of a brief, bloody melee and a
swift exit by the hunters while the rats turned on their
wounded brethren.

They now stood among the ruins of what once had been a
waste processing plant, whose pipes and tanks had been
overrun by garishly-coloured varieties of giant fungus which
evidently found the noxious fluids that now ran untreated
through a complex of sluices highly nutritious. Though he had
not admitted it to the others, Kayne was relieved to come upon
this hallucinatory landscape of broad, spotted caps and
bulbous orange-and-blue puffballs. For the first time since
guiding them through the service shafts, he was sure that they

were following the route he had taken – not from his descent
with Bael, Pitar and the others, but from his return journey to
the Spire. He had passed through here, nervously checking that
his suit's filters were proof against the mist of spores that hung
in the dense, still air.

'Perhaps you would like to take point?' Maas asked Kayne.
'After all, you are our pathfinder.'

Kayne nodded and led the way along a duckboard path
which, he remembered, would lead to a narrow bridge across a
wide culvert, running with an unhealthy-looking soup whose
rank, organic odour was strong enough to fight its way past
their filter plugs.

The hunters moved in single file down the path. At the rear,
Gyse tapped Mot on the shoulder.

'Good kill?' he asked. Mot just nodded, apparently still nurs-
ing a grievance. As long as Gyse had known him, Mot had been
a sulky, resentful person, sensitive about his place as Ty Helios
Cal's third son, quick to take offence at any imagined slight to
his status and always ready to spread damaging rumours
behind the backs of his enemies. He had once drunkenly
boasted to Gyse that he had arranged with agents from House
Ran Lo for the 'disappearance' of a daughter of another Ty family who had refused his attentions, but Gyse had dismissed it as
an alcoholic fantasy. Such a thing would be tantamount to
treason against the House.

Gyse pointed to the ears that now dangled by their thread
from one shoulder of Mot's suit.

'Why only three?' he asked.

'That was all they had between them,' Mot replied with a
shrug, making the ears dance on their thread.

'Do you think Kayne really knows where he's taking us?' Gyse
asked. There had been something in Kayne's voice – a vague-
ness, an uncertainty – whenever he had been called upon to
decide their route.

'It doesn't really matter,' replied Mot, then picked up the
pace. Gyse thought about his words, not sure of their
meaning.

'I suppose you're right. In a hundred years or so, none of this
will matter. That's what you meant, right?'

Mot looked back over his shoulder at Gyse. His face was hidden behind his mask, so Gyse could not read his expression,

but there was something in his tone – flat, non-committal –
that worried him.

'Yes,' Mot said. 'That's what I meant.'

HUNT HAD FOLLOWED hunt that first time, as Kayne, Bael and the
others moved down through the seemingly never-ending levels
of the Underhive. Sporadically their sport was punctuated by
periods when, at the centre of an intricate web of tripwires and
semi-autonomous proximity alarms, the hunters rested. While
their suits' self-repair mechanisms attended to any minor damage picked up during a hunt, or resolved any glitches that had
developed in the suits' internal systems, the hunters floated in
a narco-assisted reverie state, somewhere between sleep and
trance.

Kayne experienced this state as a feeling of deep calm, the
sense of being wrapped in a cocoon of soft white light.
Unbidden, images would coalesce out of the whiteness and he
would enjoy again the sensations of the hunt:

The shouts of surprise and alarm from the scavvy traders
when they discovered – naked, trussed in Malcadon silk and
deposited at a crossroads on one of the maze of trails between
settlements – the outriders who had been guarding the rear of
their caravan of wagons.

There had been more shouting from within the ramshackle
meeting hall when one of the Redemptionist brethren assigned
to guard the door had been lowered, again by means of Volk's
silk-spinners, through the makeshift skylight Kayne had torn in
the roof. The ecstatic cries and hysterical wailing inspired by
the priest's sermon were nothing compared to the screams that
erupted from the congregation when, rushing for the exit to
escape the unholy vision of the 'floating' brother, they discovered that the doors had been barred from the outside.

The priest's retinue had recovered themselves sufficiently
to turn their weapons towards the roof, though their first
volley succeeded only in sending their helpless, dangling
brother to the Emperor. Kayne and Volk, laughing wildly,
had jumped from the roof to avoid the next fusillade; before
following them, Aidor remained long enough to drop
through the hole where the other brother had been guarding the door. By the time the remaining brethren shot their
way through the hall's rear wall, the hunters had melted into

the shadows of the settlement's twisting, garbage-clogged
streets.

They had chased mutants, howling like unquiet spirits,
through the ash-grey landscape of a petrified forest, whose trees
were so brittle with age and poisoned by the earth in which
they grew that one blow from an Orrus suit's fist would reduce
them to powder. They had stood silently in the shadows
beyond a campfire's light, listening to the songs sung by a band
of homeless, travelling scavvies to keep their fears at bay, each
selecting their targets.

They had hunted. They had killed. And they gloried in the
knowledge that they held the power of life or death over all
who, wittingly or unwittingly, crossed their path.

'Father told me that is why we hunt,' Bael had told him after
the traps had been laid and the hunters prepared to enter the
current rest cycle. They had chosen a narrow defile in the middle of a landscape of garbage. Vast, rolling dunes of refuse
stretched for a league in every direction. On the edge of the
dunescape, the hunters had seen hivers scavenging among the
mountainous piles of waste, cooking Helmawr-knew-what on
small fires at the mouths of caves that had been burrowed into
the sides of the dunes.

Fanning out in search of a suitable resting place, they had
moved deeper into what felt like the interior of an alien
world. Cresting a dune, Kayne had been amazed to find himself looking down upon a pool of effluent, on whose bank
sat a child, hideously deformed, fishing with a stick and a
length of wire. The child had looked up, but made no sound
when it saw him. For a long moment, they regarded one
another: the son of one of the noble families of one of the
ruling Houses of Hive Primus and the barely human by-
product of the Hive's millennia of operation and growth. The
child had looked away, apparently no longer interested in the
strange figure that stood above him. Kayne, imagining that
the child had likely seen many stranger sights than he,
moved away.

As he plodded up the slope of the next dune, a sudden bird-
like chirruping made him pause and scan the space above him
– the floor of the level above was still several hundred metres
from the tops of the tallest dunes. He almost expected to see
one of the clockwork birds from the Great Gallery in the Ty

House apartments spiralling down towards him. But he saw nothing and resumed his climb.

'Father said the Houses send their young nobles below the Wall to hunt, so that they come to understand the power they will wield over those below them,' Bael had told him. 'Because, when they understand that power, they understand what it means to rule.'

His brother's words were the last thing Kayne heard before the skin-hypos set into the inner skin of his suit silently administered the sedative. The compacted layers of refuse beneath his feet seemed to melt away, leaving him suspended as the world faded to soft white nothingness.

THE PROXIMITY ALARMS had been shrieking as the milky veil was shredded from his eyes, the stimulant administered by the suit's autonomous dispensers washing the narco from his system. The rapid chatter from several of the sentry units came next, followed by the low thump of someone firing a bolter. There was another noise, one he had heard recently. A chirruping, multiplied a hundred, perhaps a thousandfold.

'Where the Llud did they come from?' Bael's shouted question was lost in the twin-bolter volley he loosed at what appeared to be a tide of Underhivers – scavvies, mutants, ratskins, the more-or-less human – advancing towards them along the defile. Georgi's bolts were already blowing holes in the advancing tide, which were quickly filled as the horde continued its advance.

A shout from Aidor, followed by more bolter-fire made Kayne turn and look up one of the defile's steep slopes. They were there too, slipping, sliding, chunks of dislodged refuse rolling down the slope ahead of them. Aidor's bolts had as much effect as Bael's. No matter how many of the attackers were reduced to bloody tatters, more stepped forward to take their place.

Attackers – that was hardly an accurate description, Kayne realised. They appeared to be unarmed. They moved at a steady walking pace into the teeth of the hunters' weapons. Kayne imagined that they hadn't broken stride even as they were raked by high-velocity rounds from the sentry units. Those whose faces weren't slack and devoid of expression seemed to be smiling, even as they lost limbs to Pitar's las-fire or their chests were pulped by bolter rounds.

And, smiling or not, they were singing – that bird-like chirruping, interspersed with weird high-pitched clicks and squeals.

'We can't just stand here and let them come to us!' Bael's voice blared through Kayne's comm-link. 'Pitar, get some altitude, find out how many of them there are.'

'On my way!' Pitar unfurled her wings – and damned them all.

The pitch of their chirruping changed, became higher still, faster, denser. Kayne's comm-link squealed as if in sympathy. As if taking the opening of Pitar's wings as some kind of signal, they rushed forward, arms outstretched, tripping over each other in their anxiety to reach the hunters. Previously blank expressions had become animated as if by some kind of ecstatic frenzy. Kayne realised with sudden, awful certainty that the hunters stood no chance of stopping them.

Pitar almost made it into the air, before grasping hands grabbed her legs. A scabrous creature vaulted onto the backs of its fellows and wrapped its arms around her waist, adding to the weight of numbers that pulled her back to earth. Las-fire hissed out from beneath the pile of bodies that closed over her, crisping flesh, but it was not enough.

A trio of ratskins hurled themselves at Kayne. Reacting on instinct, he pulverised them with bolter-fire, only to see them replaced before him by more human-looking Underhivers, arms outstretched as if anxious to greet a long-lost friend, faces alight with an unnameable joy.

Kayne crushed a skull, shattered a chest, then turned to swat away a mutant that seemed intent on clambering onto his shoulders. The defile was a cacophony of gunfire. His comm-link whooped and howled with interference, from which emerged the shouts and curses of Bael, Meela and the others. There was no time to check on their status or location. There was no time to think, only react – to pound, to crush, to fire off round after round.

He had no memory of fighting his way up the side of the defile, or of how long he had been alone. He just found himself standing there, looking down into the seething mass of bodies that filled the defile. Kayne felt as if he had overturned a rock and was looking down at a nest of outraged insects.

'Kayne!' Bael's voice rang in his ear, the comm-link momentarily clear of interference. Kayne scanned the defile, trying to locate him.

Suddenly, he saw him, in the centre of a clear space that opened in the midst of the chittering tide. His visor had been torn away. Spirals of smoke rose lazily from both empty, overheated bolters. He turned slowly, surveying the mob, massive arms swinging slowly, menacingly, as if he was an ogre from a child's story, idly selecting his next victim.

He must have caught sight of the figure standing alone atop the slope. His head jerked up.

'Kayne!' he yelled again.

Kayne almost moved, almost raced down the slope, back into the teeth of the mob to carve a path for his brother's escape, but, in the heartbeat before he took a step, he saw other heads turn in his direction, faces locked in a rictus of ecstasy, frenzied eyes fixing on him. At the fringes of the mob, figures turned, moved towards the slope.

'Kayne!' He heard his brother's voice one last time, before an intolerable shriek of interference howled from the comm-link, seeming to pierce his skull. Tearing it from his ear, Kayne turned.

Turned and ran.

## Eight

'Kayne!'

Mot's shout was followed by the ratcheting sound of autogun fire, loud enough to rupture an eardrum. From the way Schular, running ahead of him up the sloping trail between the slag heaps, slapped a hand to her ear, Kayne guessed that Mot was broadcasting on the general channel – and had forgotten to close the connection.

'Mot!' Gyse, metres above and ahead of Kayne, Schular, Maas and Telmac, shouted into his comm-link as he circled the derelict transport depot. Skeletons of heavy haulage machinery lay scattered across the yard like the remains of long-dead monsters. Container stacks, rusted together in the time since they had been left there stood like ancient monoliths, patterned with moss and lichen stood like tombstones in a titans' graveyard.

Figures moved between the stacks, ducking, dodging, fanning out in a bid to encircle a lone figure, clad in a suit of

off-world design. Muzzle flashes illuminated the shadows cast
by the stacks. The lone figure ducked, froze, then moved on.

'Mot! For Helmawr's sake, close your comm-link!' Gyse
shouted, ears ringing with the sound of bullets ricocheting off
metal. 'I've got a fix on you. The others are on their way. They'll
arrive at the gate to your left, on the far side of the depot. Make
your way there, I'll give you some cover!'

As he began his dive, Gyse glanced towards the towering
rookery – originally a vast complex of workers' residences, now
home, he imagined, to all kinds of Hive Bottom detritus –
which stood a short way off. He saw groups of figures heading
towards the depot, drawn by the sound of gunfire, hoping for
fresh pickings.

'There's more company heading our way,' he reported via his
comm-link. 'And I'll lay odds that they're not the only ones. We
really don't want to still be here when they arrive!' Gyse tilted
his wings, powered up the las-tubes mounted on his suit's forearms, and began his dive.

SCHULAR RACED BETWEEN the drunkenly tilting gateposts – and
was forced to leap aside, diving and rolling to avoid the gunfire
that tore into the ground around her. A group emerged from
behind a container stack, weapons tracking her. Gangers,
allied, judging by their heavily muscled physiques and multicoloured crests of hair, to House Goliath.

'Hah! Lookit the skinny go!' bellowed one.

'It's a woman!' shouted another. 'Keep 'er in one piece – I
wan' 'er first!'

Their shouts and laughter turned to cries of surprise and pain
as Kayne, Maas and Telmac charged through the gateway,
bolters spitting death. Three of the gangers went down, chests
gaping, before their remaining fellows rallied, turning their fire
on the new arrivals.

Grabbing the corpse of a ganger by the straps that criss-
crossed its chest, Kayne hefted the carcass off the ground,
using it as a shield to absorbs the impact of a stub charge
another ganger fired in his direction, then hurled the twice-
eviscerated cadaver in his attacker's face. By the time the
stub-wielding Goliath had pushed his dead comrade off him
and half-regained his feet, Kayne was standing over him, fist
raised.

Telmac fired a volley at the ganger who turned a melta in his direction. Two bolts missed, tearing holes in a nearby stack. The monolith rang with the impacts, teetered for a moment, but did not fall. His last bolt hit the weapon, not the man who held it, but the effect was the same: the Goliath was vaporised by the suddenly unleashed power of his fully charged weapon. For a moment, an after-image of the ganger's almost comical look of surprise hung before Telmac's eyes.

Schular, back on her feet, had to duck almost immediately, to avoid the wild swing of a ganger's chainsword. She rose behind the chattering weapon's swing, lifting her own monomolecular blade as she did so.

The bisected ganger fell back. Behind him stood another, armed with a las-pistol. Seeing the blood fountaining from both halves of his dead comrade, he paused before opening fire. That pause doomed him.

The las-beam seemed to disappear as it struck Schular's buckler shield. The gems that studded its rim flashed once – then the beam re-appeared, heading back the way it had come. The ganger didn't have time to realise what had happened before his headless corpse hit the ground.

A rapid cannonade of explosions sounded from the far side of the depot, followed by a grinding and tearing as a container stack toppled over. There were more shouts – battle cries – and the sound of gunfire – bolters, autoguns, the dull report of a heavy stubber.

'Sounds like that company Gyse mentioned has arrived,' Maas said, a broken Goliath hanging limply from each fist.

'These scum must have arrived from another direction,' added Telmac, kicking a corpse that had been reduced to little more than a smoking torso by the impact of multiple bolter rounds. 'Mot's presence here has attracted a lot of attention from the wrong sort of people.'

'I want to know what the idiot was doing here in the first place,' Schular said.

'Chasing trophies most likely,' Maas replied. 'I told him: there'll be other hunts.'

'Not if we aren't somewhere else – and soon.' Kayne opened his comm-link. 'Mot, we've waited long enough. We're leaving. With you or without you.'

'No need to shout, brother. I'm here.' Mot's reply came from the shadows between two nearby stacks. 'We should move. Gyse distracted them long enough for me to slip away, but they're bound to head this way eventually.'

'We wouldn't be here if you hadn't sneaked off to cause trouble with the locals,' Schular pointed out.

'There were only two of them,' Mot explained, defensively. 'A pair of scabby prospectors. I followed them here, expecting to deal with them, then have the pick of whatever paltry treasures they might have stored around here somewhere. How was I to know there'd be more of them?'

'This nonsense is getting us nowhere,' Kayne declared. More grenade rounds exploded, nearer than before. Kayne opened his comm-link again.

'Gyse, Mot's with us. Get back here. We're leaving before those grenade-happy low-levellers bring this place down around our ears.'

'Incoming!' came Gyse's reply. Kayne jerked his head up, scanning the air.

'There!' Maas shouted, pointing towards the winged hunter, who had shot out from between two of the taller stacks. The smooth outline of one wing had been spoiled by a near miss from a las-bolt but otherwise his Yeld suit appeared to be undamaged. Gyse arrowed toward the waiting hunters.

'Don't wait for me,' he advised them over the comm-link. 'Get–'

The first autogun rounds punched through the metal of Gyse's wing almost before anyone had time to register the weapon's chattering bark. Another joined it, bullets raking the air before slamming into Gyse's body, drawing a line of impact wounds from hip to shoulder. The winged hunter was falling now, tumbling through the air, the ground rushing up to meet him.

'Gyse!' Schular screamed. Gyse made no reply as he hit the ground, bounced brokenly, then lay still. A horde of Underhivers emerged from between the stacks, all well-armed, all baying for blood.

'There weren't that many, last time I looked!' breathed Mot. Kayne shot an uncomprehending look at his half-brother, unable to decide whether Mot was too stupid to acknowledge the fatal chain of events he had set in motion or whether he was, quite simply, insane.

'Gyse!' Schular repeated, taking a step towards the inert hunter. Maas planted a restraining hand on her shoulder, shook her head when Schular turned to face her. When she looked back, she saw that the baying mob had almost reached Gyse's body. Several of the front-runners raced ahead, anxious to tear what trophies they could from his suit.

'Helmawr's blood, Mot!' Telmac shouted. 'You've killed us all!'

The deep, grinding rumble followed so closely on Telmac's words that it sounded as if the Hive itself was offering a reply. The ground beneath the hunters' feet shifted, seemed to sag, then lifted, reminding Kayne of the sensation of being aboard an aircraft at the moment it lifted from the landing pad.

Another rumble followed. The sound of containers torn loose from their corroded embrace and tumbling to earth resounded around the depot. Kayne looked down at his feet, expecting to see the ground ripple like the surface of one of the ornamental ponds in the Great Gallery. Instead, he saw a tracery of cracks had appeared. The cracks were spreading, growing wider.

'Hive-quake!' he shouted. 'Time we were gone!' Grabbing Mot in both hands, he spun him round, then propelled him out through the depot's gateway, whose already unsteady-looking gateposts had keeled over completely. Mot almost tripped over one of the fallen posts, stumbled, regained his balance, shot a look back at Kayne, then carried on down the track.

'Telmac, keep an eye on Mot. Don't let him wander off!' Telmac nodded, then followed Mot through the gateway. Kayne shouted to Maas and Schular, beckoned them to follow. Beyond them, Kayne saw that a wide fissure had split the earth a short way from Gyse's body. The mob of Underhivers had recoiled from it as if they were single entity. Their shouts of alarm became cries of fear as a nearby container stack toppled, its constituent parts loosing their ages-old grip on each other and tumbling into the midst of the horde. Kayne took some small satisfaction from knowing that Gyse's killers might be lying, crushed beneath one of the heavy metal boxes.

'Come on!' Maas shouted, cuffing him on the shoulder as she and Schular ran past him and out through the gateway. 'This is no time to start admiring the view!'

'Your half-brother he may be,' Schular said as she and Kayne pounded down the trail in Maas's wake, 'but he's going to wish he stayed and took his chances with the quake when I get my hands on him!'

'You'll have to join the queue,' Kayne replied grimly.

THEY RETRACED THEIR route to the service shaft at which they had waited for Mot, before finally heading off in search of the errant hunter. As suddenly as it had begun, the quake subsided, leaving an eerie silence in its wake. Telmac speculated that the Underhivers' successive volleys of grenades had set off some weakness in the surrounding structure, but no one cared to join in the geological debate. First Nikol, now Gyse. They climbed into the shaft one by one in a brooding silence, then edged their way cautiously through the network of ramped tunnels that it led into, checking for rats, milliasaurs or other such monstrosities that were known to lurk in such places. Mot, whether from some sense of shame or simple self-preservation, chose to keep his mouth shut.

Whenever they came upon another gaping shaft-mouth, they took the opportunity to descend, finally finding themselves in a wide tunnel, running calf deep with a stream of viscous ordure. Unconcerned, they waded through it, heading in the direction from which they heard the low rushing roar of falling water: a weir of some kind, perhaps, or a drainage shaft. The sounds of scuttling life reached them from both ahead and behind, but did not grow in volume. Whatever life existed down here had obviously chosen to keep a safe distance.

The stream dropped over the edge of a vertiginous down-shaft. Designed to handle vast quantities of run-off sewerage, the drain was too wide to cross to reach the tunnel on the opposite side, with no ladder or handholds to enable the hunters to climb down. Retracing their steps a short way they found a rusted metal ladder, up which they had little choice but to ascend.

As he climbed, Kayne offered a silent prayer of hope that, when they emerged from the shaft, it would be into a landscape that he would recognise from his journey back to the Spire.

As he surveyed the ash dunes that ran steeply away from the door of the pump-house into which the service shaft had led them they felt like an answer to his prayer. The ash-scape rippled like sand at an ocean's edge, the ripples gradually growing larger, becoming dunes that grew larger as they swept away towards the horizon. He remembered trudging along the paths between these dunes for what seemed like days, occasionally climbing to the top of one of the taller dunes in the vain hope of getting some kind of bearing, some clue that he was heading in the right direction. In the end, he settled for following the dune-scape's generally upward slope.

Looking down upon the dunes from just outside the doorway of the pump-house, which stood alone in the landscape like a bizarre monument to a forgotten civilisation, Kayne felt almost elated. He had to search within himself for several heartbeats before he was able to identify the sensation: *hope*.

'WE'VE GOT COMPANY.'

Maas didn't sound pleased to be passing the information on from the rear of their five-man column, moving, well-spaced, along the trail between two ranges of ash-dunes. Kayne half-turned as he walked, looked back along the line, saw nothing.

Then he looked up.

Three robed and cowled figures stood atop the long, flat dune that flanked one side of the path. Behind them stood a line of gangers – House Delaque from the look of their long duster coats and wrap-around goggles.

'Oh no,' Telmac, walking in the middle of the column behind Schular and ahead of Mot, sounded even less happy than Maas. He was looking up at the dune on the other side of the trail. Kayne looked up at the other dune – and all hope turned to ashes to match the dunes that rose around them.

Two more of the robed cloaked figures stood on this other dune, flanked by roughly the same number of gangers as the first three Kayne had seen.

As if on some unheard signal, the cloaked figures pushed back their cowls. Beneath them they wore helmets and eye-pieces of familiar design.

Not just gangers.

'Spyrers!' Kayne unconsciously used the Underhive term for hunters such as he. The injured scavenger he had last seen running between the conveyor supports in the smelting works, many levels and what felt like ten times as many years ago, sprang unbidden to his mind. Is this how the man had felt in the long moment he spent, staring at Kayne who, seconds before, had torn off his friend's face?

'Hunters of House Ty,' one of the new arrivals called down to them. Judging by his visored helmet and the bulky outline of his cloak, he wore an Orrus rig. 'I tell you, according to the Rules of Engagement, that I am Mordecai Gyre of House Ulanti. I tell you that we could have taken you in the sewer, but that would not have been seemly.'

As Gyre spoke, Mot moved slowly along the trail until he reached Telmac.

'What is this?' Telmac whispered, eyes still fixed on Gyre. 'Are they going to take up back up-Spire? Ransom us back to House Ty?'

Mot shook his head slowly, saying nothing.

'I also tell you that this is not a hunt. This is a kill, bought and paid for.' Gyre's voice continued to float down from the dune-top.

'You remember, back at that depot, just before the quake, you told me that I'd killed you all?' Mot asked Telmac. Telmac looked down at him, not understanding.

'I also tell you,' Gyre concluded, 'that you have been betrayed.'

'Well,' Mot continued, smiling behind his mask. 'You were right!'

Telmac felt something long and hard punch him in the chest, at a point where two of his suit's thick armour plates met. He took an automatic step back, then looked down. All he could see was Mot's fist, as if he had simply thumped Telmac on the chest, but Telmac knew that was not the case. The claws fitted to Mot's combat rig were now buried deep inside him.

'Why?' he asked, already feeling faintly detached from the scene around him. It had suddenly become, he realised, very hard to breathe.

'Why not?' Mot answered, then withdrew his claws with an oblique, slashing motion, opening the wound further, tearing flesh and suit material away as he did so. One of Telmac's chest plates fell away from his suit. Telmac took another backward step, then dropped heavily to his knees.

Schular sprinted to Telmac, dropped to her knees and held him against her. Telmac looked up at her with heavy-lidded eyes. He frowned slowly, seemed puzzled.

'Nikol?' he asked, then died, blood running in a sudden gush from his mouth as his head lolled forward onto his chest.

By the time Schular had reached Telmac, Mot was halfway up the slope of a dune, moving with long, suit-assisted strides, heading for the other hunters and their ganger support. A number of the Delaques opened fire. Mot jumped sideways to avoid the sudden rain of bullets.

'Not the Malcadon!' Gyre bellowed the order. 'The others!'

The gangers obediently shifted their aim. Ash kicked up around Maas and Schular. Maas returned fire immediately, blowing several gangers backwards, out of sight over the lip of the dune. She swung round, hoping to take out some of the attackers who were now moving down the side of the opposite dune. The sliding ash made their progress unsteady. None, gangers or hunters, were willing to risk a shot while they half-marched, half-slid towards the trail. She triggered both bolters.

Nothing. Two red lights had started to blink in her eyepiece's head-up display.

'Kayne!' she yelled, looking past where Schular half-lay behind Telmac's corpse, her sword useless against the long-range attack, the energy absorbing properties of her mirror shield nullified by the fact that the gangers – no doubt under instructions from their Ulanti commanders – were all using solid projectile weapons. It occurred to Maas that the gangers were also under instructions merely to keep them pinned down, to allow the hunters to move in for a close kill.

'Kayne! I'm out of ammunition!' Maas called. 'Cover me!'

Kayne didn't remember taking so many backward steps down the trail, eyes fixed on Maas, Schular and the dead Telmac. A small voice in the back of his head told him that Maas carried more ammunition in pouches set into the thigh armour of her suit. All she needed was the time to reach for them and reload.

His eyes flicked from side to side, taking in the scene on either dune. The hunters and some of their retinue, advancing down each slope, the rest laying down a pinning fire from the dune-tops. He saw Mot, standing with the gangers atop one of the dunes.

'This time, I shall be the only hunter returning from the hunt.' Mot's voice over the comm-link startled Kayne. 'I shall stand ready to assume our father's place when the old man finally gives up the fight. It almost worked for you. Why not for me? As you see, I already have developed a most fruitful relationship between the Helios family and certain members of House Ulanti.'

'Mot, you motherless piece of sewer-scum!' Maas's words stabbed into Kayne's ear. 'Kayne! We need you!'

But Kayne had already turned, was already pounding along the trail, pursued by autogun fire from the dune-tops. As before, as if in a dream, he tore the comm-link from his ear as he ran.

Ahead the trail divided, curving around a tall, steep-sided dune. Kayne ignored both trails and drove himself up the slope, almost losing his footing as one foot plunged knee-deep into the shifting ash. Righting himself, he continued.

Gunfire raked the ash all around him, ricocheted off the armour across his back. Something stung past his cheek, drawing blood. Still he ran, reaching the top of the dune and suddenly finding himself staring down at an unexpectedly long, steep drop. Again his foot sank into the ash and he overbalanced, arms pinwheeling uselessly as he fell forward, tumbling end over end, unable to control his descent.

## Nine

KAYNE CROUCHED beneath the outlet pipe and tried not to think. A foul-smelling liquid gurgled from the pipe above his head, splashing merrily into an open drain a metre or so from his feet. He had crawled into the space beneath the pipe a while ago. How long exactly, he couldn't be sure. To be sure would mean having to think. Having to remember.

*The sport to come, eh?*

Kayne flinched, jerked his head round, expecting – no, fearing – to see Bael, about to deliver a brotherly slap on the shoulder. And, in remembering Bael, he couldn't help but think of the others of his hunting party. Georgi, who he had seen, carving the ecstatic, chittering attackers into odd-sized chunks, before the sheer weight of their numbers overwhelmed him; Pitar, being dragged from the air by so many grasping hands. He had no memory of seeing how Meela, Volk and Aidor met their fates, but it took little imagination to guess. He remembered well enough how the attackers had seemed to fill the defile between the garbage dunes, like a tide, rushing along the defile from nowhere, washing the hunters from his sight.

He remembered how the tide had seemed to part, revealing his brother. He remembered Bael, calling his name, looking up at him.

He remembered seeing the attackers also turn and look in his direction.

But most of all, he remembered running, at first with no thought of direction. Then, later, he thought of only one thing: the Spire. He had to make his way up-hive, back above the Wall and away from the nightmares that stalked the lower levels.

Judging by the condition of his suit, that was not going to be easy. His visor's head-up display was a kaleidoscope of warning indicators, all glowing or blinking accusingly. He should have stopped, allowed the rig's self-repair mechanisms to at least make a start on bringing the suit back up to somewhere near optimum efficiency. But to do that, he would have had to stop running.

He remembered clambering up a chute, as wide as the broadest thoroughfare in the Spire, clogged with yet more waste, until he reached a gallery along which were ranged vast compactors, presumably intended to process detritus from the levels above. Most were silent, a few were still operating, collecting, grinding, compressing as they had from the moment they were set to work, centuries, perhaps millennia ago.

He had drawn fire from a group of scavvies camped among the compactors. When he tried to return fire, to cover his escape, he found that the firing mechanism of one of his bolters was jammed and that the bolt magazine of the other was empty. He couldn't remember pumping so many bolts into the faces of the chittering attackers, but there was the indicator, glowing red at the edge of his visor. Grabbing a wheeled skip from beside one of the compactors he hurled it in the general direction of the scavvies and made off, his headlong flight given renewed urgency by the gunfire that spattered against the machinery around him.

Beneath the pipe, Kayne shifted his position, felt more than heard the grinding of one of his suit's knee joints. A stray scavvy bullet, perhaps, had damaged the hydraulics. A yellow-green fluid stained the suit's lower leg, though it was hard to make it out, given the slick brown mush in which he sat, and which now coated most of the lower half of his body.

Left unrepaired, the joint would surely seize up, leaving him limping through the Underhive like a wounded animal, easy prey for the predators – human or otherwise – that lurked down here. But, to effect the repair, he would have to trigger the suit's restorative mode and submit to narco-assisted sleep state. Given his suit's current condition, how could he be sure that it would administer the correct dose of sedative? He might never wake, starving to death while his suit repaired itself then lay, quiescent, in the mud. Years from now, he might be found, his suit opened like the burial casket of a forgotten race, his desiccated corpse crumbling to dust at the first breath of air.

Appalled as much by the grotesque avenues along which his imagination was running as by the apparent hopelessness of his situation, he clambered out from beneath the pipe, splashed across the open drain and stood upright for the first time in what felt like days. As he did so, it became clear that his knee joint wasn't the only one in need of attention. His right shoulder clicked loudly, then, for a heart-stopping moment, froze completely. A sharp downward movement freed the joint, the actuators again operating smoothly. But for how long?

For the first time, Kayne allowed himself to consider what would normally be the unthinkable: that he might have to abandon the suit.

He might as well walk into a pit-fight naked.

Fighting down the panic that rose, threatening to choke his resolve and send him scurrying back under the pipe, he forced himself to consider his options. There was only one: to acquire some other weaponry, albeit less sophisticated than the off-world marvels of his combat rig.

'Right now, I'd settle for an antique stub pistol, if I knew it would work.'

The sound of his voice surprised him; he hadn't intended to speak out loud. Worried that he may have been overheard, he looked both ways along the trench in which the pipe ran. Off to his right, the pipe disappeared beneath what looked like a tumbledown collection of buildings. One thing he had learnt during his time in the Underhive: no matter how old, how derelict a building may look, how long-forgotten was its original purpose, if it offered shelter, it would be inhabited. Scavvies, mutants, it didn't matter what kind of barely human refuse might be living there. They would be armed – and Kayne was suddenly very anxious to meet them.

* * *

THE BUILDINGS, he discovered, were little more than hollow shells. Originally several storeys high, they appeared to have been scythed away as if by some dark god's axe. Walls bowed outward, or else teetered on the brink of collapsing atop the piles of debris that already littered their interiors. Anyone fool-ish enough to seek shelter here would more than likely wake from their slumber to find a wall falling on top of them.

No shelter, then. But the buildings were evidently of interest to someone.

There were ten, maybe fifteen of them – more than Kayne would have liked to be facing with his suit in its current state. Most of them looked to be scavvies, but a couple, stripped to the waist as they all were, were more seriously deformed. Kayne was surprised to see them working together, salvaging building materials from one of the ruins that lined the opposite side of what once might have been a street from the crumbling shell in which he crouched, watching them. Mutants were the least wel-come members of the Underhive population, treated with open disdain, if not outright violence by all other classes of Hiver.

One member of the working party stood out from the others. Taller, more heavily muscled, he seemed to be directing opera-tions. As Kayne watched, the figure pointed at a beam that was protruding from a clump of concrete slabs, then joined in with the others who gathered round, working to free it.

Three of the Hivers were not joining in the salvage operation. They stood, autoguns cradled in their arms, scanning the street in either direction. If they were the ones with weapons, Kayne decided, they were his targets.

A mutant and a scavvy staggered crab-wise towards one of the two tractor-drawn wagons that stood a short way from the ruin on which they were working, a heavy-looking slab of ragged concrete between them. As they approached the wagon, the scavvy stumbled, almost dropping his end of the slab. The guard nearest to them turned. Seeing the situation, he propped his weapon against one of the wagon's wheels and moved to help. Together, the three of them manoeuvred the slab towards the inclined plank that led up to the wagon's flatbed.

Kayne seized the chance. Charging through the ragged hole that once had been the doorway of the building in which he had been hiding, he targeted one of the two guards who still held their weapons and fired.

The bolt hit the corner of the neighbouring building, punching a large hole through the crumbling structure. Kayne silently cursed his suit's failing systems, but ran on. He was committed. There was no turning back.

The working party reacted to his appearance and to the bolt's explosion with unexpected efficiency. Dropping whatever tools they were using to free the slabs and beams from the rubble, they ran towards the wagon and tractors. They might have been seeking shelter, but they moved more calmly that Kayne had expected. There were no shouts of alarm, no sense of panic.

Autogun fire raked the dirt in front of Kayne, bringing him to a skidding halt. He jinked sideways, only to jump back as another volley kicked up tiny dust devils in front of his feet. Changing direction yet again, he pivoted on one foot.

The wrong foot.

The damaged knee joint clicked – the sound all too familiar – and locked. Kayne completed his spin, arms outstretched like some ludicrous children's toy, then sprawled, face down, in the dirt. As he lay there, breath blowing tiny clouds of dust up into his face, the last dregs of his strength draining away, he heard it: wheezed out through deformed throats, barked out with more than a little derision, or simply pealing out with the gusto normally associated with a damn good night's drinking. Laughter.

They were laughing at him.

Stung by the sound, he hauled his face out of the dirt and found himself staring up at the tall figure he had noticed earlier, the apparent leader of the working party. He held a bolt pistol loosely in one hand, but the weapon was not aimed at Kayne. He was looking down at Kayne, not laughing, but the broad smile he was wearing showed that the absurdity of the situation wasn't lost on him.

Kayne swung his still-functioning bolter from beneath his body, aiming it directly into that smiling face.

'You could kill me,' the man said, his voice betraying no hint of fear. His voice was deep, the kind of voice Kayne could easily imagine addressing and holding the attention of a crowd. The voice of an politician, perhaps, or a priest. 'But what good would that do you?'

He gestured for Kayne to look past him, towards the wagons and tractors, around and between which were ranged the rest of the working party, each of them armed. These were not the average type of Underhiver, disorganised and concerned only with their own survival. These had been trained.

'Y'all right, pastor?' called a short, stubby specimen. There seemed to be something wrong with his face, Kayne noticed.

'I'm fine, Micc,' the man replied, without taking his eyes off Kayne. For all his soothing reassurance that Kayne held the upper hand in their one-on-one situation, there was something in the man's eyes that made Kayne suspect that the opposite might very well be true. 'Our friend here is just weighing up the odds.'

'Pastor?' Kayne asked, not sure whether he did so to play for time, or because he was genuinely interested. Was this why he abandoned Bael – to delay his own death by a few hours?

'The title's a relic,' came the answer. To Kayne's amazement he almost looked embarrassed. Then he reached down with his free hand, offering to help Kayne to his feet. 'My given name is Monad. And my family name is Vex.'

'Pastor?'

Vex closed the book and turned to face the door. He had been reading the words of the Arch-Zealot concerning the Last Days and the Final Crusade with which the Redemption would greet them. Every follower of the Redemption would rise up, take arms and, led by their priests, sweep away the sins of the Hive in blood and fire. As a young man, Vex remembered, he would lay awake at night, on his bare wooden pallet in the novice's dormitory of Sin's Defeat, one of the oldest Redemption strongholds in the Underhive, praying that he would live to see it, be a part of it.

And now, it seemed, his prayers were being answered – though not in the way his younger self would have expected.

For some reason, as he read, his thoughts had also turned back to Kayne, the Spyre Hunter who had passed through their lives for a short time, back then. It had been more than a year since he had left Hope's End, during which Vex had had more than enough to occupy his mind. The settlement had grown to an unmanageable size as Underhivers abandoned their homes in the face of escalating paranoia, superstitious dread fostered by the Redemption and, of course, good old-fashioned right-eous violence. So many people looking to the pastor for guidance, for protection that he knew he would be unable to provide.

So why should he be thinking about one more privileged thrill-seeker who, when Vex met him, was struggling with the realisation that he was not as invincible as life in the bosom of the Spire had led him to believe?

'Micc's back.' Neesa stood in the doorway. Since her arrival at Hope's End, she had somehow become a part of Vex's unofficial retinue. Vex was sure that Micc had something to do with it; he had taken an almost paternal interest in the girl since they had rescued her ragged group of refugees from the attentions of a roving band of Cawdor gangers. There had been a worrying increase in the numbers of such bands of murderous zealots roaming the Underhive at the time. In the short while since then, their numbers had doubled.

*And the faithful shall rise up and smite the unbelievers. Their souls shall burn in the fires of the Redemption and Mankind shall be cleansed, for it is our destiny!*

The last words he had read before closing the book came back to him. Once he would have seen them as Holy Writ. Now they sounded like a justification for slaughter on an industrial scale.

'Thank you, Neesa,' Vex replied. 'Is he in the barracks?'

The building in which the militia rested while on duty had once been a school. Now there were too many children in Hope's End to fit in the building, so lessons had been transferred to what, judging by its size and layout, had once been a church. Whenever he thought about it, Vex allowed himself a moment to appreciate the irony.

'No,' Neesa said. 'He's in the infirmary.'

'THERE WERE TOO many to count. Coming over the ash-dunes. Too many to keep to the trails.'

Micc sat on the edge of a cot. A grubby strip of cloth had been wound around a head wound and he had been told to rest for a few hours – which, of course, wasn't going to happen.

'We stayed out of sight, watched them pass. It took a long time. There were all sorts: a priest, obviously...'

'Obviously,' repeated Vex. When he had entered the long, low-ceilinged building, everything had gone quiet. Conversations stopped in mid-flow, all heads turned in his direction, the same question on every face: who has he come to bless?

Who's dying?

'Pastor,' Micc broke off from his report. 'I didn't mean…'

'I know.' Vex smiled ruefully down at Micc and waved for him to continue. 'We all make mistakes when we're young.' He plucked at his faded, tattered robe. 'This was mine. Carry on.'

'Yeah, well, sorry anyway,' Micc coughed, then continued. 'Like I say, there was a priest, deacons, brethren, more zealots than I ever wanted to see in one place and an army of gangers – Cawdor, taking point, guarding the flanks. It was like they're going to war.'

'They are,' Vex added quietly, almost to himself.

'Then there were the regular hivers – settlers, traders, I even saw a bunch wearing guilder colours.' Micc paused, raised a hand unconsciously to his head wound.

'We were heading back, trying to stay outta sight. Must've not been careful enough,' he continued. 'Cawdors blind-sided us. We were trying to outflank them. They outflanked us. Almost funny.'

He paused again, stared at the floor. When he spoke again, his voice was little more than a whisper. 'Lost three – Komo, Ludi and Dieko – before we managed to shake them off. Lost a lot of time. Rate that mob was moving, they'll–'

'Pastor.'

Vex turned. Neesa was standing at his side. 'There's something you should see. Outside the walls.'

'I'll come with you.' Micc eased himself up from the cot and walked with them towards the door.

'There was something I noticed about the priest,' he said. 'He wore a black hood.'

'Zydo,' Vex said absently. 'An old acquaintance. Renowned for his piety and fervour. I studied with him. Took it very badly when I suggested people might be more willing to accept redemption if it wasn't offered at the point of a gun.

'He'll have been waiting for this chance for a long time. The Final Crusade is just the excuse he's been looking for.'

As they followed Vex out of the infirmary, Micc turned to Neesa and grinned.

'I feel so much better knowing that, don't you?'

* * *

## Ten

IT HAD BEEN Vex's suggestion that Kayne take off his suit.

'It makes you look more war machine than man,' Vex told him, a hint of a smile playing about his lips. Kayne wondered if he was enjoying the memory of this war machine's shambolic, self-defeating performance against his men. 'When the people here have seen such things, they – or someone dear to them – have often been its next victim.'

People? Under normal circumstances, Kayne would not use such a word to describe the ragged collection of misbegotten creatures he had seen since arriving at the settlement. The two-wagon caravan had ground its way from the site of the salvage operation, both tractors wheezing and coughing with the effort. Kayne had sat amidst the jumble of salvaged materials in the rearmost wagon, closely flanked by most of Vex's men. No one spoke. Kayne got the impression that most of them would have preferred Vex to have killed him where he lay, not help him to his feet and offer him a ride. But, Kayne noticed, no one argued with Vex.

Kayne's first impression of Hope's End was that it looked little different to the collection of uninhabitable shells they had left behind. As the tractors inched down one of the trails into the basin in which the settlement sat, overlooked by the hanging crag at its back, he saw just another conglomeration of buildings whose purpose, perhaps vital to the development and construction of the Spire that now towered unreachable leagues above their roofs, was now long-forgotten.

But, where the salvage site had been deserted apart from Vex's reclamation team, Hope's End was alive, seemingly with every kind of human and semi-human refuse. Much of the activity was focused on the wall that had been erected around the town, constructed, it seemed from every broken down vehicle for levels above and below, shored up by salvaged spars and irregular chunks of concrete.

As the caravan passed through the gate it was greeted by shouts from the settlement's inhabitants. Those not involved in the construction of a pair of unsteady-looking towers on either side of the gate hurried over to help with the unloading. When they caught sight of Kayne, however, they stopped in their tracks.

'Spyrer!' The word was hissed by what might have been a man, had his skeletal frame not been so hideously twisted, his skin not a scabbed and mottled collage of grey and green. He took one limping step forward and spat in the dirt.

'All who need help are welcome at Hope's End.' Vex had climbed down from the lead wagon. The moment he spoke, every face turned towards him. 'All are welcome because all can be saved. All can find peace.'

Vex signalled to his men in the second wagon, who dismounted, then waited while Kayne also climbed stiffly down. Every joint in his suit had grown stiff; his locked shoulder still refused to budge, though a little play had returned to the knee joint that had pitched him into the dirt. The warning indicators on his visor display continued to glare at him. He couldn't even be sure that his suit had enough power left to enable him to walk unassisted to wherever Vex intended to imprison him.

'My quarters,' Vex instructed. 'Assuming he can fit through the doorway in that armour.'

Kayne, still flanked by Vex's men, followed the pastor across what might once have been the town square. More and more of the settlement's inhabitants appeared, drawn by the news of their unwelcome visitor. They kept their distance and Kayne found himself walking along a wide avenue lined with expressions of fear and hate.

Kayne was escorted towards a crumbling two-storey structure – some kind of meeting hall, he guessed. A few paces from the door, he stumbled, his knee joint locking for a moment. Two members of his escort grabbed his arms, preventing him from falling on his face for the second time that day. Someone in the crowd hissed a remark. Kayne didn't catch the words, but the tone was unmistakable. Not fear. Not even hate. Contempt.

Vex ordered that the double doors of the meeting hall be closed behind them, then ushered Kayne into a small room that opened off to one side at the far end of the hall. Kayne had to edge gingerly through the doorway, the chest and back plates of his suit squeaking against the ancient wood of the frame. The scavvy with the lopsided face made to follow Vex into the room, but the taller man shook his head and closed the door.

'You know what I am?' Kayne asked in reply to Vex's suggestion that he remove his suit. 'Your people clearly do.'

Vex nodded.

'Your kind are the stuff of legend in the Underhive,' he said. 'Mothers warn their children to behave, or else the Spyrers will come and carry them away.'

'Then why am I still alive?' Looking past the winking kaleidoscope of warning indicators that edged his vision, Kayne assessed his chances of taking Vex hostage, using him to force his way out of the settlement. Not good. The pastor was a powerfully built man and something about the way he carried himself suggested that he was no stranger to physical combat. And, encased in this crippled piece of off-world technology, Kayne might as well have been bound hand and foot in Malcadon ironsilk. He'd be lucky to get his hands on Vex in the first place, let alone restrain him for any length of time.

'That's a good question,' Vex replied. 'Your kind usually hunt in packs. Yet you attacked us alone and your equipment is clearly in need of repair. This leads me to surmise that your fellow Spyrers are dead, or else they are too far away to be of any help to you – in which case, they might as well be dead.'

'Hunters!' Kayne shot back, stung by Vex's use of the Underhivers' term for Kayne and his kind. 'We are hunters!'

'I doubt your prey would see much honour in that name,' Vex replied smoothly, unperturbed by Kayne's sudden display of anger. 'To them you are killers, pure and simple.'

Vex paused, glanced down at his hands, then rubbed at a discoloured patch on his robe's tattered skirt.

'There is no honour in killing,' he added, quietly. Silence hung in the room for a long moment, during which Kayne had the acute sense that Vex had suddenly forgotten that he was there, that he was unwittingly intruding on the pastor's most private meditations. And he was suddenly very glad that he had not attempted to attack the priest.

Vex lifted his gaze from his robe. 'We can offer you shelter,' he said. 'Time to make repairs to your equipment, though I doubt any tools that we have would be of much use.'

'My rig will repair itself, as far as it is able,' Kayne replied, surprised by the rush of gratitude he felt upon hearing Vex's offer. A profound sense of his own exhaustion had settled about him like an iron cloak.

'All it needs – all I need – is time.'

* * *

UNTIL HIS LAST day at Hope's End, Kayne had seen no more of Vex. The priest gave the hunter the use of his quarters; Kane had no idea where Vex slept. Never much of a reader, Vex's meagre library – two shelves of battered print volumes – offered no escape from the boredom that settled over him. After seeing the Underhivers' barely concealed hostility during his first tour of the settlement – without his rig, wearing borrowed rags over his skin-tight undersuit – Kayne decided that to leave the meeting hall again would be to invite a blade between the ribs.

Twice a day, two armed members of what Kayne took to be Vex's personal retinue delivered a bowl of slops to his room. The food's appearance and consistency reminded Kayne of something he would more usually expect to flush down a waste disposal unit – it occurred to him that Vex's foot-soldiers might be trying to infect him with some kind of fatal disease. When at last he summoned the courage to try a spoonful, he invariably found that it tasted like oil scooped from the bottom of a tractor's sump but, no longer sustained by the Orrus rig's intravenous feeding system, he was always too hungry to set the bowl aside.

When he wasn't eating he would pace the room, listening to the sounds of activity outside the hall: shouts, the congested wheeze of a tractor, the sounds of construction. He wondered whether the gate towers had been completed – and how long the jerry built structures would stay upright.

When he wasn't eating or pacing, he would sleep. Unsupported by his suit's bio-boosters, his body seemed to sag beneath the accumulated weight of every step of the hunt, from the moment he, Bael and the others left the Spire, to the moment he pitched into the dirt at Vex's feet. He felt hollow, weak, barely able to lift himself from Vex's hard metal cot. Like a clockwork bird whose mechanism had wound down.

He slept heavily, like a baby. And when he slept, he dreamed – and the dream was always the same.

*They had invaded the Spire. Their inhuman chittering filled the corridors of the Helios family apartments as they moved from room to room, searching.*

*Searching for him.*

*He ran from them, through deserted halls and galleries, the insectile nonsense growing louder as they gained on him.*

*Daring not to look back, he fled the Helios apartments, racing through deserted halls and minor galleries, lungs burning, breath coming in gasps. He knew that, should he try to call out, his voice would be little more than a whisper.*

*His flight always brought him to the same place: the Great Gallery, where the others were waiting for him to join the hunt. Bael, Pitar, Volk, Aidor, Georgi and Meela. Alive. And every time he saw them, he felt the same rush of relief.*

*Until, smiling, they opened their mouths and greeted him with a stream of high-pitched clicks and squeals.*

He would wake screaming, eyes wide, staring up at the Orrus rig which stood impassively against the wall at the foot of the cot. He would lay there a moment, allowing his panicked breathing to slow, letting the sounds of the settlement reassert themselves over the ghostly chittering that still echoed in his mind. Then he would ease himself up off the cot and move over to the suit to check on the progress of the rig's self-repair systems. The visor read-out's estimate of how many cycles were required before the rig would be anything like combat-ready counted down with agonising slowness. Kayne reckoned his time by this clock, rather than the alternating periods of activity and quiescence that he heard through the wall.

'The ratskins tell stories about a creature called a *khalem*.' Kayne hadn't heard Vex enter the room. He spun round from his rig, helmet held in one hand. How long had Vex been standing in the open doorway, watching him check the suit's functions? All but a number of minor systems had been returned to operating efficiency. Kayne had been considering when would be the best time to leave Hope's End. And, as if hearing his thoughts, Vex had appeared.

'What?'

'According to the stories, the khalem is a man-like creature, made from a hollow shell of mud and sticks, baked in a fire, then filled with a jumble of machine parts. A shaman creates it, then, through some blasphemous ritual, breathes life into his creation, magically sets in motion the machinery within, then sends it out to do his bidding. Seeing your armour standing there reminded me of the story.'

Kayne looked down at the helmet, then up at the suit. A hollow man? The description seemed appropriate somehow.

'Micc tells me that you have recovered your strength. I came to tell you that, should you wish, you are welcome to stay. The people here will get used to your presence. They are already aware of my feelings on the matter. You would come to no harm.

'If you decide to stay, you should be aware that life here is hard, much harder than the life I imagine you are used to, but it does have its rewards. Also, I should tell you that times are changing. Though I am no favourite among my former brethren, their attempts to disturb the peace of this settlement have, until now, been few.'

Looking at Vex standing there, all but filling the doorway, and listening to his deceptively gentle voice, Kayne had a pretty good idea why.

'Recently, however, their attacks upon our working parties have increased. New arrivals at Hope's End speak of raids on smaller, less well defended settlements, forced conversions and purges. I fear that the Arch-Zealot has declared a crusade. If that is so, I can think of at least one of my brothers who would welcome the chance to lead it to Hope's End.'

'Why are you telling me this?' Kayne asked. 'I'm a Spyrer. A hunter of those you call your people. I came here to win honour and glory for myself, my family and my House; that is all.'

'All are welcome here. There is no man who cannot find redemption if he is willing to look for it,' Vex smiled ruefully. 'Though my brethren might argue that the only true path to salvation is through fire. But there is another reason: should the crusade come to Hope's End, a man wearing an offworld combat rig would be a useful addition to our defences. And even if my fears of a crusade prove groundless, there are the rumours.'

'What rumours?' Kayne couldn't help but ask, though he was far from sure that he wanted to hear the answer.

'There are some who say the Hive has given birth to a new kind of creature, that looks like a man, but speaks like a machine. That is growing in number. That it may, at some point in the future, rise up and overwhelm us all.'

'They're not rumours,' Kayne said quietly. Vex stared at him, saying nothing. The silence stretched between them.

'They attacked us,' Kayne continued, suddenly anxious to say anything to break the silence. 'An ambush. We were unprepared. I was the only survivor.'

Vex held Kayne's gaze for a moment longer, then nodded, giving Kayne the uncomfortable impression that he had told the priest far more than he had intended – far more than his words alone had conveyed.

'Then perhaps the khalem is not merely a story after all,' Vex said. 'My offer stands,' he continued, stepping back through the doorway, turning to go.

'I will consider it,' Kayne replied, already knowing that he had made his decision.

THE RIG WELCOMED him back into its embrace like a long lost lover. His spine tingled with feedback from the bio-booster. Flexing his hands inside the massive gloves, he felt he could tear the building down around him, uproot the whole settlement without breaking sweat. He felt like a hunter once again.

He opened the meeting hall's double doors slowly, looked out across the deserted square. He had waited until the sounds of activity from outside had subsided before donning his rig, easing out through the narrow doorway of Vex's room, and moving quietly to the building's main doors.

The gate towers had been completed. A guard stood atop the tower to the left of the gate. His visor's photo-enhancers showed Kayne that the guard was facing outwards, away from the settlement. If he moved swiftly, the guard would not notice him until he was already through the gates. The gates were closed, but he felt confident in his ability to tear them aside if he had to.

'Y'leaving?' Micc stepped around the corner of the meeting hall. Kayne, no more that four or five steps from the doors, turned. The stocky scavvy with the lopsided face cradled a stub gun in his arms. He appeared relaxed, unafraid.

'I like to swing by here when things are quiet,' Micc continued. 'Make sure there's no trouble.'

'No trouble,' Kayne repeated, feeling like a flat-footed idiot.

'That's good,' Micc nodded. 'Come on. Let's see you on y'way.'

THE TRACK ROSE up to the lip of the depression in which Hope's End sat. Standing at the top of the incline, Kayne looked back at the settlement. The gates had been closed behind him and he had moved swiftly out of range of the tower guard's autogun. The figure of the guard was visible to Kayne's enhanced vision, but he was facing in another direction, paying him no heed. There was no sign of Micc.

The scavvy had given Kayne a set of directions, which, he said, would enable him to pass unseen, up through the next ten levels. Kayne had considered the possibility that they were intended to lead him to some Helmawr-forsaken dead end, inhabited by creatures, human or otherwise, who did not share Vex's attitude to unexpected visitors, but discounted it. Micc, he decided, simply wanted to see the back of him.

By now, Kayne imagined, Vex would have heard of his departure. There was no reason why he – a son of a family of one of the Ruling Houses of Hive Primus – should care a whit for the opinions of a broken down apostate priest living in the squalor of the deep Underhive. But that did nothing to ease the nagging sense that he had disappointed Vex – by doing exactly what the priest had expected of him.

Turning his back on Hope's End, Kayne shrugged these thoughts aside, forced himself to focus on the journey that still lay ahead. Far above him rose the Spire, his home. By the time he got there, he would have his story prepared. They were attacked, his fellow hunters and he. The others died fighting against their attackers who were, of course, heavily armed. The tide of battle swept him away from them. He killed those who sought to kill him but, by then, the others were dead. He could do nothing to help them – at least that was true. And there was something else. The most important thing of all: he did not run.

So why was it that, as he marched away from the settlement, that one thought filled his mind – that he was running still?

## Eleven

Now Kayne stood on the edge of the depression and looked down at the killing ground Hope's End had become.

Much of the scene was obscured by the thick smoke from the burning remains of the shacks. It hung low in the still air, turning much of the battle into a shadow play. Groups of indistinct figures clashed; brief muzzle-flashes sparked like fireflies in the gloom, counterpointed by the deeper reports of grenades. By setting fire to the shanties, the attackers had unwittingly offered a helping hand to the defenders. Under cover of the smoke,

Vex's men slipped out through the gates in small teams, striking at the Redemptionists, harrying them, sowing confusion among their ranks before withdrawing.

Kayne stepped back as a group of the attackers returned to the rise, carrying between them a number of wounded. He bowed his head, anxious that the folds of his newly acquired deacon's robes should hide his Orrus rig. The deacon had been a generously proportioned man, his voice surprisingly high-pitched for one of his size as he stood at the rear of a column of Redemptionists, urging them forwards with wild cries and exhortations. Kayne had waited until he paused for breath before stepping out from behind an irregular pile of rock fragments – perhaps some of the long-discarded remains of the excavation which had formed the depression in which Hope's End sat – and wrapped an oversized hand around his face.

Fastening the robe about him, pulling the hood around his face, Kayne had joined the tide of people that was moving through the ragged, slag-strewn landscape of this level. Though he had managed to outdistance the hunters and their Delaque cohorts among the ash-dunes before tumbling down a series of connected ramps, he knew that they would not give up their pursuit of him. For the hunters from House Ulanti it would be a matter of honour. For Mot it would be a matter of survival: if Kayne were to return to the Spire and expose his treachery, Mot would be condemned to end his days in one of the House Ty oubliettes. Sealed in a cell barely tall enough for a man to stand, fed increasingly rarely, left to waste away, knowing that his name had been struck from the records of his family and his House. Forgotten. Removed.

Kayne had intended to lose himself in the throng, whose members were all well-armed, their faces alight with religious fervour, long enough to enable him to get his bearings and strike out along one of the trails that led to Hope's End. He had not imagined that Vex's settlement would be the destination of this savage carnival.

*I fear that the Arch-Zealot has declared a crusade.*

Vex's words came back to him as he watched the wounded zealots scramble past, the light of righteous bloodlust gone from their eyes. They didn't spare him a glance as they passed.

Kayne coughed. The dune ash had clogged his mouth and nose as he fell away from the hunters' gunfire. As he had hauled himself to his feet at the bottom of the steep slope, anxious to put some distance between himself and his would-be killers. He found it virtually impossible to breathe. The fine ash grains had clogged his nasal plugs, rendering them worse than useless. It took valuable moments to remove them, the operation hampered by the cumbersome Orrus gloves. With every heartbeat that passed, he had expected gunfire to rain down on him from above. He wondered whether Maas and Schular might have put up a last fight, delaying the Ulanti, then forced the thought from his mind. He should have been there with them.

But, once again, he was alone. Alone and running.

Shaking the unwelcome memory from his mind, Kayne looked along the curving lip of the depression. For every member of the crusade who returned injured or did not return at all, there seemed to be three more eager to rush down into the smoke-clogged amphitheatre. The priest who led them had assembled an enormous force, drawn, it seemed, from every section of Underhive society. Eventually the fires would die down, the smoke would clear and sheer weight of numbers would win the day.

Kayne noted that the priest and his retinue had remained atop the rise, well clear of weapons' range. As he watched, the black-hooded priest appeared to be in conference with his advisors. Arms were pointed in his direction and, for a moment, Kayne feared that his disguise had been penetrated. But they were pointing above him, out across the depression, towards the crag that hung menacingly over the rear of the settlement. The pointing arms moved, tracing a series of ledges that led to the base of the crag. The priest was nodding now, issuing orders. A number of Cawdor gangers followed a deacon away from the main group, disappearing into the jostling throng.

Kayne thought of Vex, his calm acceptance of what he believed to be a lost cause, and found that he was still unable to decide whether he was a hero or the worst kind of fool. He would die here, Kayne was sure. Perhaps he was already dead, taking with him the information Kayne had hoped to acquire.

Time to move on.

'I DON'T NEED to tell you what they'll have in those bags, right?'

'Explosives,' Vex replied, eye still pressed to the macro-glass. He had been helping a wounded mutant to the infirmary when

Micc caught up with him, handed him the metal-and-glass tube and pointed towards the crag.

There were eight of them, Vex saw. The deacon who led them and one of the gangers carried a heavy leather bag slung over their shoulders.

'Mining gear, most likely,' Micc told him. 'Excavation charges. They're looking to bring the whole thing down on top of us. Must've got sick of chewing smoke.'

'Do you think they could do it?' Vex asked, lowering the glass and looking down at the squat scavvy.

'Who knows?' Micc replied, blinking away the blood that ran down one side of his face from a fresh head wound. He had led three teams out through the gates to strike at the attackers, each time returning with fewer men. 'We got lucky with the smoke. Maybe that's all the good luck we're gonna get.'

As if in confirmation of this, a deafening, explosive crack resounded across the settlement. Instinctively, Vex and Micc ducked, then turned towards the source of the noise. The platform set atop the tower to the right of the gates had gone. The salvaged building spars that formed the tower jabbed upwards into the smoke-clogged air.

'Krak grenade,' Micc muttered. 'Good shot, too. Square on.'

Not for the first time Vex wondered about Micc's life before they had met. He had appeared to be just another itinerant trader, down on his luck after one too many bad deals, but his knowledge of weapons and tactics had always indicated another, more military past. Micc had never seemed interested in talking about it, so Vex had never asked. Now it seemed he would not get the chance.

'Give me as many of your best as you can spare,' Vex shouted, ears still ringing from the explosion.

'No!' Micc shouted back, alarmed. 'That's my job.'

'I recognise the deacon who's leading them. He was one of my brethren. It seems he has advanced himself under Zydo,' Vex smiled down at Micc. 'It would be a shame not to take this opportunity to renew our acquaintance.'

THE SMOKE WAS beginning to clear when the gates opened and Vex and Micc led their men out of Hope's End. A rain of gunfire and the remainder of the settlement's small cache of grenades had cleared a space directly in front of the gates,

which were slammed shut behind the last of the strike force.
The Redemptionists had retreated across the corpse-strewn and
crater-pocked ground, seeking shelter behind the burnt out
ruins of the shanty dwellings, expecting a full-scale counter-
attack to follow the vicious bombardment.

When they saw that only twenty-five men had stepped
beyond the gates, they rose up and charged.

Vex didn't wait for them to close in. He and the nine men
assigned to follow him sprinted away, staying close to the settlement's wall. The defenders positioned along the wall gave a
smattering of covering fire but it was up to Micc's contingent to
provide the greater diversion.

Stub gun in one hand, auto rifle in the other, Micc led the
charge to meet the Redemptionists. His stub round blew an
axe-wielding zealot off his feet. Micc then swung the empty
stubber across the face of a ganger who rushed at him from the
side. The ganger went down flailing in a spray of blood and
teeth, but clawed the stubber from Micc's grasp as he fell.
Something sang past Micc's ear and he spun on his heel, steadied his autogun with his free hand and returned fire, dropping
another ganger.

'Keep moving!' he yelled to his men. 'We buy the pastor
enough time to get clear, then head back to the gates!'

He glanced over his shoulder to check on Vex's progress and
so didn't see the bullet that slammed into the side of his head.
He stumbled sideways, then dropped to his knees. He seemed
to be falling forward, but the ground had disappeared. In its
place was a vast, yawning darkness. With nothing beneath him
to arrest his descent, he fell – and the falling seemed to last forever.

CORVEQ STUMBLED, clutched his leg and went down. Hearing
his cry, Vex turned. Beyond the fallen man he saw a line of
Redemptionists, racing towards him. Evidently, Micc's men
had not managed to draw their attention away from Vex's
team as they made for a set of steps carved, centuries ago, by
those unknown miners who excavated this part of the
Underhive.

Corveq squirmed round in the dirt, levelled his rifle at the
oncoming group and fired. The pain of his wound spoiled his
aim; the shots went wide.

'Pastor?' Goresh called. Kayne turned and saw that the rest of his team had halted a short way ahead of him. He waved them on towards the steps.

'Go!' he ordered. They hesitated, eyes flickering from Vex to the injured Corveq.

'We'll be along in a moment!' Vex shouted. 'Now go!'

This time they moved, running towards the rock wall that loomed above them. Vex ran in the opposite direction – towards the fallen Corveq.

'I… I'm sorry, pastor,' Corveq gasped as Vex dropped to one knee beside him. Corveq was a young man, though his mottled, sagging skin gave the impression of great age. Below one knee, the fabric of his trousers was already soaked with blood. It was a bad wound; he would have to be carried.

'Let's not worry about apologising right now,' Vex replied before depressing his bolter's trigger. One of the approaching gangers flew backwards, his chest a ruin. The pace of the attackers' run faltered momentarily, until one of their number levelled his rifle and fired.

Corveq's head snapped back, then dropped forward into the dirt. The exit wound in the back of his skull gaped wetly up at Vex as he returned fire, hitting another ganger low in the body and vaporising a hip and the upper section of his leg. This time, however, the rest of them didn't slow down. They came on faster than before, raking the area with auto-fire.

Something that sounded like an angry insect whipped over Vex's head as he dropped to a prone firing position beside Corveq's body, which jerked as two more rounds punched into it. Firing as they ran, the Redemptionists' marksmanship was erratic. Soon they would be too close to miss.

KAYNE DREW A bead on a member of the approaching line, only to see the man stumble as if he had been shoved hard from behind. There was something wrong with his chest: most of it wasn't there any more.

As Kayne's original target fell forwards into the dirt, the ganger to his right was flung violently aside, one of his arms parting company from the rest of him and spinning away on its own trajectory. The others' headlong rush faltered again as half their remaining number turned to meet the new, unexpected threat. Another ganger and a scavvy were punched backwards into oblivion before they could bring their weapons to bear.

As he selected another target, Kayne couldn't help but smile. Micc had disobeyed yet another of his instructions. Instead of leading his men back behind the settlement's gates he had brought them to protect the rear of Vex's team.

Kayne fired. Headless, his target spun round, finger clamped in a death-grip around the trigger of his rifle. The arc of his auto-fire cut down two of his fellows. At the edge of his vision, Kayne saw another of his attackers turn and run. Shuffling round in the dirt, he sought a target among those who had turned to meet Micc and his men.

The corpses of the gangers lay strewn across the ground, a hulking robed figure looming over them. The sleeves of its robe were ragged and singed. Thin trails of smoke rose from the nozzles fixed along the knuckles of the oversized gloves that jutted from the sleeves. The robe's hood had fallen back, revealing a skullcap helmet and visor. Not Micc.

VEX CLIMBED TO his feet, cradling his bolter in what appeared to be a relaxed, non-threatening posture, but which would allow him to bring it to bear in a heartbeat. The hulking figure moved towards him, stripping off the robe as it approached.

'Pastor Vex,' it said.

'Ah, Kayne,' the pastor replied.

## Twelve

THE CHARGES HAD been set. Mylec, a ganger with some experience of working with explosives, had checked the fuses and connected them to the detonator. He turned the crank handle that protruded from the side of the detonator – a battered black box – then stepped back and nodded to the deacon.

'All set, worship,' he grunted.

Deacon Fek stepped past him – there was barely enough room on the ledge for two men to stand side-by-side – and, intoning a prayer to the Emperor and his representative on this world, the Arch-Zealot, knelt before the detonator.

That simple action saved his life.

The bolt hit the rock wall above Fek's head, showering him in sharp-edged fragments. He recoiled in shock and fear and almost pitched himself off the ledge. All around him shouts erupted, accompanied by the harsh ratcheting of autogun fire and the deeper concussive reports of bolters. Something heavy landed across his legs. Twisting round and kicking out to free himself, he saw it was Mylec, missing half his face.

Looking back along the ledge, he saw that a number of the unholy mongrels from the settlement had somehow made their way onto the ledge and were attacking his demolition team from the rear. In the confusion, Fek's men struggled to turn and face their attackers, but surprise and the width of the ledge were against them. A hulking figure, clad in some kind of armour, stood to the rear of the attackers, pumping bolts into the midst of his men as the unarmoured scum rushed forward. Fully half of his men had already fallen but, Fek saw with satisfaction, those who remained cut down one of the unclean scum, bisecting him with a close-range volley.

Turning away from the fight, Fek hauled himself to his knees and shuffled towards the detonator. Vex's hybrid abominations might claim the lives of he and his men, but, Fek swore to himself, the crag would fall like the Arch-Zealot's fist, crushing the settlement beneath it.

Gripping the plunger handle set into the top of the detonator, Fek pulled. The handle rose smoothly, then stopped with a click. Fek paused. One last prayer and he would bring damnation to all those Vex claimed blasphemously were worthy of salvation.

Then it felt as if a giant had seized him by the shoulder, shook him once, then tossed him aside. There was a moment of surprise, then searing pain. And blackness.

'PULL THE FUSES,' Vex ordered as he yanked the wires from the contacts on the top of the detonator box. 'Collect the charges – I'm sure we can find a better use for them.' The five remaining members of his team hurried along the ledge, ducking under the overhang.

He looked down at Fek, whose hand had been clamped around the detonator's plunger at the moment Vex's bolt had severed his arm at the shoulder. His hand and a short length of forearm still dangled grotesquely from the handle.

'Vex?' Fek's voice was barely a whisper. Blinking slowly, the deacon stared up at Vex with rolling, unfocused eyes. His face was deathly pale, his robe soaked in blood. Vex knelt beside him, remembering the young trader's son who had presented himself after a rally held among the ruins of a mutant settlement, recently purged of those Vex had then truly believed to be unclean. Fek had begged to be allowed to join his retinue, to become an instrument of the Redemption. Vex had recognised the fire in the young man's eyes and welcomed him into the fold. He had been an apt pupil, hungry to learn, his fervour growing as Vex's began to falter.

'So this is what we brought you to, Zydo and I.' Vex felt an immense sadness as he looked down into Fek's face. The fire still burned in the deacon's eyes.

'My faith is still strong, apostate!' Fek croaked defiantly. His eyes were beginning to glaze over. Vex was amazed that he still had the strength to speak. 'I go to my reward.'

'For your sake, I hope you're right,' Vex replied softly, but Fek could no longer hear him.

'Vex.' Kayne stood over him, smoke trails still rising from the barrels of his bolters. 'We had an agreement.'

Vex straightened, looked away from Kayne, along the ledge that ran under the crag. His men were on their way towards him, explosives cradled carefully in their arms. Turning back to Kayne, he nodded.

'You wanted information,' he said. 'I was in the middle of something. I'm grateful you decided to help us. Now ask.'

Kayne regarded Vex for a moment, still unable to decide whether he was a hero or a madman. Had he not spotted Vex running with his team away from the settlement, towards the rock wall, the priest would be dead now, lying in the dust beside the scavvy he had sought to save. His borrowed robes had enabled him to move unmolested through the press of bodies at the fringes of the killing ground, before sprinting into bolter range of the gangers who were bearing down on Vex. And, when he stood before the priest, surrounded by the Cawdor dead, what did he say to Kayne's demand?

'Later.'

Vex returned Kayne's gaze, saying nothing. The first of his team edged past them, heading for the steps by which they had climbed to the ledge.

'Well?' Vex asked.

'I told you, we were ambushed,' Kayne began. 'That I was the only survivor. I was wrong. The others are still alive. I have come back for them. I had hoped you could tell me the way.'

Kayne described the landscape of refuse in which he, Bael and the others had been attacked. Vex listened, eyes flicking to one side as he counted each of his men as they passed.

'I have no memory of how I got to where I... met you,' Kayne concluded, surprised by the sense of relief that washed over him as he spoke, the feeling that he was at last unburdening himself of a poisonous secret. 'I had been running and climbing for, well, I don't know how long. I was lost. By rights, I should have died.

'By rights, you should have killed me.'

Vex said nothing. Goresh, the last of his men, edged past. Goresh paused, looked at Vex then glanced questioningly at Kayne. Vex nodded in answer to Goresh's unspoken question, motioned for him to carry on along the ledge.

'Do you know the way? Will you help me?' Kayne asked, more pleadingly than he had intended. Suddenly he doubted the wisdom of coming back to Hope's End, of the whole descent. Why was he here? For Bael and the others? For honour and glory? For himself? Whatever the reason, it had already cost too much.

'The level you describe is still some way below us,' Vex replied at last. 'A couple of salvage teams went down that far, but didn't find much we could use. I think we can see you on your way.' Vex's last words reminded Kayne of the scavvy with the lopsided face who had confronted him when he last left Hope's End. For some reason he now felt the same mixture of embarrassment and shame that he had felt then.

Vex looked out across the battlefield below. The smoke had all but cleared. Zydo's horde was gathering for another assault on Hope's End. For all the casualties that had been inflicted upon them, there still looked to be more than enough of them to overwhelm the settlement.

'After all,' he added, looking back at Kayne, 'you'd be mad to stay here.'

'Pastor!'

Vex and Kayne both turned in the direction of Goresh's shout in time to see the scavvy standing a few steps ahead of him slammed against the rock wall by a volley of gunfire. A group of Redemptionists – brethren backed up by a contingent of gangers – was creeping along the ledge towards them. As the ledge curved, following the rock wall, it gave the attackers at the rear of the group a clear shot at Vex's men as those at the front of the group advanced. Goresh and the others returned fire. The first of the carved steps was agonisingly close, but they would have to shoulder their weapons in order to make the climb.

'Time you were going, I think,' Vex told Kayne as he checked the load in his bolter's magazine. Spitting a very un-priestly oath, he threw the empty weapon aside. He bent to kneel once again beside Fek then straightened, the deacon's autopistol in one hand, his chainsword in the other.

'No,' Kayne said firmly. 'I have the better range and the armour. Just the sight of me might buy you some time. Get your men on the ground, then cover me.'

Vex stared at him for a heartbeat, then nodded. Moving quickly ahead of Kayne along the ledge, he barked orders to his men. Turning, Goresh shot a puzzled look at Vex, then Kayne. The hunter came to a stop a short way back from Vex and the others, raised both fists and fired a volley of bolts over their heads. The first line of the advancing Redemptionists dissolved in a confusion of blood and bone. A shower of rock shrapnel cut into those behind them. Their advance faltered in a chorus of screams.

Autogun fire pattered against his armour like hard rain. A ricochet scored a hot trail across one cheek. Switching his aim to the rear of the attackers' column, he fired again. More screams. More ruined bodies. In a desperate attempt to escape the bolts, several gangers threw themselves off the ledge.

Kayne risked a glance towards the steps. Goresh's head was just disappearing from view. Only Vex remained on the ledge, emptying the autopistol at the milling Redemptionists at the front of the column. His other arm hung limply. Kayne saw fresh blood staining his robe.

'Go!' Kayne shouted. Vex glanced at him, then, tossing the empty pistol aside, lowered himself awkwardly over the edge.

Maybe it was his rig's bio-boosters kicking in, or perhaps it was the example of Vex and his men, who had nothing more to live for than an idea but who were still willing to die in its defence, but Kayne felt a wild exhilaration thrill through him. There would be no more running, no matter what the odds. He was Ty Helios Kayne and he would make his stand here.

He triggered his bolters again, prompting nothing more than a chorus of dry clicks. In his visor display, two red lights flashed. Empty. A fusillade from the Redemptionists caused him to half turn, taking the impacts on the thick armour across his shoulders. Another warning light blinked into life. A bullet had nicked an actuator line.

None of this mattered, he decided as he turned back to face the Redemptionists. The front of the column was only metres from him, too close for those at the rear to risk firing on their own. The two brethren at the head of the column were bringing their weapons to bear, but none of this mattered, because…

*No one hunts like House Ty!*

A savage, howling laugh escaped his throat as he charged at the brethren, arms outstretched.

## Thirteen

'FOR A MOMENT I thought you had changed your mind,' Vex told him as they ran at a fast trot towards Hope's End. The open ground around the settlement's wall was eerily deserted but for the ruined shanties and numberless corpses. Zydo's horde had drawn back to the top of the rise. There was to be one more assault, it was clear, and this one would not stop until the wall had been breached.

Kayne's ears still rang from the detonation that had brought down the section of the ledge upon which he had been standing minutes ago. The first of the men at the head of the column had already been reduced to a smear on the rock wall, and the other had been punched, screaming off the ledge, when a volley of gunfire had cut into the Redemptionists, claiming two lives and driving the others back from him. A shout from Vex had reminded him of the plan. Head buzzing, limbs trembling almost uncontrollably, he had clambered unsteadily down the carved steps; halfway down he had slipped, lost his footing and landed heavily at the priest's feet.

Goresh had set one of the excavation charges at the foot of the steps and paid out a length of fuse. Several paces away from the wall he crouched beside the detonator. Standing in front of him, the remainder of Vex's team provided covering fire as Kayne and the priest raced away from the steps. As they ran past him, Goresh depressed the plunger.

'For a moment I had no mind,' Kayne told the priest. 'No thoughts. Do you understand?'

'Only too well,' Vex replied. He slowed, came to a stop. 'You have my thanks. It's time you were on your way.' He beckoned to Goresh, who was bringing up the rear.

'Our friend here needs a guide,' Vex told him. 'The Wasted Land. What is it, five levels down? Take Filep with you.'

Goresh looked as if he was about to argue, but Vex waved away any objections he might have.

'You saw what he was willing to do for us. We had an agreement, he and I. I need you to honour my side of the bargain.'

Goresh nodded, shot Kayne an unhappy, resentful look, then called to the others, who had run on ahead. He jogged towards them, handed the detonator to one and beckoned another to follow him.

They didn't stop as they passed Kayne and Vex. Looking past them at the apparently featureless wall of rock, cast into shadow by the overhanging crag, Kayne's visor-enhanced sight managed to pick out an area of deeper shadow: a tunnel mouth.

'If you have a way out, why in Helmawr's name don't you take it?' he asked.

'You must have some idea of how many people there are in Hope's End,' Vex explained. 'It would take days for them to get through that hole.' He gestured towards the massed ranks of Zydo's crusade. 'And I don't think they're going to give us more than a few minutes, do you?'

'Then come with me,' Kayne suggested. 'It makes no sense for you to stay. You've already done more for these creat– I mean, these people – than they ever had a right to expect.'

'I stay because it's right,' Vex replied. 'Because everything that I believe means that this is where I must be. Redemption has its price. Mine is atonement for those things I did while I followed the Arch-Zealot. If you didn't feel the same, why did you come back?'

Kayne stared at him dumbly, struggling to find an answer.

'Come on, Spyrer!' Goresh stood at the edge of the crag's shadow, beckoning.

'Go,' Vex told him, nodding in Goresh's direction. 'Whether you know it or not, you are seeking redemption. I hope you find it – and that the price is not too high.'

Kayne opened his mouth to speak but Vex had already turned away. Kayne watched him run towards the remaining members of his team. He shouted something, the words of which Kayne didn't catch, and they ran ahead of him towards the settlement.

Goresh shouted again and Kayne turned his back on Vex, on the doomed settlement of Hope's End, and sprinted off towards him.

THE TUNNEL MOUTH was wide enough to allow two men to enter side-by-side, but soon narrowed. There was barely enough room for Kayne to move between the heavy metal struts that supported the irregular rock ceiling. Goresh unclipped a small battery-powered lantern from his belt and led the way; Filep brought up the rear. Both were silent and sullen, clearly unhappy at leaving Vex.

They reached a junction, the tunnel splitting. One passage widened and led upwards. Goresh led them along the second branch, which angled sharply downwards and remained as cramped as the tunnel they had left.

The tunnel floor was rough and unfinished. Several times Kayne stumbled, foot skidding away from him on a jumble of loose fragments, shoulder slamming into one of the roof supports. The first time this happened, Goresh stopped and turned to regard him with a sneer.

'Want to bring the Hive down on us?' Goresh growled. 'Watch where you're puttin' your feet.'

The tunnel branched again and again. Even when all the alternatives led downwards, Goresh seemed to choose the most cramped. Kayne began to wonder if, now they were clear of Vex's influence, his guides planned to lead him into a tunnel so narrow that he would become wedged, stuck fast, and where they might leave him to starve.

The tunnel opened halfway up the wall of a high gallery. Goresh turned, lowered himself over the lip of the opening and, after hanging by his fingertips for a moment, dropped lightly to the floor.

Kayne had no choice but to jump. He landed heavily but stayed on his feet. A dry, mechanical clack came from one of his suit's knee joints and the warning light in his visor display flashed more urgently – the jump had done nothing to help his rig's already damaged actuator system.

Filep dropped easily from the opening and Goresh led the way across the gallery floor. Ranged around the walls were huge machines, equipped with devices for drilling, others with jaws that looked capable of grinding rock to paste, mobile conveyors and flatbed wagons. Kayne's attention was caught by a splash of colour revealed by the beam of Goresh's lantern. Focusing his visor's enhancer, he saw that it was a yellow helmet, perched jauntily atop the engine grill of one of the gargantuan steam-powered earthmovers. Kayne wondered how many centuries it had been since its owner had left it there.

There were six or seven possible exits, wide and high enough to accommodate the forgotten monsters that slept in the gallery. Goresh led them towards the furthest from the opening through which they had arrived. Kayne discovered with relief that its floor had been covered with plates of ridged metal, to aid the progress of the machines up and down its slope. Bizarrely, a number of the lighting panels bolted to the high ceiling still shone down, dotting the tunnel floor with broad pools of yellowish light. The ramp led down to another, as wide as one of the processional thoroughfares through the Spire, that spiralled through the rock above and below them.

There were more machines on the level below, together with long-disused workers' quarters – tall prefabricated rookeries which might accommodate upwards of a thousand people. Kayne glimpsed them as they passed the wide gallery entrance, as Goresh impatiently led them on down the spiral thoroughfare.

A ROCK FALL had sealed the entrance to the next level. Kayne surprised himself by hoping that the collapse had occurred after the gallery had been abandoned. Why should he care whether hundreds of nameless, House-less drones had been crushed beneath a million tonnes of rock?

Goresh stopped at a wide, oval opening in one wall.

'Down there,' he said, pointing into the darkness.

'Garbage chute,' Filep added, with more than a trace of amusement in his voice.

'The Wasted Land is down there?' Kayne wanted to be sure. Goresh nodded.

'This is as far as we go. The Pastor asked us to show you the way. Here it is.' He nodded at Filep and the pair of them turned, ready to retrace their steps.

'I know that you wanted to stay with Vex,' Kayne said. Goresh and Filep paused, looked back at him. Kayne suddenly had no idea why he had opened his mouth, but could only think of one more thing to say.

'I'm sorry.'

Filep snorted – whether in amusement, derision or surprise, Kayne couldn't tell.

'A Spyrer, sorry?' Goresh replied. There was no mistaking the mocking tone in his voice. 'That'll be the day.'

'I hope Vex survives. I hope there's a future for Hope's End,' Kayne said, stung by Goresh's words, but Goresh and Filep had turned their backs on him and were already moving quickly up the slope. Kayne watched them for a moment, then turned to the oval mouth of the chute and cautiously stepped inside.

'SO WHAT ARE we gonna do?'

Goresh looked at Filep, but didn't slacken his pace. They were marching through the darkness between two pools of light, two levels above where they had left the Spyrer and he didn't want to waste any more time on this fool's errand.

'What?' he asked.

'I mean, it'll all be over, right? You saw it – the Redemptionists were getting ready for a big one. Hope's End'll be in pieces by the time we get back.'

'So you figure we should cut and run?' Goresh stopped suddenly, turned to face Filep squarely. 'You figure we should leave the pastor an' everybody else to burn?'

'The pastor knew what was gonna happen,' Filep reasoned. 'He wouldn't want us to go back to that.'

'You do what you like,' Goresh sneered dismissively. 'I'm going back. If I can take a few more of the scripture-spoutin' scumbags with me, that'll be my redemption.'

'Your reward is closer than you think, Underhiver.'

Goresh and Filep spun round, trying to locate the source of the voice. Goresh brought his autogun to bear, the rifle braced across the hand in which he held the lantern.

He felt a light tap on the barrel of his gun, then a sudden numbness in his arm. The lantern beam jumped, spun crazily then stabbed upwards as it hit the floor. For a moment, the thought it had slipped from his fingers.

Filep's yelp of alarm made him look down at the lantern – and the hand that was still clamped around it. His hand.

There was still no pain, even as he dropped his rifle and clutched to his chest the fresh stump of his wrist. Eyes wide with surprise, he thought he saw something flash towards him through the lantern beam.

Goresh's body remained standing, its neck gouting blood, for several heartbeats after his head hit the floor. Its knees buckled, slowly at first, then, as if to make up for lost time, it hit the floor like a heavy sack dropped form a great height.

His killer stepped into the light. It wore some kind of form-fitting armour. The small circular shield attached to one forearm sparkled as if inlaid with precious gems. In the other hand it held a slim sword.

It was not alone.

Filep turned a full stumbling circle as the others stepped towards him. Five of them – six, counting Goresh's killer. Two wore the same bulky armour as the Spyrer he and Goresh had recently left, two wore close-fitting suits of what might have been some kind of polished leather, from the bulbous forearms of which long, wicked-looking claws extended. The last of them was the hardest to make out; it seemed to be wearing some kind of cloak that blurred the outline of its body.

'We thought we'd lost you in the tunnels,' one of the heavily armoured Spyrers said.

Filep knew that he should raise his own rifle, at least try to take a couple of them with him, but found that he couldn't move. Something was pinning his arms to his sides. Looking down, he saw that some kind of wire had wrapped itself around him.

'I am Mordecai Gyre of House Ulanti,' the Spyrer continued, ignoring Filep's vain attempts to break free of the ironsilk. 'My fellow hunters and I seek the one, like ourselves, whom you were escorting through these levels. If you wish to spare yourself some pain, you will tell us where to find him. Should you choose to resist, the pain shall be greater than is strictly necessary.

'But, believe me, Underhiver, you *will* tell us.'

## Fourteen

KAYNE'S DESCENT WAS more rapid that he had planned. The curving metal floor of the garbage chute was slick with the rotten remains of ages-old refuse. He had only taken three or

four precarious steps down its sharp incline before losing his
footing and sliding the rest of the way on his back, arms and
legs kicking up a spray of the grey-green filth.

His fall was arrested by a mass of slightly more solid waste
that plugged almost half of the chute's exit. His arms and legs
sank into the semi-congealed mass as he clambered over it and
emerged, on hands and knees, into a landscape of memories.

The surface fell away from the chute. As he climbed to his
feet, Kayne found himself looking out across the undulating
dunes. Unbidden images from his first visit to this place
flooded his mind: climbing over dunes in the company of Bael
and the others; the boy fishing in the pool of effluent; laying
proximity alarms and positioning sentry units around the
defile in which they had chosen to spend the next rest cycle;
and, inevitably, the ambush.

As if pursued by the memory of the insane chattering of their
attackers, Kayne hurried down the slope, liquid filth collected
during his slide down the chute squirting from the joints of his
rig as he moved.

'WE'RE STILL THERE, *where you left us.*'

Bael's last words ran through his mind again as he plodded
up the side of yet another dune. Reaching its top, he scanned
the landscape, searching for some sign of Pitar, Aidor and the
others, though he had little enough idea of what form such a
sign might take. Smoke from a cooking fire, perhaps, or some
kind of encampment? If they had been unable to accompany
Bael on his final, fatal journey back to the Spire, then their suits
must have been disabled during the ambush, or perhaps they
were themselves too badly injured to risk making the trip.
Perhaps they had spent the intervening time eking out an exis-
tence down here, reduced to the level of the pitiful creatures
that lived out their entire lives among the refuse.

And, even if he should find them, how would they greet him?
How pleased would they be to see the man who abandoned
them to the chittering horde of their attackers?

And what might he find to say to them? Should he beg for
their forgiveness, or invent some fiction to cover his cowardice?
Should he tell them that he had come to lead them home – but
that they would have to face the Ulanti hunters, their Delaque
cohorts and his own treacherous brother if they wanted to see

the Spire again? Alone, his bolters empty and his suit damaged, they would surely consider him a sorry-looking rescuer.

The cave mouth was small, easily missed. At first, Kayne thought it was just a shadow cast by a slight overhang on the lower slope of the next dune along. He had already encountered two such pathetic dwellings, both of which had been empty. Peering cautiously in through the openings, he had noticed how the floors had been levelled, how salvaged artefacts had been arranged around the low, cramped spaces according to patterns that would have made sense only to the occupiers. At the rear of each cave there had been a reeking pile of what he imagined to be bedding materials. The thought of Meela and the others living under such conditions made him shudder and burn with shame.

A cooking fire sat in the centre of the first cave he had explored, its embers still glowing dully. Had the cave dwellers seen him coming? Perhaps they were hiding behind a neighbouring dune, waiting for him to move on – or lurking until he was fully inside the cave, without an escape route, before they attacked.

Kayne had backed hurriedly out of the cave, straightened and, senses suddenly alert, scanned the area. Nothing. Moving on across the dunes, he had seen no sign of the activity that he remembered from his first visit, no sign of what passed for life this far down in the Underhive.

This new cave was probably empty, too, but he had to be sure. He took a first step – then spun round as a las-bolt hit the impacted garbage to his right.

At first he saw nothing, then looked up. A shape wheeled in the air, metres above. Kayne recognised the shape of the wings: Yeld. Instinctively, he raised a fist, before the blinking red lights in his visor display reminded him that his bolters were empty. Two more ruby beams flashed downwards, hitting the dune to his left. Something on the loose surface ignited with a pop. Kayne spun round again and broke into an uneven run down the dune's slope, heading for the cave.

A volley of las-fire hit the ground ahead of him, forcing him to turn sharply away from the cave. The beams' after-images glowed in his vision as he ran.

He didn't remember seeing a Yeld among the Ulanti hunters, though the robes they had worn would have disguised the rig's outline. That the airborne hunter had not led the ambush among the ash dunes confirmed what Kayne already suspected about Gyre: that he was not one to settle for a long-distance kill. He liked to get close to his prey, close enough to watch the life fade from its eyes.

The next volley from above must have hit a pocket of gas. A column of blue flame jetted out of the ground in front of Kayne, who cut right, then right again, heading back towards the cave in the hope that, as well as offering cover, it might contain something he could use as a missile. Though he would have little hope of bringing the Yeld hunter down, he might at least force him to back off, give him a chance to think. Having come this far, Kayne was determined not to die meekly, like some cornered animal.

As if sensing his intention, the Yeld hunter's next shot seared through his left knee. Pitching forward, he cried out, as much in frustration as pain. The sickening scent of cooked meat leaked from the wound as he rolled over onto his back and leant forward to grasp the ruined joint.

The Yeld wheeled, swooped low, then turned again, finally coming to rest halfway up the slope of the dune upon which he has been standing when he first spotted the cave.

'He's not going anywhere,' Kayne overheard the Yeld report into her comm-link. Her voice was soft, well educated. 'He awaits your pleasure.'

Nerve-endings cauterised by the las-beam, Kayne's leg below the knee had gone mercifully numb. As he sat there, staring at the Yeld, he raged at himself. To stand atop one of the tallest dunes for kilometres around – how could he have been so stupid? He might as well have erected a sign, sent up a flare to tell the Ulanti where to find him!

'Hello, brother.'

Kayne lifted his gaze to the top of the dune. Mot stood there, evidently enjoying the scene, flanked by the Ulanti, all of whom had divested themselves of their robes.

'What happened to your Delaque lapdogs?' Kayne shouted up at Gyre. 'Without them at your back, are you sure there are enough of you to handle a single, crippled quarry? I'd not expect any help from my brother, if I were you.'

'Come now, Kayne, where's your pride?' Mot sneered. 'Surely you can face your destiny, however distasteful, without resorting to childish insults.'

'The Delaques were no longer necessary,' Gyre called down to Kayne. 'You were our prime target. Your companions were merely unfortunate witnesses who could not be allowed to live. It seemed appropriate that we end this hunt without their involvement.'

Gyre led the hunters down the slope. Kayne watched them come – until a sudden noise made him look up, over their heads, to the top of the dune. A line of ragged figures stood there, pressed shoulder-to-shoulder and swaying slightly as if with barely restrained excitement. As he watched, more figures joined the line, rising up from the far side of the dune, and the noise that had alerted him to their arrival grew in volume: a dry, insectile chittering.

Mot was the first to notice them. He turned, let out a startled shout and, losing his footing, stumbled into Gyre. The others turned, got their first glimpse of the new arrivals and opened fire. Bolter fire and las-beams tore into the line, but the gaps it made were quickly filled. The chattering grew yet louder and the line began to advance down the slope, revealing itself to be a vast, ragged tide.

At the foot of the slope, Kayne smiled. His hunt was over. He would die here, as he should have done months ago.

And, this time, there would be no running.

# Fifteen

'KAYNE!'

The name drifted like a phantom through the clicks and squeals, the background chatter of the creatures that carried him through the tunnels beneath the dunes. Kayne didn't know what he found more surprising: that someone had bored these narrow, twisting passageways down through the compacted, millennia-old detritus that lay beneath the rolling dunes, or that these no-longer-human creatures were still capable of uttering a recognisable word.

He was sure, however, of what he found the most surprising of all: that he was still alive.

It had felt as if he had become a spectator at his own nightmare as the chittering tide had rushed down the slope of the dune, their cries growing wilder, punctuated by the Ulanti hunters' gunfire. Their man in the Malcadon gear had been the first to disappear, still slashing wildly with his long claws, beneath the wave of misshapen bodies. Like Pitar, the Yeld had tried to take to the air, only to be brought down by the grasping hands of the throng. For every body that the hunter wearing the Jakara rig carved into bloody pieces, three more would take its place, hands reaching for her, faces twisted in the same ecstatic rictus.

Kayne watched with a dark satisfaction as Mot tried to bolt, racing down the slope then turning sharply in an attempt to outflank the oncoming tide, only to find that those at the ends of the line had moved past the hunters' position and were now swinging round to encircle them. Seeing this, Mot stumbled to a halt – and, in a moment, was gone.

Gyre and the other Orrus-clad Ulanti held out the longest. Kayne was irresistibly reminded of Bael's last stand, though, oddly, he felt no guilt at the memory. The sight of the throng, the realisation that his life had only heartbeats left to run, had purged him of all emotion, leaving only a vague yearning for the peace of the grave.

By the time their bolters fell silent, they were already hidden from Kayne's sight. He was surrounded.

'Well?' he asked. 'What are you waiting for?' Their frenzy seemed to have subsided. The faces that returned his gaze had slackened. One of their number bent down to get a closer look, her cheek twitching. No, Kayne realised, not twitching.

Something was moving beneath her skin.

'Kayne!'

The word didn't come from the woman. It seemed to resolve itself out of the unintelligible warbling of all those who stood over him. Kayne thought he had imagined it, but then it came again, like a snatch of conversation overheard through the murmur of a vast crowd.

Others bent to join the woman. Reaching out, they began to unfasten his suit, lifted away his helmet. He knew that he should try to stop them, but discovered that he no longer had the energy or the desire. Only when they removed the plates around his ruined knee did he cry out and thrash against their grasp, using up the last of his energy. Those working on his leg paused until he stopped struggling and then, almost tenderly, completed their task.

Once free of the rig, they had lifted him gently between them and, like a hero fallen in battle, bore him across the dunes.

When darkness closed about him, he assumed they had brought him to a cave, though for what purpose he had no idea, but they kept moving. The angle of the floor changed abruptly, leading downwards. Kayne felt as if he was being swallowed by the Hive itself. The darkness was total, blotting out all sense of time and direction. Kayne wondered whether he was, in fact, already dead, his body lying in pieces at the foot of the dune. Perhaps this journey was one last hallucination, or the path taken by all cowards and failures to a special hell reserved for them by the Emperor.

*Redemption?* He thought of Vex as he continued his slide through the darkness. *I doubt it.*

KAYNE OPENED HIS eyes to the sound of water. He had no memory of his eyes closing, nor any idea of how long he had been unconscious.

He opened his eyes slowly and eased his head up off his chest. He was standing, supported under each shoulder by one of those who had borne him through the tunnels, on the rocky bank of what appeared to be a wide, open sewer. The stench was appalling; the water moved slowly, as if weighed down by the effluent it carried. Looking around him, he saw that a crowd had gathered at the water's edge, some carrying primitive torches. A low, unintelligible murmuring ran through their ranks as they stood, swaying gently as if engaged in some form of communal prayer.

Kayne recalled stories he had heard of forces that existed beyond the warp, the unseen interstellar ocean that stretched between worlds and through which the ships of the Imperium travelled to do the bidding of the Emperor. These forces could twist the minds and bodies of men, he had heard, bending them to their perverse will. Entire worlds had been lost to the Imperium when their inhabitants had turned to the worship of these forces. With a sudden rush of fear, it occurred to him that he might have fallen into the clutches of just such an unholy cabal, here in Hive Primus, and that he had been brought here to witness one of their blasphemous rituals. Such a ritual, he imagined, would require a sacrifice.

Ripples had begun to spread across the water. Bubbles rose from its depths in greater and greater numbers. The slick, iridescent surface seemed to boil.

Kayne sagged against the arms that supported him, almost overcome with relief when he saw that what had emerged from the depths was a machine, not some unspeakable abomination summoned from beyond. A long, tapering metal teardrop, topped by a stubby tower, it wallowed for a moment in the wake of its own emergence. The water ran slickly over the riveted plates of its hull. A hatch towards the rear of the vessel clanged open. Figures appeared through the hatch and set about loosening the ropes that secured one of a number of smaller craft to the hull. The skiff was set down in the water and a number of the figures climbed aboard. An engine coughed into life and its crew steered it towards the shore.

Kayne found himself moving closer to the water's edge. For a moment, he dug in his heels, tried to halt his progress, but those who supported him merely lifted him off his feet. He was delivered to the narrow beach as the skiff's prow ran aground and three of the boat's crew jumped ashore. One of them was a huge specimen, built like a pit-fighter, but, like his two companions, he wore the same slack expression as all those who had gathered on the shore to greet them.

Kayne was handed over into their care. The pit-fighter grasped him under the shoulders while one of the others lifted his feet. Any hope of escape evaporated the moment Kayne felt the power in the larger man's hands. The third member of the skiff's crew to come ashore aided them as they carried him aboard the boat, then pushed the prow away from the beach, jumping lightly aboard as the engine coughed into life once again. The fourth member of the crew steered the boat towards the waiting submersible.

As the skiff came alongside its mother ship, Kayne noticed a brass plate riveted to the side of the stubby tower. Etched into it was a single word: *Queequeg*.

Kayne was lifted aboard the submersible with as much ceremony as a sack of meal. The pit-fighter held him at arms' length, as one might hold a new born child, and lowered him through the hatch to waiting hands below while the rest of the skiff's crew secured the boat. As he was manhandled along a cramped corridor leading to the wider end of the vessel, Kayne heard the hatch slam shut behind him. The ship vibrated as the engines powered-up and the deck over which he limped began to dip.

The incline of the deck had steepened by the time he reached the control room. A low, continuous hum filled the slightly less cramped space – a sound which, Kayne was sure, did not originate from the ship's machinery. The room was lined with a tangle of pipes and gauges; cables hung in thick bunches from the ceiling. In the dim, red-tinged light it appeared that yet more cables hung between the various workstations and those who occupied them.

As his eyes adjusted to the gloom, Kayne saw that these cables were thicker and paler than those that ran across the ceiling. And they were alive. Tendrils of flesh connected each crewmember to their controls. These pale extrusions flexed and swayed as, without any recognisable command being given, they brought the *Queequeg* to a level course.

A member of the crew stood in the centre of the control room, eye pressed to the viewing glass set into a thick pipe that entered the control room through the ceiling – some kind of viewing scope, Kayne decided. The figure wore a heavy jacket of thick animal hide, still covered with a layer of its previous owner's short coarse fur. He turned away from the pipe to glance at Kayne, a reassuringly human gesture of curiosity, Kayne thought – until he saw the tendril that snaked from around from the far side of the pipe, terminating at his temple. Kayne watched, appalled, as a ripple ran the length of the tendril's flesh. Something was moving beneath its skin, using it as a fleshy tunnel to travel from the vessel's machine parts, to the organic haven of the crewman's skull.

At that moment he knew what, standing on the shoreline, he had only feared: that fate had delivered him into the hands of the damned.

THE FIGURE BY the viewing scope had emitted a short series of clicks and those who still supported Kayne had conveyed him to a tiny cabin in the mid-section of the vessel. The room was furnished with a small bunk, a metal table and chair. The cabin had a neglected, disused look, as had the threadbare hammocks he had glimpsed, hanging forlornly between the submersible's bulkheads. Evidently, the creatures that manned this vessel had once required sleep, like any other human beings. Lying on the cramped bunk after his handlers had departed, Kayne wondered whether mercy was another human trait that had been lost in their transformation.

Kayne awoke with a start, first wondering when his eyes had closed, how long he had been asleep. Then he noted that the engines' dull, monotonous throb had changed pitch. The deck, the walls of the cabin were canted up at an acute angle. The ship was surfacing. They would be coming for him soon.

He swung his legs off the bunk – and cried out at the excruciating pain that exploded in his damaged knee, erasing all hope of a last-minute escape attempt. Whatever fate had in store for him, he would have no choice but to face it.

The cabin door opened. Two crewmembers he had not seen before stepped into the room, arms outstretched, reaching for him.

Kayne was carried, unresisting, to the rear of the submersible, then lifted up towards the already-open hatch. The crewman Kayne had decided might once have been a pit-fighter stood over the opening, reached down with his massive arms and lifted him easily into the reeking air. A skiff had already been set in the water beside the *Queequeg*. Kayne was manhandled aboard the swaying boat and the pit-fighter followed him aboard.

The submersible had surfaced in a wide, dome-roofed cave. Some kind of light-producing fungus hung in ribbons from the ceiling. The skiff sped towards a wide ledge that ran around part of the curved wall. Shadows hung in drapes over the rear of the rock platform.

There were figures standing on the ledge, awaiting the skiff's arrival. The boat's helmsman kept the engine running, holding the craft tight against the vertical rock as Kayne was lifted – by the pit-fighter, yet again – to the waiting hands above. The hunter looked down at the pit-fighter, expecting him to follow, but he remained aboard the skiff. His job, it seemed, was done.

Though he would not have believed it possible, those into whose hands he had been passed were an even more unsettling sight than either the horde of chittering idiots who had carried him to the shoreline or the crew of the *Queequeg*. Tendrils of flesh hung between them, their surfaces in constant motion, as if a flurry of activity was going on beneath their skin. One of them appeared to be the product of a fusion of two bodies. It scuttled sideways on four legs, grinned slackly at him with two mouths. Four eyes gleamed wetly at him in the pale light.

Kayne was conveyed away from the edge, towards the shad-ows and what appeared to be a large rock that protruded from the ledge's uneven surface. No, not a rock, Kayne decided: some kind of sculpture. Had he been brought to be sacrificed before a representation of these creatures' blasphemous god? Metal gleamed dully in the diffuse light. Kayne made out curved plates, the outline of which reminded him of something.

Kayne's handlers came to a halt and, as he watched, the sculpture began to move, breaking apart along invisible seams. The single monolithic shape became five, six separate figures, connected by the now all-too-familiar tendrils of flesh. The fleshy tunnels also broke apart, withdrawing quickly, sliding out of sight through self-sealing slits in the figures' armour.

Panic welled up within Kayne. He struggled against the hands that held him, kicked uselessly at the air. He knew what he was about to see – and wished with all his heart that he would be hurled into the poisonous murk at the foot of the ledge before he was forced to see it.

One of the figures stepped forward, oversized gloves reaching up, unfastening the helmet that obscured its eyes. When it lifted the helmet away, Kayne found himself staring looking into a face that he had last seen, lying dead on the floor of the Great Gallery.

'Greetings, Kayne,' Bael said, apparently having some diffi-culty with the words. 'We have so missed you.'

## Sixteen

'IF ONLY YOU hadn't run,' Bael told him, 'you would already know our joy.'

For long moments, Kayne had been unable to speak as his mind struggled to comprehend what he saw. Bael was dead, yet here he stood, together with Meela, Pitar, Volk, Georgi and laughing Aidor, all of them looking as they did the day they left the Spire, all of them wearing the same slack smile.

Bael's mention of his cowardice broke the spell and words tumbled out of him in a torrent: stammered apologies, half-formed excuses, attempts to explain why he had returned. Then finally, despairingly: 'What have they done to you?'

'They have set us free,' Bael replied. 'Free of the bonds of indi-viduality. Free of the lonely confines of a single body, the narrow limits of a single mind.'

Kayne shook his head violently. He would have pressed his hands to his ears to shut out Bael's words – and the inhuman clicking that accompanied them – but his handlers maintained their iron grip on his arms.

'This is madness!' he gasped. 'Blasphemy.'

'This is science,' Bael replied. 'Lost, long forgotten knowledge, buried among the roots of the Hive.

'The Underhivers call such knowledge archaeotech – lost examples of the massive, world-shaping technologies our forebears used to spread the human race across the galaxy, to colonise the worlds they found, to raise this and the other hive-cities of Necromunda. But not all archaeotech exists on such a scale. Some of it is minute, designed not to manipulate base materials such as metal and rock, but blood and flesh and bone. To move within us and between us, to make mind and body one and to bring all minds together.' Bael swept his arm in a gesture that included the other hunters and those monstrosities that still held Kayne, mind reeling, in their grip.

'That is what flows through us now,' Bael continued. 'Its creation is lost in time, but we believe it was created to ease the process by which worlds might be re-modelled, made more suitable for human habitation – or else to alter the bodies of colonists to fit the world on which they chose to live. Once lost, it must have lain dormant for centuries until it was found, its cracked containment vessel salvaged from among the debris of a hive-quake. We know this because we share the memories of the first one who found it – an outcast, a scavenger named Drell. Free at last, it entered the body of its first host, then moved quickly among his associates.

'They were the first to know the joy of connection, their minds and memories co-mingled, and, in their joy, they wished to share it with others.'

'This isn't freedom!' Kayne shouted. 'This is mind-control! You've become the slaves of this unholy nonsense!'

Bael regarded Kayne calmly. The idiot grin didn't fade.

'Is it madness to know that you will never feel lonely again?' asked Bael. 'To never again live in fear of your fellows, to know that they share your thoughts and feelings? That is a gift. That is freedom.

'Those who found us among the waste dunes wished only to share this gift with us. The destruction of a body means ıothing since the mind survives. Should it be desired, another body can be constructed from any organic material. We created such a body in my image, to call you back to us. We knew you would come. You are our brother.'

As he spoke, Bael stepped closer and raised his hand. The Orrus glove peeled back, like the petals of some impossible metal and ceramite flower, revealing the pale, long-fingered hand beneath.

As his brother reached out towards him, Kayne saw that something was moving beneath the skin of the man's palm. A seam appeared, running from the base of his thumb to that of his fourth finger.

Kayne whipped his head desperately from side to side. From behind him, a pair of hands clamped themselves around his head, forcing him to stare, wide-eyed with fear, at his brother's hand as it covered his face, stifling his last human scream.

THEY ROSE THROUGH bands of light, the elevator car clattering and jolting around them as it carried them up the shaft. Kayne stood, clad once again in his Orrus rig, flanked by Aidor and Mot. His brother had joined them, chattering with joy and wonder at his new, liberated state, as they had journeyed up through the Hive, past the deserted, smoking ruin that had once been Hope's End and onwards, upwards, towards the Spire.

'*Whether you know it or not, you are seeking redemption.*' Kayne remembered Vex's last words to the man he had once been. '*I hope you find it – and that the price is not too high.*'

The only price had been to shed a lifetime of loneliness, fear and isolation – and that had been no price at all. Now he looked forward to sharing his redemption with the rest of his family, his House, with every inhabitant of Hive Primus, of Necromunda itself. Imagine it – no more need for petty politicking between Houses, between hives! No more fear. No more lies.

A smile hung loosely about his lips as his mind hummed and buzzed with the lives of everyone he had communicated with during his ascent – and the lives of all those they had communicated with. Distance was no obstacle; the language produced and translated by the minute machines that now flowed through him could convey unbelievable amounts of

information across vast distances, beyond the range of huma.
perception. Words now seemed so slow, so clumsy, but he
would have to use them again soon, when the elevator arrived
at the Ty House apartments.

He would tell the members of his House what they wanted
to hear: that he and Mot had found the lost hunters, though at
the cost of their own companions. He and Mot would return to
the bosom of the Helios clan, Meela, Aidor and the others to
their own. Then, when they were safe and secure, they would
begin to share the gift they had already received. The deception
was regrettable, but the end – the glorious vision of a united
hive, a united world! – would justify the means.

The elevator rattled one last time as it reached the top of the
shaft. Through the grille of the car door, Kayne saw the assembled honour guard that always greeted returning hunters. One
of the ornately uniformed House Guard opened the door and
saluted. Two ranks of the guard lined the corridor, at the end of
which stood Lord Ty himself, resplendent in the robes he
reserved for high ceremonies. Beside Lord Ty stood Kayne's
father, Ty Helios Cal, face pale with the illness that had dogged
him for so long, supported by two of his personal guard. Kayne
was surprised to see them here – normally, the formal greetings
would take place in the Great Gallery.

'We return in honour and glory,' Kayne announced, according to the long-established ritual, as he led the hunters between
the ranks of the honour guard.

'And you are welcome,' Lord Ty gave the ritual reply, then
turned, leading the way through the corridors. Kayne's father
tottered unsteadily in his wake. The hunters, escorted by the
honour guard, followed.

As was the usual practice, the corridors had been cleared of
House servants. The procession moved in silence until it
reached the doors which led to the Great Gallery. Two members of Lord Ty's retinue hurried forward to open the doors. As
Lord Ty, Kayne's father and the others stepped through into the
gallery, Lord Ty's chamberlain turned to face the honour guard
holding up his hand to bring them to a halt.

'You will wait here a moment,' he announced, 'to allow our
Lord to take his place.'

The chamberlain then disappeared through the doors. Kayne
noticed that the guard to his right seemed to be shuffling

nervously. Normally these ceremonial warriors were the very model of correctness. Before he could give the matter any more thought, the doors swung open again and the guard moved forward, escorting the hunters into the gallery.

The sound of heavy bolts slamming home across the doors echoed briefly around the almost-deserted gallery, rapidly followed by the sound of running feet as the honour guard sprinted away from the hunters. Kayne stared in incomprehension at the group of massively armoured figures that stood facing them, weapons trained on Kayne and his companions. There were fifteen of them, Kayne counted. Half as tall again as a man, their armour was midnight black, but for unit markings on their shoulder plates and a grey heart emblazoned on their chest plates. Half their number carried bolters, etched with the two-headed Imperial eagle; the rest carried more bulky-looking weapons: meltas.

'Welcome home, Ty Helios Kayne – if that is truly who you are.' A black-robed figure stood to one side of the armoured figures, flanked by his similarly attired retinue. Cinar, Kayne remembered: the inquisitor. Then Kayne remembered something else: among Cinar's retinue there had been a tech-adept. Had the adept probed the remains of the simulacrum that had been sent to call him? Had he found something?

Kayne looked past Cinar, to where Lord Ty and his retinue stood. Desperately, he searched for a face.

'Father?' he called.

The only answer he received was the dull roar of a melta being triggered.

Ty Helios Cal looked down at the remains of his son. The old man felt grief, of course, but he also knew the pain that came with the certain knowledge that his family's disgrace would last for generations. His reputation, honed and crafted over the decade of his long life, the services he had performed for this Lord Ty and his father before him, would count for nothing. He would be known to history as the father of not one, but three, sons who consorted with blasphemy.

'Your sons' example shall stand as a warning to all who would seek after forbidden knowledge.' The inquisitor stood beside him. 'Had my tech-adept not examined the corpse of your first-born, had he not uncovered the unclean creatures within him, think of the horrors that might have been unleashed throughout the Hive.' Cinar did not mention that these creatures were now safely stowed aboard the Thunderhawk that rested on one of the Spire's larger landing pads, ready for transport to the distant laboratories of the Adeptus Mechanicus.

'I have no sons!' Cal spat weakly. The eerie, inhuman squealing that erupted from the throats of Kayne and the others as they died still rang in his ears. 'I disown them!'

'That is as it should be,' Cinar nodded, then turned to address Sergeant Lycidius of the Iron Hearts, whose men, under the supervision of Cinar's tech-adept, were busy collecting the still-smouldering remains of the other hunters. 'As planned, I shall depart on the *Blessed Redemption* and make my report to my Ordo's superiors. I have informed Lord Ty that your unit will remain here, held ready in case any more of these creatures attempt to enter the Spire. Should this occur, you have been given full authority to deal with them. Lord Helmawr has been made aware of the situation.'

The massive Space Marine nodded, then strode back into formation. Cinar turned back to the old man, who was still staring down at his son.

'Emperor be blessed that the *Blessed Redemption* arrived on schedule. It can only have been divine providence that a Chapter of the Emperor's finest warriors were aboard. The campaign on Livius Nine went well, they tell me.'

Cal nodded.

'Emperor be blessed,' he repeated quietly.

## Nineteen

THE MAN WHO had once been Ty Helios Bael stood on the ledge, flanked by his brothers and fellow hunters. It had been a small thing to create new bodies for them to house the copies of their intelligences that were stored in the archaeotech which swam through his veins. It was not necessary, of course. The personalities of the men and women who had been Kayne, Mot, Volk, Pitar, Aidor, Meela and Georgi could have remained within him for eternity, but he found their physical presence somehow comforting.

Together they watched as the *Queequeg* slipped beneath the water of the pool, where the vessel and its crew would remain, dormant, until it was needed again. Waiting at the bottom of the elevator shaft, Bael had received Kayne's last communication from the Great Gallery. Moving swiftly back down through the Hive, Bael had broadcast the news: an ambush.

Somehow their strategy had been uncovered, but it did not matter. Time was on their side. Given time, their kind would become mere rumour once again. Given time, these rumours would fade, become half-forgotten stories. No one posted guards against stories.

But he knew: one day, decades, perhaps centuries from now, they would rise. And Necromunda would be theirs.

Also from the Black Library

# INTO THE MAELSTROM

## An anthology of Warhammer 40,000 stories, edited by Marc Gascoigne & Andy Jones

'THE CHAOS ARMY had travelled from every continent, every shattered city, every ruined sector of Illium to gather on this patch of desert that had once been the control centre of the Imperial Garrison. The sand beneath their feet had been scorched, melted and fused by a final, futile act of suicidal defiance: the detonation of the garrison's remaining nuclear stockpile.' – **Hell in a Bottle** *by Simon Jowett*

'HOARSE SCREAMS and the screech of tortured hot metal filled the air. Massive laser blasts were punching into the spaceship. They superheated the air that men breathed, set fire to everything that could burn and sent fireballs exploding through the crowded passageways.' – **Children of the Emperor** *by Barrington J. Bayley*

*IN THE GRIM and gothic nightmare future of Warhammer 40,000, mankind teeters on the brink of extinction. INTO THE MAELSTROM is a storming collection of a dozen action-packed science fiction short stories set in this dark and brooding universe.*

### Also from the Black Library

# REALM OF CHAOS
## An anthology of Warhammer stories
### edited by Marc Gascoigne & Andy Jones

'Markus was confused; the stranger's words were baffling his pain-numbed mind. "Just who are you, foul spawned deviant?"

The warrior laughed again, slapping his hands on his knees. "I am called Estebar. My followers know me as the Master of Slaughter. And I have come for your soul."'
– **The Faithful Servant,** *by Gav Thorpe*

'The wolves are running again. I can hear them panting in the darkness. I race through the forest, trying to outpace them. Behind the wolves I sense another presence, something evil. I am in the place of blood again.' – **Dark Heart,** *by Jonathan Green*

*IN THE DARK and gothic world of Warhammer, the ravaging armies of the Ruinous Powers sweep down from the savage north to assail the lands of men. REALM OF CHAOS is a searing collection of a dozen all-action fantasy short stories set in these desperate times.*

Also from the Black Library

# RAGNAR'S CLAW
## A Warhammer 40,000 novel
## by William King

One of the enemy oficers, wearing the peaked cap and
greatcoat of a lieutenant, dared to stick his head above the
parapet. Without breaking stride, Ragnar raised his bolt
pistol and put a shell through the man's head. It exploded
like a melon hit with a sledgehammer. Shouts of
confusion echoed from behind the wall of sandbags, then
a few heretics, braver and more experienced than the rest,
stuck their heads up in order to take a shot at their
attackers. Another mistake: a wave of withering fire from
the Space Marines behind Ragnar scythed through them,
sending their corpses tumbling back amongst their
comrades.

*FROM THE DEATH-WORLD of Fenris come the Space Wolves, the
most savage of the Emperor's Space Marines. Ragnar's Claw
explores the bloody beginnings of Space Wolf Ragnar's first
mission as a young Blood Claw warrior. From the jungle hell
of Galt to the polluted cities of Hive World Venam, Ragnar's
mission takes him on an epic trek across the galaxy to face
the very heart of Evil itself.*